"It may regrettably be true that there are
those who customarily use the expression 'Tarra'
as a form of valediction, but such a solecism is as
offensive to the eye of the reader as it is
to the ear of the hearer, and who, it may be
wondered, is presumed to derive satisfaction from
the contemplation of a husband enjoining
the contemplation of a husband enjoining
his wife to silence by telling her to shut her hole ?"
South Wales Argus

"A delicious houseful has been assembled in
this hilarious first novel"
Yorkshire Post

"One of the best comic first novels to come
out this decade"
Daily Express

"Joe Orton crossed with Coronation Street"
Observer

—— MOG ——

PETER TINNISWOOD

—— MOG ——

HODDER AND STOUGHTON

I

"My plan is quite simple," said Mrs Mortensen, who was Danish. "I shall set up a small lunatic asylum in an ordinary suburban house in an ordinary suburban street."

It was spring, and the weather was cool. It was also 1960.

Philip Manners, who was English, stood up. He was a small man, and he was the owner of a large property company. His elder son, Tom, who was an MP, ran the business for him. His younger son, Oliver, was a lunatic.

He walked across the drawing room to the french windows and looked out over the lawns of Mannersville. A few of the lunatics in his private asylum were enjoying the fresh air.

His son, Oliver, was sitting in a deck chair under the monkey puzzle tree. Horace A'Fong was mending his butterfly net. 'Baldy' Hogan was jogging a football up and down on his right instep.

"It is an experiment, of course," said Mrs Mortensen.

She was wearing a black velvet jacket, flared at the waist. Her plum-coloured trousers were speckled with ash from her small cigar.

"Without experiment one cannot have progress," she said, and she smiled. Her teeth were very white and even.

Philip Manners said nothing. He just stared out of the windows. Group Captain Greenaway was whispering through a crack in the vaulting horse, glancing furtively over his shoulder from time to time. Brother Herbert and Wyndham Lancaster were playing chess. The pug dog, Lord William, sniffed at them and then bounded towards Nurse Mooseman, who was pushing a trolley laden with tea things.

The lunatics gathered round the nurse, and he poured out cups of privet tea for them. Oliver Manners took his cup, and, when no one was looking, he emptied its contents into the goldfish pond.

"What do you want to go and disturb them for any road?"

said Philip Manners. "They're all as happy as Larry. They're all getting on grand here, aren't they?"

"Of course they are," said Mrs Mortensen, and she went and stood beside Philip Manners. "But they are not part of the world. They are locked away from it."

"I thought that was the whole idea of a lunatic asylum."

"Don't call it a lunatic asylum. It is a home for mentally disorientated invalids, if you please," said Mrs Mortensen, who was, of course, a trained psychiatrist. "And it is not the whole idea of an asylum any way."

Nurse Mooseman began to hand out sandwiches. There were pumpkin seed sandwiches, grated fig sandwiches and shredded sprout sandwiches.

Oliver Manners took one, peeled back the upper layer of bread, wrinkled his nose and threw the sandwich to the Old English sheepdog, Quimby.

"You'll starve them to death feeding them on that rubbish," said Philip Manners.

"Stuff and nonsense," said Mrs Mortensen. "Look at yourself how well you are thriving on it."

Philip Manners looked down at the sagging waistline of his trousers and nodded glumly.

"Oh aye," he said. "Oh aye."

Mrs Mortensen sat down cross-legged in front of the carved marble fireplace.

"The curse of modern civilisation is artificial food," she said. "The prize bull is fed on the choicest of natural foods. So is the champion stallion at stud. Yet our menfolk are fed on artificial foods, and we expect them to be champion lovers."

"But I don't want to be a champion bloody lover," said Philip Manners.

"Stuff and nonsense," said Mrs Mortensen.

That night as they lay side by side in bed Philip Manners said to Mrs Mortensen:

"How many of them will you put in this suburban asylum?"

"Three or four," she said. She had firm, full breasts and she made Philip Manners kiss them. Then she whispered: "That was pleasant, wasn't it?"

"I'm getting too old for that sort of work," said Philip Manners.

She bit the lobe of his left ear. When he tried to push her away, she laughed and tickled his scrotum.

"I wish you'd give over;" he said.

"When my husband was alive, it was his great pleasure for me to do that to him."

"That's what probably killed him," said Philip Manners. "You can have too much of a good thing, you know."

"Pig!"

The clock on the summer pavilion by the lake struck midnight. Away in the distance a steam locomotive whistled, and a small bird chattered and then fell silent. A heron stood motionless on the edge of the goldfish pond.

"How will you set up this asylum any road?" said Philip Manners.

"Simple. You will buy a house in the normal way and place them into it."

"Rubbish," said Philip Manners. "Bloody rubbish, woman. The neighbours will be forced to notice if a bunch of lunatics move in next door to them."

"Not if we choose the correct neighbours. They will think that they are simple lodgers," said Mrs Mortensen.

She had long legs, and she wound them tightly round Philip Manners's ribs.

"You're squashing me," he said. "Give over."

She unlocked her legs and sighed deeply.

"Are you sure you took your bone meal today?" she said.

Philip Manners climbed stiffly out of bed. He put on his dressing gown and sank down on the chaise longue, over which Mrs Mortensen had draped her clothes.

"If they're going to be the lodgers, who's going to be the bloody landlord?" he said.

"Simple," said Mrs Mortensen. "Ambrose Tierney."

Ambrose Tierney was chauffeur and odd job man to Philip Manners. He lived in a cottage in the grounds of Mannersville.

Next morning his wife, Megan, sat in the kitchen of the cottage. Oliver Manners sat next to her. They were looking at a snapshot album.

"This is my granddad Cardiff, but he have died of old age by now he have," said Megan. "And this is grannie Ross-on-Wye, and she have died, too, unfortunate like owing to the simple fact that she didn't take her medicine proper when the doctor told her. And this by here is my brother,

7

Watkin, what is a catering officer in New Zealand and sitting next to him by there is my brother, Mog, what have come to no good owing to the simple fact of him getting into bad company."

Oliver Manners smiled.

"Very interesting, Meg," he said. "Very interesting."

He had been a captain in the army. However, after his court martial he had been cashiered and stripped of his rank.

"And by there is my Uncle Windsor," said Megan, pointing to a photograph of the battle cruiser, *HMS Lion*. "Well, you can't see him owing to the simple fact that he was stoking the boilers for Early Beatty at the time the picture was took, but you can rest assured that one half the smoke coming out of the funnels was caused by him."

It was a mews cottage. Below it were the garages, which had once been the stables. There were two Rolls Royces, a Humber and a Lanchester in the garages. Ambrose Tierney was cleaning the maroon Humber.

The first swallows of the year had arrived earlier in the week, and they swooped low over his head as they made for their nests in the rafters.

Ambrose stepped back from the Humber and smiled at it.

"There we are, my old son," he said. "How does that feel then?"

Then he went out into the cobbled yard and threw the dirty water out of the bucket down the grid, which lay at the foot of the rusty pump. He wiped his hands on his overalls and climbed the wooden spiral staircase, which led into the kitchen of his cottage.

"How do, Meg," he said, and, when he saw Oliver Manners sitting next to her, he said: "How do, Captain Manners."

"Hello, Ambrose," said Oliver Manners, smiling. "Your wife's showing me some of your snapshots."

"And I was just telling Captain Manners, informing him like, about the letter what we received from Mog this morning," said Megan.

"Oh, that," said Ambrose, and he ran cold water into the sink and began to swill down his face and arms.

"My brother, Mog, have just come out of prison, been discharged like, and he have nowhere to go and he have only one shirt to call his own and his fallen arches is playing him up something cruel and could we lend him a postal order to the

8

value of 13s 9d to tide him over," said Megan, and she began to sob softly to herself.

Ambrose rubbed himself furiously with the striped towel. When he had finished, he said:

"The balmy pillock didn't even put his address on the letter neither."

"That's so we wouldn't know the desperate straits and conditions what he's living in," said Megan.

"Then how can we send him the money?"

"Oh dearie me, I hadn't thought of that I hadn't."

Ambrose snorted and began to button up the tunic jacket of his chauffeur's uniform.

"Cooee," called a voice from the foot of the stairs.

Megan's face broke into a smile. She wiped the tears from her eyes with the corner of her pinnie and shouted down:

"Come on up, Miss Miranda my lovely."

Footsteps clattered on the wooden stairs, the door of the kitchen burst open and in stepped Mrs Mortensen's daughter, Miss Miranda. She was sixteen, and she had long golden hair.

"Oh, hello, sexy pants," she said, pointing at Oliver Manners. "Isn't he gorgeous, Megan? Isn't he simply super?"

Oliver Manners smiled at her.

"Hello, Miranda," he said. "Has your mother told you about her plan to set up another asylum?"

"Yes, she has," said Miss Miranda crossly. "And I think it's a diabolical fucking liberty."

"Oh dearie dearie me, what a naughty word to use," said Megan. "You'd make God turn over in His grave, if He could hear you using words like that, Miss Miranda, my lovely "

Oliver Manners laughed loudly.

"I don't see why you're laughing," said Miss Miranda. "You'll be a dead cert to go and live in the new place."

"Well, it is supposed to be for my benefit, isn't it?" said Oliver Manners.

"Bollocks," said Miss Miranda. "You know perfectly well you're completely sane."

"I know," said Oliver Manners. "But your mother doesn't think so."

"'And after all, Miss Miranda, she have been trained for the job, haven't she?" said Megan. "I mean, no disrespect to Captain Manners by here, but if your mam says he's a lunatic, there's nothing we can do about it, is there?"

"I know," said Miss Miranda sulkily. "It's just not fair."

"Never mind, my lovely," said Megan. "Come over by here and look at my snapshots of my relations and Barry Island on a Bank Holiday."

Ambrose came out of the bedroom, where he had been brushing down his uniform.

"Hiya, Ambrose," said Miss Miranda. "Gosh, you do look handsome today. Isn't he gorgeous, Megan? Isn't he simply just too super for words?"

Ambrose grinned and patted her on the head.

"Cor, you sexy old dog," said Miss Miranda, and then her face clouded and she said: "You're not going to take Oliver away with you, are you, Ambrose?"

"Well, it's got nowt to do with me, Miss Miranda," said Ambrose. "It's your mother what'll be making all the decisions, not me."

Miss Miranda stood up and went to the window.

"Honestly, the whole thing is just too beastly for words," she said. "Fancy having a mother, who's an out and out shit house."

When Tom Manners, MP, heard of Mrs Mortensen's plan, he said to his father:

"The whole idea is utterly insane."

"That makes it very appropriate under the circumstances, doesn't it?" said Philip Manners.

They were in the study at Mannersville. Philip Manners was drinking a large whisky and soda. Tom Manners was drinking a large gin and tonic.

"That bloody woman is just twisting you round her little finger," said Tom Manners.

"I know," said his father. "But it's none of your business, is it?"

"It most certainly is my business," said Tom Manners. "As a Member of Parliament I have a certain status to live up to in this city, and when I hear remarks being passed in the Constitutional Club which are tantamount to an open assertion that my father is living in sin with a woman who is not his wife, I find it exceedingly difficult to live up to the high standards required of me."

"Bollocks," said Miss Miranda, who had crept into the study, when no one was looking.

"I beg your pardon?" said Tom Manners.

"You couldn't care less whether Philip here is getting his end away with the old bitch," said Miss Miranda. "All you care about is that Oliver's getting more attention than you."

"I think that's enough, Miranda," said Philip Manners.

"Everyone known that old flop belly here is trying to diddle you out of your business. Everyone knows he's trying to get you to cut Oliver out of your will," said Miss Miranda, pointing at Tom Manners.

"I said, that will be enough, Miranda," said Philip Manners sternly.

"He just doesn't want Oliver to be cured," said Miss Miranda. "He doesn't, he doesn't, he doesn't."

And then she fled, sobbing, from the room.

Tom Manners banged down his glass on the mantelpiece.

"Well," he said. "That, my dear father, well and truly takes the biscuit."

Philip Manners chuckled and poured himself another glass of whisky.

"You didn't believe a word of what she said, of course," said Tom Manners.

Philip Manners held his glass up to the light, examined its contents carefully and then smiled at his son and said:

"Cheers."

"I think it's an absolutely topping idea, Tierney," said Horace A'Fong. "All the chaps in the dorm think it's a perfectly wizard idea to come and live with you and your good lady wife."

"Good," said Ambrose Tierney.

It was still spring, but the weather was warmer. Ambrose was driving Horace A'Fong back to Mannersville after his visit to the dental hospital. They were in the navy blue Rolls Royce, and Horace A'Fong had had two fillings.

"When I heard about the plan, I went straight up to Mrs Mortensen, doffed the old topper and said: Congratters, old horse. Take me hat off to you. Spiffing wheeze,'" said Horace A'Fong.

He was of minute size. There was not a hair on his head. His front teeth protruded over his lower lips, and his slanting eyes and yellow skin were unmistakeable tokens of his Oriental antecedents.

11

"Had a dashed good wank in the dorm last night," he said.

"Good," said Ambrose.

The streets of the city were crowded, for it was six in the evening, and the workers were making their way home. The car crawled in bottom gear behind a blue and white flat-topped tram, which bucked and bounced over the cobbles.

"Do you think I'm going off the old hairymacchump as far as sex is concerned?" said Horace A'Fong.

"I don't know," said Ambrose, overtaking the tram. "It's not for me to say, is it?"

"Absolutely, old sport. Mind your own business." said Horace A'Fong, and he took off his silk topper and rubbed his bald pate with a scarlet handkerchief.

Ambrose followed the tram tracks for three miles past the foundries and the mills, the warehouses and the snuff factory, the abattoir and the rows of soot-flecked terraced houses. As soon as the tram tracks stopped, the countryside began.

There were scrawny fields. Pit ponies grazed there. There was a river. Anglers sat on its banks. There was a machine spraying tar on the road. Shortly after this Ambrose turned off the main road and drove along a winding country lane with beech woods on either side.

"Now you take Mrs Mortensen," said Horace A'Fong. "Dashed handsome woman, if ever I saw one. Fine set of teeth. Good jaws. A1 biceps, and the best pair of shoulders I've seen since Bombardier Billy Wells. Now she says I'm sexually disorientated."

"Oh aye," said Ambrose, and he slowed down as they came to the first houses of the pit village.

"Absolute rot," said Horace A'Fong. "When it comes to the old hairymacsexual intercourse, you won't find me going AWOL, you know. Only yesterday I saw Miss Miranda walking round in her bathing togs. I tell you frankly, Tierney, man to man, I'd a dashed good nerve to go up to her and volunteer to cut her toenails."

"I see," said Ambrose, and he waved to Arthur Topcliffe, who was leaning his bicycle against the wall of the Rocket public house.

The car passed a colliery, a row of miners' cottages and a marshalling yard. Then it turned left through a pair of large wrought iron gates into a gravel-surfaced driveway. In the

12

distance over the tips of the trees could be seen the towers and turrets of Mannersville.

"If you ask me, if anyone round here is sexually disorientated, it's that beast Nurse Mooseman," said Horace A'Fong. "Did you know the chap puts talcum powder in his socks?"

"No."

"Well, keep it to yourself, old bean. Wouldn't want to get the chap gated, even if he is an out and out bounder."

The driveway was lined by well-kempt copper beeches, and there were wild flowers on the grass verges. Butterflies flew above them.

Horace A'Fong wound down the window and breathed in deeply.

"The scents of spring, Tierney," he said. "How adorable they are."

They came to an arched timber bridge, and Ambrose dropped into bottom gear and edged the car slowly over the springy wooden planks.

"Stop! Halt!" shouted Horace A'Fong, and Ambrose followed the minute Oriental's instructions to the letter by halting the car in the centre of the bridge.

Horace A'Fong leaned out of the window and looked to his right along the course of the stream, which ran into a large lake.

There were rhododendron bushes ringing the banks of the lake, and in the shallows moorhens and coots picked their way delicately across the water lilies.

"What a topping view," said Horace A'Fong.

There was a small wooded island in the middle of the lake. A summer pavilion with a gilded cupola stood on the near bank, and in front of it a small lawn flanked by box hedges sloped down to a clapboard boat house.

To the left of the bridge the stream meandered snugly in its gentle floodbanks through the parkland, where Friesian cattle and Club Forest sheep grazed. A green woodpecker made its dipping sagging flight between the clumps of horse chestnuts.

"Absolutely ripping," said Horace A'Fong, inhaling deeply. And then he said: "I say, Tierney, would you be a brick?"

"Certainly."

"Well, when it comes to the point of deciding which of us

13

chaps are going to live with you and your hairymacspouse in this blasted suburban house, I wonder if you'd be a good sport and put in a good word for me?"

"I'll do me best," said Ambrose.

"Capital. Top hole," said Horace A'Fong. "Remind me to give you some boiled sweets when my next tuck box arrives."

And then Ambrose drove him to the house.

Next morning there were chiff chaffs singing loudly in the grounds of Mannersville. Philip Manners complained of pains in his back, and Mrs Mortensen prescribed a day's rest in bed and an increased dosage of wheat germ oil.

Coots fought on the lake, Nurse Mooseman had two poached eggs for his breakfast, Lord William was stung on the muzzle by a wasp and 'Baldy' Hogan told Wyndham Lancaster he had scored a hat trick against Ironville United.

On the lawns the other lunatics were disporting in the gentle noon time sun.

Brother Herbert and Group Captain Greenaway were playing quoits. Lance Tippett was repairing the struts on his kite, and Horace A'Fong was throwing a hoop for the old English sheepdog, Quimby.

Ambrose Tierney watched them from his cottage. He was sitting in the rocking chair, puffing slowly at his pipe.

Megan came out of the kitchen and placed her arms round his neck. She had high cheek bones and long lustrous auburn hair tied in a bob at the nape of her neck.

"You does love me, Ambrose, doesn't you?" she said.

"Aye, I do that, me old ducks," said Ambrose, and he patted her arm with the stem of his pipe.

"If we has a child, Ambrose, a baby like, and if he turns out to be a little boy, can we call him Mog after his uncle? I knows he have come to a sticky end in Splott, but fair do's he was a dear gentle soul in his boyhood and had a smashing way with dad's ferrets."

"We'll see, we'll see," said Ambrose.

"If we has the time, Ambrose, could we go to Cardiff for a weekend? I likes it there being as how it's my birthplace, where I was born like, and it would be smashing to visit mam's grave and the church where we was married and see if we can catch any sight of our Mog and his whereabouts."

"We'll see, we'll see," said Ambrose.

"If we dies, Ambrose, who would you as sooner goes first—me or you?"

"We'll see, we'll see," he said, and he reached round the chair, pulled Megan onto his knee and began to stroke her thigh.

"Oooh, Ambrose, kid, wait till my dinner goes down before that sort of thing," said Megan, and she broke free from his grasp. But she was smiling to herself as she returned to the kitchen.

Ambrose leaned forward and rubbed the window pane with the sleeve of his jacket. Through a gap in the cedars he saw Miss Miranda lie down at the feet of Oliver Manners, who smiled at her and began to stroke her hair.

He stood up and went into the kitchen.

"What do you think to this idea of us moving house then?" he said.

"Oooh, I doesn't think nothing, my lovely," said Megan, who was working on a patchwork quilt. "Where you goes, I goes. You knows that, doesn't you?"

"I don't like change," said Ambrose, pulling on his gardening boots. "Wherever there's a change, there's trouble."

"There'll never be no trouble as long as you and me's together, God love you," said Megan.

Ambrose smiled. He picked up a hunk of cheese from the dresser and kissed Megan on the cheek.

"I've got a few days owing me," he said. "We'll go to Cardiff this weekend, if you like."

"Smashing, kid," said Megan. Then she smiled and said: "I think my dinner's gone down now."

2

The journey to Cardiff was most pleasant.

They took a hamper of food with them, and they had to change at Derby, Birmingham and Newport (Mon).

Throughout the journey Megan read the morning paper. She

read it slowly, mouthing the words and licking her forefinger to turn over the pages.

Just outside Birmingham the train began to gather speed. Half-timbered houses became a blur. The wheels of the carriage hammered over the joints in the rails. The couplings creaked, and the ashtrays rattled.

"If the train should crash, I hope we both die instantaneous like," said Megan. "I should hate to think of us being mutilated for the rest of our lives."

"Aye," said Ambrose. "It'd be a bit inconvenient, wouldn't it?"

After a while the River Severn came into view. Small waders scurried over the sandbanks, and a tug pulling three lighters nosed its way into the mouth of the canal at Sharpness.

"I can't help worrying about Miss Miranda," said Megan.

"Why?" said Ambrose.

"Using all them naughty words. I never heard language like it since the day Uncle Windsor discovered they shut the VD clinic on Sundays."

The Tierneys stayed at Grangetown in Cardiff at the home of Megan's elder sister, Mrs Prosser.

It was a terraced house with an outside lavatory. Mr Prosser made fretwork models, and Mrs Prosser worked in the greengrocer's next to the chapel.

"Sanctimonious old bitch she is," said Ambrose to Megan as they sat on the pier at Penarth.

"And she haven't even invited our Mog to Sunday tea neither," said Megan, dabbing at the corner of her eyes with a handkerchief. "Two months he've been out of gaol, and she haven't even gone so far as to invite him over the doorstep. She don't even know sight nor light of his whereabouts, God love him. It do really upset me, do that, Ambrose."

The tide was coming in. A Finnish steamer with an upright smoke stack and timber lashed to its decks let out three long, mournful hoots from its siren. On the other side of the Bristol Channel the hills of Somerset were deep purple.

"I'll find him for you, don't you mither," said Ambrose, putting his arm round Megan.

"Oh, I wish you would, sweetheart. I'd be so much happier in my own mind, if I knew where his whereabouts was."

Next day Ambrose went to the Horse and Groom public house in the centre of the city. It had faded pennants and old

16

rugby club favours pinned to the walls. It was the local of Basil Yorath.

"How are you? All right, is it?" said Basil Yorath, when he saw Ambrose. "Pint of Home Brewed, is it?"

"Aye, go on," said Ambrose.

"Well, well, my old son. Long time no see, eh?" said Basil Yorath, and then he whispered: "I got a red hot donkey for the two thirty at Ripon. Lovely Melissa. Can't go wrong. Dead cert."

He was a small stout man with a wet lower lip. He was wearing an ankle-length black and white tweed overcoat with epaulets. On his head he wore a black Anthony Eden hat.

"Have you seen Mog Williams in your travels by any chance?" said Ambrose, when he had finished his pint and wiped the froth from his lips.

"Mog Williams? Owes you money, do he?"

"No. It's the wife what's looking for him."

"Oh yes. The old trouble and bleeding strife. Isn't they related or something?"

"Brother and sister."

"Well, you couldn't get more related than that if you tried, could you?" said Basil Yorath, and then he turned and raised his eyebrows at a ginger-haired half caste, who stood in the doorway.

"Wizard's Fancy, thirteen to two," said the half case.

"Shit," said Basil Yorath, and the half caste grinned and waited by his side while he wrote out another betting slip. As he was writing he said: "As a matter of fact I has seen Mog recent."

"Do you know where he is now?" said Ambrose, buying a pint of Home Brewed beer for himself and a rum and raspberry for Basil Yorath.

"Well," said Basil Yorath, folding up the slip and giving it to the half caste, "I does know and I doesn't know in a manner of speaking like."

He stood on tip toe and put his arm round Ambrose's shoulder.

"It's like this, kid," he said. "There's people what I'd tell, and people what I wouldn't tell, see? If it's personal like, well, I might think about it. If it's business . . ."

He shrugged his shoulders and grinned.

"It's personal," said Ambrose.

17

"Be here tomorrow same time, and I'll see what I can do for you," said Basil Yorath, and he dismissed Ambrose with a wave of his arm. The corgi dog he held by a piece of string looked up and snarled.

Ambrose presented himself in the Horse and Groom on the very day and at the very time stipulated by Basil Yorath, but there was no sign of Mog.

He bought himself a pint of beer and chatted to the man who worked on the turnstiles at Cardiff Arms Park.

"They want to pull the whole bleeding place down, man," said the turnstile operator. "Turnstiles? They wouldn't know a good turnstile from my old grannie's arsehole. Lumbago? I've had it five years, man, through working on them bleeding turnstiles. Compensation? They don't want to know about it. If you wants a job on the turnstiles, take my tip and go to Llanelli. They knows how to treat their turnstile men there, they does."

Three pints later Ambrose felt a tap on his shoulder. He turned, and there in front of him was his brother-in-law, Mog Williams.

"Hey up then, Mog?" he said. "How are you diddling?"

Mog blew on his hands and then glanced shiftily round the faces of the people in the bar.

"Do you fancy a vessel then?" said Ambrose.

He moved to pat Mog on the arm, but his brother-in-law jumped back and raised his arms to protect his face.

Ambrose smiled slowly and bought two pints of beer. They went into the back room and sat in the corner by the fire out of sight of the customers in the bar.

Mog sat on the edge of his seat and tapped his feet nervously. His long raincoat was ripped under the arms and stained with mud and grass.

"What do you want?" he said hoarsely, and he glanced round the room rapidly before taking a sip from his pint. It made him cough.

"Calm down, old lad. Calm yourself down. I've come to help you," said Ambrose, and at that Mog put his hands over his eyes and burst into tears.

When he had finished sobbing, he looked through his fingers at Ambrose and said:

"You couldn't lend us a couple of bob till tomorrow, could you, Ambrose?"

Ambrose raised his glass to his lips and stared at Mog over its rim.

"It's Meg," he said. "She's worried about you."

"Is she?" said Mog, and he took hold of Ambrose's sleeve. "One and six would do nicely. Only till tomorrow, mind, till I gets some capital together."

Ambrose brushed away Mog's hand and said:

"Don't you want to know how she is then?"

"Oh, I does, I does, Ambrose," said Mog. "How is she? A bob would be better than nothing I suppose."

They sat in silence until they had drunk their pints, and then Mog said:

"You didn't ought to have mentioned me to Fat Bas, you know."

"Bugger Fat Bas," said Ambrose. "Do you want to see her or not?"

"Who?"

Ambrose threw a threepenny bit on the table and stood up.

"Go and rot yourself," he said. And then he walked out of the pub and set off for the Castle, where he had arranged to meet Megan.

When he told her what had happened, she burst into tears and insisted that they return to the pub. Mog, however, had disappeared. The half caste with ginger hair winked at them and said:

"He've gone, my old son. Dispersed like."

Later that evening as they lay in bed Megan said:

"What are we going to do, Ambrose? I mean, we can't stand by and do nothing, when he's my brother like that. It's not doing right by him to do nothing, when he's in trouble like that."

"He had his choice," said Ambrose sleepily.

"Ah, love him, I knows he have had his choice, but you know him and how independent he is, when it comes to the matter of making a choise. He've got a mind of his own, worse luck, when it comes to doing the right thing."

"Mm," said Ambrose, and he rolled over onto his side and buried his cheek in the pillow.

A ship's siren wailed, and Mr Prosser's fretwork cuckoo clock struck one. And then after five minutes it struck seventeen.

"Ambrose?" said Megan.

"What's up now?"

"I thinks we ought to take Mog home with us and fatten him up and get him on his feet again. What does you think, my lovely?"

"No bloody chance," said Ambrose, and he rolled over on his back and fell asleep.

Next day Ambrose and Megan took a Campbell's steamer from Cardiff to Ilfracombe. There was a thick sea fog in the Bristol Channel, and they had haddock and chips for lunch and bought a souvenir tea spoon for Mrs Prosser.

On the return journey as the paddle steamer was churning against the tide off Flat Holm island Megan put her arm round Ambrose's waist and said:

"I mean, if we doesn't do something about our Mog, he'll turn out nothing more or less than a common or garden vagabond owing to the simple fact that no one cares about him."

"I wish you'd give over," said Ambrose.

Megan sighed and her body fell limp. She spoke softly with a hint of a sob in her voice:

"I knows he've not led a good life, Ambrose. I knows he've done wrong and been a bad egg. I knows he've brought shame and disgrace on the family and had his name in the *Western Mail*. But basic like, underneath it all, when you looks at it basic like, he's a good man with a heart of gold and a lovely way with kiddies, and he'd give his last penny to charity if he had a last penny to give, and, oh Ambrose, I can't bear to think of him with no one to air his vests and breaking into tears when he seen you like that, and not having one and six to call his own and being in such distress. It runs through me like a cold dagger when I thinks of him. I didn't sleep a wink of sleep last night, and it wasn't the tripe and onions we had for supper, and I'll not never sleep again proper till I sees him and sets my mind at rest, Ambrose."

"All right, all right, we'll have another go," said Ambrose. "Do you fancy a bottle of stout or owt?"

"Oh, Ambrose, you are a lovely man," said Megan.

And so Ambrose went to the Horse and Groom once more. Basil Yorath was not there, but the landlord said he might be found in Hallinan's.

Sure enough he was there. He was sitting by the leaded

windows with a thin woman, who had a fox fur wrap round her shoulders.

"Well?" he said gruffly, when Ambrose came over to him.

"Where's Mog?" said Ambrose.

"Him? He didn't turn up then, is it?"

' Oh aye, he turned up all right, but then he disappeared."

Basil Yorath turned his back on him and said over his shoulder:

"Well, if you was to ask my opinion, my old son, I'd say that was your problem. I'd say it was nothing to do with me, and that you was making yourself highly unwelcome bothering me with such unimportant trivialities."

The woman saw the angry flush appear on Ambrose's face, and, without saying a word, she stood up and left the room.

"Where is he?" said Ambrose.

Basil Yorath said nothing. Deliberately and slowly he lifted up his glass and finished off its contents. Then he stood up and put on his Anthony Eden hat.

"I'll give you a little tip, my son," he said still with his back to Ambrose. "If you wants Mog for a job, lay off. He's no good to no one no more, see? If you wants someone for a job, come and see me at Icky's gym tonight, nine thirty—and bring a few bottles with you."

Ambrose followed him outside into the street. The woman in the fox fur wrap was waiting in the back of the car with the corgi sitting by her side.

'All right, Winnie?' said Basil Yorath, opening the front door.

Ambrose grasped him by the shoulder and spun him round so that they were facing each other. He lifted him up under the arm pits and began to shake him.

"Where is he?" he said.

"Now then, now then, don't let's have no violence," said Basil Yorath, his feet waving wildly in mid air.

"Well?"

"Look under Canton Bridge. That's where he's been kipping these past few nights."

Ambrose dropped him, and he staggered backwards into the car.

"You bastard," he shouted as Ambrose strode away. "You big bastard, you've torn one of my bloody epaulets."

Mog was not under Canton Bridge, but on payment of a

florin an old man in a naval greatcoat tended the information that he might be found in the Castle Market.

Mog was indeed in the Castle Market. He was standing by a tea stall, clutching a half-eaten turnip to his chest. When he saw Ambrose, he waved his arm and said:

"Ambrose, my old son. How are you, boy? How's Meg, eh? Fit and well, is it? I was only thinking about her the other day and hoping she was in the pink and not under the weather. Right?"

"Now listen here, bugger," said Ambrose. "Meg wants to see you. Now do you want to see her? Yes or no?"

'Well now, my old flower, that's a proposition that sounds most appealing. I'd have to consider, think about like, whether it could be fitted in with my current commitments, what I got on at the moment like, but I'll certainly see what I can do for you. Right? When are you going back?"

"Tomorrow morning."

'What train?"

"The 9.15."

"Right. Being as how it's family I'll see if I can accommodate you this evening. Royal Arcade, eight o'clock, prompt. Right?"

"You'd better be there," said Ambrose.

But Mog was not there at eight o'clock. They waited for an hour, and then Ambrose said:

"I'm off."

"Oh dearie dearie me," said Megan, panting as she struggled to keep up with her husband. "I bet he have had an accident. I bet he's in the Infirmary with tubes sticking out of him. I bet he's at death's door at this very moment."

"Well, I wish he'd knock and walk right in, said Ambrose.

The train left Cardiff General station at precisely 9.15 next morning.

At precisely 9.17 the door of the Tierneys' compartment opened, and Mog Williams entered.

"How are you?" he said. "I've decided to honour you with my presence for the next few months. Right?"

"Oh, Mog, Mog," said Megan, clasping him to her bosom. "Look at your fingernails, my love. They're as black as the ace of spades and there's terrible rust on your collar stud."

Ambrose stared silently at his brother-in-law. His jaws began

22

to work, and he clenched his fists behind his back. Then he stepped out into the corridor, saying:

"Right. I'll leave you two to it."

He leaned out of the window and watched the countryside slip by. On the flat marshlands round the mouth of the Rhymney river there were flocks of black-headed gulls and lapwings. Ponies grazed on the soft water meadows, and the water sparkled in the Channel.

When he returned to the compartment Mog looked up with his mouth full of cold faggot and said:

"Howdie, Ambrose, my son. Sit down and help yourself to the grub. Have a beer, if you wants one."

Ambrose sat down on the seat opposite and took out a roll of black pudding from the food hamper. He cut it up into slices with his clasp knife and tore off pieces from the cottage loaf, which Megan had bought fresh from the baker's that morning.

"I was just telling Megan, Ambrose, that you're in luck as far as me coming to stay with you is concerned."

"Oh aye?"

"Well, I had this big proposition proposed to me, see. Very attractive it was. Right? But I thinks to myself, no, I hasn't seen Megan and Ambrose for such a long time it would be criminal to disappoint them by not coming to stay with them for a month or so. Right?"

"Thank you," said Ambrose.

"Don't mention it, my old flower. Pass the black pudding, eh?"

Mog ate and drank steadily. And as the food and liquid passed through his digestive processes the colour returned to his cheeks, and his gums began to glow pink and healthy.

Halfway towards Birmingham he leaned back in his seat and rammed a fistful of Ambrose's tobacco into his pipe.

"Yes," he said, "There's so many things on the horizon I just doesn't know what decision to make for the best. You see, in my business it doesn't do to be too hasty. Right? You has to sit back and think, contemplate like, before you commits your capital, see. Now you take Fat Bas as an example."

"Fat Bas?" said Megan. "Who's he, my love?"

"Fat Bas? You doesn't know Fat Bas?" said Mog. "For your information, just so's you'll know like, Fat Bas is one of the most respected figures in the whole of Cardiff. Well, more like

23

the whole of the Principality if the truth be known. Right? Well, him and me, see, what we does when we gets a business proposition is to sit down with our thinking caps on and work it all out with regard to the various possibilities possible in the venture. Right?"

"Under Canton Bridge, I suppose," said Ambrose softly, but Mog ignored him and continued:

"Yes, me and Fat Bas has got our capital tied up in a hundred ventures. Well, a thousand more like the truth. Right? The trouble is you got to make sure, ensure like, that you uses it, deploys it like, to its best advantage. Now Fat Bas, fair do's to him, is never one to see a business associate short of a penny or two when it comes to considerations of the old ready, and after I comes back from my visit . . ."

"Visit, Mog?" said Megan. "Where've you been visiting, God love you?"

"Clink," said Ambrose. "The nick. Over the wall. Inside. Jail. That's right, isn't it, Mog?"

"Give a dog a bad name," said Mog and tears came into his eyes. He did not speak again until they approached the outskirts of Derby, when he said: 'I suppose you wants to know about my misfortunes then?"

"Not if it's going to upset you, my lovely," said Megan.

Mog shrugged his shoulders and then tapped his chest rapidly.

"This is where it gets you," he said. "By here. The old ticker. Deep down in your heart. There's wounds there will never heal in a hundred years. Well, more like a thousand years if the truth be known. Right?"

"Well, you wants to see a doctor, love you," said Megan. "You doesn't want that sort of trouble hanging round all that time, does you?"

"How was I to know he knew Wynford Vaughan Thomas?" said Mog. "You don't expect a sanitary engineer in Wrexham to be a personal buttie of Wynford Vaughan Thomas does you, fair do's?"

"What's that got to do with it?" said Ambrose.

"Well, I cashes this cheque in Swansea, see, on behalf of Talbot Baines Reed, don't I?"

"Who's he?" said Megan.

"Talbot Baines Reed? Cor blimey Charlie, you doesn't know who Talbot Baines Reed is? For your information, to

24

put you in the picture like, Talbot Baines Reed is a famous writer of boys' stories. Well, more like a bleeding literary genius if the truth be known. Long since deceased, I grant you, but nonetheless a dab hand when it comes to the old scribbling."

"I don't know, my love, you've got me beat," said Megan. "I just can't keep up with you."

"Well, things starts to get a bit hot in Swansea, see, so I takes the train to Bristol, where I'm known as F.S. Seymour. Right? Like?"

"But that's not your name, Mog," said Megan. "I always thought you was very fond of the name Maurice Mansell Williams. What do you want to go and change it to F.S. Seymour for?"

"For purposes of capital," said Mog, and he winked at Ambrose. "Well, it seems the police, suspicious bastards, starts asking questions. So I takes the train to Wrexham, changing at Shrewsbury like, and I goes to this sanitary engineer and buys a dozen lavatory seats on behalf of Wynford Vaughan Thomas."

"What did he want with a dozen lavatory seats?" said Megan. "He don't sound like the sort of man that would need a dozen lavatory seats when he commentates on the Queen opening Parliament."

"Well, the bastard takes one look at my cheque, and he says: 'You're not Wynford Vaughan bleeding Thomas,' he says. 'I knows I'm not, you daft twat,' I says. 'I'm his buttie.' 'You're bloody not,' he says. 'How do you know?' I says? 'Because you're bloody not,' he says. Well, next thing I knows I'm in the Bridewell in Swansea and this bobby's saying to me: 'Maurice Mansell Williams, alias F.S. Seymour, alias Wynford Vaughan Thomas, alias Audrey Russell, I'm charging you with false pretences.'"

"Well, I never," said Megan. "Fancy thinking up all them names. Still, you always did have a way with names as a little boy, didn't you?"

"It was the judge what upset me, though," said Mog.

"Why was that, Mog?" said Megan.

"Because of what he says to me. 'Maurice Mansell Williams,' he says. 'I'm sending you down the old swanee for five years on account of your false pretences and on account of you

25

being the biggest fucking rogue unhung in the whole of South Wales. Right? Like?' "

"What language," said Megan. "He didn't ought to be a judge using language like that—especially in front of criminals."

"No, no, fair do's to him, he didn't use the exact words identical like. But you could see what he was bloody thinking, and I don't care who he is, I'm not having no one speaking to me like that. It's bloody near blasphemy using language like that. 'I don't dispute the pretences, me lud,' I says. 'What I'm disputing is the implication of falsehood you've put on them,' I says. Five bloody years in jail, and I could have been doing my stuff with the boys in the Rhondda. There's no bleeding justice in the world, when you thinks how they was crying out for man power in the coal industry."

The train broke down outside the station, and they had to wait half an hour until a relief locomotive came out from the depot and pushed them to their destination.

As they got off the bus outside the main gates of Mannersville, Mog looked about him, breathed in deeply and said:

"Ah, I smells capital."

3

"But you didn't tell me this place was full of bleeding lunatics," said Mog.

"I didn't think it would interest you," said Megan.

"Interest me? Cor blimey Charlie, it bloody petrifies me."

"Why?"

"Well, I got my head to consider, hasn't I? I doesn't want it lopped off by some bloody nutter running round with a cleaver in his hand. That's the last thing in the world I wants. Right?"

"Oh, them lunatics is all proper gentleman," said Megan. "I'm sure they wouldn't do nothing like that to you."

"Don't you be so sure," said Mog. "Look what they done to Lady Jane Grey. 'Fancy a bit of a stroll round the Tower of London?' they says. 'Ta very much,' she says. 'I don't mind if I do.' Then what happens? All nice and matey one minute. After you, Claude. No, after you, Cecil—you knows the sort of thing. And then next minute this geyser creeps up behind her with a bloody great cleaver in his hand, raises it above his head, and, bang, Lady Jane Grey is minus one napper. Cor blimey Charlie, I learned my lesson from that, I tell you. The history of mankind's full of people what had their nappers decapitated by cleavers. Right?"

Megan smiled at him. They were sitting in the kitchen of the cottage.

It was the annual visitors' day at the asylum. On the lawns the lunatics chatted to their friends and relations. The sun was shining, and Mrs Mortensen was wearing a white linen suit with bell bottom trousers. There was to be a ball that night for the visitors.

"Why don't you go out in the sunshine and enjoy yourself and get some colour into your cheeks?" said Megan, who was working on her patchwork quilt.

"Not bloody likely," said Mog. "I'm staying here where I can keep an eye on my head. Right?"

He went to the window and looked out. The towers and turrets of Mannersville glinted in the sunshine above the great bank of cedars.

"Yes," he said after a while. "Yes, I smells capital all right. There must a couple of hundred quidsworth of lead on them roofs. Well, more like a thousand, if the truth be known. Right?"

Philip Manners and his son, Tom, were drinking whisky in the study.

"I don't see why I should have to bring every paper connected with the business for you to sign," said Tom Manners.

"Simple," said Philip Manners. "Because I don't bloody trust you."

"In that case why don't you take over the responsibility for running the business?"

"Because I'm too ill," said Philip Manners. "I'm proper poorly."

Tom Manners took a long sip of his whisky. A dry cleaner's staple could be seen on the cuff of his black jacket.

"You've got a career of your own as a politician," said Philip Manners. "When I die, I want the business to go to Oliver."

Tom Manners sighed, and he straightened the wings of his stiff white collar.

"As you well know, father—as I myself have informed you on countless occasions—under present company law it is impossible for a lunatic to inherit a business corporation of this kind."

"That's why I'm going to all this trouble to get Oliver cured," said Philip Manners. "And that's why I'm making sure you don't transfer the business to the control of your cronies down at the Constitutional Club."

"Preposterous," said Tom Manners. "I've a damned good mind to resign from the business here and now and leave you to carry the can by yourself."

"You wouldn't dare," said Philip Manners. "Not now while Sir Peter Wakefield has got his clutches so deep into you."

Tom Manners gulped back his whisky and poured himself another large glassful. His father smiled at him and raised his glass in salutation.

On the lawns the lunatics and the visitors were enjoying themselves.

There was a buffet lunch provided in the marquee. Stalls had been set up, too. Brother Herbert was running the tombola, and F.K. Henderson was in charge of the "Guess the weight of 'Baldy' Hogan" competition.

In the Lunatics versus Fathers sack race there was a dead heat.

Horace A'Fong took hold of Alderman Samson Tufton's arm and steered him to the fountains. The alderman was Lord Mayor and chairman of the Friends of the Asylum committee.

"I must say it's absolutely ripping to see all the chaps with their maters and paters," said Horace A'Fong.

"Oh, aye," said Alderman Samson Tufton, glancing nervously over his shoulder.

"Are you a wanking man by any chance?" said Horace A'Fong.

"Pardon?"

"Do you go a bundle on the old hairymacself abuse?"

The water hissed and gurgled in the fountains. A dog yapped, and a pied wagtail flew onto the roof of a garden shelter and flicked its black and white tail.

Alderman Samson Tufton glanced rapidly from side to side. Horace A'Fong smiled sweetly at him.

"Topping day, what?" he said.

"Aye," said Alderman Samson Tufton.

"Perfect for a spot of gardening, eh?"

"Oh aye. Perfect for gardening," said Alderman Samson Tufton.

"'And perfect for bird nesting, too, I'd wager."

"Perfect. Aye. Couldn't be better for bird nesting."

"It's also perfect, of course, for butterfly collecting."

Alderman Samson Tufton nodded vigorously. Then a broad smile came to his face, and he said:

"And it's perfect for a garden fete, too, isn't it?"

"Rather," said Horace A'Fong. "Dashed good job we're having one, what?"

The two men smiled at each other. Alderman Samson Tufton offered Horace A'Fong a cigarette, but the minute Oriental declined with a polite bow.

"And I'll tell you something else it's perfect for," he said.

"What's that, old son?" said Alderman Samson Tufton, patting his companion warmly on the shoulder.

"A good stiff wank," said Horace A'Fong.

"I think that's my wife beckoning to me over there," said Alderman Samson Tufton, and he stood up and walked off rapidly, breaking into a trot, when he heard Horace A'Fong shout:

"Toodle-pip, old fruit. Oodles of toodles what?"

Oliver Manners and Miss Miranda were sitting side by side on the two berth garden swing.

"I think it's rotten not allowing you to come to the ball tonight, Oliver," said Miss Miranda.

"It's understandable, I suppose," said Oliver. "After all, I *am* supposed to be a lunatic, aren't I?"

"Nonsense," said Miss Miranda. "Stuff and nonsense. I think you're the sanest lunatic I've ever met, and I don't think it's fair they should stop you coming to the ball."

Oliver Manners smiled.

"Never mind, Miranda," he said. "You'll enjoy yourself.

You'll be able to dance and dance all night, and everyone will say you're the belle of the ball."

"What's the use of being belle of the ball, if you're not there to dance with me?" said Miss Miranda, pulling hard at the chains of the swing and kicking her feet in the air.

"One day, when I'm cured, I'll take you to the most splendid ball in the world. You'll be wearing the most ravishing dress anyone has ever seen, and all the young men will be green with envy because you won't dance with anyone but me."

"Why can't it be tonight?" said Miss Miranda.

"Because your mother says so."

"Balls to my mother," said Miss Miranda. "She's an old bitch and all she can think about is sex, sex, sex."

"It's all part of our treatment," said Oliver Manners with a sad smile, and then he kicked his feet high in the air and giggled.

The sounds of the jollifications wafted faintly across the lawns to the small garden of the Tierneys' cottage, where Ambrose was standing with Mog.

"I comes here with the best of intentions," said Mog. "I comes here determined to turn over a new leaf and see you and Meg doesn't get into no trouble, and what happens? I finds I'm living in an asylum surrounded by a load of bloody nut cases."

"You know what you can do about it," said Ambrose.

"No chance," said Mog. "I'd never forgive myself if I walked out on you now. You needs an ex-paratrooper to look after you at a time like this. Right? Unarmed combat? Cor blimey Charlie, I'm like a bleeding gorilla when I gets started."

There was a faint rustle in one of the bushes surrounding the garden.

"What's that?" said Mog, jumping towards Ambrose and clasping him round the waist.

"It's only one of the bloody hens," said Ambrose.

"It better not come near me," said Mog. "I'll break it's bloody neck for it. I wasn't a marine commando for nothing, I tell you."

Ambrose pushed him away and sat down on the edge of the water butt. He took out his pipe and began to puff at it slowly.

Mog walked up to him and stood by his side.

"What's the set-up here ?" he said.

"How do you mean?"

"Well, let's face it, my old bath bun, you doesn't come across a bloke with an asylum in his back yard every day of the week, does you? It's not often you meets a bloke what wants to buy an ordinary suburban house and stock it up with nut cases, is it? Fair do's, Ambrose."

"It's because of his son."

"Wants to set him up in business as a trick cyclist, do he?"

"No, you balmy prat, it's his son, Oliver, who's the lunatic."

"Oh."

"Apparently he did something wrong in the army and got court martialled for it. And then when he come home he done something to his mother, and he can't remember nothing about it all, because he's lost his memory."

"And that's why they've set up this asylum?"

"That's right," said Ambrose, knocking out his pipe on the heel of his boot.

"They wants their bloody heads testing," said Mog. "I'd soon cure him. I'd soon get his memory back for him. Well, I seen a lot of lunacy in the Ministry of Labour, hasn't I? Course I bloody has. What I'd do, see, is I'd go up to him all nice and friendly like and I'd say: 'Now then, bacon balls, what's all this about losing your memory? You tell your old Uncle Mog all about it or he'll get cracking on you with a spot of the old ju-jitsu. Right?' "

Ambrose stood up and took hold of Mog by the shoulders and began to shake him.

"You mention one word of this to Oliver Manners, and I'll give you such a going over they'll have to take you back to Cardiff in an ambulance. Understand?"

"All right, all right," said Mog as Ambrose released his hold on him. "There's no need to be violent about it. Cor blimey Charlie, you're worse than a bleeding gorilla."

He walked away sulkily, his hands deep in his trousers pockets.

A narrow gravel path led from the cottage to the main driveway of Mannersville. He began to walk up it tentatively and nervously.

He had not gone far, when he met Horace A'Fong, who was walking towards the Tierneys' cottage.

Horace A'Fong doffed his top hat and said:

"How do you do, sir. Who's pater are you?"

"What's that?" said Mog quickly. "Who are you?"

"I'm one of the chaps," said Horace A'Fong. "As a matter of fact, old sport, I'm ink monitor."

"Are you trying to take the piss?" said Mog.

"Crumbs, no," said Horace A'Fong. "The point is I wouldn't know how. I'm a lunatic, you see."

"A lunatic?" said Mog, jumping two feet backwards.

Horace A'Fong smiled sweetly.

"I say, old chap, let's play a game. Come into the old hairymacbushes with me and we'll play doctors and patients. I'll be the doctor and you can be the patient," he said.

"If you doesn't clear off, you'll need to be a bloody surgeon by the time I've finished with you."

Horace A'Fong smiled sweetly again and began to move towards Mog, unbuttoning his trousers.

Mog retreated, and then suddenly he turned on his heel, fled down the path, raced into the garage and locked and bolted the doors behind him.

"Where's Oliver?" said Sir Peter Wakefield to his nephew.

"I don't know," replied Tom Manners.

Sir Peter Wakefield was the brother of the deceased wife of Philip Manners. He was a stout man with a cluster of hard-capped warts on the back of his neck.

"Did your father sign the papers?"

"No."

Sir Peter smiled, and they continued their walk through the rose garden. They climbed a flight of shallow marble steps and stopped in front of the sanctuary. There was a marble bust of Philip Manners' wife, and in front of it was an urn.

Below them was the summer pavilion and the lake. To their right was the parkland, in which the cattle and sheep grazed. There were one or two fallow deer there, too.

"It was her favourite view," said Tom Manners, nodding at the bust.

"Not quite," said Sir Peter. "I think more than anything she preferred the view of those small black figures on her bank balance, don't you?"

"Possibly, possibly," said Tom Manners.

32

"A quite appalling woman, your mother, I always thought," said Sir Peter, knocking off the ash from his cigar into the urn.

Tom Manners shrugged his shoulders.

"That Mrs Mortensen," said Sir Peter. "A fine woman, don't you think?"

"You always say that when you come here."

"Do you think we could regard her as an integral part of your father's assets?"

"Pardon?"

Sir Peter slowly re-lit his cigar and dropped the spent match into the urn.

"When we have finally taken control of your father's business, I was wondering whether Mrs Mortensen could be legitimately regarded as belonging to us."

"I think you're being decidedly over-optimistic," said Tom. "My father is well aware of what we are doing, you know."

"Exactly," said Sir Peter. "Splendid. Perfect. That means he'll be completely off his guard against those things we are doing without his knowledge."

"I don't follow."

Sir Peter laughed and began to walk back to the house. Halfway along the rose garden he stopped and smiled.

"I enjoy being surrounded by nastiness, Tom," he said. "It's a great comfort to me, you know."

Slowly he extended his right hand and swept it in a wide circle to encompass the house and the lawns, the cedars, the fields with their grazing cattle and sheep, the verges of the driveway with their wild flowers and butterflies, the pale green spring foliage of the oaks, the misty blue of the lake, the sunlight glinting golden on the cupola of the summer pavilion, the banks of white clouds soaring above the craggy peaks of the distant moorlands, and he said:

"It's all so exquisitely, perfectly nasty, isn't it, Tom?"

In the marquee tea was being taken.

Alderman Samson Tufton filled his plate with smoked salmon sandwiches and sausage rolls and drank a glass of claret before walking over to Mrs Mortensen and saying:

"I wonder if I could have a word in your ear, Mrs Mortensen."

"Certainly," said Mrs Mortensen, and she led him to a quiet corner of the tent and said: "Fire away."

"Well, it's about that Chinaman," said Alderman Samson Tufton.

"Mr. A'Fong, you mean? A delightful little man, don't you think?" said Mrs Mortensen.

"Aye, mebbe, mebbe. But some of the things he comes out with . . . well . . . well, there are ladies present, Mrs Mortensen, and there are some subjects that are not talked about in mixed company. Do you follow my meaning?"

' Masturbation for example?" said Mrs Mortensen.

Alderman Samson Tufton ran his finger rapidly round the inside of his shirt collar, and then he mopped his brow with his handkerchief.

"Mrs Mortensen," he said, "I am a man of the world. Do you follow my meaning?"

Mrs Mortensen smiled at him and shook her head.

"No," she said.

"How shall I put it to you?" said Alderman Samson Tufton, and he took another large bite from his sausage roll. "During the last and highly regrettable world war I had occasion to do my bit as a fire watcher. Do you follow my meaning? Well, come the blitz and I and four of my colleagues are doing our stint on the top of Burton's building. Now then, Gerry come over round about eleven. In force, he were. Now then, before you had time to blow your nose the whole city was ablaze. Do you follow my meaning?"

He finished off his sausage roll and began to nibble at the first of his smoked salmon sandwiches.

"It's on occasions like that with the incendiaries whistling round your ears and the whole of the Moffatt Street tram sheds burning from end to end that a man begins to think about the fundamentals of life. How shall I put it? Well, he gets to talking about the basics. Do you follow my meaning?"

"No," said Mrs Mortensen, and she nodded her head in greeting to the wave of Hedley Nicholson, who was standing at the far side of the marquee.

Alderman Samson Tufton moved a little nearer to her, and he dropped his voice to a whisper.

"Man talk is what I'm talking about, Mrs Mortensen," he said.

"Ah, now I see," said Mrs Mortensen, and she waved a greeting to Hedley Nicholson's daughter, Estelle, who was talking earnestly to Tom Manners.

"And so we have arrived at the crux of the matter, Mrs Mortensen," said Alderman Samson Tufton, smiling broadly. "The discussion that memorable night on the top of Burton's buildings was in private. Things was said on that never-to-be-forgotten occasion that none of us would ever dream of discussing in public. Now do you follow my meaning?"

"What sort of things were said?" said Mrs Mortensen.

Alderman Samson Tufton winked and said between bites from his sandwich:

"You're a woman of the world Mrs Mortensen. Do you follow my meaning?"

"I do," said Mrs Mortensen. "And did you, in fact, discover who had the largest penis?"

The plate dropped from Alderman Samson Tufton's hand, and he took a step backwards. Mrs Mortensen smiled.

"Don't be so shocked," she said. "You see, the whole trouble with society today is that it is riddled with sexual taboos. We are captives of what I like to call our self-made human zoo. We are naked apes desperately trying to cover our pubic regions with the wallpaper of respectability. Do you follow my meaning?"

"These smoked salmon sandwiches are right tasty, aren't they?" said Alderman Samson Tufton, stepping backwards again.

"My patients here at Mannersville are the victims of this society," said Mrs Mortensen. "The trouble with them is sexual disorientation."

"Pardon?"

"It's all bottled up inside them, Alderman Tufton. So that is why I encourage them to talk about their inhibitions. I am delighted that Mr A'Fong talked to you about his problem. It shows he is getting better."

"Oh aye?" said Alderman Samson Tufton, who found himself jammed against one of the wooden struts supporting the marquee. Mrs Mortensen moved very close to him and said:

"You see, Alderman Tufton, whether we like it or not, we are all naked apes. And in his natural state the ape has no sexual problems. It is my theory, that all these problems are caused because man has trapped himself in that masterpiece of unnaturalness—the human zoo. You and I, my dear Alderman, are simply exhibits in that zoo."

"Aye well, don't you think we should be making the most of feeding time then?" said Alderman Samson Tufton, pointing to the buffet table.

Mrs Mortensen smiled and tapped Alderman Samson Tufton on the chest with her forefinger.

"I foresee a time when we shall rid ourselves of all these inhibitions," she said. "Within quite a short time we shall see the sexual act being performed on the stage. Sunday newspapers will show pictures of men and women copulating. The pubic regions will be considered fertile oases of enchantment rather than dark, dank groves of sin. Society will rid itself joyously, rapturously, riotously of its inhibitions, and we shall experience a spiritual and physical freedom that sets our souls soaring to new heights of self expression."

Alderman Samson Tufton drew himself up to his full height, grasped the lapels of his jacket, coughed and said:

"Mrs Mortensen, as chairman of the Watch Committee I can state this quite categorically—there will be public displays of the sexual act in this city over my dead body."

The ball started at eight o'clock. There was a seven-piece orchestra, and the pug dog, Lord William, bit the ankle of the lady trombonist.

Upstairs in the dormitory Horace A'Fong said:

"Well, the beaks certainly seem to be enjoying themselves."

F.K. Henderson snorted scornfully.

"F.K. Henderson loathes occasions of this sort," he said.

"Hear hear," said Group Captain Greenaway. "Still, with all the racket they're kicking up the Goons won't hear the men tunnelling.

"Father gave a ball in 1938. I was 18 at the time, and Delia Sibley was exactly seven months younger," said Lance Tippett, who was lying on his bed, arms behind his neck.

"Delia Sibley! Ah, that name brings back memories," said F.K. Henderson.

"I don't see why it should," said Lance Tippett crossly.

"Oh?" said F.K. Henderson. "You don't see why it should, don't you?"

"No, I don't," said Lance Tippett.

F.K. Henderson struck ponderously off his bed and

36

immediately Lance Tippett curled himself up into a little ball and began to shiver.

"No, no, no, please. Not again," he said.

There were footsteps in the corridor outside.

"Cave, you chaps. A beak," shouted Horace A'Fong.

The key turned in the lock. The door opened, and in came Mrs Mortensen. She was wearing a long black evening gown. Her shoulders and arms were bare.

"Well my little men," she said. "Well, well, well."

"I trust the festivities are proving to your liking, Mrs Mortensen," said Brother Herbert. "Verily I say unto Thee, with hypocritical mockers in feasts they gnashed upon me with their teeth. Amen."

Mrs Mortensen patted him on the arm.

"Thank you, Brother Herbert, we are all enjoying ourselves immensely," she said. "And how did you all enjoy your visitors' day?"

"Perfectly ripping," said Horace A'Fong. "Tippett's pater was an absolute brick."

"Was he?" said Lance Tippett, turning over on his side.

"Rather, old sport. He showed me a picture of Delia Sibley in her gym slip."

At this Lance Tippett began to sob once more. Mrs Mortensen smiled and blew a long stream of cigar smoke through her nostrils.

"Well, it's time for our confessions," she said.

"Oh, crikey, not tonight," said Horace A'Fong.

"Every night without fail. You know that," said Mrs Mortensen. "And we'll start with you, Mr A'Fong."

Horace A'Fong bowed his head and scratched his nose.

"The usual," he said softly. "Three times."

"You'll go blind," said F.K. Henderson.

"Rot," said Horace A'Fong.

"And what about you Mr Henderson?" said Mrs Mortensen.

"F.K. Henderson has nothing to confess," said F.K. Henderson. "Try 'Baldy' Hogan."

'Well, Mr Hogan?" said Mrs Mortensen.

"I missed an absolute sitter against Seahampton Town, and Nick Smith got sent off for passing remarks to the referee," said 'Baldy' Hogan.

"What did he say?" said Mrs Mortensen.

"He said Cannonball Kid was a cissy."

"I've got something to confess," said Group Captain Greenaway.

"Very good," said Mrs Mortensen. "Do tell me."

'On the prurience front—no activity," said Group Captain Greenaway. "Slight troop movements are recorded in the concupiscence sector, but venery and lubricity are being well contained, and the morale of the men is high."

"Splendid," said Mrs Mortensen. "And what about you, Lance?"

Lance Tippett took off his spectacles and wiped them on a corner of his pillow.

"I thought about Delia Sibley again," he said quietly.

"Good," said Mrs Mortensen. "That's the eighth time this month, isn't it?"

"The tenth actually," said F.K. Henderson.

"Even better," said Mrs Mortensen. "We really seem to be making a breakthrough with you, Lance."

"No, you're not," said Lance Tippett, and he began to weep softly to himself again.

"There he goes again—the old waterworks," said F.K. Henderson.

"Don't be such a stinker, Henderson," said Horace A'Fong. "Why can't you leave a chap alone, when he starts to blub?"

"Why aren't we making a breakthrough, Lance?" said Mrs Mortensen gently, and she went across to his bed and put her arms round him. He buried his head in her chest and said between his sobs:

"I just can't think of a single erotic thing about her."

"Poor chap," said Group Captain Greenaway.

"I can," said F.K. Henderson. "F.K. Henderson thought about her last night, and she was riding a bicycle."

"What's erotic about that?" said Lance Tippett, looking out from Mrs Mortensen's chest with a tear-stained face.

"If you can't see the erotic symbolism in that, you're not trying," said F.K. Henderson.

"Can you, Lance?" said Mrs Mortensen.

"No."

"Think of the mudguards," said Group Captain Greenaway encouragingly.

"Think of the chain case," said Wyndham Lancaster helpfully.

"Think of the handle bar grips," said F.K. Henderson crossly.

"Think of her showing her knickers," said Brother Herbert.

"I can't. I can't," cried Lance Tippett.

He fell back on the bed. His limbs shook, and his teeth chattered. Mrs Mortensen pulled the sheets up to his chin and mopped his brow with her handkerchief.

"No imagination, that's his trouble," said F.K. Henderson, and Oliver Manners, who was reading the evening paper, smiled to himself.

The buffet was served at half past nine. Hector Tippett and Mrs Tippett went onto the terrace and looked out at the fairy lights, twinkling in the trees. They were joined by Alderman Samson Tufton.

"Mrs Tufton's had another one of her diplomatic migraines," he said.

"Lance was looking well, though, didn't you think, Sam?" said Hector Tippett.

"They all were," said Alderman Samson Tufton. "They all look as fit as bloody pigs."

"Quite right, Sam," said Mrs Tippett. "And it's such a relief to know they're being so well looked after, poor souls."

An aeroplane passed low overhead. Its landing lights were winking, and for a moment the noise of its engines drowned the music coming from the ballroom.

"They come out with some right funny things, though," said Alderman Samson Tufton.

"They're forced to, aren't they, Sam?" said Hector Tippett, wholesale coal merchant and chairman of the public libraries committee. "I mean, after all, they are a bit short of change on the top deck, aren't they?"

"I've told you before about saying things like that, Hector," said Mrs Tippett. "You know perfectly well what Mrs Mortensen says. They are simply mental invalids. There's no difference between them and someone suffering from heartburn. The only difference is they've got heartburn of the brain. That's how Mrs Mortensen explained it to me, any road."

"Mrs Mortensen! The merry bloody widow," said Hector Tippett.

"Don't be so disgusting, Hector, mentioning such words in

39

company," said Mrs Tippett. "If you're going to talk like that, I'm not stopping a minute longer. I'll go and see how Mrs Tufton's going on, poor soul."

After she had gone the two men lit cigars. It was still warm. The scent from the wallflowers was strong. In the distance mallards were quacking on the lake.

"You're not wrong about Mrs Mortensen, Hector," said Alderman Samson Tufton. "You're spot on, in fact."

"I've seen her sort before," said Hector Tippett. "By the heck, I could tell you some tales about the days I was on the waggons what would make your hair stand on end. What you don't learn about women, delivering coal isn't worth knowing."

"You're not wrong, Hector. You're right," said Alderman Samson Tufton after a few moments' contemplation. "Do you know what she said to me in the tea tent this afternoon?"

"No."

Alderman Samson Tufton looked over his shoulder. Then he leaned forward and whispered into Hector Tippett's ear.

Hector Tippett's eyes widened, and his mouth sagged.

"I didn't know you was a fire watcher, Sam," he said. Then he stroked his chin thoughtfully: "Who had got the biggest one, any road?"

"That isn't the point," said Alderman Samson Tufton, stamping his left foot angrily. "The point is, she didn't ought to talk about such subjects in the presence of ladies."

Hector Tippett nodded gravely.

"Mind you," he said. "When I were on the waggons delivering round the back of York Street some of the conversations you overheard the women having in the privvies would make your hair stand on end. It bloody would."

"That's nowt," said Alderman Samson Tufton. "You should have heard what she said to me about what were going to happen in the future."

"What?"

"Well, in a nut shell she were implying that come 1970, and all you'll get will be unrestrained hanky panky."

'Mm," said Hector Tippett, and he leaned his elbows on the stone parapet of the verandah.

The music grew louder. Another plane passed overhead. The light from the Tierneys' cottage twinkled through the gap in the cedars.

"I don't know what the world's coming to, Hector," said Alderman Samson Tufton. "Morals? They don't want to know. The sanctity of the marriage vows? Up your arsehole. Society is being corrupted in front of our very eyes. And do you know what's at the bottom of it all?"

"No," said Hector Tippett.

"Hanky panky," said Alderman Samson Tufton with a shake of his head.

Megan sat in the rocking chair in the cottage. On her knee was the open snapshot album. Miss Miranda sat on the window ledge.

"And this by here is a snapshot of my brother, Mog, what has just come to live with us," said Megan. "It was took on Remembrance Sunday just before Cuthbert Loosemore hit him on the head with a bottle for not keeping the two minutes silence."

"Do you think I'm beautiful, Megan?" said Miss Miranda.

"Oh, I does, my lovely, I thinks you're as pretty as a picture."

,'Do you think I'm a grown-up woman?"

"Well, I doesn't know about that, love you. I mean, you're only sixteen, aren't you?"

"Women mature these days much earlier than they used, if you must know. And, in any case, you know Mary Queen of Scots? Well, she was married at the age of fifteen and in Samoa girls are ready for sex at the age of twelve. And you know the heart of darkest Africa? Well, the women there . . ."

She giggled and stood up. She twirled herself round, and her green eyes flashed, and her dress spun up round her thighs.

"Look at my bust, Megan," she said, and she stuck out her chest. "I think I've got the best pair of tits at the ball tonight."

"Oh, Miss Miranda, you didn't ought to use words like that. You ought to use the proper word when you're talking about your dingle danglers like that," said Megan. "I don't know what God would say, if He heard you. I knows what He'd say most probable. He'd say: 'Oh dearie dearie me, what a naughty word Miss Miranda just used. Though, fair do's, Jesus, she don't use them often, do she?' "

Miss Miranda laughed and kissed Megan on the cheek.

"I'm not as beautiful as you, though, Megan. You're as pretty as a picture, my lovely," she said.

41

The moon had disappeared behind the clouds, and there was a single shaft of light from the study window gashing the darkness of the lawns. Someone staggered out of the shrubbery, reeled drunkenly in the beam of light, and then disappeared. Through the open window they could hear laughter and the notes of a piano.

"Megan?" said Miss Miranda. "You know Lord William?"

"Of course I does. I never seen such big fleas as what he've got on him."

"Well, he's got a bald patch on his muzzle, and there's a sore there."

"I expect he've got a rash, love him."

"Will he die, Megan?"

"Eventual like. We all has to die sooner or later, hasn't we, Miss Miranda?"

"Has your mother died yet, Megan?"

"Yes, she have, my love. She took a nasty attack of TB, and she never was the same till she passed on the day after Bonfire Night."

"Is your father dead yet, Megan?"

"Well, he come over badly after his trip to Tredegar, see. He come home like a drowned rat, and mam says: 'Oh, Tudor, look at your clothes, boy, they're soaked to the skin. Take them off and rub yourself down with liniment.' But he wouldn't have it. Out he goes to the pub, and that's the last time I seen him on his own two feet."

"Do you think I've got sex appeal, Megan?"

"Shockin' pneumonia it was. Shockin'. The neighbours said they never heard anyone spit so loud. And the coughin'? Shockin' Shockin' it was. Morning, noon and night. Shook the whole house it did. After he'd passed on, we had to have five new slates on the coal shed."

"I'm 36 round the bust. Antoinette Lilley's 38½, but everyone knows her back's much wider than mine, and she weighs eleven stone, so that doesn't count, does it, Megan?"

"The whole trouble was he hadn't got the constitution for pneumonia, see. All that drinking and walking round in wet trousers. Well, it affected his pipes, see. The pipes in his chest just gave up the ghost."

Miss Miranda pointed out of the window.

"Look, Megan," she cried. "Isn't that Tom with a woman?"

"I blames his resistance. He'd no resistance, see. 'He'd no

42

resistance, see, Mrs Williams,' the doctor says to mam. And mam says to our Mog: 'Let that be a lesson to you, Mog.' But he didn't take no notice. Dad was hardly under the sods, when he was off to Splott boozing and keeping bad company."

"It is Tom," said Miss Miranda. "I wonder who the woman is."

Tom Manners and Estelle Nicholson sat on the lawn in front of the wooden summer pavillion. He put his arm round her waist, and she rested her head on his shoulders.

"Estelle?" he said.

"Yes, Tom?"

He coughed, stood up and walked the three feet to the edge of the lake. Then he turned to her, clasped his hands tightly to his chest and said:

"As you are no doubt aware, Estelle, Parliament is at this moment in time in recess."

"That's right, Tom. You're on holidays."

"That being the case, I consider the moment is now opportune to put a certain question to you."

"Yes, Tom?"

"There comes a time in every Member of Parliament's life, when he or she has to consider his or her marital status. The exigencies of public life are such as to render the status of batchelor—or spinster for that matter—undesirable, when one reaches 'that certain age'. Accordingly I am compelled to ask myself the following question—am I, all things being equal, doing the right thing by my constituents?"

Estelle began to giggle softly to herself, and Tom Manners bounced up and down on his heels.

"Estelle, what are your feelings with regard to changing your spinster status to that of the wife of a Member of Parliament?"

"Tom, my sweetheart, are you asking me to marry you?"

"Just so. Just so."

Estelle burst into roars of laughter. She threw herself full length on the ground and rolled from side to side.

"Yes, Tom, I accept," she said, and then she lay back and sighed deeply.

"Estelle, you have made me . . ."

He paused and looked down at her. She beckoned to him slowly and closed her eyes.

43

"Etc etc etc," he said, and rushed over and threw himself on the ground by her side.

"Well," said Miss Miranda sadly, "I suppose I'd better be getting back to the ball."

"Please yourself, my lovely," said Megan. "But don't press yourself too close to the gentlemen when you're dancing with them. That sort of thing gives gentlemen ideas, see?"

"What sort of ideas, Megan?"

"Oh, I didn't ought to tell you, my lovely. They're nasty ideas that a girl of your age didn't ought to know about."

"You mean, they might want to try and get their end away?"

"Oh dearie dearie me, there she goes again," said Megan.

At that moment there was a heavy clumping of feet on the stairs. Mog stumbled through the kitchen door and sank down on a chair.

His hair was covered in cobwebs, his collar was covered in oil and there was a rip in the knee of his trousers.

"Mog, my lovely, where have you been, my son?" said Megan.

"Locked in the garage," said Mog. "Cor blimey Charlie, I been in there five hours. I had to climb out of the fanlight in the end, didn't I? Course I bloody did."

"But what was you doing in the garage, Mog?" said Megan. "You can't drive, can you?"

"I was attacked by a bloody Chinaman. Talk about the yellow peril. Stone me, it was worse than being in the bloody Chindits."

He began to remove the cobwebs from his hair. Miss Miranda giggled, and he looked up and glared at her.

"Now then, Miss Miranda," said Megan. "I'd like to introduce you to my brother, Mr Williams. Mr Williams, this is Miss Miranda. Miss Miranda, this is my brother, Mr Williams."

"Are you the one who's spent all his time in clink?" said Miss Miranda. "How super, I've never met a real live criminal before."

"Is she another one of the loonies then?" said Mog.

"No, I'm not one of the loonies," said Miss Miranda angrily.

"Miss Miranda is the daughter of Mrs Mortensen what is in charge of all those poor gentlemen lunatics, aren't you, my lovely?" said Megan.

44

"I don't care if she's the daughter of Lord Chief Justice Parker," said Mog. "She've no right to mention my record before the verdict have been reached. Right?"

Miss Miranda giggled and said:

"I'm sorry. It's just that I was so excited to meet you. I've always wanted to meet a genuine criminal."

"Listen to me, sweetheart," said Mog. "It's not only criminals what is stuck in clink. Right? Oscar Wilde? It wasn't nicking bobs from gas meters what got him in Reading Gaol. Right? Lord Haw Haw? They didn't stick him in the Tower of London for not having no dog licence, did they? Right? Mrs Pankhurst? You'll be telling me next they put her inside for bloody soliciting. Right?"

"Doesn't he have the most super way of talking, Megan?" said Miss Miranda. "He talks through his nose all the time as though he's got catarrh."

"Catarrh? You'd have a bloody sight more than catarrh if you went through what I experienced in the Battle of the North Cape, my lovely," said Mog. "Count yourself lucky you wasn't old enough to be called up. Right?"

Megan began to prepare supper, and when Ambrose came in, Miss Miranda said:

'Isn't he super, Brosey? Isn't it super he's going to be staying with you?"

Ambrose looked across at Mog and grunted.

"I hope you told Mr Williams that all the lunatics here have got the most frightful sex problems," said Miss Miranda to Megan.

"Sex problems? They doesn't only apply to lunatics, my lovely," said Mog, helping himself to a mug of nettle beer.

"Why? Have you got them?" said Miss Miranda.

"Me? Course I hasn't," said Mog. "I got too much on my mind with my business commitments to bother myself about sex, hasn't I? Course I bloody has."

"Don't you bother with women then?"

"Women? Members of the opposite gender? I detests them, my sweetheart. Well, not exactly detests them. More like hates their guts."

"Gosh. Are you a homo?"

Ambrose chuckled, and Megan fiddled nervously with the knot on her apron strings.

"How old did you say she was?" said Mog to Megan.

"I'm nearly seventeen if you must know," said Miss Miranda.

Mog looked her up and down and said to Megan:

"Well, she either needs her tonsils out or a bucket of water thrown over her."

"Oh, no I don't," said Miss Miranda. "If you must know, I'm fantastically mature for my age. I know all about biology and how frogs copulate, and when we went to the zoo, Oonagh Liddel and I saw the orang utang doing something absolutely unspeakable."

"I'm not surprised he did with you gawping at him," said Mog.

"Oh, piss off," said Miss Miranda, and she flounced out of the room and ran down the stairs.

After she had gone Mog filled his pipe with tobacco from the bowl on the dresser and said:

"I don't know what you two would do without me to look after you. Innocents? You're worse than new-born babes. Yes, my old cream cakes, we got a long hard job on our hands with this lot, I tell you. Right? Like?"

4

Three days after the ball Mrs Mortensen chose the house, in which the lunatics and the Tierneys were to live.

It was Victorian. It was part of a terrace, and it was built of stone. There were three storeys, too, and there was a small fuchsia bush in the front garden.

"Well, Ambrose, what do you think?" she said.

"Very nice," said Ambrose.

They were sitting in the black Rolls Royce outside the house. For most of the morning there had been a light drizzle, but now it was fine and the pavements were beginning to steam.

"Do you want to live there?" said Philip Manners.

"I'm easy, sir," said Ambrose.

"I think it is exactly perfect," said Mrs Mortensen. "It is precisely what I had in mind."

"It's up to him," said Philip Manners. "He's the one what's got to live in it. Go and have a look round, Ambrose, and tell us what you think."

Ambrose got out of the car, went into the house and made his inspection.

He looked briefly in all the rooms and then went up to the attic. There were two rooms there. He went to the back room, opened the window and looked from side to side. In the next door garden to his right two men were standing by the side of a greenhouse. One of them was smoking a pipe. They were talking softly.

A woman came to the back door and called to them:

"Les! Mort! How many more times have I to tell you your dinner's going stone cold?"

"Has our Carter come yet?" said the man with the pipe.

The woman sniffed hard and tugged at the strings of her pinnie.

"No," she said. "Pat's probably made him stay on at her mother's for dinner."

"Poor sod," said the man without the pipe.

Ambrose shut the window, climbed down the stairs, walked down the front path, got into the car and said:

"It's champion."

"Good for you, Ambrose," said Mrs Mortensen, slapping him on the shoulders. She was wearing a navy blue anarak and tartan trews. "Well, will you buy it?"

"I suppose so," said Philip Manners, and he coughed drily into his handkerchief.

On their way home they called in at a public house. It was called The Green Man. It had green carpets and red, low-slung chairs. Above the bar was a lobster pot and two brass navigation lights. The barmaid's name was Rikki, and there were poodle hairs on the front of her jumper.

Philip Manners bought three large malt whiskys to celebrate the purchase of the house.

"I hope you're doing the right thing," he said to Mrs Mortensen.

"Of course I am," she said. Then she turned to Ambrose and said: "There is one thing, though, Ambrose. You will have to get rid of your brother-in-law. I cannot allow him to come and live with you in the new house."

"Brother-in-law?" said Philip Manners.

"He's staying with us in the cottage at the moment, sir."

"Well, why can't he go and live in the new house?" said Philip Manners.

"Because from what Miranda tells me he would be a most disrupting influence and would undoubtedly destroy the whole point of the experiment," said Mrs Mortensen.

"Well, you'll have to get shut of him then, won't you, Ambrose?" said Philip Manners, ordering three more malt whiskys from the waiter.

When Ambrose told Mog what had been decided his brother-in-law said:

"There's no justice in the world, is there? No wonder the criminal fraternity flourishes. You try to get out of it. You try to turn over a new leaf. And what happens? You gets a swift kick in the goolies and they tells you to sling your bleeding hook."

"We could always smuggle him in, Ambrose," said Megan. "We could always put him in that big sea chest of my Uncle Windsor's and then hide him in the attic so no one will know he's there."

"Listen to me, sweetheart," said Mog. "I got my pride, hasn't I? Course I bloody has. If I can't go through the front door with my head held high, I doesn't go at all. Right?"

And then he went out of the front door of the cottage with head hung low and made his way slowly towards the lake.

Horace A'Fong was playing croquet with Wyndham Lancaster on one of the lawns, and Mog crept hurriedly through the shrubbery to avoid being seen.

As he walked slowly down the driveway he picked up a switch of ash and struck at the wild flowers and the butterflies.

Oliver Manners was sitting alone on the wooden jetty which stuck out into the lake from the boat house. He was throwing tiny pebbles into the water. They made tiny ripples.

He turned and saw Mog, standing by the summer pavillion, staring at him.

He called out:

"Morning."

48

Mog hesitantly raised his switch in acknowledgement.

"Beautiful day, isn't it?" shouted Oliver, and then he stood up, walked across to Mog, extended his hand and said: "How do you do. My name's Oliver Manners."

"Oh aye?" said Mog. "You're the chief loonie round here, aren't you?"

"That's right," said Oliver Manners, laughing. "And who are you?"

"F.S. Seymour," said Mog.

"Are you a new patient?"

"Pardon?" said Mog, and then his face broke into a wide smile. "That's right, my old flower. I'm the new patient. Just come this morning I has. Well, more like arrived half an hour ago. Right?"

They began to walk side by side along the banks of the lake. Warblers sang from the reed beds, and a heron flapped lazily overhead, ignoring the mobbing thrushes.

"What's your problem then?" said Oliver Manners.

"Problem?"

"Well, we're all supposed to have the most appalling sexual problems. I haven't the faintest idea what mine is, I must confess."

"Oh, I knows what mine is all right, my old bath bun," said Mog.

"What?"

"Pardon?"

Oliver Manners smiled at him warmly.

"Are you too shy to tell me?" he said.

"Course I'm bloody not," said Mog, and then he took hold of Oliver's arm and whispered into his ear: "I thinks I got no balls."

"Good Lord," said Oliver.

"I has, of course, don't you worry yourself. Cor blimey Charlie, my equipment's second to none. Right? Where I falls down is I thinks part of it's missing. I goes for the interview with the gaffer, Mrs Mortensen, OC loonies. Right? And she says to me: 'What's up with you then, Mr Seymour?' 'It's my stones,' I says. 'Well, more like the old testicles. I keeps misplacing them,' I says. 'Poor bastard,' she says. 'Why don't you put them in a glass at the side of your bed at night?' What do you think I am?' I says. 'A bleeding contortionist?' Don't you swear at me like that,' she says. 'I can't help it,' I says.

'I'm a bloody nut case, aren't I?' 'That's right,' she says. 'And I hopes you'll be very happy here,' she says."

Oliver Manners laughed warmly again and said:

"She's a strange woman, Mrs Mortensen, isn't she? Did you like her?"

"I doesn't like any women, my old fruit," said Mog. "Look what Salome done for John the Baptist. Right? Look what Bathsheba done to Uriah. Right? Poor bastard, he's doing his stuff in the trenches with Joab, and his wife's shacking up with David. Right? Well, fair do's, you can't blame David. He wants his bit of nookie like the rest of them. Right? Well, he's been busy destroying the children of Ammon, see, so he decides to put his head down and have a bit of a kip. When he get up, he goes for a stroll on the roof, and there's this tart, Bathsheba, having a bath in the back yard. Down to the canvas, she is, having a rare old do with the loofah. Well, you know as well as me that class of people could afford indoor bathrooms. Even the bleeding miners wash themselves in their own back parlours. There was no need for her to do it in the back yard. Right? Provocative? More like an open invitation. Right? Well, old Dai knows when he's onto a good thing. He sends a messenger down to tell this tart he fancies her and to come up and see his etchings. Right? Well, she's no mug. She's got her head screwed on. Right? She don't take no precautions and a couple of months later she tells old Dai she's in the club. Right? No wonder he has to go and do the old dirty on Uriah. That's women for you, my old son. You steer clear of them like me. Right?"

Oliver Manners' face glowed with pleasure. He shook Mog warmly by the hand and said:

"Marvellous, Mr Seymour. Wonderful. You and I are going to be tremendous pals, aren't we?"

"Are we?" said Mog.

"Of course we are," said Oliver. "Meeting you has bucked me up no end. I feel like a new man. We'll form a partnership, Mr Seymour. Just you and I. We'll show them. We'll cure each other."

Mog looked at him thoughtfully for a moment and then shook him vigorously by the hand.

"You're on, my old fruit cake," he said. "And you'll see me right, when I've cured you, eh? You won't see me go short of a copper or two. Right?"

"Of course I won't. You shall have all the money you want," said Oliver Manners. And then the bell rang for lunch, and he said: "We'll discuss it further over lunch, Mr Seymour."

Mog stopped dead in his tracks.

"Lunch?" he said. "Ah yes, well, I won't be taking lunch today. What it is, see, I haven't taken permanent residence here yet. Well, more like I haven't moved in. I'm still clearing up a few business matters at home, see. I got to make sure, ensure like, all my business commitments is looked after before I becomes a full-time nutter. Right?"

"Well, hurry up and do it." said Oliver. "I can't wait for the day you move in with us."

That evening Mrs Mortensen sat in front of the mirror of the ladies' powder room in the Royal Edward Hotel. Next to her sat Estelle Nicholson.

They were the guests of Sir Peter Wakefield, who had organised a small dinner party to celebrate the engagement of Tom Manners to Estelle Nicholson.

Philip Manners, Tom Manners, Sir Peter Wakefield and Estelle's father, Hedley Nicholson, were in the cocktail bar.

"Did you ever know Tom's mother?" said Estelle Nicholson.

"No, I did not," said Mrs Mortensen, fixing a diamond clip into her hair.

"Tom doesn't talk about her much, you know."

"Indeed?"

"Apparently she died under rather mysterious circumstances."

"Is that the case?"

"I was asking father about it last night, and he said there were terrible rumours flying round town at the time."

Mrs Mortensen took out her compact and began to apply powder to her nose.

"He wouldn't tell me what they were, though," said Estelle.

Mrs Mortensen snapped shut the compact and stood up.

"Are we ready?" she said.

Estelle did not move. She looked up at Mrs Mortensen and said earnestly:

"It's all very mysterious, isn't it, Mrs Mortensen?"

"Terribly," said Mrs Mortensen. "Now shall we go?"

Estelle looked at herself in the mirror, and began to prod at

51

her mass of listless brown curls. Her lipstick was smudged, and there was a purple spot at the corner of her mouth.

"I wish you and I could become friends," she said softly.

"Come along, my dear," said Mrs Mortensen firmly, and she led the way out of the powder room, across the lobby and into the cocktail bar.

The men were standing at the bar, talking to Alderman Samson Tufton.

"Well, I'll be off," he said hurriedly, when he saw Mrs Mortensen enter the room. "I don't want to intrude on your celebrations. Do you follow my meaning?"

"Very good, Sam," said Sir Peter Wakefield, and he led his party to a table by the window, which overlooked a small stone-flagged courtyard.

When the drinks came, Sir Peter raised his glass and said:

"Well, here's to Tom and Estelle."

They toasted the health, happiness and future prosperity of the couple, and then Sir Peter said:

"You must be a very happy man, Philip."

"Why?" said Philip Manners.

"Seeing your son become engaged to a charming, sensible and eminently eligible young lady like Estelle."

"Mm," said Philip Manners, and he took another sip from his whisky.

"I must compliment you on your dress, Mrs Mortensen," said Sir Peter. "Most attractive. Most becoming."

"Thank you," said Mrs Mortensen.

Sir Peter stared pointedly at her bosom and then looked her straight in the eyes. She stared back without blinking.

"I must say, Tom, the constituency party is highly delighted with your news," said Sir Peter, turning to his nephew.

"Good," said Tom.

"A man needs a woman behind him in public life," he said. "I know that only too well since Margaret died. She was a great support to me. A great comfort. A great solace in times of stress."

"A great bitch, too," said Philip Manners, and he slowly and painfully hauled himself to his feet. "Shall we go and eat? I'm bloody starving."

There was little talk over dinner. Philip Manners picked gloomily at his vegetarian goulash and ate not a mouthful of his herb-flavoured junket.

52

Sir Peter watched him throughout the meal and smiled to himself with satisfaction. When the coffee and brandy had been brought he said:

"I'm sure I couldn't tackle vegetarian food with Philip's gusto, Mrs Mortensen."

"It's very much an acquired taste," said Philip Manners flatly.

"I can't see the point of it myself," said Estelle.

"It stimulates sexual activity, my dear," said Mrs Mortensen.

"Really?" said Estelle. "I didn't know that. How does it work?"

"Could we please have one evening, when sex doesn't come into the conversation?" said Philip Manners.

"Hear, hear," said Tom, and Hedley Nicholson nodded his agreement.

"Sex, sex, sex—that's all we hear about these days," said Philip Manners. "Can't people talk about anything else?"

"You sound just like Sam Tufton," said Sir Peter. "Personally I find the subject absolutely fascinating. Tell me, Mrs Mortensen, is Philip's diet having the desired effect?"

"How could I possibly know that, Sir Peter?" said Mrs Mortensen.

After the bill had been paid they returned to the cocktail bar. There had been a meeting of the Rotary Club in the Regency Room and a display of vacuum cleaners and food mixers in the Esmeralda Room. As a result the bar was crowded.

Francis McNeil, the editor of the morning newspaper, was talking earnestly with Alderman Samson Tufton and Councillor Mrs Mary Foulkes. A young man with a name pin stuck to the lapel of his jacket was showing a wad of catalogues to the head buyer of Haslam's Stores. The chief constable was demonstrating a trick with a match box and three cocktail sticks to the Broomhead twins and the manager of Williams Deacons Bank.

Sir Peter gave a cigar to Tom and said:

"Tell me, Philip, have you ever considered trying to re-open Oliver's court martial?"

Estelle looked up with surprise. She was about to speak, but when she saw Tom shaking his head, she closed her mouth.

Hedley Nicholson said:

"They tell me that fellow, McNeil, is a smart boy."

"Too smart for his own good," said Tom Manners. "I had occasion to write him a strong letter of rebuke only this morning. It was brought to my attention that one of his reporters, a rather disreputable scribe from north of the border, had been . . ."

"Or perhaps there's no new evidence to uncover," said Sir Peter, puffing placidly at his cigar. "Perhaps poor Oliver really did take the girl and . . ."

"Still, McNeil's brightened the sports pages up, I'll give him that," said Hedley Nicholson hurriedly.

Philip Manners stood up slowly, smiled at Sir Peter and said:

"I think it's time I got back to my maniac son, don't you?"

In the back of the car on the way home Mrs Mortensen said to him:

"You are mad with him still?"

"No," said Philip Manners. "I just treat him for the big fat bastard he is."

"He was eyeing me up all night."

"So I noticed."

"You don't seem concerned about it."

"I'm not," said Philip Manners. "After all he's not on a vegetarian diet, so I don't suppose you'd come to much harm, if he caught you."

An hour later Mrs Mortensen stood naked in front of the mirror, gently easing the muscles of her stomach with her fingers. She said:

"You know, of course, that he and Tom are carving up your business between them?"

"They're trying to," said Philip Manners. "With very little success, too."

He was lying up in bed, reading the report his trainer had made on his four race horses.

She turned to him. She had smooth skin and a deep navel.

"And you are not concerned?"

"Not at all."

She lay on her back across his knee and took the report from his hands. She laughed.

"They can't understand why a beautiful woman like me should give herself to a tired old man like you, can they?"

"Neither can I," said Philip Manners, and he picked up the report to resume reading about the progress of his six-year-old hurdler, Corporation Pop.

Over in the cottage at the other side of the grounds Ambrose and Megan lay in bed.

"Cuddle me, Ambrose," said Megan. "I likes being cuddled."

Ambrose put his arms round her and drew her into his chest. She sighed with pleasure.

"I think cuddling's better than the other thing at times, doesn't you, Ambrose?" she said.

He patted her shoulder and ran his chin along the top of her head.

"I mean, it's not so exhausting, is it, love? It don't make you pant and want a drink of water in the middle of the night, do it?"

He put his hand inside her night dress and began to scratch her shoulders.

"Oooh, smashing, kid," she grunted, and then she said: "Your toenails, Ambrose, they're like daggers. It's no wonder the sheets is full of holes and my shins is criss-crossed with scratches. Why don't you cut them some time, my lovely?"

Ambrose scratched her back harder.

"I can't help worrying about Mog," she said.

"Why?"

"Well, I thinks it dreadful having to throw him out on the street like that owing to the simple fact that we've been compelled to. When my Auntie Gertie threw my Uncle Windsor out of the house for carrying on with Mrs Duffy, he fell into the canal at Abergavenny, and that's the last we seen of him except for his pocket compass. I should hate to think of anything like that happening to our Mog."

"He doesn't seem to be concerned about it."

"Why?"

"I saw him coming out of the Rocket in the village tonight and he were singing his bloody head off. And look at him over supper. He had a grin on his face like a bloody Cheshire cat."

"It's very mysterious, isn't it, Ambrose?" said Megan. "I hopes the shock hasn't made him lose his mind or nothing like that."

In the morning Oliver Manners and Miss Miranda lay side by side in the long grass that flanked the main lawns.

The pug dog, Lord William, snapped at a butterfly. Crickets chirped, and a lawn mower whirred.

55

"Honestly, Oliver I feel fantastically sexy these days," said Miranda.

"Well, it's only natural, Miranda. You're a young woman now."

"That's just what I said to Megan the other night. I'm not a school girl any more, and it's high time I was getting my oats."

"Your oats?" said Oliver. "Where on earth did you pick up that expression from?"

"From Chloe Shoemaker, if you want to know. She had her oats last Christmas holidays, and she's three weeks and two days younger than me."

Oliver laughed and patted Miss Miranda on the knee. She brushed his hand away angrily.

"Don't laugh at me," she said. "I can't stand being laughed at."

"I'm sorry," said Oliver, and this time she did not move his hand, when he placed it gently on her knee.

"You can put your hand a little higher if you want to," she said.

Oliver began to move his hand up her thigh, and she closed her eyes and sighed deeply.

"Don't stop, Oliver," she said. "Don't stop. Keep it going right up to the collision mat."

"The collision mat?" said Oliver, removing his hand quickly.

Miss Miranda jumped up from the grass and began to giggle.

"Isn't it the most super expression?" she said. "Mary Bazely taught it to me last Easter."

'It strikes me it's a damn good thing you've left school," said Oliver, raising himself on one elbow and staring up at her. "Goodness knows what you'd have picked up, if you'd stayed any longer."

"Oh, what I've told you so far is nothing," said Miss Miranda. "Do you want to know what happened to Oonagh Liddell?"

"I'm all ears," said Oliver.

"Well, you know her parents?" said Miss Miranda, lying on the grass beside him once more. "Well, they lived in Ethiopia, you see, and what happened was Oonagh Liddell used to spend her holidays with them, you see. Well, this time a black man sat next to her on the plane, and he made her hold his Thing all the way from Rome to Addis Ababa."

"You don't say?" said Oliver.

"Of course, Antoinette Lilley had to go one better."

"Of course."

"She said that was nothing. She said her father's gardener used to take her into a corner of the paddock and make her put daisy chains round his Thing. I don't believe a word of it, though, do you, Oliver? I think she must have read it somewhere, don't you?"

Before he could answer, Nurse Mooseman jumped out from behind a rose bush and said:

"Nabbed you. Right in the middle of a snogging session, you filthy things."

"We weren't snogging," said Miss Miranda.

"Oh, yes, you was. Don't you tell fibs to me, madam."

'Piss off," said Miss Miranda.

"Honestly, what language," said Nurse Mooseman, putting his hand to his breast and clicking his tongue rapidly. "Talk about out of the mouths of babes and sucklings."

'You were saying, Oliver?" said Miss Miranda deliberately.

"You listen to what I'm saying, madam. Never mind him. You want to learn to keep control of your lusts, young lady, or you'll come to a sticky end."

"That's what Oonah Liddel came to just before Addis Ababa," said Miss Miranda, and she and Oliver burst into laughter and began to roll about on the grass.

"You—you're a damn sight worse than what she is," said Nurse Mooseman, pointing at Oliver. "You want your bloody head testing, you do."

"I am well on the way to being cured, if you must know," said Oliver, sitting up and glaring angrily at him.

"You're telling me, kid," said Nurse Mooseman. "We'll be having to put bromide in your Lucozade before long, I'll tell you."

"Why don't we just ignore the nasty little puff, Oliver?" said Miss Miranda.

"You little vixen," said Nurse Mooseman. "I'll scratch your bloody eyes out for you one of these days."

Miss Miranda turned her face away from him and said very loudly:

"Won't it be marvellous, Oliver, when we get rid of him at last?"

"Is he leaving?" said Oliver.

"When Megan and Ambrose set up their new home, he's going to live with them. And fucking good riddance, too."

"Now that's just where you're wrong, clever Dick," said Nurse Mooseman. "This kiddo's not moving nowhere. I'll tell you that for nowt, missy."

"Oh yes, you are. It's all been arranged."

"Oh no, it hasn't. That's just where you're up the creek. It so happens, Miss Sexton bloody Blake, that you're behind the times. The plans have been changed."

"Changed?"

"Aye. I knew that would put your knickers in a twist."

"Don't be so vulgar."

"My friend almost fainted, when I told him. He comes over in hot and cold flushes, poor soul. 'You want to put your foot down, Leonard,' he says. 'Don't you mither yourself, luv,' I says. 'There's no one going to push this kiddo round,' I says. Ooh, I was in a right tizzy, I tell you. I flounces into your mother's office with a face like bad fat. 'Mrs Mortensen,' I says. 'Mrs Mortensen, soft-hearted I might be, but soft-headed—never on your bloody nelly.' 'What's to do, Leonard, luv?' she says. Well, to cut a long story short, I told her that if she insisted on me going to live with the Tierneys, they wouldn't see my backside for dust."

"And she climbed down?" said Miss Miranda.

"Forced to, wasn't she?" said Nurse Mooseman. "Nurses like me don't grow on trees, you know."

"I know," said Miss Miranda. "They crawl out of little holes in the ground, don't they?"

"Hey up, don't you play the Lady Muck act with me, missy," said Nurse Mooseman, his neck flushing scarlet. "You want to think what's going to happen to you, when your fancy man here goes off to live with the Tierneys."

Miss Miranda's lower lip began to quiver, and Nurse Mooseman cackled and walked away.

"It's not fair, Oliver," she said. "It's just not fair, sending you away at a time when my whole body is being wracked by lust for you."

Oliver put his arm round her shoulders and began to stroke her hair gently.

At that moment he saw Mog skulking through the bushes, and he jumped up and shouted:

"Hoy, Mr Seymour."

Mog looked up, and when he saw Miss Miranda sitting next to Oliver, his face turned white and his knees began to tremble.

Oliver Manners took Miss Miranda by the hand and led her across to Mog.

"Miranda," he said. "I'd like to introduce you to our newest lunatic, Mr F.S. Seymour."

"F.S. Seymour?" said Miss Miranda. "But this is Megan's brother, Mog. He's the awful shifty-eyed man with the bloodshot eyes I was telling you about."

"There's no need to be personal," said Mog.

Oliver stared at him for a while, and then he said:

"Are you Megan's brother?"

"Well, in a manner of speaking, we is related by blood. Well, more like we're consanguine, if the truth be known. Right? I suppose you could say we was brother and sister being as how we've got the same mam and dad."

"Then why did you tell me your name was F.S. Seymour?"

Mog looked down at the ground, and his shoulders sagged. He spoke very quietly.

"It wasn't my fault the Marquis of Bute made Cardiff the biggest coal port in the world, was it? Course it bloody wasn't," he said. "Well, on account of his doing that, see, my dad comes down from the valleys. If he hadn't done that, he wouldn't have met my mam and married her and got his back trouble through falling down the hold of a Belgian coaster. Well, he couldn't work no more, see, after that. Mam said he'd have never fallen down the hold if he hadn't been on the piss with his mates the night before, but dad blamed it all on the Marquis of Bute. 'If it hadn't been for the Marquis of bleeding Bute turning Cardiff into the biggest coal port in the world, I'd never have had occasion to fall down the hold of a Belgian coaster, would I?' he used to say. Then comes the depression. Well, my dad couldn't help that, could he? 'That's right,' he used to say to mam. 'Blame the Wall Street crash on me.' Times was hard then, see. Dad couldn't get no work. I couldn't get no work. No one could get no work. Well, no wonder I got nicked for impersonating a minister of religion and stealing ten thousand sheets of quarto carbon paper. 'You had bad luck, son,' my dad said when he visited me in clink. 'You'd have been all right if you hadn't been wearing your bishop's gaiters when you had that punch-up with Icky Evans in the Horse and

59

Groom.' And that's how I became a member of the criminal fraternity, see. An accident of birth, it was. If I'd been born the son of the Marquis of Bute, I wouldn't have been put inside for cashing a cheque on behalf of Wynford Vaughan Thomas, would I? Course I bloody wouldn't. If I was walking round with a coronet on my napper, you wouldn't find Mrs Mortensen wanting to sling me out, would you?"

"The old bitch wants to sling you out?" said Miss Miranda.

"Because of what you told her about me."

"I didn't say anything about you," said Miss Miranda. "Except to say I thought you ponged."

"There you are, you see," said Mog. "Give a dog a bad name."

"Let's get this straight," said Oliver Manners. "Mrs Mortensen is throwing you out from the cottage?"

"More than that, my old jam sponge. She won't let me move into the new house with Meg and Ambrose. I got to sling my hook and take the next train back to Cardiff, hasn't I?"

"And that's why you told me you were F.S. Seymour?"

"That's right," said Mog. "I thought being a loonie for a few months might get me back on my feet again, see."

He shuffled his feet on the ground and then shrugged his shoulders.

"Well, I suppose I better be going," he said. "Sorry to have troubled you."

He turned to go, but Oliver called him back and said:

"But I want you to stay."

"And so do I," said Miss Miranda.

"Neither my father nor Mrs Mortensen has seen you, am I right?" said Oliver.

"Right, my old flower."

"Well then, you can still be F.S. Seymour. I'll see my father straight away and get him to fit you in as a new patient."

"And I'll tell the old bitch that you're a bosom friend of Oliver's and she's simply got to treat you."

"So you can become a lunatic after all," said Oliver.

Mog shook his head. Tears came to his eyes. He stepped forward and clasped Oliver tightly round the neck.

"Bless you," he said. "And if you ever wants Fat Bas to do a job for you, just you let me know. Right? Like?"

Oliver was as good as his word.

He told his father that it was essential for his future well-being that F.S. Seymour be taken on as a patient.

"I've only met him for about an hour, and already I'm showing distinct signs of improvement," he said.

"In that case he must move in at once," said Philip Manners.

Mrs Mortensen was a little wary of the idea.

"But I know nothing about him," she said to Philip Manners as they lay in bed that night.

"I do," said Philip Manners. "He's well on the way to curing Oliver, and what's good for Oliver is good for F.S. Seymour. He's moving in, and what's more he's going to live with the Tierneys when Oliver moves in with them."

Mrs Mortensen raised her eyebrows, and then she bit the inside of Philip Manners's thigh.

Next morning Oliver took Mog into Mrs Mortensen's office to be introduced.

"Lie down on the couch, Mr Seymour," said Mrs Mortensen.

"Right you are, my old flower," said Mog, and he took off his shoes and stretched himself out on the leather couch.

Mrs Mortensen looked down on him. She was wearing a white knee-length overall. The top three buttons were undone and a shaft of sunlight made a deep cool shadow in the cleavage of her breasts.

"Mr Seymour," she said. "What would you do, if I were to take off my clothes and offer myself to you?"

Mog sat bolt upright on the couch.

"Listen to me, sister," he said. "If you're looking for an excuse to hold my balls and make me cough to see if I've got flat feet, don't bother. I has. That's why they wouldn't have me in the Chindits. Right? It's true. It's true."

Mrs Mortensen pushed him gently on the chest, and he fell back on the couch.

"Don't worry, Mr Seymour," said Oliver. "It's all part of the treatment."

"Mr Seymour," said Mrs Mortensen. "How many times have you had sexual experience?"

"Once," said Mog. "With Mrs Harries."

"Only once?" said Mrs Mortensen.

"Well, that's the only one you could call an experience," said Mog. "Cor blimey Charlie, she put on a gramophone record and made me do it in time to the 'William Tell' overture. I was bloody knackered by the time the French horns came in."

"But you have had other women?"

"Course I has. All shapes and sizes and colours and creeds. Valparaiso, that's the place. Before the war you could buy a packet of twenty fags, a bottle of hooch, a six foot negress and a brooch for your old mam and still get change out of a ten bob note."

"Go on, Mr Seymour."

"What? About the six foot negress?"

"If you like."

"Well, her name was Doris. She was double-jointed, too. She could get hold of her fingers, pull the joints and make them crack like castanets. Cor blimey Charlie, gived you an headache, half an hour of that. Anyone got a fag?"

Mrs Mortensen handed him a cigarette and lit it for him with her gold lighter.

"Mr Seymour," she said. "When was the last time you had sex with a woman?"

"October the thirteenth, 1955," said Mog.

"Tell me about it."

"Nosey bugger, in't she?" said Mog to Oliver Manners. "Well, then, my old flower, me and Fat Bas . . ."

"Fat Bas?" said Mrs Mortensen.

"That's the name of the tart I was with," said Mog hurriedly. "Fatima Basra, they called her. A Turk, she was. Come from Turkey, see. Well, more like Cyprus, if the truth be known. Her dad was an upholsterer down the Mile End Road, wasn't he? Course he bloody was."

Mrs Mortensen smiled and returned to her desk.

"That will be all, thank you, Mr Seymour," she said.

"You agree to treat him then, do you?" said Oliver Manners.

"Indeed I do," said Mrs Mortensen. "Mr Seymour seems to have more sexual problems than the whole lot of you put together.

"Cheeky bitch," said Mog to Oliver Manners, when they left the office. "And I didn't even start to tell her about that bint I had at the back of a religious book shop in Port Said."

Ambrose came into the cottage after mowing the lawn. He

found Megan reading the morning newspaper. She looked up and smiled.

"Oh, Ambrose, I've been saving this up for you," she said, pointing to the Births, Marriages and Deaths column in the newspaper. "There's a lovely, tasteful in memoriam here. Beautiful sentiments it expresses. Shall I read it to you?"

"Aye, go on then," said Ambrose, taking off his socks and beginning to massage his toes.

Megan began to read slowly, following each word with her finger.

> "Heaven sent you, little mite,
> And now you're gone, it don't seem right.
> Still, dear Lord, in your infinite mercy
> We hopes you'll look after our little Percy."

She looked up, and on her face was a look of radiant happiness.

"Beautiful, isn't it, Ambrose?" she said. "Them's the sort of sentiments what are just right for the occasion, aren't they, my love?"

"Aye," said Ambrose.

"Ambrose?"

"Mm?"

"If we should have a little boy, and if he should go and die, be took from us sudden like, which with the good Lord's will he won't, but you never can be too sure, could we have a in memoriam for him just like that?"

"Aye. But you couldn't have it identical, could you?"

"Why ever not? Why couldn't it be identically the same, my love?"

"Because we'd have to call the lad Percy so's to get the rhyme with mercy, and I'm buggered if I'm going to call any son of mine Percy."

"Oh, you is a clever one, Ambrose. I hadn't thought of that," said Megan. "Still, we could express similar sentiments, couldn't we, my love? If we tries hard enough, we're bound to find a rhyme for Gareth, isn't we?"

She poured Ambrose a mug of nettle beer from the pitcher she kept in the press. He drank it in one gulp, wiped his lips with the sleeve of his shirt and was just about to hold out his glass for more beer, when Mog burst through the door.

"Hello there, my old flowers," said Mog. "I've just become a fully-fledged lunatic."

After he had explained what had happened Megan sank down in the rocking chair and said:

"Oh dearie dearie me, I doesn't like it, Mog. I mean to say, my love, we never had lunacy in the family before, has we?"

"What about Gladys Thomas?" said Mog. "Cor blimey Charlie, every full moon you'd find her sitting in the Castle Arcade squatting on a deck chair telling everyone she was fishing for bloody salmon."

"Yes, but she was only a third cousin," said Megan.

"Blood's thicker than water," said Mog. "Anyway, it's not me that's the lunatic. It's F.S. Seymour. He's the bloke you should be getting on to. I'm only playing a part, isn't I?"

"Does that mean you'll be coming to live with us in the new house?" said Ambrose.

"Course it does, my old swiss roll," said Mog. "And you'd better look after me proper or I'll lop your head off with my bloody cleaver."

5

Mog quickly adjusted himself to his new role as lunatic.

During the course of intensive examinations by Mrs Mortensen he revealed that kneecaps were his favourite part of a woman's body, that baked beans made him think of Mrs Harries, that his father had not been in the habit of closing the lavatory door, that he had once used Megan's knickers to clean his bicycle and that he saw no phallic significance in a stick of rhubarb.

He rather enjoyed the examinations. What he enjoyed even more, however, was the news that Mrs Mortensen had chosen him, Oliver Manners and Lance Tippett to go and live with the Tierneys in their new house.

"It was God's will that they should thus be chosen," said Brother Herbert to Horace A'Fong as they strolled in the garden.

"He is a bit of a strange cove, though, isn't He?" said Horace A'Fong.

64

"He is inclined at times to move in a mysterious way His wonders to perform, I'll grant you that," said Brother Herbert, brushing a moth away from his face.

"I mean, if a chap says the old harymacgentle Jesus malarkey every night, a chap jolly well expects to have his prayers answered."

"And yours were not?"

"No, they bally well weren't. I got down on my knees last night, hands together, eyes closed—that sort of rot—and I said: 'Now look here, old boy, how about sending down a plague of jolly old vipers or something like that to wipe out all the chaps in the dorm. And then, Bob's your Uncle, Fanny's your aunt, I'll be the only one left so they'll have to bally well choose me to go and live with the Tierneys. Amen.' A perfectly reasonable request, what?"

Brother Herbert stopped and took hold of Horace A'Fong's arm.

"But did you have faith, my son?" he said.

"Ooodles of it, old bean."

"Then somewhere, some time, my child, you must have sinned. He that sinneth and do not repenteth shall surely be doomed to eternal damnation."

"What a rotten swiz," said Horace A'Fong.

In another part of the gardens Miss Miranda threw her arms round Oliver and began to weep bitterly.

"I'll never see you again, Oliver," she said. "Never ever ever ever never."

"Of course you will," said Oliver gently.

"No, I won't," she said, snivelling into her handkerchief.

"That's nonsense," said Oliver.

"S'not," she said sulkily.

He took her by the arm, and they crossed the driveway at the front of the house and began to walk in the parkland, where the Friesian cattle and the Clun Forest sheep were grazing.

They came to the stream and sat down on the bank. There were clumps of lesser celandine in the shady spots under the trees, and they shone golden yellow. A robin sang in a thicket.

"Fancy having to leave all this and go and live in a rotten old working class house," said Miss Miranda, and she stretched herself out on her back and closed her eyes.

"It's all part of my cure," said Oliver.

E

Miss Miranda jumped to her feet and stood over him.

"But you don't need a cure, Oliver," she said fiercely. "You're the sanest person I've ever met in my life. There's nobody more saner than what you are."

"That's what I think, too," said Oliver, and he took hold of her hands and pulled her down to the bank beside him. She rested her head on his chest, and he began to stroke her long golden hair.

"Oliver?" she said after a while.

"Yes?"

"Do you mind me asking you something?"

"No."

She moved away from him and sat cross-legged, staring at him intently.

"Why did they put you in the asylum?" she said, and then she added hurriedly: "You don't need to tell me, if you don't want to. Honestly, you don't, Oliver."

A magpie chattered, and a small pale blue moth fluttered weakly over the surface of the stream.

"When I was 19, I was in the army," said Oliver.

"Super," said Miss Miranda. "Did you ever kill anyone with a flame thrower?"

"It was National Service."

"What's that?"

"We were stationed in Germany, and I caught polio."

"What's that?"

"Infantile paralysis."

"Gosh! Were you really paralysed, Oliver?"

"I was in hospital just outside Hanover for almost a year. They couldn't move me, you see, because I was in an iron lung."

"Gosh," said Miss Miranda. "How do you have a pee in an iron lung, Oliver? I've always wanted to know."

"Then they sent me back to England, and I was in hospital for three months. Then they court-martialled me."

"Why?"

"Because of something I'd done in Germany."

"What?"

"I don't know."

The magpie chattered again. The harsh rattle of its voice disturbed a party of woodpigeons, whose wings cracked as they crashed out of the tops of a clump of oak trees.

"And what happened here, when you got home, Oliver?" said Miss Miranda. "What happened with your mother?"

"Did anything happen?" said Oliver.

And then it was time for lunch. Miss Miranda walked with him as far as the house, and then she strolled over to the fountain and stared down at the goldfish.

Mog crept up behind her and said:

"How do, my old flower. You looks down in the dumps then."

"I am," said Miss Miranda. "And why aren't you at lunch?"

"Can't stand the grub. Right?" said Mog. "Too much of it, see. Cor blimey Charlie, I tell you, it's hard work being a lunatic. You doesn't realise what a skive it is being sane until you turn yourself into a nutter."

Miss Miranda smiled wanly.

"I wish Oliver weren't a nutter," she said.

"Well, that's the whole point of the operation, isn't it?" said Mog. "I'm not doing all this loonie lark for the good of my health, you know. I'm doing it owing to the simple fact that I'm going to cure old Oliver."

"You? How can you cure Oliver?"

"Listen to me, sweetheart. I'm a fully-qualified nurse, aren't I? Well, not exactly qualified in the medical sense of the word. More like I served my time with the St John's Ambulance. Right? There's not a thing you can teach me about nose bleeds. Right?"

"I don't believe you ever met a real live lunatic in your life till you came here."

"Didn't I? Didn't I? What about that bloke I knew when I was in the commandos? Thought he was Dorothy Lamour. He wasn't, of course. Right? But we just played along with him till he had his operation."

"What sort of operation?"

"For intestinal trouble," said Mog. "He'd been eating cigarette wrappers, hadn't he? Course he bloody had, the daft bastard."

Miss Miranda laughed.

"And how do you think you can cure Oliver?" she said.

"Simple, my old lovely. Simplicity itself," said Mog. "I gets pally with him, see. Gets his confidence. Swaps yarns about the old days. Has a few hands of crib in the evening. Rolls a few fags for him. And then he'll start talking, won't he? The more he talks, the more his memory will come back. And then when I gets him to tell me what happened in the army and what happened with his old lady, he'll be bloody cured. Simple. Right?"

"I know what happened to him in the army," said Miss Miranda. "I know why he was really court-martialled."

Mog grasped her by the arm, looked over his shoulder several times and then said:

"Right. Shoot."

"Well, you know Lawrence of Arabia?"

"Old Lol? Course I bloody does. Well, not exactly knows him personal like. More like I used to mend his motor bike for him when we was butties in the Tank Corps. Right?"

"Well, what happened to Oliver was the same as what happened to Lawrence of Arabia," said Miss Miranda, and her eyes opened wide. "You know the desert? Well, Oliver was fighting there on a camel and he was captured by the enemy and they tortured him something rotten."

"Lousy bastards," said Mog.

"This big fat enemy took him into his office, and he made him take down his trousers. And you know Mary Bazely? Well, she says her brother was bummed by the captain of rugger on his first day at school, and that's what almost happened to Oliver except that he was too quick and he jumped out of the window and almost died of thirst before he got to Addis Ababa and he was court-martialled because they thought Oliver was telling fibs about what the big fat enemy had done to him."

Mog stared at her silently for a moment, and then he said: "You bloody liar."

"I know," said Miss Miranda, and she giggled. "Isn't it rotten telling fibs about the man you love?"

And then quite suddenly her eyes filled with tears. She sobbed unrestrainedly.

"Never mind, my old beauty," said Mog. "You and me can work together. Well, more like in harness. Right?"

"How do you mean?" said Miss Miranda, sniffling hard.

"Well, we're both after the same end, aren't we? We both wants Oliver cured, doesn't we?"

"I suppose so."

"I tell you what," said Mog, patting her on the arm. "You

tell me all you know about Oliver and what his predicament is, how he stands like."

"I don't know very much."

"You knows more than me, my old jam tart. I knows bugger all."

"All I know is that Oliver did something awful in the army, and then he came home and did something awful to his mother, and that's why Philip Manners set up the asylum, so's he wouldn't be put in clink for it."

"What did he do to his mother?"

"I don't know. Something happened to her on that bridge by the lake. Well, apparently only Oliver and his mother were there when it happened and no one really knows what went on. Isn't it all super and mysterious?"

"Super and mysterious? More like bloody heart-breaking," said Mog. "You'd get more out of Fat Bas at an identification parade in Canton than what you've just told me."

"I can't help it," said Miss Miranda crossly. "Anyway, clever Dick, I know something much more interesting that that."

"What?"

"Not telling. So there."

"All right then," said Mog. "All right then. See if I bloody cares. I can easy go back to Cardiff, you know. I knows for a fact Fat Bas wants a job doing in Bridgewater. I knows for a fact he haven't got rid of that lorry load of sponge cakes he nicked at Cowbridge. Right?" Miss Miranda smiled.

"If I work with you, will I become a criminal, too?"

"If you wants to, my old lovely," said Mog. "I can easy get Fat Bas to implicate you in the sponge cake job, don't you worry."

"How super," said Miss Miranda. Then she looked very serious and said: "I know for a fact that Tom Manners and Sir Peter Wakefield are trying to pinch the business off Philip Manners."

Mog whistled through his teeth.

"And I know as well that Philip Manners is going to leave the business to Oliver, and Tom and Sir Peter Wakefield don't know it, but he's going to do it before he dies, and that's why Tom and Sir Peter don't want Oliver to be cured."

Mog whistled through his teeth again.

"Now you're talking my language, my old cream cake," he said. "Now we're really getting somewhere, isn't we?"

"And am I a criminal now?"

"Course you is. A fully paid-up member of the criminal fraternity. Remind me to get Fat Bas to send you your membership card."

"How super."

That evening Mrs Mortensen came into the dormitory to hear confession.

Group Captain Greenaway confessed that strong forces of salaciousness had been intercepted at Angel One Two and thoroughly routed, 'Baldy' Hogan confessed that he knew Wilson had cheated when he ran the three minute mile and Horace A'Fong confessed the usual.

"Dirty little slant-eyed bastard," said Mog.

"And what about you, Mr Seymour?" said Mrs Mortensen.

"I had a dream about Delia Sibley, didn't I? Course I bloody did," said Mog.

"Oh no, you didn't," said Lance Tippett.

"Oh yes, he did," said F.K. Henderson. "And so did I."

"Oh no, you didn't," said Mog. "Don't you try and muscle in on my dreams, my old son, or I'll give you a clip round the bloody ear hole."

"What was your dream, Mr Seymour?" said Mrs Mortensen firmly.

"Simple, my old flower. Simplicity itself. She was having it away with Lawrence of Arabia on the back of a camel. I never seen nothing like it. Cor blimey Charlie, the old camel had three humps on his back by the time they'd finished, I tell you."

Lance Tippett began to sob, and it took Mrs Mortensen a quarter of an hour to console him.

After she had gone and after the lights had been put out Oliver Manners leaned across to Mog and whispered:

"You are rotten to Lance, making up dreams about Delia Sibley."

"Who's making dreams up?" said Mog. "It was true. Every bloody word of it."

A few afternoons later the sun was shining and a cuckoo was calling in the woods that fringed the parkland.

Out on the lake Oliver Manners shipped his oars and moved into the stern of the boat alongside Miss Miranda.

"Do you think it's possible to have your oats in a boat, Oliver?" said Miss Miranda lazily.

Oliver laughed and put his arm round her neck.

"Chloe Shoemaker's sister had it away with her boy friend on a punt in Cambridge," said Miss Miranda. "And you know Oonagh Liddell? Well, she says she was conceived on the Empress of Britain."

The boat drifted slowly towards the bank. Swallows skimmed low over the surface of the lake, and there was the scent of wood smoke.

"I was asking the old bitch last night what was wrong with you, Oliver. She said you were sexually inhibited. Does that mean you're frightened of sex, Oliver?"

The boat nuzzled softly into the bank. A dragonfly alighted for a second on one of the rowlocks, and then the breese caught it, and it drifted away.

"You know when you're conceived, Oliver? Well, I wonder whether it makes any difference to you where it happens. I mean Oonagh Liddell's got bow legs when she plays hockey and Sister Concepta always gave her a beta minus for deportment and sailors all have bow legs and walk with a roll, don't they?"

"I believe they do," said Oliver, lying back and closing his eyes.

"It makes me fed up that I was conceived in a rotten old ordinary bed. I mean, it was during the war and my father was Danish and if he hadn't been living in England, the Germans would have been bound to put him in a concentration camp for blowing up bridges and helping pilots to escape, and that's where I'd have been conceived, and I'd be all willowy and slim now, because they were all emaciated in Belsen."

"You're all willowy and slim now, Miranda," said Oliver, and the sunlight made jagged, shifting patterns on the inside of his eyelids.

"Super," said Miss Miranda. Then she said thoughtfully: "You know when you were a soldier in Germany, Oliver, before you got infantile polio or whatever you call it? Well, did you ever have a German girl? I mean, did you ever have knowledge of her?"

"No, I was far too young for that, Miranda."

"Then you are frightened of sex, aren't you? Aren't you, Oliver?"

71

Oliver shrugged his shoulders and grinned.

"How super," she said. "How absolutely super."

And then she sat up and removed the top of her bathing costume.

"There, Oliver," she said. "Look at those."

"Well, well," said Mrs Mortensen, looking through her binoculars at her daughter.

"Let's have a look," said Philip Manners, and he took the binoculars and trained them on the boat. "Bloody hell fire."

"She's very well-developed, isn't she?" said Mrs Mortensen. "She's beautifully firm. Just like me."

"Should she be doing that? Will she be safe? Will he be safe? Bloody hell, she shouldn't be doing that—a girl of her age in a rowing boat with a lunatic even if he is my own son."

"She is quite safe," said Mrs Mortensen. "And it will do them both a world of good."

They were in the summer pavilion, and the door was locked.

"I sometimes think I'm living in a bloody mad house," said Philip Manners.

"You are," said Mrs Mortensen, and she looked through her binoculars once more. "Good, good. Excellent."

"What's up now?"

"She's taken off the bottom half."

"Oh Christ. And what's he doing?"

"Rowing for all he is worth back to the shore," said Mrs Mortensen, and they both began to laugh.

Mrs Mortensen was still laughing to herself a few hours later, when Miss Miranda came into her office.

"Well, well, well," she said to her daughter.

Miss Miranda ignored her. She went straight to the window and looked outside. Then she turned and said:

"I don't know if you're aware of it, but I shall be seventeen in two months three days time."

"My word, doesn't time fly?" said Mrs Mortensen.

"There's no need to be so bloody sarcastic."

"Sorry."

Miss Miranda turned away from the window and threw herself on the couch.

"Well, I've been thinking. At my age it isn't right I should be leading such a sheltered life. And it certainly isn't proper for a young girl like me to be living in a place like this surrounded by a gang of lunatics who've all got sex problems. Goodness knows what I'll pick up."

"So?"

"Well, I think it would be a super idea if I were to go out and do some work, and I've been thinking it would be a super idea if I went to live with Ambrose and Megan in their new house. I mean, now that Nurse Mooseman isn't going to stay with them, they'll need someone to help them round the house and I was always jolly good at domestic science, apart from puddings and personal hygiene and I don't mind going down on my knees in the house and buying eggs in the shops, and Megan and I get on frightfully well together, and, anyway, I'm going whether you like it or not."

Mrs Mortensen leaned back in her chair and put her feet on the desk. She was wearing a dark blue velvet jacket and black trousers.

"Would this decision have anything to do with Oliver Manners?" she said.

Miss Miranda blushed. "What do you mean?" she said.

"Well, you seem to have become very pally with him lately."

Miss Miranda turned her face to the wall.

"I approve," said Mrs Mortensen quietly.

Miss Miranda did not move.

"You seem to be having a very good effect on him."

Miss Miranda still did not move.

"When he is cured, I should like you to marry him."

Miss Miranda tugged at the lobe of her left ear.

"I shall buy you a motor scooter, and then you will be able to drive into town and see him every day," said Mrs Mortensen.

Miss Miranda turned round. Her hair was tossed, and her eyes were sparkling.

"A Lambretta?" she said.

"Anything you like."

"Well, put it in these terms," said Tom Manners to Sir Peter Wakefield. "Would you allow your daughter to form an attachment to a lunatic, even if he is my own brother?"

"But how long will he remain a lunatic?" said Sir Peter. "That's the important question."

73

Sir Peter was a patron of the city's cricket team and a member of the committee of the county club. They were standing on the balcony of the pavillion of the county ground, looking out onto the pitch, where several players were practising in the nets.

It was early evening with a hint of rain in the breeze. The light was a watery blue. Sparks flashed from the trolleys of the trams outside the ground. An old newspaper fluttered listlessly across the pitch and wrapped itself round the chains of the heavy roller. Inside the pavilion there was the smell of linseed oil, stale bear and dusty cushions.

"Damn it, she's only sixteen, when all's said and done. She's only just over the age of consent," said Tom Manners.

"A good sixteen, though, Tom. A good sixteen," said Sir Peter.

"She's too precocious by half," said Tom Manners. "Still, what can you expect with a mother like her's?"

"A fine woman, don't you think?" said Sir Peter.

They were joined on the balcony by Alderman Samson Tufton and Hedley Nicholson.

"Young Renshawe's come along a pace," said Alderman Samson Tufton. "He'll be quite an asset, will young Renshawe."

"Aye, with a bit of luck he could make the Colts' team, too," said Hedley Nicholson.

The light was beginning to fail, and the cricketers picked up their gear and trudged slowly back to the pavillion. The groundsman's dog sniffed at each of the posts supporting the nets.

"Aye, he'll be quite an asset, will young Renshawe," said Alderman Samson Tufton.

"So long as he doesn't go the same road as his brother," said Hedley Nicholson.

When they went into the bar, the club captain, Walter Farr, came up and said:

"Young Renshawe were working up a bit of pace tonight."

"Aye, he'll be quite an asset, will young Renshawe," said Alderman Samson Tufton.

"So long as he doesn't go the same road as his brother," said Hedley Nicholson.

Tom Manners and Sir Peter Wakefield drank a whisky each, and then they went outside for a walk.

The dew was falling, and their feet made damp prints on the newly-cropped grass. The groundsman's dog came up and sniffed at their ankles. In front of the score box was a battered bucket clogged with lime.

"Why did you mention Oliver's court martial in the Royal Edward the other night?" said Tom Manners.

"Tactics," said Sir Peter.

"Tactics?"

Sir Peter took hold of Tom's arm and drew him closer.

"A little bird happened to whisper in my ear last night," he said. "The little bird in question had had one gin and tonic too many. He told me your father had been to see him about drawing up some documents."

"Documents?"

"Documents which would give effective control of the business to Oliver here and now."

"Good God."

"Gives you food for thought, doesn't it?" said Sir Peter.

"It does indeed," said Tom Manners. "But where do the tactics come into it?"

Sir Peter chuckled to himself.

"Leave that to me, Tom," he said. "I'm very near to hatching up a little plot, which I'm sure will appeal to your devious politician's mind."

The car park was in darkness when they returned to collect their cars. They heard Alderman Samson Tufton say to Ernest Walmsley, the club secretary:

"Young Renshawe were working up a fair old head of steam tonight, Ernest."

"Aye," said Ernest Walmsley. "He could be quite an asset this season, could young Renshawe."

"So long as he doesn't go the same road as his brother," said Hedley Nicholson.

Mrs Mortensen switched on the angle light on her desk. It cast shadows on the walls of the office.

"She is a beautiful girl, isn't she, Oliver?" she said.

"Yes," said Oliver Manners.

"She has a beautiful body, yes?"

"Yes."

"Did you touch her in the boat this afternoon, when she took off her clothes?"

"No."

"Why not?"

"I was frightened."

"Of her?"

"No."

"Of what then?"

He did not answer. He was lying on the couch, breathing deeply and regularly under the effects of the drug. Mrs Mortensen sat down beside him and felt his pulse.

"Were you frightened of her body?"

"No."

"Then why didn't you touch her?"

"I was frightened."

"Did you touch the oars, Oliver?"

He began to twitch, and his breathing became irregular.

"You could give someone a terrible blow with an oar, couldn't you, Oliver?"

He began to move his head from side to side, and his eyelids fluttered.

"You could lift it high above your head, and you could bring it down with all your might and . . ."

"I did not touch the oars," shrieked Oliver Manners at the top of his voice. "I was going to, but I didn't. I didn't. I didn't."

Mrs Mortensen gave him another injection, and he sank back onto the couch and began to breathe deeply and regularly once more.

Miss Miranda stepped out of the adjoining surgery and looked down on him as he lay sleeping peacefully on the couch.

"What was all that about?" she said.

"Something that happened to Oliver a long time ago," said Mrs Mortensen, and she smiled at Miss Miranda. "One of these fine days I shall have to tell you about it."

6

The basement of Haslam's Stores had a remarkably good selection of health foods.

Mrs Mortensen made her purchases, and then she decided to take afternoon tea in the cafe on the top storey.

The cafe was oak-panelled with a mock minstrel gallery, on which was engraved a selection of the shields and coats of arms of the counties, cities and distinguished families of the North of England. The windows were bowed and leaded. The condiment sets were made of heavy silver, the waitresses wore black dresses, small white pinnies and starched white caps. Most of them were elderly and flat-footed. One was a grandmother twice over.

Mrs Mortensen ordered a pot of tea, toasted tea cakes and a plate of fancies.

A five piece orchestra played on a wooden dais surrounded by pots of ferns. There was a smell of freshly-ground coffee.

Mrs Mortensen had just cut up her first toasted tea cake, when she looked up and saw Sir Peter Wakefield standing in the entrance. He spotted her and walked over.

"Ah, Mrs Mortensen," he said.

"Ah, Sir Peter," she replied.

"May I join you?"

She nodded and he smiled, drew up a chair and sat down next to her. He ordered a pot of tea and three crumpets.

"Allow me to compliment you on your dress, Mrs Mortensen," he said. "Most becoming. Most attractive."

The leader of the orchestra wore gold-rimmed spectacles. He suffered from asthma, and the toe caps of his black shoes were cracked. He raised the bow of his fiddle, and the orchestra commenced to play selections from *No No Nanette*.

"Do you like music, Mrs Mortensen? said Sir Peter.

"I'm tone deaf."

"What a pity. An appreciation of music can give one such solace, such pleasure," he said. "Yes, it's a great pity. As you may know I indulge myself each year by hiring the Philharmonic Orchestra and conducting a concert of the more popular classics. It's harmless, incompetent in a way, but it gives me great pleasure. I was going to invite you to be my guest this year, but as you're tone deaf, it hardly seems appropriate."

"Possibly my being tone deaf might be an advantage on such an occasion," said Mrs Mortensen.

Sir Peter laughed and patted her on the knee.

"You're an intriguing woman, Mrs Mortensen," he said. "Fascinating. Most fascinating."

She nodded and made no move, when he rested his hand on her knee and kept it there. Then he began to stroke her knee.

"It does wonders for a man's morale to be with a woman like you, Mrs Mortensen," he said.

"That I can imagine."

The pressure of his hand became a little firmer.

"Would you care to come out to dinner with me some evening?" he said. "Just the two of us, of course. Out in the country somewhere. Perhaps we could spend the weekend together. I've a cottage in the country, you know. Very quiet. Very relaxing. Very discreet."

"All right."

"When?"

"You must ring me some time to discover when I shall be available."

He smiled broadly and removed his hand from her knee. The orchestra finished its selection, and there was a faint ripple of applause.

"I was talking to Tom the other day about his father," said Sir Peter, taking a cigar from the leather case he kept in the inside pocket of his jacket.

"Were you?"

"He tells me that Philip is considering making over the business to Oliver."

"Really?"

Sir Peter cut off the end of his cigar, licked it, held it to the light and then lit it. He puffed rapidly for a few seconds and then leaned back and blew out a cloud of fragrant, light blue smoke.

"Am I right in thinking, Mrs Mortensen, that Oliver is to all intents and purposes certifiable as being insane?"

"He is not certified."

"I didn't say that. I was asking if he was certifiable."

"Why do you want to know?"

The leader of the orchestra raised the bow of his fiddle again, and his colleagues joined him in a rendition of selections from *The Dancing Years*.

"There are certain company laws, Mrs Mortensen. Certain laws relating to inheritance," said Sir Peter, and the corner of his mouth curled up into a smile. "In the context of Oliver's condition they might well be worth Philip's perusal."

When Mrs Mortensen told Philip Manners what Sir Peter had said, he laughed.

"Good. Champion," he said.

She sat on the stool in front of the dressing table, removing the varnish from her toenails.

"He's worried, you see," said Philip Manners. "They both are. There's neither of them knows what I'm up to. Aye, they're beginning to squirm now."

"I wasn't talking about that," said Mrs Mortensen. "I was talking about his invitation to me."

"Oh, that," said Philip Manners.

She got into bed alongside him.

"Do you mind?"

"No."

She whispered into his ear:

"He might be a very ardent and accomplished lover, you know."

"And then again he might not."

"Perhaps all he wants to do is to wear my underclothes."

"They wouldn't fit him," said Philip Manners, turning away from her and switching off the light.

She took off her nightgown and then began to pull off his pyjama trousers.

"Bloody hell, not tonight," he said. "Give it a rest, will you?"

"When are we going to move into this new house? That's what I wants to know," said Mog to Megan.

They were sitting in the kitchen of the cottage, and Megan was working on her patchwork quilt.

"I doesn't know, my lovely," said Megan. "It takes longer than two ticks to move into a new house, you know."

"Cor blimey Charlie," said Mog. "It's getting on my bloody nerves over in that house there."

"I thought you would have liked it," said Megan. "I mean, it's very like a prison, isn't it?"

"I'm not saying it isn't, am I? Course I'm bloody not," said Mog. "What I'm saying, intimating like, is that it's having a very bad effect on my health."

"You're not eating kippers for breakfast, are you?" said Megan. "You knows how they doesn't agree with you and brings you out in a rash on your backside, doesn't you?"

"I knows all about my backside, don't you worry," said Mog. "That's not what's bothering me. It's my head and what's inside it, the old grey matter like, what's bothering me."

"You're not sleeping in a draught, are you?"

"It's enough to send you round the twist, spending all your time with a bunch of raving nutters," he said. "I can't even have a dream about Delia Sibley without someone sticking his schonk in and trying to claim it for his own."

"Who's Delia Sibley?"

"I wish I bloody knew," said Mog. "There I was last night having a quiet dream about Tommy Ishamel's bull terrier, and who should walk in but Delia bloody Sibley. 'Hoppit,' I says. 'Get out of my dream,' I says. But no, she wouldn't have it. She sat there in the nude with nothing on like cracking her bloody finger joints all night. Cor blimey Charlie, I had a terrible headache when I woke up this morning. Thought the back of my head was caving in."

"I'll give you two aspirins and a cup of strong sweet tea," said Megan, standing up and walking to the gas cooker.

"Cooee," came a voice from the bottom of the stairs.

"Hello, Miss Miranda, love you," said Megan. "Are you coming up for a cup of tea and an eccles cake?"

"Is Mog up there with you?" shouted Miss Miranda.

"Yes, he is," shouted Megan. "And he's having a bit of trouble with his grey matter, poor soul."

"Tell him to come down. I want a word with him. It's frightfully important."

Mog looked at Megan, shrugged his shoulders and went down the stairs to join Miss Miranda.

"Thank goodness I've found you," she said. "Something fantastically interesting has just happened."

"Oh yes?" said Mog.

"Yes," said Miss Miranda and she took him to the rose garden and told him about everything that had happened between her and Oliver in the boat on the lake and what her mother had said later in the evening.

"Smashing. Go to the top of the bloody class," said Mog. "Now we're really beginning to get somewhere."

"But what does it all mean?"

Mog tapped the side of his nose.

"Leave it to your Uncle Mog to sort out," he said. "I got the training for this sort of work, hasn't I? I wasn't in the Intelligence Corps for nothing, was I?"

They were standing in the sanctuary. Mog took off his hat, stuck it on the bust of the late Mrs Manners and scratched his head.

"What I can't understand is what your mam's doing here," he said.

"She came to run the asylum and cure Oliver."

"I knows that, my lovely. But she must have an ulterior motive as well. Everyone's got an ulterior motive, hasn't they? Course they bloody has."

"I think she plans to marry Philip Manners. In fact, I know she does."

"Cor blimey Charlie, what a bloody tangle to sort out," said Mog. "Problems? I got so many now I'm in danger of glutting the market."

"I've got problems, too, you know," said Miss Miranda, sitting down on one of the shallow marble steps.

"You're not old enough to have problems," said Mog.

"Oh yes I am," said Miss Miranda. "And they're sex problems, too."

"Not another one?" said Mog. "It must be bloody catching round here. What's your trouble then?"

"Randiness," said Miss Miranda.

"Well, don't look at me, sweetheart. I can't do nothing for you. I'm not supposed to have any cobblers, am I?"

"Cobblers? What are they?"

"If you doesn't know what they are in your mood, my lovely, you're going to be in dead stuck in nine months time, I tell you."

81

F

"There's no need to be so superior about it," said Miss Miranda crossly. "Tell me what they are or I won't give you any more inside information ever again."

"All right then," said Mog wearily. "You know what race horses is?"

"Course I do, you daft bugger."

"And you know what they do to race horses what goes over the jumps?"

"No."

"They make them into geldings, don't they?"

"Do they?"

"And cobblers is what geldings hasn't got, see."

"No."

"Cor blimey Charlie, I can't get any more technical than that, can I? They cuts their bloody cobblers off so they won't catch them against the fences. It's the classic case of not letting your dinglers dangle in the dust. Right?"

"I still don't understand."

Mog took his hat off the bust, stuck it on the back of his head and said:

"Listen, I got some books on the subject. Wrote by experts, they is. Hank Jansen and blokes like that. I'll lend you one, when I can afford to get my suitcase out of the left luggage at Wrexham station."

Miss Miranda sighed deeply.

"The only answer to it is complete chastity till the day I get married," she said.

"Well, doing without a bit of the old how's your father for a bit never did no one any harm," said Mog. "That's why the Pope got so much promotion, see."

Miss Miranda patted the marble step by her side, and Mog sat down next to her.

"What brought all this on, you see, is that I had a terrible shock last night," she said.

"So did I," said Mog. "Some bastard had tied the legs of my pyjamas together."

"You know when you go to bed?" said Miss Miranda. "Well, I always take all my clothes off and look at myself in the mirror in the nude. We used to do that at school to see who'd got the biggest pair. You know Chloe Shoemaker?"

"No, I hasn't had that pleasure, my lovely," said Mog.

"Well, she says that men don't bother about how big they

are. She says it's the shape that counts, but I think she was only saying that because her's are so small."

"She wants to use falsies, don't she? Course she bloody does."

"Well, anyway, I was looking at myself and suddenly I got this absolutely frightful shock. You know Deidre Spooner?"

"No, I haven't had that pleasure, my lovely."

"Well, you know when you're playing tennis against her, and she's always tripping up because she's short-sighted and won't admit it because she doesn't want to wear glasses? Well, sometimes you get a high smash and Deidre's tripped and she's lying on the ground. Well, you've got her at your mercy, haven't you? And that's just how I felt when I looked at myself in the mirror."

She paused for breath and to knock a small fly from her nose and then she said:

"You know my breasts?"

"No, I haven't had that pleasure, my lovely," said Mog.

"Well, they seemed so desirable. I looked at them as Oliver must have looked at them that afternoon in the boat, and they got so full and hard I thought they was going to burst. And you know those big brandy glasses Philip Manners has got in the drawing room? Well, I wanted Oliver to get them and hold them over me, and I could just imagine what he'd feel like and how he'd be sort of throbbing with desire, and I began to feel all sort of woozy and quivery, and I could almost hear the glass splintering.

"And then I looked at my tummy, and, although it was all smooth and tiny, there was a curvy sort of bulge there and I thought, Gosh, someone has only got to cast his seed there and I'll make a baby out of it. They gave us this book to read at school, and it was awful, and it showed you the inside of a woman's womb, and it was awful, and Sister Virtuous said it was the same for orang utangs and elephants and we all giggled, and Oonagh Liddell said that looking at Antoinette Lilley she could easily understand why it was the same for elephants and we all giggled. But it wasn't till I looked at myself in the mirror last night that I thought, Gosh, it *is* the same for me, and that inside my tummy I'd got this power to do something that only me in the whole wide world had got—to make a new being in my own image. And it made you forget all the horrible things that go on inside you when you're

83

pregnant, because you sort of have no power to stop them and yet only you have the power to start them."

She had her eyes closed, and Mog stared at her intently.

"I think it's a bloody good job I can't afford to get my case out of the left luggage," he said.

At nine o'clock in the evening the bar of the Constitutional Club in the centre of the city was always crowded.

Francis McNeil, the editor of the local morning newspaper, would call in that time for two whiskys and a panatella before supervising the putting to bed of the first edition of his paper.

Lord Dronhouse was often to be found there at that time. So were Ernest Knightly and Walter Huggett, the industrialists, Ben Pink, the bookmaker, the Very Reverend Cyril Chindle, Professor Graham Gurnard, Neil Simpson-Watt, Moreton Houseman, the eponymous proprietor of the firm of quality dry cleaners and Sir Alfred Wellington, philanthropist, race horse owner and triple divorcee.

"Bloody loud-mouthed old ram," said Alderman Samson Tufton, pointing to Sir Alfred, who was talking loudly at the centre of a group of young men wearing navy blue suits and gold wrist watches.

"Aye, but he's given a penny or two to charity in his time," said Hedley Nicholson.

"Charity!" snorted Alderman Samson Tufton. "He'd give the hairs out of his arse hole to charity, if he thought it'd get his name in the papers."

They were sitting side by side in a deep leather sofa. Alderman Samson Tufton had just returned from a presentation at the repertory theatre, and he was still wearing his chain of office.

"And he's just as bad, too," said Alderman Samson Tufton, pointing to Francis McNeil, who was talking earnestly to Councillor Harry Hatton. "Always bloody plotting."

"Aye, the paper's gone to the dogs since he took over," said Hedley Nicholson. "It's never been the same since old D.W. retired."

"It gets more like a bloody Socialist broadsheet every day," said Alderman Samson Tufton.

"Aye," said Hendley Nicholson. "They didn't even put a picture of Tom and Estelle in, when they announced their engagement."

"Which proves my point conclusively," said Alderman Samson Tufton.

They were joined by Sir Peter Wakefield, who said:

"I've just been talking to the secretary of the house committee about the painting inthe smoke room. What's your opinion, Sam?"

"I don't know about the painting, but it could certainly do with being re-wallpapered."

"Not that sort of painting. I was talking about the portrait of Huskisson," said Sir Peter, sitting down in a low chair opposite them.

"Oh that," said Alderman Samson Tufton. "Well, it covers up the damp patch, I suppose."

"I think it's absolutely hideous," said Sir Peter. "I've suggested that we commission a local artist to replace it with an original work."

"What? One of them long-haired layabouts from the art college?" said Alderman Samson Tufton. "Tit and bum merchants, that's all they are."

Sir Peter smiled to himself and said quietly:

"Nonetheless, Sam, I think we have a duty to act as patrons of culture in this city."

"Culture!" said Alderman Samson Tufton. "Listen to me. I've just been to the rep to make a presentation to this bloke what's written the play what's on there at the moment."

"Ah yes," said Sir Peter. "I thought it was excellent, didn't you?"

"Excellent? Bloody mucky more like. For a kick off it were set in a house of ill repute."

"Was it be God?" said Hedley Nicholson.

"It bloody was," said Alderman Samson Tufton. "And as for the language. Well, you'd not take your wife to see it. Do you follow my meaning?"

"Well, Shakespeare can get pretty ripe at times, can't he?" said Hedley Nicholson.

"Granted, Hedley," said Alderman Samson Tufton. "He can be a right mucky devil, when he's in the mood. But he writes about the olden days. This bloke at the rep, well, he's purporting to write about the present day. Do you follow my meaning?"

"It makes a difference, does that," said Hedley Nicholson.

"You're not wrong, Hedley. You're right," said Alderman

Samson Tufton. "You mark my words, it'll not be long, it'll be soon, in fact, when all you'll get on the stage will be unbridled hanky panky."

"Perish the thought," said Sir Peter softly and he went over to another part of the bar to join Tom Manners, who had just finished his business with the chief constable.

He ordered two double Irish whiskeys and then he said:

"Tell me this, Tom. How attached is your father to Mrs Mortensen? How dependent on her, is he?"

"Too much by half," said Tom Manners.

Sir Peter nodded thoughtfully

"He was, of course, utterly dependent on your mother," he said.

"He was dominated by my mother."

"Quite so. Quite so," said Sir Peter. "He seems to be remarkably susceptible to women of a positive character, doesn't he?"

"Positive is not the word I would use for Mrs Mortensen," said Tom. "Evil is the tag I would append to her character."

"You don't like her?"

"I detest her."

Sir Peter stared at his glass of Irish whiskey for a moment and then said:

"It doesn't do, Tom, to make your feelings so obvious in this matter."

"Why not?"

Sir Peter stretched himself in the chair and loosened the knot in his bow tie. It was a silver bow tie with blue spots.

"There are more subtle ways of achieving one's ends," he said. "You remember the story of the old bull and the young bull looking at a field of cows? 'Let's rush over and do one of those cows,' said the young bull. 'No,' said the old bull. 'Let's stroll over and do them all.' "

"I don't think I follow you."

"Slowly does it, Tom," said Sir Peter, and he closed his eyes and took a slow puff of his cigar.

Francis McNeil drank back his whisky and left to put his paper to bed. The chief constable sat at the bar with Moreton Houseman, demonstrating a trick involving a match box and three cocktail sticks

Suddenly Sir Peter sat up in his chair and gripped Tom Manners on the knee.

86

"This is the way we shall do it, Tom," he said. "As I understood it your father has made no further move over transferring the business to Oliver. Good. There's still time. However, we shall not attempt the head-on confrontation with your father. We shall concern ourselves with the two people, who have the most influence over him."

"Meaning?"

"Meaning that you, Tom, will deal with Oliver," said Sir Peter, and then he smiled and said softly: "You can leave Mrs Mortensen to me."

When Tom got back to Mannersville, he found Hempstall, the maid, handing round mugs of cocoa.

Oliver Manners was sitting on the sofa next to Miss Miranda. Mrs Mortensen was sketching in a notebook, and Philip Manners was reading the *Financial Times*.

"Hello, Oliver," said Tom. "What are you doing out of the dormitory at this time of night?"

"He's got a special dispensation, if you must know," said Miss Miranda. "He's moving to the new house tomorrow so he's been allowed to stay up late, haven't you, Oliver?"

"That's right," said Oliver, and then he stood up, yawned and stretched. "I'm feeling rather sleepy as a matter of fact. I think I'll go up to bed."

"That's right, Oliver, old lad," said Philip Manners. "You do just as you please."

Oliver Manners nodded and went out into the hall. He was halfway up the stairs, when Tom came from the drawing room and called up to him:

"Oliver! I wonder if we could have a few words together?"

Oliver nodded and sat down on the stairs. Tom climbed up and sat down beside him.

"We used to sit like this on the stairs, when we were lads, do you remember, Oliver?" he said.

Oliver nodded.

"We were supposed to be in bed really, but we'd creep out of the bedroom, tiptoe along the landing and make our way softly down the staircase. I wonder if that fourth step from the top still creaks?"

"It does," said Oliver.

"Ah, sweet memories. Sweet memories indeed," said Tom. "Do you remember, Oliver? We'd sit here by the hour, and mother and father would be in the drawing room and we'd hear them . . ."

"Screaming and shouting at each other. I remember."

"Yes, well," said Tom hurriedly.

"What do you want?" said Oliver.

"We were very close in those days, weren't we, Oliver?"

"Were we?"

"We used to talk about all our troubles and share all our secrets, didn't we?"

"Did we?"

"Why can't we be friends again, Oliver, like we used to be in the old days? Why can't we make an effort to recapture that old comradeship we used to have?"

"And why don't you piss off and leave him alone?" said Miss Miranda, bounding upstairs and hustling Oliver away. When they reached the top landing, she looked down at Tom and said: "I hate your guts. And so does your father. So there."

When Tom re-entered the drawing room, sticky-palmed and red faced, Philip Manners looked up and said:

"Where were you tonight? Boozing with your cronies again?"

"I happen to have been engaged on important constituency business."

"Can I get you a drink?" said Mrs Mortensen.

"I'm quite capable of getting my own drink, thank you," he said and went to the drinks tray and poured himself a large brandy and soda.

Philip Manners smiled at Mrs Mortensen, and she winked at him.

"I don't seem to have had any papers to sign lately, Tom," he said.

Tom Manners looked up sharply, and then the phone rang in the hall.

Hempstall opened the door of the drawing room and said: "There's someone on the phone for you, Mrs Mortensen."

"Excuse me," said Mrs Mortensen, and she went out into the hall, closed the door of the drawing room behind her, picked up the receiver and said: "Hello."

"Mrs Mortensen?" said Sir Peter Wakefield.

"Ah, Sir Peter."

"I hope I'm not disturbing you."

"No. What can I do for you?"

"You remember our conversation in Haslam's cafe the other day, Mrs Mortensen?"

"Yes."

"Well then, I was wondering if as a result of that, you'd care to take dinner with me on Friday evening."

"All right. "

"Splendid. Excellent. May I call for you at six?"

"Half past six, if you don't mind."

"Of course. Of course."

Mrs Mortensen smiled to herself as she replaced the receiver and returned to the drawing room. Miss Miranda, peeping round the stairs from the top of the landing, smiled to herself, too.

In the dormitory the lunatics were sleeping peacefully. The curtains were undrawn, and a shaft of moonlight played gently on the thick purple carpet.

"Oliver! Oliver!" whispered Lance Tippett. "Are you asleep, Oliver?"

"No," said Oliver. "What do you want?"

"I had an erotic thought about Delia Sibley today," said Lance Tippett.

"Good, I'm very glad for you."

"Do you want to know what it was?"

"Did I hear someone mention Delia Sibley?" said Mog sleepily. "I was just having a dream about her. Running round with brandy glasses over her headlamps, she was. Dirty bitch."

Lance Tippett began to sob, and a few minutes later Mog began to snore.

Oliver Manners leaned over and whispered into Lance Tippett's ear:

"What was your erotic thought, Lance?"

"I thought of her mixing a cake," said Lance Tippett.

"And?"

"Nothing else."

Oliver patted him on the arm.

"Jolly good, Lance," he said. "I'm very pleased for you."

"And now I'm going to go to sleep and have an erotic dream about her," said Lance Tippett, and he pulled the sheets over his head and closed his eyes tightly.

All through the night he talked softly in his sleep.

"Those are hollyhocks, Delia," he said. "Careful you don't

tread on the rosemary and thyme. Mind you don't cut yourself on the crocuses."

A locomotive whistled. Someone flushed the toilet. Owls called to each other. There was a light fall of rain for half an hour.

"That's a sparrow, Delia," said Lance Tippett. "Isn't he beautiful? Isn't he tender and delicate? I wonder if sparrows have enough legs."

Blackbirds began to sing. A few minutes later they were joined by song thrushes. Then dawn broke.

"Is it my birthday cake, Delia?" said Lance Tippett. "Has it got almond paste on it? Can I blow out the candles? Can I blow out your eyes?"

At half past eight in the morning Nurse Mooseman unlocked the door of the dormitory, stepped inside and said:

"Come on, campers. Wakey, wakey, rise and shine. Let's be having you."

The lunatics stirred, rubbed their eyes and slowly dragged themselves out of bed. Lance Tippett, however, remained motionless.

Nurse Mooseman walked quickly over to his bed and shook him by the shoulders.

"Come on, you skiving bloody A—rab. Biddy byes is over," he said.

But Lance Tippett did not move. Nurse Mooseman whipped back the sheets from his head, and when he looked down at him, his face turned white. He put his ear to his chest. He pulled back his eyelids and felt his pulse. Then he stood up and said:

"Bloody hell. He's dead."

"Oh, I say, what rotten luck," said Horace A'Fong. "Bags I take his place at the Tierneys."

7

Mrs Mortensen decided that the death of the unfortunate Lance Tippett should not interfere with the removal operations.

Despite the protestations of Horace A'Fong she decided, too, that Brother Herbert should complete the trio of lunatics, who were to join the Tierney household.

Her instructions to Ambrose and Megan were brief and explicit.

"You are to treat the three men as though they were perfectly normal lodgers," she said. "Ambrose will bring them back to Mannersville each morning for their treatment. And in the evening, when they return, you will make sure that their lives are as normal as possible. Under no circumstances must you tell the neighbours of the true mental state of your lodgers."

Accordingly the removal took place on a fine morning in early summer, and by the time dusk had settled on the city the Tierneys and their lodgers had established themselves in their new house.

Half an hour later there was a knock on the front door. Megan answered it. There was a woman standing there, who said:

"My name's Mrs Brandon. I'm your next door neighbour and I was wondering, if you'd like to come in and have a cup of tea with us and be introduced."

"Thank you very much," said Megan. "We'll come over right away."

Mog insisted that he be allowed to join the party.

"Cor blimey Charlie, I'm off duty now," he said. "I'm only a lunatic when I'm at Mannersville. Right? A man's got to have his social life, haven't he?"

The introductions took place in the Brandons' front

91

parlour. Megan presented her husband and her brother to her new neighbours, and then Mrs Brandon said:

"This is my husband, Les. This is my son, Carter, and his wife, Pat. And this is Carter's Uncle Mort."

"I knows you," said Mog to Uncle Mort.

"Oh aye?" said Uncle Mort.

"Yes. Strangeways. 1949. Embezzlement and petty larceny."

"I'll punch your bloody head in, if you talk to me like that," said Uncle Mort.

"Mort! Please! What a way to welcome your new neighbours," said Mrs Brandon. "Don't take no notice of him, Mr Williams. He's always like this when he's having trouble with his bowels."

"You're taking in lodgers, are you?" said Mr Brandon, tamping down the tobacco in his pipe with a box of Swan Vestas.

"Well, they're not lodgers in the literal sense of the word," said Mog. "More like lunatics, if the truth be known. Right?"

"Lunatics?" said Uncle Mort. "Bloody hell, we'll be having coons in the street next."

Mrs Brandon laughed.

"He's a right yell, your brother, isn't he, Mrs Tierney? Fancy calling your lodgers lunatics. They'd be right mad, if they could hear you say that."

"Do you play bowls?" said Mr Brandon to Ambrose.

"Aye," said Ambrose.

"Right. We'll have a game next Sunday."

Carter Brandon and Pat excused themselves and left for their home. Mrs Brandon refilled the cups of tea and handed round more cream crackers, cheese and pickled onions.

"What part of the world do you hail from, Mrs Tierney?" she said.

"Number 323 Proop Street, Cardiff, Wales," said Megan.

"Cardiff, eh?" said Uncle Mort. "That's where Tiger Bay is, in't it? You get a lot of coons there, don't you?"

"True," said Mog. "But most of them are Welsh coons."

"How can you have a Welsh coon, you barmy prat?" said Uncle Mort.

"Simple. Simplicity itself, my old son," said Mog. "A West Indian bloke comes to Cardiff. Right? And then a West Indian bint comes to Cardiff. Right? They gets married, and in the

92

fulness of time they has a nipper. Right? Well then, what nationality's the kid?"

"Half caste," said Uncle Mort.

"Wrong," said Mog. "In the eyes of the legal profession he's as Welsh as you and me."

"Don't call me a bloody Taffy," said Uncle Mort. "I'm English and proud of it. You'll never catch me sitting down for the national anthem."

They talked for a few minutes more, and then Megan said it was time for them to leave.

As they stood at the front door Mrs Brandon said:

"Now, if you want to borrow owt, Mrs Tierney, don't hesitate to ask. I know what it's like when you move house. There's things you just can't put your hands to, isn't there? And, if you run short of owt, don't be shy of asking."

"I wonder if you could lend us half a bar till Saturday," said Mog.

When the Tierneys returned to their new house, Megan said:

"You didn't ought to have told them about the lunatics, Mog."

"Why not? I'm one myself, aren't I?" said Mog. "I'm not ashamed of it. Well, more like F.S. Seymour ain't. Right?"

"You breathe one word of it again, mate, and you'll get my boot flush up your backside," said Ambrose.

"I don't know what society's coming to," said Mog. "First I'm threatened with a bash in the kite by that big-mouthed bastard next door, and now I'm threatened with a kick in the backside. In my own home, too. There's too much violence in the world these days. No wonder we don't get the summers like what we used to."

Upstairs in one of the bedrooms Brother Herbert was fixing his statue of Our Lady on the mantelpiece. He stepped back to admire his handiwork and then he fell on his knees and prayed.

"Oh, Lord, we beseech Thee to bless this house and all who live therein," he said. "We ask Thee to look over it with Thine infinite love and to ensure that adequate supplies of toilet paper are constantly provided. Amen."

Mog passed by the door of his bedroom and shook his head. Then he tapped softly on the door of Oliver Manners' bedroom. He was instructed to enter.

Oliver Manners was lying in bed reading a book. He snapped

93

it shut when he saw Mog, and a great grin came to his face.

"Isn't this marvellous, Mog?" he said. "A month of this, and I'll be completely cured."

Mog nodded and sat down on the side of his bed.

"Likes rowing, does you, Oliver?" he said. "Likes a bit of a heave ho on the old oars, eh, is it?"

"Why?" said Oliver.

"I'm a bit of a dab hand with the old boating myself as a matter of fact," said Mog. "Well, it's in the blood, isn't it? You don't spend fifteen days in an open boat in mid-Atlantic without learning a bit of the old in-out, in-out, does you?"

"I didn't know you'd been ship-wrecked," said Oliver.

"You'd be surprised how many people are in the same boat as you there, my old cream cake," said Mog. "Fat Bas? He didn't know. Icky Evans? Completely innocent of the fact. Well, I doesn't like to talk about it, see. I lost some good ship mates that time, didn't I? Course I bloody did. Well, old Monty Jones, he went completely potty. He'd been drinking salt water, see. Tried to attack the skipper. Well, I had to bash him on the napper with one of the oars, didn't I?"

"How dreadful," said Oliver.

Mog stared at him for a moment and then said:

"With an oar. Lifted it above my head, I did. Held it high. Then—bash. Right on the top of his crust."

"What happened to him?"

"Old Monty? Snuffed it, didn't he?"

"You killed him?"

"Well, I wouldn't be the only one what's killed somebody with an oar, would I?" said Mog.

Oliver got out of bed and put his arm round Mog's shoulders.

"Poor old Mog," he said. "It must give you nightmares when you think of it."

"Nightmares? More like the bloody screaming abdabs," said Mog, and he glanced quickly out of the corner of his eye at Oliver, whose face was full of concern.

"I've got something that will cheer you up," said Oliver, and he went to the bedside locker and took out a bottle of Irish whiskey. "I pinched this from the old man's study this morning."

"You're a toff, my old son," said Mog. "One of nature's bleeding gentlemen, that's what you are, my old bath bun."

94

Oliver poured out two large glasses of whiskey, and Mog took a quick gulp.

"Course what grieves me is that Monty Jones isn't the only one what I hit over the napper with an oar," he said. "Cuthbert Loosemore? I gived him a right walloping one day."

"In the open boat?"

"No. On Roath Park lake. Remembrance Sunday it was. The bastard wouldn't give over rabbiting during the two minutes silence so I stood up and crowned him with the oar."

Oliver looked at him with a puzzled smile on his face.

"Then there was Jean Moloney," said Mog.

"Another one?"

"You hasn't heard the half of it, my old son. Do you want to hear about Jean Moloney?"

"Yes, yes," said Oliver Manners gently. "Just you sit back quietly and tell me all about it. Get it off your chest, and you'll feel so much better."

They drank their glasses of whiskey, and Oliver poured out two more.

"Big Jean, they called her. Face like the back end of a tram and never shaved under the arm pits. You knows the sort. Well, her and me's having a bit of a row at Porthcawl, see. Nice day. Good visibility. Wind in the south east quarter. Right? All nice and friendly. Having chat about this and that. And then, bugger me, she stands up and unbuttons the front of her frock. Cor blimey Charlie, I never seen nellies like it. 'Do you mind putting them away?' I said. 'I've only just had my dinner, hasn't I' I said. It was like talking to a brick wall, man. Took no notice of me? More like lifted her frock up and took down her knickers. Well, there was only one thing to do, wasn't there?"

"Was there?" said Oliver.

"Listen to me, pudding head. What would any normal reasonably sane man do under the same circumstances?"

"I don't know."

"Course you bloody does. For argument's sake, hypothetical like, take me out of the boat, and put the Archbishop of Canterbury there instead. Well, you can put the Archbishop of Wales there, if you like. I'm not fussy. Now what would he have done under the same conditions?"

"I don't know."

95

"All right. Okay. Fair enough. Put it another way. If you'd been there, what would you have done?"

"God knows."

"Of course He do, my old sport, owing to the simple fact that He's omniscient. He's a right know-all, in't He? Cor blimey Charlie, don't try and tell me about the Almighty. Don't lay the law down about religion to me, my old son. You're picking on the wrong bloke, if you wants a row about Christianity, aren't you? Course you bloody are. I wasn't put inside for impersonating a minister of religion for nothing you know. Well, it wasn't my idea, was it? Fat Bas gives me this dog collar and a pair of gaiters and tells me to put them on and do a look out job for him outside Reece's wholesale warehouse. Got it all planned, he had. What he maintained was that the law wouldn't look twice at a bishop hanging round outside a wholesale warehouse at three o'clock in the morning. Where his plans fell down, though, was in not anticipating, forecasting like, that I'd put on my bishop's clobber go down to the Horse and Groom and have a punch up with Icky Evans. Well, you got to wet your whistle before work, hasn't you?"

Mog held out his empty glass, and Oliver filled it to the brim with whiskey.

"The Archbishop of Canterbury? The Primate of All England? Don't talk to me about him. I seen enough of that sort of caper when they forced King Teddy to abdicate. Right? You never met a bigger shit house in your life than Cosmo Gordon Land. Right? He didn't dare show his face in the Horse and Groom, did he? Course he bloody didn't. He knew he'd get a clip round the ear hole from Icky Evans if he did."

"I know what I'd have done in the boat," said Oliver quietly.

Mog swigged back his glass, took the bottle from Oliver and poured himself another large measure.

"I got nothing against the coggers, the old left footers, the red necks. Right? Well, more like I'm on their side. Right? I seen them at Chepstow Races. Old Father Nut and Bolt there studying form for the three thirty. Cor blimey Charlie, what the Catholic Church don't know about three mile handicaps isn't worth knowing, don't you kid yourself."

"I should have stood up and taken the oar in my hands," said Oliver.

Mog topped up his glass, wiped his mouth on the back of his sleeve and scratched the stubble on his chin.

"Poor old Monty Jones," he said. "Wouldn't hurt a fly wouldn't Monty. His dad got done for selling condemned corned beef at Pontypridd market. Broke old Monty's heart it did. 'My old dad,' he says to me. 'He'd got a nice line in dog biscuits. What he want to go selling condemned corned beef for?' he says. I reckons that's why he started drinking sea water. Well, the whole bloody family went off the rails after that. Last time I seen his sister she was selling *War Cries* for the Sally Ally down Wind Street on a Saturday night. Broke old Monty's heart it did. 'My old sister,' he says to me. "She got a smashing job in . . ."

"I should have raised the oar above my head, and I should have brought it crashing down on her head," said Oliver.

"Problems? You doesn't know what problems is, my old flower," said Mog, and he took the bottle from Oliver's hands and began to gulp from it rapidly so that the whiskey cascaded down his chin and ran in sticky rivulets down his neck.

"I should have beaten her and beaten her on the head," said Oliver. And then he paused and said very softly. "Like I did that time in Germany."

Mog began to snore. His chin had fallen to his chest, and there were flecks of spittle on his lips.

Oliver pulled him off the chair and heaved him to his bedroom. He took him by the shoulders and hoisted him onto the bed. Then he looked down on him and smiled.

"That's right, Mog," he said gently. "It will have done you all the good in the world getting your problems off your chest like that."

And then he put the light out and tip-toed softly back to his bedroom.

"Kiss me again," said Oliver to Miss Miranda, and she flung herself into his arms.

They were lying on the bed in the Tierneys' cottage. It was three days since the lunatics had moved to the new house, and Oliver was at Mannersville to continue his treatment.

They lay side by side, panting, and Miss Miranda said:
"Isn't it rotten being chaste, Oliver?"

Then she took off her jumper and brassiere. Oliver began to tremble. She leaned over to him and took hold of his hand. It

97

was covered in perspiration. He tried to move it away, but she held it tightly and clamped it down over her breast.

Oliver's body went rigid. Miss Miranda groaned softly.

"Oliver, Oliver," she whimpered.

Gradually his body relaxed, and tension disappeared from his hand. Slowly he began to stroke her breast, and she cried out and writhed on the bed. He began to run his hand round the inside of her skirt, and then he found the zip and pulled it.

"Oliver," she shouted, jumped off the bed, and her skirt fell down round her ankles.

Oliver raised himself, but she put her hand firmly on his chest and pushed him back onto the bed.

"Oh, Oliver," she said. "Chastity can be such a bastard at times, can't it?"

Over in Mrs Mortensen's office Mog was lying on the couch receiving treatment.

"Yes, I'm feeling bloody marvellous," he said to Mrs Mortensen. "Well, they say a change is as good as a rest, don't they? And moving in with Megan and Ambrose have done me all the good in the world. I'm feeling as sane as you are now, don't you kid yourself, my old beauty."

"Mr Seymour, tell me more about the dream you had last night," said Mrs Mortensen.

"Well, like I says, I'm lying there in the Land of Nod. Not doing no harm to no one. Minding my own business. Right? And then up comes this tart, Delia Sibley," said Mog. " 'How about having a bit of a row on Roath Park Lake,' she says. 'All right,' I says. Well, we goes down there and, bugger me, there's Monty Jones, the Archbishop of Canterbury and King Teddy all ready to climb in with us. Well, fair do's to him, the old Archbishop volunteered to row. Not bad he wasn't neither. 'I can see you done this before, colonel,' I says to him. 'Course, I bloody has, you daft twat,' he says. 'I didn't spend fifteen days in an open boat with Monty Jones for nothing,' he says. And then something happened."

"What happened, Mr Seymour?"

" 'A certain incident,' " said Mog.

"What sort of incident,' "

"A certain incident " said Mog. "Something occurred, took place like, what shouldn't have occurred. Right?"

Mrs Mortensen looked down at him and scratched the back of her head.

"I'm worried about you, Mr Seymour," she said.

"What?" said Mog, sitting up on the couch.

"Oliver and Brother Herbert are coming along splendidly since they moved to the Tierneys' but you seem to be getting worse, I'm afraid."

"Worse? What are you talking about, you daft pudding head? I'm getting better. The old grey matter? Never felt so good in its life. Right?" said Mog, getting off the couch and banging his fist on Mrs Mortensen's desk.

"You seem to be getting more excitable," said Mrs Mortensen softly.

"Excitable?" shouted Mog. "Who's getting bloody excitable? Cor blimey Charlie, I never felt so serene in my life. Serenity? It's dripping out of my bloody ear holes, I got so much of it."

Mrs Mortensen sat down behind her desk and looked up at Mog. His face was flushed, and there was a slight twitching of his right temple.

"It might be necessary, Mr Seymour, to bring you back to Mannersville permanently," she said softly.

Mog glared at her, and then his mouth hardened and he leaned across the desk towards her.

"Listen to me, sweetheart," he said. "You got to keep on the right side of me. Right? I knows what you're up to, see. I knows you got a meeting, an assignation like, with Sir Peter Wakefield tonight. Right? I knows you're up to no good. Right? You better watch yourself, my old lovely. I got my spies in action, see. You better not get on the wrong side of me, or I might start telling a certain person what I knows of your activities. Right?"

"I'm afraid I don't know what you're talking about, Mr Williams," said Mrs Mortensen.

"Williams? That's not my name. Seymour. That's my name, isn't it? Course it bloody is," said Mog.

"Is it indeed?" said Mrs Mortensen softly.

"Tell me about your husband, Mrs Mortensen," said Sir Peter Wakefield.

"He was Danish. He had ginger hair. He wore spectacles. He drank too much. He died of it. His name was Billy," said Mrs Mortensen.

They had just finished dinner. They were sitting in the

dining room of the Hare and Hounds. There were exposed oak beams overhead, polished hunting horns on the walls, horse brasses on the gritstone fireplace, and the menu was written in French.

"A fascinating story, Mrs Mortensen," said Sir Peter, holding his brandy glass up to the light. "And told with admirable economy."

Mrs Mortensen's hair was swept up from her neck, and held in place by an amber clip. She wore a low-cut dress crocheted in blue silk wool.

"It does wonders for a man's morale to be seen in the company of a beautiful woman, you know," said Sir Peter.

"You told me that once before," said Mrs Mortensen.

Sir Peter made a slight bow. The flame of the candle on the table flickered.

"I admire a woman who is not ashamed of displaying her breasts to their best advantage," said Sir Peter.

Mrs Mortensen leaned forward to re-light her small cigar from the candle. The light glowed on her breasts, and the shadow in their cleavage grew dark.

"You have very fine breasts, if you don't mind my saying so," said Sir Peter.

"I don't mind."

"The quality of your skin is very fine, too. It has the most exquisite colouring, you know. By candlelight it takes on a texture, which reminds me of the very great Venetian painters. Have you ever been painted, Mrs Mortensen?"

"No."

"I should like to have your portrait painted. Would you allow me to do that?"

"Yes."

Sir Peter took a small sip of his brandy. The heat of the room heightened the scent of the cologne he had applied to his cheeks.

"I have a very clear picture of how I should like it to be done," he said. "Are you perhaps familiar with the painting of Gustac Klimt?"

"No."

"He painted his women in exotic, but curiously formal poses. His draughtsmanship was extraordinarily unemotional, you know. Yet it had a deeply disturbing sensuousness about it. That is how I should like you to be painted, Mrs Mortensen.

I see you standing quite stiffly, woodenly almost, in front of a brocaded chinoise tapestry. You are naked to the waist and your dress . . ."

One of the commercial travellers at the table next to them suddenly banged on the table with his fork and shouted to the waitress:

"When I ask for French mustard, I mean French mustard. I don't mean English mustard. I don't mean mustard from a tube. I mean genuine French mustard from a genuine pot."

"This is French mustard, sir," said the waitress.

"Send me the manager," said the commercial traveller.

Sir Peter sighed and paid the bill. They retired to the cocktail lounge. From its windows they could see the dusk cascading down the steeply-wooded hills of the dale. The high crags stood out black, gnarled and frenzied against the deep blood red of the setting sun.

They sat together on a couch, and Sir Peter said:

"Philip seems to be very attached to you, Mrs Mortensen."

"And I to him, Sir Peter,"

"I hope you don't mind my saying this, but . . ."

"But it is a most curious alliance. Is that what you were going to say? I suppose it was. Yet, it is curious, isn't it? But then I like curious things, you see. I am a curious person. That is why I do the job I do. That is why I am dining with you tonight."

Sir Peter chuckled and patted her on the arm.

"And that is why you will come to spend a weekend with me at my cottage very soon?" he said.

"Yes," said Mrs Mortensen.

"I wonder what Philip will say."

"I have no idea."

What Philip Manners was saying at that moment was this:

"Pass us another piece of that steak and kidney pie, Hempstall."

"Are you sure, Mr Manners?" said Hempstall. "You've had three helpings already, you know."

"Aye, and I've never tasted owt so good in me life after eating all that bloody rabbit food for the past five year or so."

He was in the kitchen of Mannersville sitting at the scrubbed table in his shirt sleeves. He licked his lips as Hempstall cut another slice from the steak and kidney pie and slid it onto his plate.

"And some more chips," he said.

"You've already had four helpings," said Hempstall. "Honest to God, Mr Manners, I don't know what Mrs Mortensen will say, if she finds out."

"Bugger Mrs Mortensen," said Philip Manners, ramming a forkful of pie into his mouth.

When Mrs Mortensen returned home, he had been in bed for half an hour. He lay there and watched her take off her clothes.

"Did you have a good time?" he said.

"Quite good," she said as she climbed into bed alongside him. Then she said: "I'm very pleased the way my patients are improving since they went to live with the Tierneys."

Philip Manners pulled up her night dress and stroked the inside of her thigh.

"Brother Herbert's confessions have become positively fulsome these past few weeks," she said as Philip Manners kissed her on the hip bone. "He's admitted everything that went on with him and Hempstall."

"Hempstall?" said Philip Manners, biting the lobe of her right ear. "What went on with her?"

"Nothing, thank goodness," said Mrs Mortensen, leaning forward so that he was able to pull the night dress over her head. "And Oliver's improvement, too, has been quite spectacular."

"It's all wrong letting Miranda knock around with him," said Philip Manners, undoing the buttons on his pyjama jacket.

"Stuff and nonsense," said Mrs Mortensen, lighting a small cigar. "It is doing him the world of good. She is really drawing him out of himself. She is really making him aware of his latent sexuality."

"Bloody eyewash," said Philip Manners, pulling off his pyjama trousers. "He'll be putting her in the club before you know what's what, and then we'll be right up the creek, won't we?"

"What a crude mind you have," said Mrs Mortensen. "You're disgusting at times, Philip."

"Don't let's quarrel," said Philip Manners gently running his tongue over her stomach.

"I don't know about the patients improving," she said. "Your improvement tonight is positively sensational."

Philip Manners laughed and began to hoist himself on top of her.

"Must you smoke at a time like this?" he said.

She put her hands on his chest and pushed him away from her.

"Not tonight," she said. "Not tonight, please."

He sighed and rolled over onto his back.

"I don't know how rabbits manage it," he said.

On the following evening Mrs Brandon looked out of the window of her front parlour and saw Tom Manners walking up the front path of the Tierneys' house.

"Isn't that Tom Manners, the MP?" she said.

Mr Brandon looked over her shoulder and said:

"Aye."

"I wonder what he's doing there," she said. "I hope she's not complaining about having vermin in the house."

"She will do, when he sets foot in it. Bloody Tory pig," said Uncle Mort.

"Mort! Fancy talking about one of Sir Winston's pals like that," said Mrs Brandon. "You don't deserve to have won the war, talking like that."

She looked out again and saw Ambrose open the door and lead Tom Manners inside.

Ambrose directed him into the back parlour, and Megan jumped up from her patchwork quilt and said:

"Oooh, Mr Manners, sir, fancy you calling on us like this to see us personal like. Isn't it an honour, Mr Tierney? Isn't it an honour, Mr Williams? This is my brother, Mog, Mr Manners. I don't think you've had the pleasure, has you?"

"I'm not your brother," said Mog. "My name's Seymour, isn't it? You're barking up the wrong tree calling me your brother, aren't you? Course you bloody are."

"Very sorry, Mr Seymour," said Megan. "I must have made a mistake."

"Delighted to meet you, sir," said Tom Manners, extending his hand towards Mog.

"This is Mr Manners, Mr Seymour. He's our Member of Parliament."

"Oh yes?" said Mog. "And what denomination are you, my old flower?"

"Conservative, of course," said Megan.

"Shit house," said Mog.

"Mr Seymour! You didn't ought to talk to him like that, my boy. This is Mr Philip Manners's son."

"I don't care if he's William Ewart Gladstone's son," said Mog. "I seen 'em. Dole queues. Right? Soup kitchens. Right? Deprivation. Right? You can't teach me nothing about deprivation, my old son. What was you doing when the lads in the Rhondda was starving with nothing to eat? Where was you when my old dad was picking through the dustbins to get scraps for us to live on?"

"Oh, Mog, he never," said Megan.

"Well, not picking through dustbins in the accepted sense. More like nicking trousers from the Fire Brigade. Right? But why did he have to go in for criminal activities? Why couldn't he lead an honest life like what I done?"

"Come, come, come, Mr Seymour. I'm sure you'll agree that there are two sides to every question, you know," said Tom Manners.

"There's only one side to this question, boyo," said Mog. "And I'll tell you what it is—the bloody Jew boys. Right? Like? Stanley Baldwin? Bonar Law? Winston bleeding Churchill? Don't talk to me about them, boy. Bloody Jews the lot of them. Well, not exactly Jews in the religious sense. More like they'd all got bloody big schnozzles on them. Right?

"Quite, quite, Mr Seymour. But all that is in the past, you know," said Tom Manners. "I'm sure you'll agree that Harold Macmillan . . ."

"Don't try ramming Harold Macmillan down my throat, my old flower. I seen too much of it. I've been through the war. I seen the warrant officers flogging NAAFI cigarettes to the wogs, don't you kid yourself. I knows all about the Suez Canal and the old age pensioners not having enough to eat. Don't you come the old soldier act with me, boy. Right? Like?"

Tom Manners coughed and tapped the bridge of his spectacles with his left forefinger.

"I wonder if I could see my brother, Mrs Tierney?" he said.

"Yes, of course, Mr Manners. I'm dreadful sorry about that, Mr Manners. I hopes you'll excuse him, Mr Manners. I hopes you won't put him in the Tower of London or nothing like that, Mr Manners," said Megan.

"If I was ten years younger, I'd take him out in the back yard and give him a bloody good hiding," said Mog, as Megan

104

led Tom Manners out of the room. Then he turned to Ambrose and said: "Well, it's my tubes, see. He's the sort what would take advantage and put the boot in while I'm getting my puff back."

Megan showed Tom Manners into his brother's room and said:

"If there's anything you should want, require like, just shout down, Mr Manners, and I'll bring you up a cup of tea and a bun directly."

When Megan had gone downstairs, Tom Manners sat down on the wicker chair and said:

"Well, Oliver, and how are you getting along?"

Oliver stared at him silently for a moment, and then he said:

"What do you want, Tom?"

Tom Manners tapped the bridge of his spectacles again. He brushed a speck of dust off his pin stripe trousers and blew his nose.

"Oliver, I want to talk to you brother to brother. I want to address you man to man," he said.

Oliver smiled, and his fingers tapped on the cover of the seed catalogue, which he had been reading.

"What sort of interest, Oliver, do you take in father's business?" said Tom.

Oliver Manners opened the catalogue and smiled.

"Sweet peas," he said. "They're rather nice, aren't they?"

"You see, since father's illness more and more of the running of the business has fallen on my shoulders."

"Delphiniums are rather lovely, too, I always think."

"In fact, Oliver, it would be true to say that I am in sole control of father's business. I'm the one who has all the headaches. I'm the one who bears all the responsibility. I'm the one who has to take all the decisions," he said, and his voice grew louder. "Father takes not the slightest interest in the business, yet he insists on signing every paper that leaves my office. I do all the work, and he reaps all the benefit. I'm the one who . . ."

Suddenly he jumped up and swept the seed catalogue off the table. He stood in front of Oliver, panting heavily, his jaws grinding, his fists clenched.

"It's all your bloody fault," he shouted at the top of his voice, and at that moment the door opened, Mog walked in and grasped hold of the hem of his jacket.

105

"All right, boyo. Out," he said. "Sling your hook. Hoppit. Skidaddle. Right? I'm not having you disturbing my patients like this. Right?"

"Your patients?" said Tom, struggling to free himself. "Who the hell do you think you are?"

"Mog Williams, my old son, and proud of it," said Mog.

"So you are Megan's brother?" said Tom Manners.

Mog let go of the hem of his jacket and winked at him.

"Well, not exactly, my old flower," he said. "More like I'm masquerading as her brother owing to the simple fact that I'm a lunatic really by the name of F.S. Seymour. Right?"

"Wrong," said Tom Manners. "You are Megan's brother, and I happen to know that you have been expressly forbidden to have any access whatsoever to this household."

"I want him here," said Oliver.

"It's got nothing to do with you, Oliver," said Tom Manners. "It's out of your hands now. I shall report the circumstances of this meeting to my father and Mrs Mortensen, and then we shall see what happens to this quite disgusting creature here."

After he had left the house Mog said:

"He didn't ought to have called me a creature. Cor blimey Charlie that's the same as, tantamount like, as classing me with a bloody ant eater. I resent that, I does. No one calls me a bloody ant eater and gets away with it, I tell you. Right?"

8

"An ant eater? What was he doing calling you an ant eater?" said Ambrose.

"That's what I says. Them's precisely the sentiments I got, my old flower," said Mog. "He must be going off his bloody head."

It was Saturday morning and they were driving in the fawn Lanchester to Mannersville.

Mog had been summoned to appear before Philip Manners, and he was wearing Brother Herbert's black suit, Oliver's pink shirt, Ambrose's yellow socks and a pink tie, which had once belonged to his Uncle Windsor.

"How does I look then?" he said to Ambrose. "Pretty natty, eh? The bee's knees, is it?"

"You'll be looking like death warmed up by the time old man Manners has finished with you," said Ambrose.

Mog nodded glumly and did not speak for the remainder of their journey to Mannersville.

He was met in the entrance hall by Nurse Mooseman, who looked him up and down and said:

"Talk about Joseph and his coat of many colours. Bloody hell, you look like an advert for a confetti factory."

"I'll punch your teeth in, if you talks to me like that," said Mog.

"Oh no you won't, smarty pants," said Nurse Mooseman. "You've got enough trouble on your hands without getting had up for assault and battery."

Nurse Mooseman showed him into Philip Manners's bedroom and then left.

The pug dog, Lord William, was sitting on a cushion by the dressing table. When Mog came in, he stood up, stretched and sniffed at his trousers.

"How do, Fido," said Mog, and then he turned to Philip Manners and said: "Poorly, is it? How are you feeling then? You don't look too good to me. Well, more like you look bleeding dreadful, man. Liver, is it? You wants to look after your liver, my old son. Treat it as man's best friend, that's my tip to you. Right? Like?"

Sit down, Mr Williams," said Philip Manners.

He was propped up in bed with three large, lavender-coloured pillows. There was a thin stubble of beard on his chin. His skin was pale, and there were deep bags under his eyes.

"I ate something that disagreed with me," he said.

"You wants a good dose of Gregory Powder, my old son," said Mog, sitting on a chair by the side of the bed. "Laxative? Cor blimey Charlie, T.N.T. isn't in the same league as Gregory Powder."

"Mr Williams, I've called you here to discuss a very serious matter," said Philip Manners.

107

"Not guilty," said Mog, jumping to his feet. "Well, more like I pleads extenuating circumstances. Right?"

"Sit down, Mr Williams," said Philip Manners wearily. "As you can see, I'm not feeling too well, and I want to get this over with as quickly as possible."

"Listen to me, if you're thinking of leaving me something in your will, my old son, I'll have the Rolls Royce and that bit of carpet you've got on the landing. That's all I wants. I'm not greedy."

"For Christ sake, shut up," said Philip Manners.

Mog sat down on the chair again and said:

"I'd have brought you some grapes, if I'd known."

Philip Manners took a tablet from the box on the counterpane in front of him and popped it in his mouth. He sucked it silently and then said:

"I've known for some time that you weren't F.S. Seymour. Mrs Mortensen knew, too. She was going to confine you to Mannersville to teach you a lesson."

"Rotten dog," said Mog. "I never did nothing to her."

"I stopped her, however."

"Good for you, old cock."

"Not because I like you. In fact, I think you're rather repulsive if the truth be known."

"There's no need to be personal," said Mog. "I can't help it if my ears sticks out, can I? Genetics. The old chromosones. Them's the blokes you wants to be getting at. Not me."

"Shut up," shouted Philip Manners, and then he began to cough.

"You got a nasty cough there, colonel," said Mog. "You must have been wearing damp braces. Right?"

When Philip Manners had finished the coughing bout, he gasped for breath and then said quietly:

"Then my son, Tom, came to me and said he had discovered your real identity. He insisted that I get rid of you."

"Course he bloody did. And I knows why, don't I? Course I bloody does," said Mog. "Listen this way, my old jam sponge. I knows a thing or two about Tom. I knows why he wants to get rid of me, don't you kid yourself."

"Why?"

"Because I'm bloody near to curing Oliver, aren't I?"

"Yes."

"Pardon?"

"I don't know what it is, but you seem to be having a remarkable good effect on Oliver's health," said Philip Manners. "And for that reason I intend to keep you on at the Tierneys'."

The gas fire hissed, and the pug dog, Lord William, yawned loudly and scratched at the carpet.

"Mr Williams, you seem to be the only one who has managed to get into the minds of these poor lunatics. I don't know how you do it, but you seem to be the only one who has come anywhere near to curing them."

"Well, I wasn't a porter at St David's maternity for nothing, boy. I'd have gone in for the medical caper full-time if it hadn't been for my chest. All that cotton wool played havoc with my tubes, see."

"I'm about to make you a proposition that could work out to your financial advantage."

"Now you're talking my language, my old flower," said Mog.

Philip Manners took another tablet and paused to regain his breath. The curtains were drawn, and the heat from the gas fire made the atmosphere in the room stuffy. The pug dog, Lord William, yawned and flopped over on its side and fell asleep.

"I want you to do all in your power to cure Oliver," said Philip Manners.

"How much an hour are you paying?"

"If you can do that, then I shall reward you handsomely."

Mog stood up and began to walk up and down the room, scratching his chin thoughtfully.

"How much is handsomely," he said. "A fiver?"

"It could be a four figure sum, if you do it properly," said Philip Manners.

"Right, my old fruit cake, you're on," said Mog, and he whistled cheerfully to himself as he bounded down the main staircase and stepped outside into the summer sunshine.

Miss Miranda was waiting for him.

"Well?" she said anxiously.

Mog told her triumphantly what had happened and her eyes lit up and she hugged him and said:

"Super, Mog. How absolutely super."

"Now you see what sort of a man you got on your side,"

said Mog. "Now you sees the real calibre of the talents you've got lined up behind you."

"Meaning?"

"Meaning, my old sweetheart, that I was playing it this way all the time. I knew they knewed I wasn't F.S. Seymour, didn't I? Course I bloody did. What I was doing, see, was playing them along. Lulling them into a sense of false security. Well, more like I was playing the part, the role like, of a double agent. Right?"

"You bloody old liar," said Miss Miranda.

"Insults," said Mog. "That's all I've had these past few days. First I'm called an ant eater. Then I'm called repulsive. Then you calls me a liar, and last night Delia Sibley says I'm like a bloody gorilla. I've a good mind to take up the old lunacy lark again. You gets more respect as a lunatic these days than what you gets when you're sane. Right?"

Miss Miranda took him by the arm and led him to the fountain.

Gulls were circling lazily overhead. Their cries were faint, and their wings scarcely flickered as they spiralled on the currents of hot air.

"I'm sorry," said Miss Miranda. "It's just that I'm overwrought."

"Cor blimey Charlie, you not eaten something that's disagreed with you, has you?" said Mog.

"It's chastity that disagrees with me," said Miss Miranda. "It's just about killing me. It's no wonder Sister Virtuous was always getting gum boils, is it?"

"You wants to do a spell in clink, my lovely, then you'd know what chastity is," said Mog. "I seen men go blue in the face with it. Sister Virtuous? It wouldn't have been gum boils what was bothering her, if she done six months in Parkhurst with old Claude Mathias. It's true. It's true."

"It's having a very bad effect on Oliver, too."

"He wants to put a bulldog clip on it," said Mog.

"You know when you're riding my motor scooter?" said Miss Miranda. "Well, the accelerator's on the handlebars, and it's a twist grip, and when you turn it, it sort of throbs with power. Well, I had hold of Oliver's Thing last night, and it felt just like the accelerator on my motor scooter."

"It's a good job it didn't feel like the gear," said Mog. "You'd have bloody near ruptured him changing into fourth."

110

"Oh, you're horrid," said Miss Miranda. "You've got a mind like a cess pool. You never take anything I say seriously."

"Yes, I does, my sweetheart," said Mog gently, and he put his arm round her shoulders.

She snuggled her head into his chest and looked up at him with her big green eyes wide open.

"Do you? Honestly? Really?" she said.

"Course I does," said Mog. "I know about the pangs of growing up all right. Adolescence? Cor blimey Charlie, I had so many spots on my face that there wasn't enough room for my whiskers to grow. What it is, see, is it's all a question of glands. You gets to a certain age and the old glands say to theirselves; 'Hello, I think it's about time we started a bit of the old puberty. Right?' Well, once your glands gets in that frame of mind, there's nothing you can do about it. You just got to sit back and take what they throws at you. Right?"

"I suppose so," said Miss Miranda. "The thing is it's not me that I'm worrying about. It's Oliver. If I won't let him have his oats, it could set us back months and months in trying to cure him. I mean, he'll get so frustrated he'll turn all queer like Mother Fortuitous, and she used to make us put the lights out when we had our bath on Saturday nights."

"That's so you wouldn't see the cheap soap you was using," said Mog. "I knows her sort. Indents for a two bob bar of soap, buys it for a bob a time at Woolworth's and keeps the change to go on the piss on Friday nights."

"Gosh! Do you think she did?" said Miss Miranda.

"Course she did," said Mog. "How do you think Sister Virtuous got all them gum boils?"

Half an hour later Mog entered the office of Mrs Mortensen. She was sitting behind her desk, writing up notes in a ledger. She was wearing a white roll-collar sweater and lime green trousers.

"Sit down, Mr Williams," she said without looking up.

Mog sat down on the couch and lit a cigarette.

"I should tell you that I am totally and completely opposed to your staying on at the Tierneys," she said, still writing in her ledger.

Mog lay back on the couch and blew out a slow and steady stream of cigarette smoke.

"However, if that is what Mr Manners wants, that is what Mr Manners shall get," she said. "I am sending Group Captain

111

Greenaway over to take your place as a patient, and I hope you'll make him feel at home."

"I'd have preferred 'Baldy' Hogan, if it's all the same by you," said Mog.

"Mr Hogan was discharged this morning," said Mrs Mortensen. "And in any case the selection of patients is nothing to do with you."

"Please yourself," said Mog. "I don't mind doing it the hard way. If you doesn't want to co-operate with me, fair enough, I'll do it my way."

"Do what your way?" said Mrs Mortensen looking up from the ledger.

"Listen to me, sweetheart," said Mog. "You and me is rivals now. Right? You been looking after old Oliver for bloody near five years, hasn't you? But it wasn't till I come along that he showed the slightest sign of improvement Right? If I hadn't suggested, put forward the idea like, of setting up a new home for him with Megan and Ambrose, he'd still have been a raving bloody nutter like what he always was. Right?"

Mrs Mortensen's eyes flashed angrily. But then her face softened and she stood up and went over to the couch.

"Don't call us rivals, Mr Williams," she said, stroking the back of his neck. "We should be more like friends, shouldn't we?"

Mog sat bolt upright and brushed her hand away from him.

"Don't start any of that monkey business with me, sister," he said. "Don't come the old Salome caper with me. Right? You won't win me over to your side on a lick and a promise. Right? I'm not Sir Peter Wakefield, you know."

"Exactly," said Mrs Mortensen. "You're quite quite different from Sir Peter Wakefield."

On their way back home Mog said to Ambrose:

"That bloody woman. She gives me the bloody heeby jeebies, she do."

"Why?" said Ambrose.

"Well, she propositioned me in her office about half an hour ago."

"Don't talk so bloody wet."

"It's true. It's true. Lays herself down on the couch, gives me the nod and then invites me to give her a bit of the old Sir Peter Wakefields."

Ambrose snorted and halted the car behind a tram, which

112

was picking up passengers outside the pickle factory. In the queue were girls in bottle green overalls and white headscarves. The early leavers from the football match were there, too. They wore black and white striped scarves. They did not look happy.

"Well, you're in clover now, aren't you?" said Ambrose, as he drew out to overtake the tram. "When are you going to cure Oliver and collect your loot?"

"Ah, that's where the experience comes in," said Mog. "I might not be in such a hurry, might I?"

"Why?"

"Tactics. Deployment of resources. Compilation of capital. Availability of liquidity. Right?"

They stopped again at a zebra crossing. A man was selling evening newspapers outside a public house, and two slim Somali youths were gazing into the shop window of a gents' outfitters.

"It might not be politic, expedient like, to cure Oliver too quick," said Mog. "It might be a case of biding your time, holding your horses, not striking until the iron's hot. Right?"

"What the bloody hell are you on about?"

"The longer I drags the cure out, the more old man Manners gets desperate for results. Right? So the longer he have to wait, the more he have to pay. Supply and demand, my old flower. When what you wants is in short supply, the more you has to pay for it. Right?"

"You bastard."

Mog chuckled.

"And, of course, I got plans for using, utilising like, my new labour force to its best advantage."

"Which labour force?"

"Oliver Manners, Brother Herbert and Group Captain Greenaway," said Mog with a smile. "I'm not having them skiving away round the house doing nothing. I got plans for them, hasn't I? Course I bloody has."

Mrs Mortensen stood in front of a lattice-work screen. Paper roses of green, blue and vermilion were attached to the screen. She wore a wide brimmed black hat. Round her neck was a necklace of coiled and twisting golden serpents. Her dress was of silk embroidered with purple dragons spouting great gashes of carmine from their nostrils. She was naked to the waist.

113

The painter worked quickly. His brush strokes were pernickity, and he hissed through his teeth. Two sparrows had built their nest in one of the angles of the great sloping studio window. They chirruped and chirped.

"That will be all for now, I think," said Mrs Mortensen, and she bowed slightly to the painter and retired to the dressing room.

Sir Peter Wakefield pulled himself out of the arm chair and looked at the painting.

"Good, good," he said. "It's coming along well. You've a fair bit of talent, my friend."

The painter nodded at him.

"She has quite splendid breasts, don't you think?" said Sir Peter Wakefield. "Noble, savage things, aren't they? Ferocious. Quite ferocious."

The painter rubbed his hands on a large cloth, which smelled of turps.

"Let those two breasts loose on each other, and they'd fight to the death," said Sir Peter, and he turned to the painter and smiled. "I'd like you to get that feeling into the painting, if you can."

When Mrs Mortensen had changed into her town clothes, Sir Peter took her to dinner. They went to the Cafe Royal. Before going into dinner they sat in the small bar, which overlooked the dining room. There were heavy brocade curtains, wrought iron bar stools and gilt mirrors.

"Their improvement is quite extraordinary since they moved to the Tierneys'," said Mrs Mortensen. "These last three or four days they have really blossomed out."

"You must feel very pleased with yourself," said Sir Peter.

"Stuff and nonsense. It has very little to do with me. It is they themselves who are doing the work."

"Or possibly Mr Mog Williams?"

"Possibly."

The barman was cutting up pieces of lemon, and a young Maltese waiter in the dining room yawned silently and scratched his back against a wrought iron standard lamp.

"Does this general improvement include Oliver?" said Sir Peter.

"Oh yes," said Mrs Mortensen.

Sir Peter paused. He ran his forefinger round the rim of his glass, and then he said:

"What precisely is wrong with Oliver?"

"It's difficult to say."

"That woman he assaulted in the rowing boat."

"Lieutenant Quimby?"

"That's the one," said Sir Peter, and he paused again before saying: "I don't know whether you have thought of this line of enquiry, but I wonder if she bore any physical resemblance to Oliver's mother."

"I had thought of it," said Mrs Mortensen. "She was quite unlike Oliver's mother."

"Possibly she looked more like your sheep dog."

"Possibly."

Two more sherries were brought to their table, and then the head waiter presented them with the menus. They chose their dishes, and then Sir Peter said:

"Will Oliver ever be sane again?"

"Do you want him to be?"

Sir Peter gulped at his sherry. The liquid went up his nose, and he began to cough violently. Mrs Mortensen watched him silently as he struggled for breath. When he had recovered, he said angrily:

"That was a most uncalled for remark, Mrs Mortensen."

Mrs Mortensen smiled at him. She was still smiling at him a few minutes later, when Alderman Samson Tufton walked in with the chief constable and Alderman Vernon Hankinson.

Alderman Samson Tufton hesitated for a moment, and then he walked across and said:

"Philip's on the toilet, is he?"

Mrs Mortensen laughed.

"It is possible, I suppose," she said. "Why don't you ring him at Mannersville and find out?"

Alderman Samson Tufton's mouth dropped. He fiddled with the handkerchief in the breast pocket of his jacket and ran his finger quickly up the zip of his flies.

"Mrs Tufton's at home, too," he said. "It's her varicose veins, you see."

"Why don't you sit down and join us for a drink, Sam?" said Sir Peter icily.

"Aye. Well. Aye. It's business, you see," said Alderman Samson Tufton, pointing to the chief constable, who was demonstrating a trick with a match box and three cocktail sticks to Alderman Vernon Hankinson.

"As you wish," said Sir Peter.

"Aye. Well. Ta all the same," said Alderman Samson Tufton and then he turned to Mrs Mortensen and said: "Give Philip my regards, when you see him, Mrs Mortensen."

At that moment, however, it wasn't regards, which were being given to Philip Manners. It was a large helping of tripe and onions.

"And don't be so skinny with the onions neither," said Philip Manners to Hempstall, who was serving him in the kitchen of Mannersville.

"Don't you think you should go easy on the tripe, sir?" said Hempstall. "You know what happened to you last time you gorged yourself on meat."

"I do," said Philip Manners. "And I'd rather go to me grave with indigestion than with bloody malnutrition."

"Mail order catalogues?" said Miss Miranda.

"Yes, it's rather fun, isn't it?" said Oliver Manners.

They were sitting on the crags above the open-air swimming pool at Endcar. Miss Miranda, who had passed her driving test that morning, had taken Oliver there on the back of her motor scooter.

"Mog's got you selling mail order catalogues?" she said.

"No, we don't sell them. We take them round to houses in the evenings, show the people what's in them, and then, if they're interested in buying something, we take orders from them," said Oliver Manners. "I wish I were as good as Brother Herbert at it."

"No wonder the old bitch says you've improved so much."

The sun was shining on the surface of the reservoir below them. The wind was fresh with a slight nip on its breath.

"I think Mog gets a commission on every order we get," said Oliver. "It's jolly good for him isn't it?"

"Good for him?" said Miss Miranda. "What about you? Don't you get anything?"

"Oh, we will eventually. He says it's all very complicated to work out, and he won't know how much we've earned till he's consulted his accountants and legal advisers."

Miss Miranda began to laugh. She threw herself on the grass, and her whole body shook. Oliver began to laugh, too.

"Isn't life super, Oliver?" she said. "Isn't it simply heavenly?"

116

"Shall we kiss each other?" said Oliver.

"Yes, let's," said Miss Miranda. "But nothing more, mind."

When Oliver arrived home later in the evening, Mog looked up angrily and said:

"Where have you been? Out courting, is it? I didn't give you permission. You should have been out with the catalogues. Right."

"I'm sorry," said Oliver. "I'll make it up tomorrow night."

"See you do. Right?" said Mog. "Now then, listen this way. Tonight, gentlemen, I am pleased to report that we have cracked it. Brother Herbert, my old tea towel, you're a bramah, a real topper. For your information, Mr Manners, the Holy Father by here have sold this very evening, flogged to cash paying customers, one greenhouse, one tartan travelling rug, one suedette lumber jacket and three children's Micky Mouse wrist watches."

"And a set of apostle tea spoons," said Brother Herbert. "Don't forget those, Mr Williams."

"Right, my old bath bun. Don't let's forget the apostle tea spoons when we're dishing out the praise," said Mog. "I tell you, boy, you missed your bloody vocation, you did. You're wasting your time being a lunatic. You'd make a fortune for yourself flogging spectacle frames in Pontypridd market. It's true. It's true."

"What about me, Williams?" said Group Captain Greenaway. "I bagged three of the blighters didn't I?"

"My son, you did smashing. Well more like bloody marvellous. Corking, my old cockeroo," said Mog. "For your information, Mr Manners, old Reach for the Skies by here have flogged one floral pinafore dress for the fuller figure, one rubber torch and one manicure set in imitation leather case. Right?"

"Correct," said Group Captain Greenaway. "Quite amazing how the natives love anything that's shiny or colourful."

"So, Mr Manners, the moral as far as you're concerned is simple," said Mog. "Right, Brother Herbert?"

"Let thine finger be remov—ed from the place wherein which it resid—eth," said Brother Herbert.

"Amen," said Mog. "And if you doesn't, I might have to consider, think about like, sending you back to Mannersville and getting someone else to take your place."

"You wouldn't do that?" said Oliver. "We're supposed to be friends."

"Just you try me, boy. I wasn't in the red berets for nothing, I tell you," said Mog, and then he ushered them all off to bed, saying: "I wants you lot fresh for tomorrow evening. I don't want no one falling asleep on the job through lack of getting in the correct kipping time. Right?"

When he went into the front room for supper, Megan said:

"You won't half cop it, kid, if Mrs Mortensen finds out, discovers like, what you're doing."

"Doing? Me?" said Mog. "I tell you what I'm doing for your information. I'm giving them something to occupy their minds. Therapy. Right? That's what we calls it in the trade, see, and a bit of the old therapy never did no one no harm. I seen it in the war. There was hundreds of our lads given up for hopeless. Well, more like thousands if the truth be known. Hopeless, they was. And then they got them cracking on the old therapy, and before you knew where you was we'd knocked shit out of Graziano and sunk the bloody *Bismark*. Right? I'm doing them a favour, if the truth be known."

"You're not doing too badly out of it yourself neither," said Ambrose.

"Listen to me, boy. I'm using the old noddle, aren't I? That's how you gets your capital together, my old son. That's how you gets liquidity. Right? Like? If you wants to get on in this world, you got to work for it. Right? Like?"

"Aye, and you're working your fingers to the bone, aren't you?"

"Course I am. Metaphorical like. I supplies the know-how. They supplies the graft. Right? You can't have a better metaphor than that, can you? Course you bloody can't."

When Parliament was in session, Tom Manners returned from Westminster each Friday and held his surgery in the headquarters of the constituency party.

This was the last Friday before the recess, and Tom was hard at work dealing with the problems of his constituents.

Alderman Samson Tufton and Hedley Nicholson sat in the bar, waiting for him to finish. They were drinking pints of bitter.

"Alone, was she? With Sir Peter Wakefield on her own, was she?" said Hedley Nicholson.

118

"Aye," said Alderman Samson Tufton. "And you should have heard what they was talking about."

"What?"

"They was talking about Philip Manners being on the petty."

Hedley Nicholson stared into his pint of beer and said:

"There's something rum going on between them two."

"He's fancying her. That's what's going on," said Alderman Samson Tufton.

"Do you think he'll get anywhere?"

"Search me," said Alderman Samson Tufton. "But I'll tell you this—if he does, it'll break Philip's heart for him. Do you follow my meaning?"

They were joined by Sir Peter Wakefield, who said:

"Gentlemen. What are we drinking then?"

"I'd not say no to a drop of whisky, if it's all the same by you," said Alderman Samson Tufton.

"Neither would I," said Hedley Nicholson. "I'd not say no."

"Good. Whisky it is," said Sir Peter.

The barman brought them three double whiskies, and Alderman Samson Tufton said to Sir Peter:

"We was just talking about the state of the world before you came in."

"Really? And what conclusions about the state of the world did you reach?" said Sir Peter.

"I were telling Hedley here about the film we examined on the Watch Committee yesterday morning."

"Ah, I see."

"By gum, it were mucky. It were a nudist film. Do you follow my meaning? It were all about nudes disporting themselves. Disgusting," said Alderman Samson Tufton, and then he paused and said slowly: "It were Danish."

Sir Peter smiled and said:

"They tell me the Danes are very uninhibited in these matters."

"They tell you right," said Alderman Samson Tufton. "They had this sequence of two nude women playing ping pong. Well, I don't know how they managed. Flop, flop, flop. It were no wonder they never got a decent rally in."

"Ah, Tom," said Sir Peter as Tom Manners walked into the bar, mopping his brow. "Whisky?"

"A double," said Tom. "My God, I thought it would never end."

"That's exactly what I felt about that there film," said Alderman Samson Tufton. "I were just telling Sir Peter here about this here nude film we saw yesterday on the . . ."

Sir Peter led Tom Manners away, and they sat at a table in a corner of the billiards room.

"Well, Tom, and how are things going with Oliver?"

"They're not," said Tom Manners. "I just can't get any point of contact with him."

He took a long gulp of whisky and sighed with satisfaction.

"And how are you getting on with Mrs Mortensen?" he said.

"Splendidly," said Sir Peter. "If my assessment of the situation is correct, it shouldn't be long before we're spending a weekend together at my cottage."

"Good God," said Tom, banging his glass of whisky on the table. "It'll break father if he finds out. It'll shatter him completely."

"Precisely, Tom," said Sir Peter softly.

Brother Herbert placed his order book on his knee, took out a ball point pen and said:

"Now, Mrs Warrender, let us commence."

"Well, I'm not R.C. meself, father, but I do think it's marvellous the way you get out and about to collect money for the Faith," said Mrs Warrender. "The C of E wouldn't do it. Oh no, it would be too much like hard work for our lot. You've got to give it to your lot—they're not frightened of hard work, are they?"

"Your orders, please," said Brother Herbert.

"Number 876 stroke 5—one lady's underslip, pink," said Mrs Warrender.

"Number 876 stroke 5—one lady's underslip, pink" said Brother Herbert, writing in his order book.

"Number 390—one gent's boiler suit, navy blue, large man," said Mrs Warrender.

"Number 390 one gent's boiler suit, navy blue, large man," said Brother Herbert, writing in his order book.

"Number 997 stroke 7—one lavatory brush with blue handle," said Mrs Warrender, and Brother Herbert wrote down the details in his book.

"Now this exercise is called word and idea association," said Mrs Mortensen in her office next morning. "I say a word, and I want you to shout out the first word or idea that comes into your head. Do you understand?"

"Yes," said Brother Herbert.

"Mother."

"One lavatory brush with blue handle," said Brother Herbert.

"Pardon?" said Mrs Mortensen.

"One lady's underslip, pink," said Brother Herbert.

"Lady's underlip?"

"Mrs Warrender," said Brother Herbert.

"What do I want with a bloody brush and comb set?" said Uncle Mort.

"It's inlaid with imitation mother of pearl," said Oliver Manners.

"I don't care if it's inlaid with Queen Victoria's bloody toe nails—I'm not buying it," said Uncle Mort.

"What about a dog basket?"

"No."

"What about a set of pruning knives?"

"I'll prune your bloody ear hole for you, if you don't clear off," said Uncle Mort.

"Now this exercise is called word and idea association," said Mrs Mortensen in her office next morning. "I say a word, and I want you to shout out the first word or idea that comes into your head. Do you understand?"

"Yes," said Oliver Manners.

"Womb."

"Dog basket," said Oliver.

"Mother."

"Queen Victoria."

"Sex."

"Toenails."

Mrs Mortensen stood up and patted Oliver on the shoulder.

"Oh dear, Oliver," she said. "You seem to be having a relapse."

9

"Verily I say unto you that life is full of deceits," said Brother Herbert. "Life itself is deceit. And of all the deceits therein, the smallest and yet the largest are those which occureth between a man and his wife."

Five minutes later the unfortunate accident occurred.

The setting was the staircase in the Tierney household. The two protagonists were Brother Herbert and Mog Williams.

Brother Herbert was walking up the staircase, head bent low over his missal. Mog was walking down the staircase, carrying a large carton full of non-stick saucepans.

Halfway up the stairs they collided. The carton in Mog's arms struck Brother Herbert on the chest. He cried out, and then he fell backwards down the stairs, and was struck a succession of violent blows on the head by the non-stick saucepans. They all had green handles.

He lay unconscious for half an hour. Mog splashed two bucketfuls of water over him, Megan wafted her bottle of smelling salts to and fro beneath his nose, Oliver Manners fanned him with a tea towel, Ambrose massaged his knee caps, and Group Captain Greenaway sent for the doctor.

When he regained consciousness, Brother Herbert looked at the monk's habit he was wearing and said:

"What the bloody hell am I wearing this clobber for?"

The doctor said he was suffering from mild concussion and recommended a week's stay in bed and a course of glucose tablets.

Brother Herbert, however, leapt to his feet and said:

"I can't stand here all day, playing silly buggers. Our people have got a claim in for an extra two and six a day dirt money."

Mrs Mortensen was sent for immediately. She locked herself in the front room with Brother Herbert and after two hours she reappeared and said:

"I am glad to say that he has completely recovered. He is now sane."

Brother Herbert, however, complained of a pain in his right temple and a feeling of slight nausea. So he was confined to bed for three days in a darkened room.

At the end of this period he was allowed to get up, and he came down for breakfast wearing a navy blue blazer, a white shirt with starched collar and grey flannel trousers with braces.

"Some silly bugger's had me going round dressed like Friar Tuck," he said, and he covered his sausages and tomatoes with liberal dollops of Yorkshire relish.

At nine o'clock there was a knock at the front door. Standing there was a small middle-aged lady with rimless spectacles and a plastic raincoat. She introduced herself as Mrs Esme Herbert of Fanshawe Street.

"Eee, George, you're looking champion," she said to Brother Herbert. "Shall you be home for your dinner?"

"No, luv, I'll be back tomorrow morning first thing," said Brother Herbert. "I've just got this spot of union business to complete."

At half past ten there was another knock on the front door. This time there was revealed a stout lady with peroxided hair, who introduced herself as Mrs Hilda Herbert of Rotherham. She said to Brother Herbert:

"It's about time they got you on your feet again, Tommy Herbert. I've aired your pyjamas for you, so you'll be all right to come back tonight."

"Aye, well, I'll be back first thing tomorrow, luv," said Brother Herbert. "I've got this gold watch to present to one of the lads in Runcorn, do you see?"

Just after mid-day there was another knock at the front door. Standing there was a tall thin lady with protruding front teeth and a pram, which contained three young children. She said to Brother Herbert:

"Hello, Oswald, do you remember me? I'm your wife, Mrs Herbert, and these are your children, Clement, Stafford and Aneurin. If you hurry up, we'll just be in time to catch the Newcastle train as far as Darlington."

Twenty minutes later a detective inspector and a detective sergeant arrived and took Brother Herbert away to the police station.

Three weeks later at the Quarter Sessions he was sentenced

to five years imprisonment on two charges of bigamy and three charges of embezzlement of trades union funds.

Mrs Mortensen came round to see the Tierneys, and Megan gave her afternoon tea in the front parlour.

"I think I ought to explain about Brother Herbert and his bigamy," she said.

"Bigamy? More like trigonometery," said Mog.

"Six years ago Brother Herbert—Wilfred Ernest Herbert, I should say—came to us suffering from total amnesia and severe religious mania. Obviously it had been brought on by his matrimonial and financial difficulties."

"Crafty sod," said Mog.

"His union sent him to us on the recommendation of Hedley Nicholson. They didn't want any scandal. I think they wanted him out of the way permanently."

"And then our Mog goes and cures him by hitting him on the head with a non-stick saucepan," said Megan. "It makes you think, don't it?"

"You mustn't blame yourself, Mr Williams. I know it was a complete accident," said Mrs Mortensen.

"Well, it wasn't an accident in the medical sense of the word," said Mog. "More like part of the treatment, see. A crack on the napper never did no one no harm. Right? This old aunt of mine. Well, she hits her crust on the parrot cage, don't she? Laid her out cold it did. When she comes to, all her warts is gone and she don't need to shave her moustache for the next six months. It's true. It's true."

Mrs Mortensen finished her afternoon tea and said:

"Well, thank you for the delicious Welsh cakes, Mrs Tierney, and you can expect Mr A'Fong to be moving in tomorrow evening."

"She's taking liberties," said Mog to Megan after Mrs Mortensen had been driven back to Mannersville by Ambrose. "I knows your average Chinkie customer. Before we knows where we is, he'll be insisting on a special diet—chop suey, bean shoots, mah jongg, octopus."

"Oh, I doesn't think so, Mog," said Megan. "He don't look the sort to me what would eat octopus, and, fair play, I knows he wouldn't mind eating laver bread instead as a substitute like."

"Laver bread!" said Mog scornfully. "I'd sooner eat engine drivers' snots."

Horace A'Fong arrived the following evening. He was wearing an Eton boater with pink ribbon, white Oxford bags and a blue and yellow striped blazer.

"What ho, Mrs Tierney," he said. "Isn't it a ripping wheeze spending the old harymacvacs with you and your hairymac-spouse?"

"I hopes you'll not mind us not having no octopus for breakfast, Mr A'Fong, but the local fishmonger don't have no call for that sort of food," she said.

"I should think not," said Horace A'Fong. "Beastly chappies, octopii. Squirt ink in a feller's eye, when they get their rag out, don't you know?"

He was shown to his bedroom, and after supper he went out into the garden.

The sky was overcast, and a heavy haze hung over the tops of the cooling towers in the valley below. There was a sickly sweet smell from the brewery.

Uncle Mort leaned on the garden wall, watching Horace A'Fong. He called to Mog, who came over and said:

"What do you want then, my old son?"

Uncle Mort pointed with his thumb at Horace A'Fong.

"What did I tell you? I told you it wouldn't be long before we had coons moving into the street."

"He's not a coon," said Mog.

"Oh no, oh no?" said Uncle Mort. "I suppose he's just got a bad attack of jaundice, has he?"

"He's not a coon. He's a chink," said Mog.

"Same bloody thing."

"Now that's just where you're wrong. That's just where you shows your lack of education, isn't it?" said Mog. "It wasn't coons what built the great wall of China, was it? It wasn't coons what invented Chinese laundries, was it? It wasn't coons what discovered the use of chop sticks, was it? It wasn't coons what discovered Roman candles was it? Chinamen. Chinkies. Little slant-eyed bastards. They're the ones what did all that. Right?"

"I know my history as well as what you do, mate," said Uncle Mort. "Why do you think Chester's got walls round it? To keep the bloody Welsh out, that's why. Who did all the pillaging and looting in the Middle Ages? Who's always bottom of the International Soccer table? Who keeps their pubs shut on Sundays? The bloody Taffies. I'd rather have an Irishman

125

any day of the week than a bloody Taffy. It wasn't a Taffy what invented Guinness, was it?"

"You're just racially bleeding prejudiced," said Mog, and then it began to rain, and they retired to their respective houses.

Up on the moors and in the dales the rain delved down.

It gurgled in the runnels of the parched beds of the reservoirs. It soaked the fleeces of the mountain sheep huddling into the sides of the dry stone walls. It hammered on the canvas sight screens of village cricket grounds, pocked the surface of the slow and lazy trout streams and sent bus tickets, orange peel and rose petals swirling down the gutters of village streets.

It also drenched Miss Miranda and Oliver Manners.

Miss Miranda pulled up her scooter in the courtyard of an inn, and she and Oliver jumped off it and ran into the public bar.

"A bit damp, in't it?" said the landlord, watching them shake the rain from their clothes. "Unseasonable, too, for the time of the year."

They sat on a bench next to a large stone fireplace, in which was an iron hob with an iron kettle and iron tongs. There was no fire.

"I've never been in a real pub before, Oliver," said Miss Miranda. "Isn't it super?"

"What will you drink?" said Oliver.

"What does one drink in a pub? I don't know, do you?"

Oliver Manners went to the bar and ordered a pint of Mansfield's bitter beer for himself and a port and lemon for Miss Miranda.

"It's the sheep dog trial tomorrow," said the landlord. "It always rains for the sheep dog trial. You can bank on it. You can set your watch by it."

Oliver Manners licked his lips as he watched the landlord draw his pint slowly and tenderly. It was clear and sparkling, and it brought out beads of moisture on the outside of the glass.

"You rotten old thing," said Miss Miranda, when Oliver came back with the drinks. "Why couldn't I have a glass of beer? I've always wanted to drink a glass of beer."

"That will be better for you," said Oliver, pushing across the port and lemon.

126

"Ugh!" said Miss Miranda. "It's hateful. I want a beer. If you don't get me a beer, I shan't tell you the marvellous piece of scandal I picked up this morning."

Oliver went to the bar and ordered a half pint of bitter beer.

"It always rains for the flower show, too," said the landlord. "Do you want the peg board?"

"Pardon?" said Oliver.

"For the dominoes. I thought you and your young lady might fancy a hand of dominoes."

"No thank you."

"Please yourself," said the landlord. "It's no skin off my nose."

"Well, what's the piece of scandal?" said Oliver, when he returned to Miss Miranda with the beer.

Miss Miranda took a sip of it and said:

"Ugh! How hateful. Can I have something else?"

"No," said Oliver. "And in any case you shouldn't be in here really. You're under age."

"Oonagh Liddell says it doesn't matter what age you are, when you're staying with your aunt and uncle in Ireland," said Miss Miranda. "She says she's always going into pubs there with her boy friends."

"She's quite a lass is Oonagh Liddell by the sound of things."

"Oh, I don't know about that. She's very immature in other things, you know. She thinks it's being frightfully grown-up to smoke cigarettes, for example. She thinks it's terribly daring to ride her bicycle with no knickers on, and in any case I'm not under age. Well, hardly anyway, and, if you were a gentleman, you wouldn't mention my age. Gentlemen aren't supposed to talk about things like that. Can I have a sip of your beer, please, Oliver?"

"You've got your own."

"But your's is bound to taste nicer, and, if you don't let me, I won't tell you about the piece of scandal I heard."

She took a sip of his beer and tried hard not to wrinkle up her nose. Then she sighed and said:

"Do you want to know the piece of scandal I heard? Well, this morning I was in the drawing room and the old bitch was on the phone in the hall so I picked up the extension and listened in. And do you know who she was talking to? She was talking to Sir Peter Wakefield, and she was making arrangements to spend a weekend with him as his cottage."

"Good Lord."

"Isn't that the most super piece of scandal you've ever heard in your life?"

"Does my father know?"

"I don't know," said Miss Miranda. "It's all gorgeously promiscuous, isn't it?"

"It's horrible," said Oliver.

"Oh, I don't know," said Miss Miranda. "This is the age of promiscuity after all, isn't it? I mean, there are hundreds of married women being poked right left and centre by men who aren't their husbands. Oonagh Liddell says her aunt's been having it away with the manager of the creamery for years and years, and that's in Ireland, where the Pope doesn't even allow you to use precautions. What are precautions, Oliver?"

"Do you mind if I have another beer?"

"Course not. And you can buy me an orange juice. I hate alcohol."

Oliver bought a pint of beer for himself and an orange squash for Miss Miranda. While he was at the bar a stout man with a leather waistcoat, gaiters and a red face came in and said:

"There was a silly bugger through here this morning with a donkey. He said he were from the newspapers. Did you see him?"

"Aye," said the landlord. "He asked me for a ham sandwich and a bucket of water."

"I think it's a publicity stunt," said Oliver.

"It weren't shod proper, weren't donkey," said the stout man, and then he went to a corner of the bar and took out his evening paper.

"Bloody donkeys," said the landlord, handing Oliver his drinks. "They want to spend more time getting their weather forecasts right, never mind gallivanting round with bloody donkeys."

Miss Miranda drank her orange squash in one gulp and said:

"When we're married, Oliver, would you mind if I were promiscuous?"

"I rather think I would, you know."

"Honestly, Oliver, you are old-fashioned. Fornication's all the rage these days. Chloe Shoemaker says her father

fornicates his secretary every Friday night. Of course
Antoinette Lilley has to go one better. She says her father did
it so much, he had to go to hospital to get his fornicater seen
to."

"I think we'd better be going," said Oliver.

It was still raining, when they went outside into the
courtyard.

Miss Miranda put her arm round Oliver's waist and
whispered:

"One day very soon, Oliver, I'm going to fornicate you.
Won't it be absolutely super?"

Then she kicked the scooter into life, and they chugged off
back to the city. It began to rain even more heavily before
they had travelled half a mile.

In the city, however, the rain had stopped, and a missel
thrush was singing softly to itself in the Tierneys' back garden.
Mog turned from the bedroom window and faced Horace
A'Fong, who was lying in bed staring at him attentively.

"Fire away then, old bean. I'm all ears," said Horace
A'Fong.

"Right. Now this is what I calls my pep talk. Well, it's more
like telling you what's what in this household and how you've
got to behave yourself and not get up to no mischief or you'll
get the end of my boot up your Oriental backside. Right?"
said Mog.

"Absolutely, old horse," said Horace A'Fong. "You won't
find me going AWOL when it comes to observing the old
hairymacrule book."

"There's one thing to remember above all, paramount like,
see. You play ball with me, I play ball with you. Right? I
wants to see your bed nice and tidy each morning and with
your shaving gear and similar ablutions accoutrements neatly
laid out on your bedside table. Right? There's to be no
smoking in the bogs, no sticking your bogies on the corner of
the tablecloth, and if you doesn't eat all your dinner, you
doesn't get no pudding. Right?"

"Rather."

"Now then, as far as discipline's concerned, I'm the boss
man. Well, put it another way. I'm the gaffer. Right? What I
say goes. If I tells you to jump out of the window, you jumps.
Right? If I tell you to cover yourself with suet and pretend
you're a suet pudding, you does. Right?"

"Can't I be a Cornish pastie?"

"Listen to me, Mr Hoo Flung Dung, don't you try and take the old Michael out of me. I didn't want you here in the first place. I didn't want no renegade starch-basher from a Chinese laundry, did I? Course I bloody didn't."

"I wish you wouldn't be so beastly."

"Beastly? Me? You pin back your lug holes, boy, and listen to what I've got to tell you. I knows you're on the skive. I knows you're swinging the old lead. I knows all the dodges, doesn't I? I served my time as a nutter same as you, don't you kid yourself. Right? Well, I knows how to settle your hash for you. I knows how to cure you, and if you doesn't behave yourself and show a bit of respect, that's just what I'll do. Right? Like?"

"Oh, you wouldn't cure me, would you, Williams? You wouldn't be such a rotter, would you?"

"Don't you try me, my old flower. What I done for Brother Herbert I can easy do for you."

The front door banged as Oliver Manners and Miss Miranda entered the house.

They went into the front room and Miss Miranda said:

"Wasn't it super news about Brother Herbert being cured, Brosey?"

"It was that," said Ambrose.

"Fancy him being a bigamist, though. It's no wonder he was all in favour of chastity. He must have been worn out, poor old thing."

"Why doesn't you take Mr Manners into the back kitchen for a cup of Bovril, Ambrose?" said Megan.

"Aye, righto," said Ambrose, and the two men left the two women alone.

"You didn't ought to talk about things like that in front of gentlemen, love you," said Megan. "That sort of thing gives men ideas."

"Does Ambrose ever get ideas, Megan?"

"Sometimes he do. He had an idea this morning about putting a formica top on the kitchen table."

"I don't mean ideas like that, Megan. I mean ideas about getting randy and forcing you to submit to his lusts."

"Oh dearie dearie me, a young girl of your age didn't ought to know nothing about lusts and things like that. Lusts is only what grown-ups has, when they go to X films and reads books."

130

"Antoinette Lilley lent me this book, and it was about this man and this woman, and they were married and . . ."

"Now I doesn't want to hear vulgar talk like that, Miss Miranda," said Megan. "I don't know why people bothers writing books about private things like that of a personal nature. People what writes books like that don't have no manners. It's bad manners to write books about what grown-ups does when they kisses each other."

"You know when you were courting Ambrose, Megan?"

"Oh, I does, my lovely. I remembers it as well as if it was yesterday."

"Well, do you remember the first time he kissed you?"

Megan hid her face in her hands and giggled. Then she said:

"We'd been on the chara to Porthcawl, see, and it only cost 2s 6d each return. Well, when we gets home, mam says: 'Hello, Megan,' and I says: 'Hello, mam,' and she says: 'Hello, Ambrose,' and he says: 'Hello, Mrs Williams,' and she says: 'Does you want to go in the front parlour for a while?' and I says: 'Righto, mam,' so in we goes. Well, my dad always had a fire in the front parlour winter and summer. He said it benefitted the damp courses, but I thinks it was on account of his chest, see, because there was no shortage of coal in them days owing to the simple fact that my brother, Watkin, worked on the docks loading coal for Egypt before he became a catering officer in New Zealand. So we sits on the sofa like side by side, together like, and the next thing I knows is Mr Tierney says: 'Well, I suppose I'd better kiss you, hadn't I?' And I says: 'I suppose you had,' so he blows his nose on his hankie and then he kisses me. 'Thank you very much,' I says. 'I think we got faggots for supper. Does you want one?' "

"How romantic," said Miss Miranda.

"Oh, it was, love you. I didn't sleep a wink all night after it, which was a good thing cos my dad comes home the worse for wear, see, with Billy Montgomery, God rest his soul, and they had a fight in the back yard and I had to run down to Mrs Emmanuel's to get their Ossie to separate them. Oh, you should have seen the blood. 'Mind his dentures, Ossie' my mam kept shouting, but it wasn't a bit of good, see, cos Ossie had fought professional in Wolverhampton, and when our Mog comes back with Tommy Ishmael, they has a right set-to, and Mrs Davies from number 154 starts to have their Cyril, and I has to run down Bute Street to fetch the midwife."

They had a cup of Horlicks each, and then Miss Miranda asked to see Mog before she left for home.

In the back parlour she told Mog what she had overheard on the telephone that morning.

"We got to bloody stop them," said Mog.

"But how?" said Miss Miranda.

"If we doesn't stop them, they'll cock up everything I got worked out here for myself."

"What have you got worked out here for yourself?"

"Don't be such a nosey bloody parker."

"It's a good job I am a nosey parker or we'd never have found out about the old bitch and Sir Peter Wakefield," said Miss Miranda.

Mog nodded and then began to pace up and down the room.

"And there's another thing, too," said Miss Miranda. "I can't hold out for much longer."

"What's that?" said Mog.

"I think I'm getting the most wopping great gum boil, and I know what's causing it," said Miss Miranda.

"Cor blimey Charlie, you're worse than Delia Sibley," said Mog. "Why can't you exercise a bit of the old self control? Why don't you start collecting stamps or something?"

"You know Oonagh Liddell? Well, she says it's quite safe, if you take precautions," said Miss Miranda. "What are precautions, Mog?"

"What Tommy Ishmael flogs for three bob a dozen at the back of the fire station. Now shut up, and let me think, will you?"

"Who's Tommy Ishamel? How will I recognise him if I go to the fire station?"

"Cor blimey Charlie, who's this, what's that—you're worse than the Spanish bloody Inquisition," said Mog, and then he snapped his fingers and said: "Got it. You find out where this cottage is. Right? You come back and tell me. Right? And then we'll have a council of war to decide what action to take, what we're going to do like. Right?"

"Super," said Miss Miranda. "Absolutely super."

On her way home Miss Miranda passed by the Philharmonic Hall, where Sir Peter Wakefield had been giving his concert. She saw Tom Manners and Estelle Nicholson getting into a car, and she pipped her horn and waved.

"Wasn't that Miranda Mortensen?" said Estelle, settling herself in the front seat.

"Yes," said Tom Manners, engaging first gear and drawing away from the kerb. "Did you see old Sam Tufton? He was snoring his head off during the Beethoven symphony."

"Brahms," said Estelle. "There wasn't any Beethoven tonight."

"I can't see the difference myself."

"Miranda's a very forward girl for her age, isn't she?" said Estelle.

"In what way?"

"Physically. Last time I was at your place she asked me whether we used precautions."

"Good God. I hope you informed her that nothing of that nature had occurred between us?"

"I wish it had," said Estelle.

When they arrived at the Nicholson residence, Estelle invited Tom inside for a drink.

"Is Hedley in by any chance?" said Tom Manners. "I have a spot of business it might be opportune to discuss at this juncture."

"Daddy's in Antwerp," said Estelle. "And in any case I've got a lot of business I want to discuss with you."

She led him into the drawing room. There were chintz covers on the chairs and sofas, a picture of Estelle's dead mother and a cockatoo on a stand. It blinked its eyes, when the light was switched on, and then it raised its sulphur crest and scratched it with its right foot.

"Pour me a tonic water, will you?" said Estelle.

Tom Manners poured out a tonic water and filled himself a glass of malt whiskey.

"Well?" he said. "What's the business?"

Estelle settled herself on the rug in front of the fireplace and said:

"What's going on between you and Sir Peter Wakefield?"

"Pardon?" said Tom Manners, gulping hurriedly at his whisky.

"Last week Sir Peter Wakefield offered daddy a piece of your father's property for a quite ludicrously low price."

"Good Lord," said Tom, gulping at his whiskey again.

"He told daddy that he was acting on your behalf."

"Yes, well, Estelle, there are—how shall I put it—there are

133

certain aspects of business procedure, which the average layman, a person such as your good self, Estelle, cannot possibly understand without detailed and expert knowledge of the aspects of business procedure in question."

Estelle stared at him as his face slowly turned a deep shade of scarlet.

"Sir Peter's picking on the wrong one, if he thinks daddy will do the dirty on your father," she said. "Daddy refused the offer, of course."

"Of course, of course," said Tom. "I'll look into the matter first thing in the morning. Another tonic water?"

"And I hope, too, that Sir Peter's picking on the wrong one, if he thinks you will do the dirty on your father," she said slowly.

Tom Manners looked at his watch and said:

"Well, if that's the end of the business discussions, Estelle, I think I'd better be going."

"Sit down, Tom," said Estelle sharply. "I haven't finished yet."

Tom sat down and hung his head.

"You can pour me another tonic water," said Estelle. "And this time you can put a whisky in it as well."

"That's the ticket, Estelle. That's the ticket," said Tom and he poured out two more drinks.

Estelle took a sip of her drink, and then she said:

"I don't think it's right that we should both go to our marriage beds as virgins, Tom."

"Come, come, come, Estelle," said Tom Manners. "This is neither the time nor the place to be drawn into an argument on that vexed question."

"When is the time and the place?" said Estelle calmly.

Tom Manners coughed, tapped the bridge of his spectacles and began to scratch the cockatoo's breast.

"Estelle, you are shortly to become the wife of a public figure. More than that, you are to become the spouse of a member of the most democratic parliament in the whole of the western hemisphere," he said.

"Now, the traditions, which we uphold in the Palace of Westminster are admired, revered even, wherever parliamentary democracy is cherished. Now, as the putative wife of a member of that assembly it is beholden on you to do your utmost to ensure that those traditions are not undermined."

"Yes, Tom," said Estelle wearily.

"What are those traditions? Briefly they are these—we believe in the sanctity of the principle of one man, one vote. We believe in the principle of the secret ballot. We believe in . . ."

"Don't you believe in sex?" said Estelle.

"I'm coming to that," said Tom. "Presently."

Before he could resume his account of the virtues of parliamentary democracy, however, the cockatoo leaned forward and sank its beak into the fleshy part of his right forefinger.

He let out a howl of pain, jumped back, and spots of his blood spattered onto the rug.

"And there's another thing, Tom," said Estelle. "Sir Peter told daddy that he was taking Mrs Mortensen away for the weekend at his cottage."

"Did he, did he?" said Tom, wringing his hand and hopping up and down in pain.

"I hope you're not involved in any of this jiggery pokery with Sir Peter," said Estelle. "If you are, you better uninvolve yourself pretty quickly."

"Why's that, why's that?" said Tom, ramming his injured hand under his left armpit.

"You'll find out, when the time comes," said Estelle, and she stood up and gently scratched the cockatoo's crest.

IO

"Are you sure you don't mind?" said Mrs Mortensen to Philip Manners as she stood with her suitcase in her hand at the front door of Mannersville.

"Of course I don't," said Philip Manners. "You run along and enjoy yourself."

"You look positively delighted to see me going."

Philip Manners hastily removed the smile from his face and said:

"Of course I'm not delighted. I only wish I could come with you."

"Why don't you then?"

"Pardon?"

Mrs Mortensen laughed and linked arms with Philip.

"Get Hempstall to pack you a bag quickly, and then we'll walk out arm in arm to Sir Peter's car," she said, and she laughed gleefully again. "Yes, Philip, do that. I'd just love to see the expression on that big fat bastard's face when he sees you."

"I can't," said Philip Manners.

"Why not?"

"Business."

Sir Peter walked up the steps outside the front door and picked up Mrs Mortensen's suitcase.

"Are the farewells over?" he said.

"Yes," snapped Mrs Mortensen, and without looking back she climbed into Sir Peter's car, and they drove off.

"Poor old Philip," said Sir Peter as they turned out of the front gates. "He looked like death."

"Did he?" said Mrs Mortensen.

"How's he taken it? Pretty badly, I imagine," he said.

"Very badly."

Sir Peter chuckled to himself.

"You wait till the gossip starts. That's when he'll really start to feel it."

Sir Peter drove slowly. The needle of the speedometer rarely rose above the 40 mph mark, and his handling of the gears was inexpert. He spoke very little except to offer Mrs Mortensen chocolates from the large box he had placed in the open glove box in front of her.

They took lunch at an inn in a small market town at the edge of the wolds. From the windows of the dining room they could see the plain rolling away into the distance with church towers sticking up here and there out of islands of trees.

"So?" said Mrs Mortensen finishing off her veal cutlet. "Why don't you come out into the open?"

Sir Peter smiled at her and poured out more wine.

"What's the proposition you want to put to me?" she said. "I presume that's the reason for inviting me away for the weekend."

"You have a very alarming way of talking, Mrs Mortensen," said Sir Peter. "I find such bluntness quite startling."

A herd of black and white cows slowly padded past the inn. One of the cows tried to enter the car park, but the dog snapped at its ankles, and it lowered its head and galloped off.

"Philip intends to leave Oliver the business," said Mrs Mortensen. "Oliver is insane, therefore he can't take control over it. So you want me to keep him insane, is that it?"

Sir Peter threw back his head and roared with laughter.

"Okay," said Mrs Mortensen. "What do I get out of it?"

Sir Peter stopped laughing. For a moment he did not speak. Then he leaned across the table and took hold of her hand.

"What I want you to do, Mrs Mortensen, is to use your influence on Philip," he said. "Tell him how foolish his idea is. Tell him, perhaps, that Oliver's health would not stand up to the excitement and controversy his decision would certainly provoke."

"Tell him that unless he follows my advice, I'll run off with you?"

Sir Peter chose a portion of sherry trifle off the dessert trolley and watched with satisfaction as the waiter heaped up a plate with fresh strawberries for Mrs Mortensen.

"At the end of this weekend, when you have got to know me a little more, you will realise that I'm much more subtle than that, Mrs Mortensen," he said.

When the cheese board was brought to their table, Sir Peter chose red Cheshire, and Mrs Mortensen chose Danish blue.

"Even in our choice of cheese, Mrs Mortensen, you can see my subtlety at work," said Sir Peter.

Mog, Miss Miranda and Oliver Manners sat in Megan's back parlour, poring over a road atlas.

"That's it," said Miss Miranda, stabbing at the page with the stick of her ice lollie. "That's where the cottage is."

"Right," said Mog. "Action stations. Clear the decks, and let's be off."

"Are we going there?" said Miss Miranda.

"Course we're bloody going there," said Mog. "On the back of your scooter."

"Super," said Miss Miranda.

"Can I come, too?" said Oliver.

"No, you're staying at home," said Mog.

"But why?" said Oliver.

"It's not fair," said Miss Miranda. "I'd much rather go with Oliver than go with you."

"Listen to me, sweetheart," said Mog. "In times of warfare a man's personal preferences don't count for nothing, does they? Course they bloody doesn't. Old Nelson? Before the Battle of Trafalgar he didn't say to hisself: 'Cor blimey Charlie, I wish I was at home having a bit of the old leg-over with Lady Hamilton.' Course he bloody didn't. He hoisted his sails and went into battle so's that England could be saved and made a land where a man could get his end away any time he bloody wanted. Right?"

"I don't see what that's got to do with my staying at home," said Oliver.

"Oliver, my old shirt tail, it's time you was taught a few of the facts about the tactics of modern warfare," said Mog. "When you gets a battle, the whole of the bloody army doesn't go dashing into the front lines. What happens is this: the privates go to the front and gets theirselves killed, and the generals stays at headquarters and thinks up new tactics what will get a hell of lot more privates killed in the next battle. Right? Well, in this case Miranda and me's the privates, and you're the general at headquarters."

"But I don't want you to get killed," said Oliver.

"Course we won't get bloody killed," said Mog. "I knows how to look after myself, don't you worry. I didn't serve with the Ghurkas for nothing, you know. Cor blimey Charlie, they'd lop your head off as soon as look at you."

"It all sounds super and exciting," said Miss Miranda. "I'd love to chop Sir Peter Wakefield's head off. I'd chop his cobblers off, too, if I knew what they were."

"There's to be no cobbler-chopping going on while I'm in charge of operations," said Mog. "We plays fair. Right? We sticks to the rule book. Right? Officers and bleeding gentlemen. Right?"

"Did I hear someone mention officers and gentlemen?" said Group Captain Greenaway, poking his head round the door.

"That's right, boyo," said Mog.

"Splendid," said Group Captain Greenaway. "Well, men, the collection of bed boards is coming along well and soil disposal is causing no problems. The tailor's shop has already turned out two uniforms of an Oberfeldwebel, and the forgery shop is hard at work producing forged rail tickets from Mainz to Stettin."

Then he looked at the road atlas and said:

"Damn fine job, getting that. Bribed one of the Goons, did you?"

"Isn't he just too super?" said Miss Miranda.

"Well, men, I'm happy to tell you that the new issue of Red Cross parcels will be made at 17.00 hours this evening," said Group Captain Greenaway, and then he went to the door and said before leaving the room: "Remember our motto at all times—coughs and sneezes spread diseases. Carry on, Flight Sar'nt."

"See what I mean?" said Mog. "Still an officer and gentleman even though he is bloody crackers."

He picked up the road atlas and put it under his arm.

"All right, let's be off," he said.

"But what are we going to do when we get there?" said Miss Miranda.

Mog tapped the side of his nose with his left forefinger.

"Flexibility. That's what you got to have in good battle planning. Right?" he said. "You got to be able to adapt to changing conditions, hasn't you? Course you bloody has."

Miss Miranda threw her arms round Oliver's neck and kissed him long and hard on the lips.

"Farewell, Oliver," she said. "If I should die, think only this of me. That in some foreign land . . . oh, shit, I can't remember the rest of it."

"I still don't think it's fair that I've got to stay at home," said Oliver.

"You are doing a vital job, my old son," said Mog. "Without your aid, your assistance like, the whole operation would fall flat on its arse. What I wants you to do is get a lot of little red pins and stick them in the map to show how me and Miss Miranda is progressing in our advance. Right?"

"How super," said Miss Miranda. "Isn't that super, Oliver?"

"What you does is to act as co-ordinator. Right? And if we wants reinforcements, it's your job to see they gets to us as quickly as possible. Right?" said Mog.

Oliver nodded, and then he smiled.

"Terrific," he said. "I'll set up a liaison co-ordinating committee at once. Then I'll establish a joint signals and

139

ordnance command working directly under the control of GHQ."

"There's no need to be so bloody enthusiastic," said Mog.

Miss Miranda kissed Oliver passionately once more, and then she led Mog out to her motor scooter.

She revved up hard so that the whole machine shook, and then with a screeching of tyres and a gushing of blue smoke she roared off down the street.

"Cor blimey Charlie, don't go so quick," shouted Mog, clinging tightly to the pillion bar. "I'm too young to die, aren't I? Course I bloody am."

Sir Peter nosed the car slowly out of the car park of the inn. It stuttered and shuddered as he grappled with the gears, and then the engine began to whine.

He stopped the car, put the gears into neutral, and then started off again cautiously and slowly.

"You don't appear to be very much at home with a motor car," said Mrs Mortensen.

"I'm not," said Sir Peter. "I bitterly regret the passing of the horse and carriage. They were such pretty things apart from anything else, weren't they?"

"I suppose you have heard of the theory that a man's sexual ability can be judged by his ability with a motor car?" said Mrs Mortensen a few minutes later.

Sir Peter smiled to himself and nodded.

"I suppose there's something in it," he said. "But it's much too crude a theory for my taste, Mrs Mortensen."

An hour later they were driving through fen country. The roads were straight and broad with high dykes on either side, but Sir Peter still drove slowly. Mrs Mortensen yawned.

"Are you bored?" said Sir Peter.

"Yes," said Mrs Mortensen, and Sir Peter grunted with satisfaction and drove even more slowly.

At length they came to a village. It was small. The houses were squat and pebble-dashed. The bank building was made of clapboard, and there was a brackish pond, on which a lone Muscovy duck drifted aimlessly. The east wind sent the sand rasping in a fine curtain across the surface of the road.

At the far end of the village was the church. The graveyard was overgrown, and there were many slates missing from the roof of the lych gate.

Next to the church was a flint-faced house screened from the road by a high and parched privet hedge. Sir Peter drew up outside it, switched off the engine and said:

"Well, Mrs Mortensen, here we are."

"You call this a cottage?"

"It's the old vicarage," said Sir Peter. "It's exquisitely nasty, don't you think?"

He pushed open the creaking iron gate and led her over a pebbled path. The grass on the lawn was scorched yellow, and there was sand everywhere.

He opened the front door, and they stepped into a large square hall. The floor was tiled, and the windows were made of stained glass. There was a smell of must.

Sir Peter showed Mrs Mortensen into the living room at the back of the house. There were french windows, which looked out onto a small patch of singed lawn. Behind it rose a sheer bank of sand dunes.

"The sea is behind there," said Sir Peter, pointing to the dunes.

"The sea? You told me your cottage was in the countryside," said Mrs Mortensen.

"Seaside. Countryside. It is all the same to me, Mrs Mortensen. Both are equally deliciously nasty," said Sir Peter. "Now I have a spot of work to do. Do please make yourself at home."

Back at Mannersville Philip Manners stood in the kitchen, rubbing his hands.

"Right," he said to Hempstall. "Tonight I'll have a T-bone steak. Tomorrow morning I'll have bacon and three eggs for breakfast, steak and kidney pud for lunch and a good thick mutton stew for supper."

"I don't know what Mrs Mortensen will say, if she finds out," said Hempstall.

"I've said it before, and I'll say it again," said Philip Manners. "Bugger Mrs Mortensen."

"This is the third pub we've stopped in, and we've only been on the road for an hour," said Miss Miranda crossly.

"An army marches on its stomach, my old sweetheart. Right?" said Mog, and he marched into the bar and ordered a pint of bitter and a bottle of Coca Cola.

Two old men in flat caps were playing dominoes, and Mog

went up to them, looked over their shoulders and said to the man with a yellow muffler wound tightly round his neck:

"Play your double five, my old son. You got him by the short and curlies if you plays your double five. Right?"

Half an hour later they stopped off at another pub.

"Call of nature, kid," said Mog to Miss Miranda.

She looked at him disdainfully, and he winked at her and said:

"Well, I'm no different from the Duke of Wellington. I got to have a pee same as him, hasn't I?"

And then he went into the pub and ordered a pint of bitter and a glass of lime cordial.

The next pub they stopped at was on the bank of a wide and listless Fenland drain.

Its walls were white-washed and on the shelves behind the bar were glass cases with stuffed fish inside. There was a jar half full of pickled eggs on the bar counter. The landlord's shirt was unbuttoned to the waist. He hadn't a hair on his chest.

Mog took his beer and strolled out onto the bank of the drain. An angler was sitting there on a wicker basket. The bell on his rod tinkled, and he pulled out a tiny fish, which wriggled silvery in the sunshine.

"You don't call that a fish, does you?" said Mog, standing behind him. "Cor blimey Charlie, I seen bigger things than that come out of our hot water tap."

The angler unhooked the fish and placed it in his keep net.

"What bait are you using?" said Mog. "Maggots, is it? You won't catch nothing here with maggots, my old flower. My old dad used to use his false teeth as bait when he went fishing from Penarth pier."

"I'll use you as bait, if you don't clear off," said the angler.

Mog walked slowly back to the pub. Miss Miranda was sitting on the wall, swinging her feet.

"You gets some right know-alls around, don't you?" he said. "You gets people who thinks they knows it all and threatens to drown you when you offers them a piece of advice."

Miss Miranda turned her face away from him and said:

"I hate you."

"What have I done now?"

142

"You couldn't care less about curing Oliver, could you?"

"Course I could. What makes you say that? It's the thing what is most nearest and most dearest to my heart at this very moment in time," said Mog. "My whole life is dedicated to the cause. Right? Every one of my waking moments is filled with plans of how to get old Ollie on his feet again. Right?"

"Then why don't we get to the cottage instead of stopping off at pubs boozing every five minutes?"

Mog climbed onto the wall beside her and put his arm round her waist. She knocked it away, but he only grinned.

"Boozing, my old sweetheart, is one of them noble activities what separates man from the apes," he said. "Have you ever seen a gang of orang utangs having a night out on the piss? Course you hasn't. And why? Well, for one thing most pubs wouldn't let them in in case they started swinging from the lampshades when they went on the gin. Right? And for another thing they hasn't got the intelligence to think up such a creative activity as boozing. Right?"

"Honestly, you do talk a lot of rubbish," said Miss Miranda, but the anger had disappeared from her voice, and there was the hint of a smile on her face.

"Rubbish? What I'm telling you now is what the experts has been saying for years. Charles Darwin? What's the first thing he noticed about the bloody giant turtles? I'll tell you. He noticed that they didn't go on the batter every Saturday dinner time. Well, he puts two and two together after that, doesn't he? He says to hisself: 'Hello, the Bible's up the creek here,' he says. 'All that Adam and Eve malarky? Cor blimey Charlie, it's not worth the paper it's wrote on,' he says. 'I knows what I'll do,' he says. 'I'll invent the theory of evolution.' And that's how it was discovered that we're all descended from bloody monkeys. Right?"

Miss Miranda laughed.

"But what's all this got to do with you boozing?" she said.

"Very simple. I'd never have heard of the theory of evolution if I hadn't gone boozing with Tommy Ishmael the night after Icky Evans done the sub post office at Newcastle Emlyn. Right?"

A light breeze snuffled at the surface of the drain. A mallard drake raised itself out of the water, flapped its wings, shook its head and quacked.

"Well, Tommy Ishmael was a red hot Catholic, see. He

143

could have had an audience with the Pope any day of the week, if he'd wanted. Well, his old lady used to slip nips of rum into the parish priest's cocoa, see, and he tips her the wink, see. Tells her any time she wants an audience with the Pope not to bother queueing for tickets cos he's got a buttie of his working in the box office at the Vatican. Right?"

"I'd love to have an audience with the Pope," said Miss Miranda. "We did go to Lourdes two years ago, though."

"Who was playing? The West Indians?" said Mog.

He went into the pub and ordered another pint of bitter and a large bottle of dandehon and burdock. When he came out, Miss Miranda was staring into the drain, her arms resting on the stone wall.

"I wish I knew the truth about creation," she said. "I wish I could really believe what it says in the Bible."

"That's precisely what Tommy Ishmael says to the desk sergeant at Canton police station," said Mog. "Well, they'd hauled us in for creating a disturbance in a public house. I'm not a Catholic, see. I eats the old lamb chops on Fridays. Right? But I'm not having Cuthbert Loosemore telling me I'm related to a bleeding monkey and neither would Tommy Ishmael. You should have seen him when he heard what Cuthbert said. Like a bloody gorilla, he was. Gets hold of old Cuthbert by the right ankle, throws him over his shoulder, puts the old boot in, lifts him up by the scruff of the neck and throws him straight through the door of the ladies bogs. Well, we'd have been all right if Estonian Johnny's girl friend hadn't been coming out of the door at the same moment as Cuthbert was going in. Caught her in the mouth with his elbow he did and knocked out three of her fillings. You should have seen Estonian Johnny's face. Well, I was under the table at the time and I only seen his ankles, but that was bad enough. Paddy Sullivan was in hospital three weeks after that, and he only come in for a packet of crisps.

"Well, this bloody sergeant didn't want to understand. 'What's the difference between man and the apes?' I kept saying to him. 'Brain's Best Bitter, that's the difference,' I says to him. Uneducated bastard he was. He didn't want to improve his learning. What it was, see, was he was prejudiced. I knows for a fact he only drank draught Worthington's."

Miss Miranda sighed deeply.

"Sister Concepta was always having doubts," she said. "At

least that's what they told us. You know Elaine Robertson? Well, she said she didn't believe there was a God, because if there was, He wouldn't have allowed her pony to die in agony from liver fluke. And we all thought, Gosh, Sister Clemency won't half clout her round the ear hole, but she didn't. She said that Sister Concepta wasn't there that term, because she'd had doubts and been sent away to a place in Ireland to try to resolve them. Of course, Antoinette Lilley said she knew better. She said the real reason was that Sister Concepta had been caught kissing the little man who came to fix the parallel bars in the gym and they'd sent her away to have her baby where no one could find her. And Oonagh Liddell said that was a load of balls because you had to do more than kiss to have babies, and Antoinette Lilley pretended she'd known that all the time, but I caught her the next day reading this book Chloe Shoemaker's sister had been given just before she got married."

The angler walked slowly past them, his wicker basket slung over his shoulder, his rod and keep net stuck under his arm. Mog nodded at him, but he ignored him and plodded on into the pub, his Wellington boots squelching soggily.

"Oh come on, Mog, drink your beer and let's get going," said Miss Miranda. "At the rate we're going on we won't get there till halfway through the evening."

"Exactly, my old flower. That's the precise time we wants to arrive there. Right?" said Mog. "We wants to give them time to settle in. Lull them into a false sense of security. And then, when they thinks no one's watching, and they gets on the job, we barges in and catches them red-handed. Right? Simple, my old lovely. You just leave it to Mog."

They walked slowly back to the motor scooter.

"I wonder what the old bitch is doing now?" said Miss Miranda. "I bet she's already had it three times."

It took Mrs Mortensen five minutes to climb to the top of the sand dunes. When she got there, she squatted in the coarse hummocky grass and lit a cigarette.

There was a wide, flat sea in front of her. The strand was wide and flat, too, and it glistened where the sun shone on the retreating tide. A little tern hunted above the bank of powdery shingle. A lazy chevron of herring gulls flapped high above her and then wheeled steeply and raggedly down to the water's

K

edge. There was a plume of smoke far out on the horizon, and the faint breeze came straight from the east.

She slid down the steep angle of the dunes, and when she reached the strand, she began to stride firmly to the water's edge. The gulls yapped and shuffled away from her.

She stood there for some time, staring out to sea. Suddenly she felt a tap on the elbow. She looked round to see a small man smiling up at her. He was wearing a white linen cap, a Fair Isle pullover and long khaki shorts.

"Excuse me, but are you from the caravan site?" he said.

"No."

"I am. Me and my brother just come up from Walsall this morning. My brother went to Jersey last year with my cousin. My brother says you can't beat the continent for holidays. Mind you, I maintain that your own country takes a lot of beating for holidays. It's very deceptive is your own country. Familiarity breeds contempt, you see, and you don't realise how beautiful your own country can be, if you only get the weather."

"Exactly," said Mrs Mortensen moving a few paces away from him.

"Very deceptive, isn't it, the weather?" said the little man, shuffling after her. "The weather's quite warm till you get outside in it, and then you realise how deceptive it is, don't you?"

Mrs Mortensen turned away from him, but he did not move. He stood there, hands in pockets, smiling and humming tunelessly to himself.

"Excuse me, but do you like having fun, missus?" he said.

"Pardon?"

"Well, excuse me, but there's only me and my brother in this caravan, and we both like having fun, you see. We could get a crate of light ale in, if you like, and we could all have fun together, couldn't we?"

"Go to hell," snapped Mrs Mortensen.

Half an hour later she returned to the cottage to find Sir Peter Wakefield cooking dinner in the kitchen. He was wearing a light green silk kerchief knotted round his neck.

"I've taken the trouble of preparing a vegetarian dinner for you." he said, and then he pointed to the steak he was cutting into strips on the chopping board and said: "This is for the other guests."

"Other guests?"

"Yes. Oh, of course, I forgot to tell you. I've invited Sam Tufton and his wife to spend the weekend with us. You've no objection, have you?"

Mrs Mortensen smiled slowly at him. She walked over, put her arms round his waist, her cheek next to his ear and whispered:

"And did you forget to tell them I would be here?"

Sir Peter chuckled and said:

"Do you know, I rather think I did."

Miss Miranda and Mog arrived in the village, where Sir Peter's cottage lay, half an hour after evening opening time. They had had two punctures on the way.

"They didn't have this trouble when the Royal Artillery was mounted," said Mog, climbing stiffly off the scooter. "Cor blimey Charlie, say what you like about horses, but they never had punctures, did they?"

"What are we going to do now?" said Miss Miranda, taking off her scarf and smoothing down her long, golden hair.

"What do you bloody think?" said Mog, pointing at the public house, which stood next to the bank.

"Oh, not again," said Miss Miranda.

"Listen to me, sweetheart, some of the greatest benefits to mankind was thought up in pubs, wasn't they? Course they bloody was. Penicillin? Hearing aids? Nuclear fission? Leg theory? All rustled up in pubs, my old darling," said Mog. "And that's where we're going to think up our plan of campaign for tonight. Right?"

Although it was hot outside, the pub was icy cold inside. There were three wooden benches along the side of the walls, and a large oak table, stained and dusty, filling the whole room except for a gap by the door and the bar.

The fireplace was full of cigarette butts and dirty beer mats. A strip of fly paper hung down from the naked light bulb, and there was a faint smell of burned cabbage everywhere.

"I didn't know Conrad Hilton had moved in round here," said Mog, squeezing past the table to get to the bar.

Miss Miranda held her nose and giggled, and when Mog brought over the pint of beer and the glass of lemon cordial, she said:

"Isn't it absolutely super?"

147

"Super? Cor blimey Charlie, I been in better de-lousing sheds than this, don't you kid yourself," said Mog.

"Well, I think it's absolutely heavenly," said Miss Miranda. "It's all sort of working class and horrid. Super."

"That's the trouble with you bloody toffs," said Mog. "You thinks all working class pubs are like this. You thinks you're right daring little buggers venturing into a place like this.

"I don't," said Miss Miranda. "I've been in worse places than this in my time. So there."

"Where, for example?" said Mog.

"Well, when we had our school trip to Paris, Oonagh Liddell and I went to this night club in Montmartre, and this super Negro came up and asked me to dance with him and he pressed me all close to him and I almost broke my suspenders and then this super grey-haired Frenchman came up and asked me to be his mistress and go and live in sin with him on his yacht in the Riviera. And he was a marquis and he was fantastically old—about 41, I think—and he said he was fantastically evil and perverted and I could have my breakfast in bed every day and put bath salts in the bath if only I'd give my body to him."

Mog looked at her. Then he took a drink from his pint. When he had finished, he said:

"You bloody liar."

"I know. Isn't it awful?" said Miss Miranda. "I can't help it, though."

Two men in navy blue pullovers came in. They were wearing thigh boots, and their faces were ruddy and gnarled. They did not look at Mog and Miss Miranda and sat down at the far end of the table.

"You know," said Mog, leaning back in his seat and looking at Miss Miranda. "You know, you're not a bad-looker when you gets down to brass tacks, are you?"

"I think I'm extremely good-looking, if you must know," said Miss Miranda.

"Well, I know lots of blokes what wouldn't kick you out of bed, I'll give you that," said Mog.

"Do you fancy me, Mog?" said Miss Miranda. "I mean, would you like to have knowledge of me?"

"Not really. It's my tubes, see. I hasn't got the puff no more for that sort of thing. I can always put you in touch with Icky Evans, if you fancies a bit on the sly, mind."

The little man from Walsall came in, smiled at the company, bought a bottle of light ale at the bar and sat down at the table. A few minutes later three youths with sideburns, donkey jackets and acne came in and sat down at the table opposite the little man from Walsall.

No one spoke. Feet shuffled on the dusty floorboards. Glasses clinked. Adams apples wobbled. Beer glistened on chins. One of the men in a navy blue pullover belched loudly without looking up from his pint pot.

"Friendly lot in here, isn't they?" said Mog in a loud voice to Miss Miranda.

"Absolutely divine, aren't they, my dear?" said Miss Miranda equally loudly, and she winked at Mog. "Do you remember that simply too divine evening we were dining in the Savoy Grill?"

Mog looked up sharply, and then a slow grin came to his face.

"Course I does," he said. "You was wearing that transparent dress what shows off your tits, wasn't you?"

"What a simply too remarkable memory you have," said Miss Miranda.

The two men in navy blue pullovers did not look up from their beer. Neither did the three youths in donkey jackets.

"Wasn't that the time Lady Celia took out Lord Oswald's Thing and used it as a dip stick in her consommé?" said Miss Miranda.

"That's right," said Mog. "And I took down my trousers and farted three verses of the Peruvian National Anthem."

Miss Miranda put her hand to her mouth, and her whole body shook.

"What I didn't like, though, was what Oonagh Liddell done," said Mog. "Well, there was no need for her to stick the menu up her backside and do the dance of the Flaming Arseholes, was there?"

"Excuse me, mister, but do you like having fun?" said the little man from Walsall.

"Go and get stuffed," said Mog, and then he went to the bar and bought two pints of beer.

"A pint? For me?" said Miss Miranda.

"Go on, get it down you," said Mog. "We got work to do tonight, hasn't we?"

Miss Miranda lifted up the pint glass, and the two men in

navy blue pullovers and the three youths in donkey jackets looked up and stared at her with interest.

When Alderman Samson Tufton arrived at the cottage with Mrs Tufton, he said to Sir Peter Wakefield:

"We had the devil's own job finding this place. She can't read a map for love nor money. Do you follow my meaning?"

Sir Peter showed them into the drawing room, gave them sherry and said:

"Oh, by the way, I forgot to tell you. Mrs Mortensen is spending the weekend here with me. She'll be down presently. A charming lady, don't you think, Mrs Tufton?"

Mrs Tufton looked at her husband, sniffed hard three times, put her glass of sherry on the table, stood up, walked out of the room and went upstairs to her bedroom.

"Oh, bloody hell, that's torn it," said Alderman Samson Tufton, and he followed his wife upstairs.

When he came down again, Mrs Mortensen was in the drawing room, sipping a glass of sherry. He nodded to her and said to Sir Peter:

"I hope you'll excuse Mrs Tufton, but she's got a very bad migraine and she's had to retire for the night. I think it must be the air. Very bracing here, isn't it? It can do you a lot of no good, if you're not accustomed to it. Do you follow my meaning?"

"Is there anything I can do?" said Mrs Mortensen.

"No," said Alderman Samson Tufton sharply, and then he coughed and said: "She's not one for being fussed, isn't Mrs Tufton. She wouldn't thank you for fussing over her, wouldn't Mrs Tufton, thank you all the same for your kind offer."

During dinner Sir Peter said to Mrs Mortensen:

"Sam was telling me about a film he'd been to the other day. One of those nudist efforts, wasn't it, Sam?"

"I didn't know you went to that sort of cinema," said Mrs Mortensen.

"Good God, no," said Alderman Samson Tufton. "I was viewing it in my capacity as chairman of the Watch Committee."

"It was Danish, wasn't it, Sam?" said Sir Peter.

"Well, with due respect to present company—yes," said Alderman Samson Tufton.

150

"Do you favour public nudity, Mrs Mortensen?" said Sir Peter.

"Yes, if the body is worth displaying," said Mrs Mortensen.

Sir Peter looked her up and down.

"What do you say, Sam? Do you think Mrs Mortensen's body is worth displaying?"

Alderman Samson Tufton hunched his head into his shoulders, glanced swiftly at the ceiling and began to ram celery and cheese into his mouth.

"Well, Sam? Do you?" said Sir Peter.

Alderman Samson Tufton gulped hard, took a long swig of his wine and said:

"I bet you can get bloody good mackerel in this part of the world, eh?"

At half past eight he excused himself and went upstairs to join Mrs Tufton in bed.

"She can't sleep by herself on her own, can't Mrs Tufton," he said. "She needs someone to warm her feet for her. Do you follow my meaning?"

At half past nine Sir Peter Wakefield and Mrs Mortensen walked hand in hand up the staircase. They paused on the landing and Sir Peter said loudly:

"Well, good night, Mrs Mortensen. Sleep well. See you in the morning."

Then he put his finger to his lips and winked at her. She kissed him on the forehead and whispered:

"Half an hour. Right?"

She went into her bedroom and undressed quickly. She stood naked in front of the mirror. She breathed in and placed her hands under her breasts. They were full and firm, and she smiled and stuck out her tongue at her reflection.

"Woozy, poozy, ooozy, woozy," said Miss Miranda. "I feel all woozy, poozy, oozy, woozy."

"Cor blimey Charlie," said Mog. "You're not stoned, are you?"

"I'm as high as a kite. I'm sailing high high in the sky and there's a super draught up the leg of my drawers."

"Very deceptive the beer round here, isn't it?" said the little man from Walsall.

"Shut up, you little Brummi bastard," said Mog. "Who asked you to stick your schonk in?"

151

"Woozy, poozy, ooooooooooooozy, wooooooooozy," said Miss Miranda, and she reached out for her beer and sent it cascading all over the table.

Mog took hold of her under the armpits and dragged her out of the chair.

"I'm a hat stand," she said. "I'm a bag of coal. Help, help, help, he's taking me away to his cave to rape me."

Mog nodded to the landlord, who was glaring at them from over the bar.

"All right, colonel," he said, "I doesn't live in a cave. More like a house. Right?"

As he pulled her out of the door one of the men in a navy blue pullover looked up and said:

"Shut the door behind you, will you?"

Outside in the street Miss Miranda sank giggling to the pavement. The fresh air hit Mog, too, and he had to cling hold of the wall of the bank to keep himself upright.

"Bloody hell, old Raich Nelson didn't have these problems before Trafalgar," he said to himself as he shook his head, trying to clear away the fuggy alcoholic haze.

Suddenly Miss Miranda leapt to her feet, took him by the arm and began to drag him along the street.

"Come on then," she said. "Up and at 'em."

"Wait a minute, hold your hurry," shouted Mog. "I hasn't decided on our bloody tactics yet."

"I have," said Miss Miranda firmly.

They came to the iron gate of the cottage. Miss Miranda pointed at it and said to Mog:

"Right. Over the top for you, my boy."

Mog stood there, reeling slowly from side to side. Then he began to hiccup.

"It's a bloody good job one of us can hold his drink," he said, and then he stumbled forwards, and Miss Miranda had to put her arms round him to hold him up.

"Oh, come on," she said. "Pull yourself together, man."

Mog hiccupped again and then slowly began to hoist himself over the gate. He was sitting astride it, about to lift his leg over and then drop to the ground, when Miss Miranda pushed open the gate.

"Oh, sorry, I thought it was locked," she said.

The movement of the gate caused Mog to overbalance. His feet and hands waved wildly in the air. He let out a muffled cry of panic, and then he was propelled head first into the privet hedge.

Miss Miranda looked down at his prostrate body and giggled. A series of deep baying snores wracked his body.

"Oh, shit," said Miss Miranda.

There were footsteps behind her, and someone tapped her on the elbow.

"Excuse me, miss, but you are requiring any assistance?" said the little man from Walsall.

Mrs Mortensen closed the door of her bedroom softly behind her. She looked to the left and the right, and then she tip-toed across the corridor to Sir Peter's bedroom.

She tapped softly on the door. There was a smile on her face, and her long hair hung loosely over her shoulders.

She knocked again. There was no response.

"Sir Peter," she whispered through the keyhole. "Sir Peter, it's me."

Outside in the garden the hinges of the gate creaked. She stood up and listened. Silence came again.

She knocked more sharply on the door.

"Sir Peter," she whispered. "Come on, open up."

There was still no response from the other side of the door. She put her ear to the keyhole. All she could hear was the ticking of an alarm clock.

"Come on, you big fat bastard," she shouted, and she began to beat on the door with her fists. "Open up. Open up this minute."

At that moment there was a violent crashing of glass from downstairs in the front hall. She dashed to the top of the stairs and looked down.

A panel of glass had been broken in the front door, and a hand poked through it, unfastened the catch and then withdrew. A few seconds later the door opened and in stepped the little man from Walsall.

"Excuse me, missus," he said, "but I think you've got company."

"What the hell's going on here?" shouted Sir Peter, rushing out of his bedroom. He was still fully-dressed.

"What's all the commotion? Have we got burglars?" said Alderman Samson Tufton, coming out of his bedroom, holding an umbrella in his hand.

They looked down onto the hallway, where the little man from Walsall and Miss Miranda were dragging Mog through the front door.

They deposited him on the floor and he rolled over onto his side, curled up and began to snore.

"Caught you red-handed, you old cow," shouted Miss Miranda, pointing up at her mother.

"What language," said Mrs Tufton, who had come to stand by her husband's side.

"Language? You haven't heard anything yet," said Miss Miranda. "For a start we're all as pissed as newts."

She began to giggle, and then she reeled backwards, fell over Mog and collapsed in a heap on the floor.

"Excuse me," said the little man from Walsall, "but do you like having fun?"

Alderman Samson Tufton and Mrs Tufton left the cottage at six thirty next morning.

Sir Peter Wakefield and Mrs Mortensen left for home two hours later.

At half past eleven Mog and Miss Miranda were still sleeping soundly in the caravan belonging to the little man from Walsall. He hadn't got a brother.

Mrs Mortensen arrived at Mannersville shortly after one o'clock. She did not speak to Sir Peter Wakefield as she got out of the car and slammed the door behind her.

She let herself in through the front door and stopped dead in her tracks, when she heard Philip Manners' voice coming from the kitchen. The house was full of the scents of cooking.

She marched into the kitchen just in time to catch Philip Manners placing an enormous portion of steak and kidney pudding into his mouth.

"So," she said.

Philip Manners dropped his fork, and his face turned white.

"So this is what you do when I am away? So this is why you don't mind my dining with Sir Peter Wakefield in the evening? So this is why you looked so pleased with yourself when I went away for the weekend?"

Philip Manners pushed his plate away. His whole body sagged, and the stoop returned to his shoulders.

"You have been eating this poisonous filth every time I set foot outside the house, haven't you?"

154

Philip Manners did not reply, and Mrs Mortensen turned to Hempstall and shouted:

"He has, hasn't he?"

Hempstall glanced nervously at Philip Manners, who stood up and said quietly:

"Yes I have. There's no need to blame her neither. It was all my doing."

Mrs Mortensen stood with her hands on her hips, tapping her foot angrily on the stone flags of the kitchen. Her lips were quivering, and her eyes were flashing.

"Your body needs a complete purge," she said. And then she snapped: "And your mind, too."

She took hold of him by the collar of his jacket and began to pull him out of the room. For a moment Philip Manners acquiesced meekly. Then suddenly he swept her hand away.

"Take your bloody hands off me," he shouted.

"I beg your pardon?"

"You heard," he shouted. And then he turned to Hempstall and shouted: "Well, what are you gawping at? Get some more steak and kidney pud dished out, will you?"

He turned back to Mrs Mortensen and began to wag his finger slowly in front of her nose.

"I've had just about all I can stomach from you," he said. "This is my house. I'm the boss. You're the servant. You're just as much a servant of mine as Hempstall. Do you understand?"

Mrs Mortensen stepped back from him. Her eyes were filling up with tears.

"If I want to eat steak and kidney pud, I'll eat it," he shouted. "If I want to eat boot polish and stewed pyjama cords, I'll eat it. This is my house, and I eat what I want in it. Do you understand?"

Mrs Mortensen slowly backed down the corridor. Philip Manners stalked after her, still wagging his finger in front of her nose.

"If you want to go off for a dirty weekend with Sir Peter, all right. That's your business," he shouted. "But it's my business to know which side you're on. Are you on my side, or are you on their side?"

She shook her head slowly, and the tears came spilling and tumbling down her cheeks.

"Well, you'd better make a decision pretty bloody quick,"

he shouted. "And if it's the wrong one, you can pack your bags and clear off out of this house. Understand?"

II

Three days later Philip Manners was dead.

The circumstances surrounding his death were curious.

On the morning of his decease he rose from his bed at five thirty. He went into his bathroom, washed, shaved and gargled.

He whistled happily as he put on his black and white check suit, his blue flannel shirt and his yellow tie with its motif of horses' heads.

He breakfasted in the kitchen. He ate four rashers of smoked bacon, three thick pieces of Cumberland sausage, two fried eggs and a slice of fried bread.

He was just starting on the toast, when Mrs Mortensen came down from her room. She was wearing an Arran jumper and blue and white striped trousers.

"Please let me come with you, Philip," she said.

"No," said Philip Manners.

Hempstall left the kitchen, and Mrs Mortensen sat down at the table opposite him.

"I've told you I'm on your side," she said. "Why do you have to keep on behaving like this?"

"Because I want to," said Philip Manners.

At half past six Ambrose arrived with Oliver Manners and Mog. Philip Manners went out into the hall, took his binoculars off the stand and said to Miss Miranda, who came bounding down the stairs:

"You're just in time. We'd not have waited for you, you know."

Mog yawned and rubbed his eyes. Oliver yawned, too. and sat down on the window ledge.

"Come on, come on," said Philip Manners. "What's to do with you? You look as though you're still half asleep."

156

"We are," said Oliver, and he stretched his arms and yawned deeply again.

"I don't know what the younger generation's coming to," said Philip Manners.

"Neither do I," said Mog. "No bloody stamina. That's what they hasn't got."

Philip Manners began to usher them out of the front door. Mrs Mortensen tugged at his sleeve.

"Please, Philip," she said.

"No," he said, and slammed the door in her face.

The purpose of the trip was to visit the stables, where Philip Manners kept his four race horses.

The long grass and the wild flowers on the verges of the main driveway in Mannersville were laden with dew, which sparkled in the early morning sunshine.

To their right the mist coiled and curled round the trunks of the horse chestnuts. Three fallow deer trotted rapidly across the clearing and disappeared into a tangle of young oaks.

"Marvellous. Wonderful," said Philip Manners.

Miss Miranda yawned. Oliver yawned, and Mog dug them in the ribs and said:

"Come on, show a bit of interest, will you? Cor blimey Charlie, you don't see me looking as though I'd sooner be in my bed. Right? That's the last place I wants to be at this moment."

And then he had to place his hand over his mouth hurriedly to stifle a yawn.

They drove quickly up the main road to the north. There was little traffic about.

"The old Turf, eh? The Sport of Kings. Right?" said Mog. "Cor blimey Charlie, you can't beat a day out watching the old donkeys, can you?"

"You like horse racing, do you, Mr Williams?" said Philip Manners.

"Like it? I'm bloody addicted to it, man. Well, what I doesn't know about starting prices could be wrote on the back of a tram ticket. Right? Nossie Sherman? I could have been his right hand man, if I hadn't gone down with mumps. Well, me and Fat Bas used to run a book at the point to points, see. We'd have been all right if Cuthbert Loosemore had seen the sparking plugs was working proper. Cor blimey Charlie, the last race and the evens favourite comes up. Well, there was only one thing for it—up and off and scapa. Gets to the car, jumps in, settles down with the hip flask, all fine and dandy, and we only goes ten yards and the bloody thing breaks down.

"Well, the bloody desk sergeant at the Shepton Mallett cop shop didn't want to know. Called us a load of bloody Welshers, he did. Cheeky bastard. I told him the only reason we was leaving was because we'd had a message that Fat Bas's old grannie had been run over by a trolley bus. He didn't care. She could have died without Fat Bas being at her bedside for all he was bothered. I kept telling him it was a matter of life and death. I kept asking him how he'd like it if his old grannie was run over by a pantechnicon."

"I thought you said it was a trolley bus?" said Miss Miranda.

"Same bloody thing," said Mog. "The end product's the same whether it's a trolley bus or a bleeding steam roller, isn't it? Course it is."

They turned off the main road and followed the course of a river valley. The banks were lined with beeches. Dippers flicked their tails on the stones in the shallows. A large Aberdeen Angus bull stood fetlock deep in the water, and its breath writhed around its nostrils.

When they came to the stables, Philip Manners wound down the window and shouted across to a young girl in jodhpurs and headscarves:

"Is Walter in?"

"He's up at the gallops, Mr Manners," said the girl. "Shall you go up directly?"

They drove up a narrow, winding lane, which led them away from the floor of the valley and up to the rolling moorlands.

The heather was young and green. Red grouse called to each other, and curlews trilled. Below them the river wound its way upwards into the high barrier of hills to the north.

The sun glinted on the rails of a distant railway viaduct. A meadow pipit fluttered weakly into the air, and then glided down, singing loudly. In the far distance was the faint whine and scream of a circular saw.

The road levelled off after crossing a small stone pack horse bridge, and they saw a small man in flat cap and riding breeches sitting astride a chestnut hack.

They stopped the car and got out. The man on the hack dismounted, came across to them, grunted and shook hands with Philip Manners.

158

"Everything all right, Walter?" said Philip Manners.

The trainer grunted again, and Philip Manners introduced him to the rest of the party.

Mog shook his hand warmly and said, pointing to the hack:

"Not a bad donkey you got there, colonel. What is it, a four mile chaser? Looks a good National prospect to me."

"It's his hack," said Miss Miranda.

"All right, smarty pants, I knows that," said Mog. "I was just testing him out to see if he knows his onions. Right?"

And then he took the trainer to one side and whispered into his ear:

"If you wants a horse fixing, my old son, just you get in touch with me. Right? Feed them an old dish cloth soaked in treacle half an hour before the off, and they bloody near strangle theirselves going over the first fence. Right?"

The trainer pushed him away and returned to Philip Manners.

"A right bloody know-all, him," said Mog to Oliver Manners, pointing to the trainer. "I knows a villain when I sees one, don't you kid yourself. And he's the biggest villain of the lot. He'd strangle his old grannie as soon as look at her. Right?"

Then they heard the drumming of hooves and four race horses, galloping abreast, appeared over the brow of a low rise to their left and flashed past them, their jockeys crouched low over their necks.

"By gum, that's a grand sight is that, Walter," said Philip Manners, and the trainer grunted again.

The jockeys pulled up the horses and then cantered them back to the trainer. The horses snorted and grappled with their bits. Steam rose from their flanks, and one of them lowered its head and lashed out with its back feet.

"Vicious bloody things, aren't they?" said Mog. "Well, it's the in-breeding, see. It's the same in the Welsh valleys. They're all in-bred up there. That's why you gets so many punch-ups on pay night. Right?"

Miss Miranda beckoned to Mog and said:

"Now you can show me what cobblers are."

"What?" said Mog, as she led him up to one of the horses.

"Well, you told me that cobblers are what geldings haven't got," she said, and then she said to the lad who was riding the horse:

159

"This is a gelding, isn't it?"

"That's right, miss," said the lad with a slow smile.

"Well, show me," she said to Mog.

"Bloody hell," said Mog. "You can count yourself lucky I was a personal buttie of Lord Mildmay, or you wouldn't get this expert tuition. Right?"

Then he pointed beneath the horse's belly and said:

"Have a gander at that, and you'll see what I mean."

Miss Miranda bent down and looked.

"I can't see anything," she said.

"Course you can't," said Mog. "You can't see nothing for the sole and simple reason that this here nag's a gelding, so it hasn't got nothing for your little beady eyes to see. Right?"

The horse tossed its head and stamped its feet. The lad tightened his grip on the reins.

"I still don't understand," said Miss Miranda.

Then she picked up a stick, and moving closer to the horse jabbed it under the belly.

The horse reared up with a whinny of anger. The lad was flung from the saddle. Miss Miranda and Mog jumped back. For a moment the horse stood there, tossing its head, and the lad staggered to his feet, rubbing his shoulder.

The trainer shouted across and began to run towards them. He was just about to catch hold of the horse's reins, when it lashed out with its back feet, and then trotted off and stood there, pawing the ground.

"Now you've bloody done it," said Mog.

Suddenly the horse began to gallop towards them. They flung themselves out of its way. Its eyes were flashing wildly, and its tail was swishing from side to side.

It galloped past them and jumped over a low dry stone wall. As it landed on the other side one of its hooves caught Philip Manners on the side of the head.

He had been standing there, obeying a call of nature. He was dead by the time they brought him back to the stables.

The funeral was an impressive and solemn affair.

The Lord Lieutenant of the county, the lord mayors of three cities, two peers, five knights and the chairman of the local gas users' consultative council were among the congregation at the service in the cathedral.

A detachment of soldiers from the county Territorial Army

regiment fired a salute from their rifles as the body was lowered into the grave, and all the women wore long black veils.

The reception was held at Mannersville.

"Dreadful affair," said Alderman Samson Tufton to Hedley Nicholson. "Tragic. Right tragic. Do you follow my meaning?"

Hedley Nicholson nodded and moved over to Mrs Mortensen who was sitting alone on a couch in the entrance hall.

Her face was white and drawn. There were red rims round her eyes, and on her fingernails were flecks of white.

Hedley Nicholson looked down on her for a moment, and then he sat down beside her and took hold of her hand.

"I'm very very sorry," he said softly.

She looked at him, and a weak smile came to her face.

"Thank you," she said.

He hesitated and then said:

"I don't know what your plans are, Mrs Mortensen, but if you feel you would like to take a holiday, you could easy spend a few weeks at my cottage in Cornwall."

She shook her head slowly.

"Nothing like that, Mrs Mortensen," he said quickly. "You'd be quite on your own."

Estelle Nicholson who had been watching them from the foot of the stairs, walked over and said:

"You could always come and stay with us for a bit while you're making up your mind about what to do in the future."

"It's very kind of you," said Mrs Mortensen. "But I shall be staying on here. I've still got my patients to look after, you know."

"Aye, that's right," said Hedley Nicholson gently. "That's right."

Miss Miranda and Oliver Manners were standing together by the fountain.

"It's all my fault, Oliver," she said. "I'm the one who killed your father. If I hadn't wanted to know what cobblers were, none of this would ever have happened."

She began to sob once more, and Oliver put his arms round her.

"It was a pure accident, Miranda," he said. "I've told you that over and over again. You weren't to blame in any way."

She stopped crying and looked him straight in the eyes.

L

"Was it the same with your mother, Oliver? Was that a pure accident?" she said.

He took hold of her hand and led her quickly to the timber bridge, which spanned the stream╱which led down to the lake. A redstart flicked its tail and flew off into the bushes.

"What the hell happened?" he said, gritting his teeth.

Miss Miranda shook her head slowly.

"What the hell happened?" he shouted, and he gripped her hand so tightly that she cried out in pain.

Over in the kitchen of the cottage Megan was sobbing unrestrainedly.

"Cor blimey Charlie, it's not the end of the bloody world," said Mog. "We all got to snuff it sooner or later. At least it was his own bloody horse that killed him, wasn't it?"

And then he turned to Ambrose and said:

"From the way he jumped that wall, I'd say he was a real good bet for the Champion Hurdle at Cheltenham. Right?"

"Give over," said Ambrose.

Still sobbing, Megan got up from her chair and opened a drawer in the Welsh dresser. She took out a leather-bound album and began to flick through the pages. On them was stuck her collection of in memoriam notices cut from the local newspaper.

She paused at a page and began to read out one of the cuttings.

" 'Flemthwaite. Flight Sergeant Victor. Lost on active service over the Humber. Always in our thoughts. Mam, Dad, Ernie, Rita, Serena, Freda, Wilf, Harry, Stan, Noreen, Sandra and baby Hamilton.' "

She looked up from the page and said:

"Now them's lovely appropriate sentiments, isn't they?"

"Course they isn't," said Mog. "What you wants to be looking for is a tribute to a bloke what copped his lot through being hit on the napper by a racehorse. Right?"

Megan stood up and went to the window. Through the gap in the cedars she could see Horace A'Fong and Wyndham Lancaster walking together on the lawns.

Blackbirds and thrushes were singing. House martins swooped round the gables of Mannersville, the scent of roses came in through the open window.

"Oh, I wish we could stay here, Ambrose," said Megan. "I wish we didn't have to go back to that house in the city."

"So do I," said Ambrose. "Still, you never know. Now that Mr Manners has died, they might decide to pack in the experiment."

"Pack it in?" said Mog. "What would they want to go and do that for?"

"Well, it's Tom Manners what's in charge now," said Ambrose. "And he were never keen on the idea from the start, were he?"

"Cor blimey Charlie, you'll have to find an in memoriam for me, if he goes and does that. Right?" said Mog.

Most of the mourners had already left, when Tom Manners called Mrs Mortensen into the study.

"Sit down, Mrs Mortensen," he said, drawing up a chair for her in front of his desk.

Sir Peter Wakefield handed her a whisky, and she took it from him without speaking.

"Well, Mrs Mortensen, I think it's high time that we applied ourselves to considering the change in our respective circumstances, don't you?" said Tom.

"Very well," she said.

"As you no doubt know my father has left the business to Oliver," he said. "However, you are no doubt equally aware that owing to the state of Oliver's health it is I who will be running the business until such time as Oliver is in a position to take on those responsibilities himself."

"I see."

"The house, of course, has been left to me, and I can tell you that it doesn't form part of my plans for the future to keep open this private asylum, which was established by my father."

"You're giving me notice to leave in other words?" said Mrs Mortensen.

"Not exactly, Mrs Mortensen," said Sir Peter.

She did not look at him as he came from the mantelpiece and stood next to Tom.

"We want you to continue to look after Oliver," he said.

"And if I refuse?"

Sir Peter shrugged his shoulders and looked at Tom, who coughed, tapped the bridge of his spectacles and said:

"Then we shall have no alternative but to get him certified as being insane and thus commit him to an institution."

"Oliver is very nearly cured," said Mrs Mortensen softly.

Tom Manners glanced at Sir Peter. He coughed again and tapped the bridge of his spectacles.

"And for that very reason, Mrs Mortensen, it is our belief that his cure could be more swiftly expedited if he were to return to Mannersville to be looked after in the bosom of his own family as it were."

"That is why Tom wants you to stay on at Mannersville, Mrs Mortensen," said Sir Peter.

"And what happens to the other patients?"

"I intend to get rid of them immediately," said Tom.

Mrs Mortensen stood up, went to the drinks tray and poured herself another whisky.

"Well, Mrs Mortensen, what is your decision?" said Sir Peter.

She looked at each of them in turn. Then she tossed back her whisky in a single gulp and smiled at them.

"I may be wrong, but it's my impression from talking to Sir Peter that certifying Oliver is the one thing that you would want most in the world," she said.

Tom's face flushed red. He was just about to speak, when Sir Peter pressed him down into his chair and said:

"I've told you many times, Mrs Mortensen, you are completely mistaken in your impression. Tom's whole life is dedicated to the cause of restoring Oliver's soundness of mind. Isn't that so, Tom?"

Tom Manners nodded vigorously and Mrs Mortensen smiled broadly.

"In that case I shall give you my decision," she said.

"Splendid," said Sir Peter. "I'm sure you're doing the right thing in staying on."

"My decision is that Oliver will continue to live with the Tierneys, and that my patients will not be got rid of."

Tom Manners smashed his fist onto the table and jumped up from his chair.

"Now, you listen to me, you old whore," he shouted.

"No, you listen to me, Tom," said Mrs Mortensen. "If you do not do what I say, I shall create such a scandal for you and your family that your whole political career as well as your business career will be completely destroyed."

"May I ask how?" said Sir Peter.

Mrs. Manners took out a small leather notebook from her hand bag.

"With this," she said.

Sir Peter held out his hand for it, but she snatched it from his grasp and smiled.

"In here, Tom, is the true account of the circumstances surrounding your mother's death," she said. "It's written by your father, too."

12

"Isn't it smashing to be on our own at long last, Ambrose?" said Megan.

"Aye, it's champion," said Ambrose.

It was Saturday morning. It was a few days after Philip Manners' funeral, too. Mog had taken Oliver Manners, Horace A'Fong and Group Captain Greenaway into town, and the sun was shining.

They were sitting in the back parlour, drinking coffee. The windows were open, and they could hear the sounds of a summer's morning. Birds were singing, an electric razor was humming, milk bottles rattled, a steam pile driver throbbed, a car door slammed and Uncle Mort from next door shouted:

"Has anyone seen my best cap?"

Megan was immersed in the morning newspaper. She sighed contentedly as she turned to the Births, Marriages and Deaths column.

"I thinks I likes the engagements best now, Ambrose," she said. "You don't get no verses in engagements, worse luck, but you does get nice sentiments expressed, and there's no hint of blood like what there is in the deaths and births."

Ambrose took off his slippers and began to pull on his gardening boots. Megan smiled at him and said:

"Does you remember our engagement, Ambrose?"

"Oh aye," said Ambrose, and he caught hold of Megan by the waist and pulled her into him.

She kissed him and then went into the kitchen and said:

165

"Oh, we did have a smashing party that night, didn't we, Ambrose? I never seen so much blood in my life. 'Mind his dentures, Ossie,' mam kept shouting, and when they'd put the fire out, we gived all the lads from the Fire Brigade a bottle of brown ale each. Do you remember?"

"Aye," said Ambrose, coming into the kitchen and putting his arms round her waist.

"And does you remember our wedding day, Ambrose?" she said.

"Aye."

"Tommy Ishmael was sick all down the front of Cuthbert Loosemore's demob suit, wan't he?"

"Aye," said Ambrose, and he kissed her on the back of her neck. "And do you remember our wedding night?"

Megan giggled and pressed herself closer into him.

"Oh, I does, Ambrose, I does," she said.

"Should we go and have a bash in the bedroom then?" said Ambrose softly, and he kissed the back of her neck again.

"Righto, lovely," she said. "But promised to keep your eyes closed."

At that moment there was a commotion at the front door. They went into the hall in time to see Oliver Manners and Group Captain Greenaway heaving in a large cardboard carton. There were two similar cartons on the path outside, and Horace A'Fong was unloading an assortment of packages from a taxi pulled up outside the front gate.

"What's all this then?" said Ambrose.

"It's my clobber. Right?" said Mog. "Well, more like my entrepreneur's kit if the truth be known. Give them a hand by there, will you?"

The cartons and packages were stowed in the front parlour and Mog said:

"Right, you three skiving dogs, you can have a smoke and a mug of tea, but I wants you back here on the job in half an hour's time. Right?"

"What's it all about?" said Megan to Horace A'Fong as he scurried upstairs to his bedroom.

"It's a sort of prep, I think," said Horace A'Fong. "Looks absolutely wizard, though, doesn't it?"

She went into the front parlour and was just in time to hear Mog starting his explanations.

"There's a hundredweight of horse hair stuffing in this
166

carton. Right? There's forty yards of simulated fur in this one and another forty yards of sackcloth in this one. Right? Now then, in this package you've got your templets, in this one you've got your artificial eyes and in this one you've got your doings for turning the whole bang shoot inside out. Right?"

"But what's it all for?" said Ambrose.

"Cor blimey Charlie, I'd have thought that was obvious, my old cream cake," said Mog. "This equipment by here is for making hares for greyhound tracks, isn't it? Course it bloody is. They provides the materials. I provides the labour. Right? Like? Twenty two bob a kick I gets for each completed hare and an extra half dollar for each one what is completed within three days. Home industry, my old son. That's where the money is. That's where you finds your liquidity. Right?"

"And what are all the other packets for, Mog?" said Megan.

"Simple. Simplicity itself, my lovely," said Mog. "I got my leaflets in one, my envelopes in the other and my list of addresses in the other. Right? Now then, all I does is address each envelope, stick a leaflet in it, send the completed job lot back to the agency, and I gets nineteen and six a gross. Right? Then I got my semi-precious stones in these two packets, my mountings in this packet and my cement in this one. Right? Three and six for each completed brooch is what I gets. Right? Like?"

"Well, I never," said Megan, sitting down heavily on the sofa.

"Mind my stalks," said Mog. "There's two bob for each dozen artificial flowers completed. I doesn't want you squashing my bleeding stamens, does I?"

"What's going to happen to your mail order business then?" said Ambrose.

"Oh that," said Mog. "That's thrown to the winds, my old flower. That's chicken feed compared to this lot. Well, it was the returns, see. You doesn't get enough returns for your labour outlay, does you? Course you bloody doesn't. Any fools knows that. You doesn't have to be a genius like me to know that. Right?"

"Well, I hopes you knows what you're doing, Mog, love you," said Megan. "I hopes it's all above board with no trace of fishiness about it."

"Above board? Course it's above board. I don't know, there

167

are some suspicious minds round here. They didn't ask Henry Ford, when he was inventing his motor cars, if it was above board, did they? They didn't ask Florence Nightingale where she'd nicked her lamp from, did they? Right? Well, keep your nose out of my affairs," said Mog, and then he went to the door and shouted upstairs: "Right, you skiving dogs, time to get cracking. Right?"

That evening the lunatics laboured long and hard at the tasks set them by Mog and did not go to bed until two in the morning. They were up at eight on Sunday morning, and all day until nine in the evening they cut out patterns, licked envelopes, stuck in artificial eyes and sneezed when the horse hair stuffing got up their noses.

On Monday evening Mog went into town with six hares and three dozen artificial flowers. On Tuesday he dispatched five gross of addressed envelopes, and on Wednesday afternoon he took in five more hares and twenty nine brooches.

On Thursday morning Mrs Mortensen said in her office:
"Sex."
"Hares," said Horace A'Fong.
"Don't you mean rabbits?"
"Z-z-z-z-z-z-z," went a sound asleep Horace A'Fong.

Over the weekend they addressed and sealed six gross of envelopes, made fifteen hares and completed three dozen artificial lilies of the valley. Oliver Manners showed great talent in sticking on the stalks.
"Sex," said Mrs Mortensen on Monday morning.
"Stalk," said Oliver Manners.
"Babies."
"Stalk."
"Really, Oliver, how innocent you are about such matters," said Mrs Mortensen. Then she tapped her pencil on the side of her nose and said: "Erection."
"Stalk."
"Ah, that's much better."
"Zz-z-z-z-z-z," went a sound asleep Oliver Manners.

During the rest of the week Mog sent off another fifteen hares, two dozen brooches and twenty plastic ashtrays hand-painted with the legend, "A Present from Dunkirk".
"Women," said Mrs Mortensen on Friday morning.
"Dunkirk," said Group Captain Greenaway.
"Hares,"

"His," said Group Captain Greenaway.

"Stalk."

"Five thousand feet. Fieseler Stork dead ahead. The blighter hasn't seen us. Going in to attack. Wow-wow-wow-wow-wow Ratatat-ratatat-ratatat. Got him. Bagged him. Wizard prang, the blighter's in the drink," said Group Captain Greenaway.

"Ah, that's much better."

"Z-z-z-z-z," went a sound asleep Group Captain Greenaway.

"Don't you think you're working them too hard, Mog?" said Megan one Sunday morning. "I mean, God love them, they never stops sleeping these days."

"It's the demand, my lovely. The laws of supply and demand. Right? It's not my fault if the greyhounds rips the bleeding hares to pieces at the end of each race, is it? Blame the theory of evolution, my sweetheart. Don't blame me. Right?" said Mog. "Anyway, it's doing old Oliver the world of good, isn't it? You never seen him looking so perky and full of hisself, has you? Course you bloody hasn't. Them stamens has really brought him out of hisself. Right?"

A little later in the week on an afternoon of watery sunshine and sullen breezes Tom Manners called Oliver Manners into the study of Mannersville.

Oliver took Miss Miranda with him. Tom had Sir Peter Wakefield by his side as he sat at the desk.

"And how are you feeling, my dear Oliver?" said Tom Manners, handing him a glass of whisky.

"Never felt better in my life, thank you," said Oliver, yawning loudly and stretching his arms.

"I trust you are quite satisfied with the way I am conducting the affairs of the family business."

"I suppose so."

"I trust, too, that you are satisfied with the financial arrangements I have made on your behalf."

"Yes, thank you," said Oliver.

"Well, I'm not," said Miss Miranda. "You give him ten pounds a week pocket money, and, for Christ's sake, he owns the place. I think you're absolutely stinking rotten."

"I don't think that the arrangements Tom has made for his brother are anything to do with you, my dear," said Sir Peter Wakefield.

169

"Oh, fuck off, warty neck," said Miss Miranda.

"Now, now, Miranda," said Oliver.

"You know Mog Williams? Well, he thinks you're nothing less than a couple of bleeding criminals. Right?" said Miss Miranda. "If Icky Evans was here, he'd give you such a going over with the old dusters, you wouldn't know what hit you. Right? Like?"

Tom looked at Sir Peter and arched his eyebrows.

"I think, Miranda, it's high time I had a word with your mother about your behaviour," he said.

"Go on then. See if I care," said Miss Miranda. "The only person I take any notice of these days is Mog Williams, isn't it, Oliver?"

"That's right," said Oliver.

"He's absolutely super. He's gorgeous," said Miss Miranda. "And he's keeping close tabs on you, don't you worry yourselves. He's been in the army. Right? You can't come the old soldier on him. Right? Unarmed combat? Cor blimey Charlie, if he got going on you, you wouldn't have a single cobbler to call your own. Right? What are cobblers by the way?"

After Oliver and Miss Miranda had left the room Sir Peter went to the window and looked out for a while.

The pug dog, Lord William, was digging a hole in the centre of the lawn. Wyndham Lancaster was playing quoits with F.K. Henderson. Black, purple-bellied clouds with wind-frayed edges were lumbering in from the high moorland crags.

He turned, rubbed his chin thoughtfully and said:

"I think it's high time, Tom, that you and I arranged to meet this Mog Williams."

Tom Manners had to wait half an hour in the lobby of the Constitutional Club before Mog turned up for his appointment.

"Sorry I'm late, tardy like, my old son, but I had a bit of trouble with my boot laces," said Mog.

"Better late than never," said Tom Manners, and he led Mog into the bar.

"Good bit of furniture you got here," said Mog, looking round with approval. "If ever you wants to flog a bit on the side, let me know. I'll get you a good price, and we'll split the profits fifty fifty down the middle. Right?"

"Would you care for a brandy?" said Tom Manners. "Or possibly whisky's your favourite tipple?"

"I'll have a pint of Guinness in the old straight glass, my son," said Mog, sinking back into the leather arm chair and stretching out his feet on the thick-piled carpet.

"I don't think they have draught beer here actually," said Tom.

"Bastards," said Mog. "It's always the same in these places. They don't take into account the tastes of the working man. Money talks, see. If you're born with a silver spoon in your mouth, you hasn't got enough room to get your chops round a pint pot, has you?"

"Whisky then?"

"Make it a double."

The waiter brought two whiskys on a silver salver and poured in water from a Bohemian glass jug.

"I thought you and I would take dinner first, and Sir Peter will join us for drinks after," said Tom. "Does that meet with your approval?"

"Spot on, my old bath bun," said Mog, stubbing his cigarette on the carpet.

They had two more double whiskies, and then they went into dinner.

"I'll have two portions of potted shrimps, one oxtail soup, a couple of melons and a bit of the old whitebait. Right?" said Mog.

"You can't have all those at one sitting," said Tom. "You just have one as a first course."

"Listen to me, boy. Don't you tell me how to conduct myself in a cafe. I knows what they gets up to in the kitchens. Right? I been in the kitchen of Tommy Ishmael's cafe, don't you kid yourself. Cor blimey Charlie, he'd cockroaches as big as bull mastiffs in his bleeding pantry, hadn't he? Course he bloody had."

Tom Manners sighed and gave the order to the waiter.

Mog followed his first course with grilled sole, chipped potatoes, cabbages, carrots, peas and spinach. After this he had roast rib of beef, Yorkshire pudding, roast potatoes, creamed potatoes, boiled potatoes and chipped potatoes. The saute potatoes were off.

"I thinks I might find room for a bit of sherry trifle next," he said.

171

He followed the sherry trifle with plum tart and custard and baked apple and cream.

Over the cheese and biscuits he said:

"You hasn't eaten much, my old son. You've only been nibbling. What's up with you? Got a spot of the old colly wobbles, is it?"

Tom Manners slipped another indigestion tablet into his mouth and said:

"I never could stand the sight of over-eating."

"Neither could I," said Mog. "You gets some dirty pigs what stuff theirselves so much it bloody near comes out of their ear holes. Right? Talk about a surfeit of lampreys. Cor blimey Charlie, Cuthbert Loosemore's old lady snuffed it through guzzling too much pickled cabbage, didn't she? Course she bloody did. I think I'll have some more of that trifle, if you don't mind."

Tom Manners slipped three more indigestion tablets into his mouth, and then he led Mog back into the bar.

The chief constable was demonstrating a trick with a match box and three cocktail sticks to Alderman Samson Tufton.

"I'll show you a better trick than that, my old cock," said Mog, sweeping the match box and the three cocktail sticks off the bar counter. "Now then, has anyone got a five pound note, a candle and half a parsnip?"

Tom Manners pushed him away to a corner sofa and ordered him a double whisky. He ordered a tonic water for himself.

"Right, my old flower, fire away," said Mog. "You didn't invite me out just to ram a bit of the old fodder down my gullet, did you? Right?"

Tom belched discreetly into his handkerchief.

"I'd get your gut looked at, if I was you," said Mog. "You only had half a slice of haddock and look at you—you're green round the gills and your tongue looks like the inside of a Japanese wrestler's jock strap."

Tom stood up quickly and hurried out of the room. When he returned, his hair was flattened down with water, and there was a slight flush on his cheeks.

"Spewed your ring up, has you?" said Mog. "I thinks it must have been the cabbage. I found a couple of slugs in my helping."

Tom jumped up again and fled to the toilet.

When he returned, he was told that there was a telephone call for him from Sir Peter Wakefield. He excused himself, went out into the lobby, picked up the receiver and said:

"Well?"

"Tom, I'm most dreadfully sorry, but I shan't be able to make it this evening," said Sir Peter.

"Oh, my God."

"There's nothing wrong, is there?"

"No," said Tom weakly, and he belched again.

"It really is most infuriating, but we're dreadfully involved in the question of council subsidies to the orchestra, and I just can't leave the meeting at this stage," said Sir Peter. "How are things going anyway?"

"Up and down," said Tom.

"Good, good. Well, it's up to you. Put the proposition quite bluntly to him. Cards on the table. There's no need for subtlety with a person of his character."

"I wish you could do it."

"Nonsense, Tom. You'll do it splendidly. Cheerie bye."

Tom Manners paused for a moment outside the telephone box before striding briskly into the bar, sitting on the sofa and saying:

"Mr Williams, I suggest we conclude this business as quickly as possible."

"Fire away, old cock," said Mog, taking a handful of potatoe crisps from the glass dish on the table in front of him.

"I have a certain proposition to make to you."

"I'm all ears. Well, only in the metaphorical sense like. Right?"

"As you know, Mr Williams, during the last few years of my father's life most of the responsibility for running the family business fell onto my shoulders."

"And you've not been behind the door helping yourself to the petty cash, eh?" said Mog. "Well, if you wants a crooked lawyer, just you get onto Fat Bas. He's got half a dozen of the most crookedest ones in the whole of South Wales in his pocket, I tell you."

"Will you shut up and listen to what I am about to say?" shouted Tom Manners, and then he turned pale and slipped another indigestion tablet into his mouth.

"Them pills will do you no good," said Mog, taking an olive from the dish. "I knowed a bloke, name of Patterson, what

173

spent all his life taking pills. Cor blimey Charlie, when they opened him up at the post mortem, he'd so many coloured pills inside him, he looked like a bloody snooker table. It's true. It's true."

Tom Manners half-rose out of his seat. There was a series of tiny convulsive movements in his throat, and he had to gulp rapidly. He mopped the perspiration off his brow, and Mog sipped his whisky placidly.

When he had regained his composure, Tom leaned forward and said:

"I want you to tell me something in the strictest confidence, Mr Williams."

"Confidence? You come to the right man, my old cream cake. They'd have to pull my toenails out before I'd split on a confidence. Right?"

Tom looked over his shoulder and whispered:

"What is the precise state of Oliver's mental health?"

"It'll cost you a tenner," said Mog.

"Oh, come, come, come, come, Mr Williams."

"All right, I'll do it for a fiver being as how it's family."

"If my brother is insane, then legally he can have no claim to the family business. Do you understand me, Mr Williams?"

"I understands you, boy," said Mog. "What's in your mind?"

"If my brother were to be certified as insane and placed in a mental home, then the person who helped bring it about might find substantial gains accruing to him. Do you understand me, Mr Williams?"

"I understands."

"The gains, social as well as financial, which this person would derive would be quite considerable, I do assure you, Mr Williams."

" 'This person?' 'This person?' Me, you means, doesn't you? You wants me to stick Oliver in the old nut house so's you won't have it on your conscience. Right?" said Mog. "You dirty Tory swine. You Fascist vermin. Cor blimey Charlie, I fought the whole of the Second World War to defend democracy against the likes of you. Right?"

"Please, please, not so loud," säid Tom Manners, smiling nervously at Alderman Samson Tufton, who had interrupted his conversation with Hedley Nicholson to look at them.

174

"Typical of the bleeding Conservatives that, isn't it?" said Mog, leaning back in the sofa. "Mrs Simpson? You had it in for her right from the start, didn't you? Who sent the troops into the Rhondda? Winston bloody Churchill. Who declared war on Hitler? Neville bloody Chamberlain. Who sent the Black and Tans into Ireland?"

"That was Lloyd George. He was a Liberal."

"Liberal? You're telling me, the randy little git. There was no one in the history of promiscuity more liberal than him in spreading his seed around. Bible-punching little bastard he was. Typical of North Wales. All day Sunday dipping his head in chapel. All the day the rest of the week dipping his wick with his fancy women. Right?"

"I don't see what this has got to do with my brother," said Tom, smiling weakly at the chief constable, who was looking across the room at them.

"Oh, you doesn't, doesn't you?" said Mog. "Well, it don't surprise me. You lot never thinks of no one but Number One. Look at the state of the world today. Famine. Drought. Earthquakes. Typhoons. Don't talk to me about natural bleeding disasters, man. Right? At this very moment in time there are millions starving in India. Well, they hasn't got no grub to eat, has they? And what do you do about it? You comes here, stuffs yourself with so much food you spends half the evening spewing up in the lavatory, the toilet like. Dirty Tory pig you are."

Tom Manners wiped the palms of his hands on his handkerchief, coughed, tapped the bridge of his spectacles and said:

"I think you'd better be going, Mr Williams. Your behaviour is quite disgraceful. Quite disgraceful."

"I knows it is. And I'm doing it on purpose, isn't I?"

"On purpose?"

"That's right, my old son. So's you can see what it's like to be on the receiving end, when someone is behaving disgraceful like what you're doing with Oliver. Right?"

Tom Manners shook his head and began to rise from his chair. Mog took hold of him by the sleeve and dragged him down again.

"What you suggested to me about your brother was the most disgraceful thing I ever heard in my life. Right?" he said. "Talk about conspiring to pervert the course of justice. You'd be lucky to get away with twenty years. Thirty more like, if you was up at Chester Assizes. Right?"

"I don't wish to prolong this discussion any further, Mr Williams."

"But I does, my old son. And if you doesn't stay and hear me out, I'll kick up such a rumpus you won't be able to hear yourself speak no more in this club through the rattling of black balls. Right?"

"I bitterly rue the day I first set eyes on you, Williams," said Tom Manners.

Mog smiled and ordered another double whisky off the waiter. When it came, he took a slow sip, lit a cigarette and said:

"Loony bins? Smashing places they are, my son. You doesn't know Hubert Morgan, does you? Well, there's no reason why you should. He lived next door but one to my old mam in Splott, didn't he? Epileptic he was. Suffered from the old epilepsy, see. Bit screwy, too. Off his rocker like. Harmless enough, mind. Pass the time of day with you. Did his pools regular. Didn't go round exposing hisself. Couldn't be diddled out of small change in the chip shop. Right? Well, one day his mam gets herself a fancy man. A Polak he was. Couldn't stand the sight of old Hubert. Feelings was mutual, mind. Well, more like Hubert couldn't stand the sight of him neither. Right? Well, one day poor old Hubert goes up to his mam's bedroom. He doesn't know what's what, see. The door isn't locked. In he goes, and there she is on the job with this great hairy Polak. So what does they do? They sticks him in the loony bin. Certified he was. All above aboard. No jiggery pokery or line my palm with silver. Right? I'll have another whisky while you're at it, too."

Tom ordered a whisky for Mog, and then he recalled the waiter and ordered one for himself. He kept looking at his watch, but Mog only smiled.

"Well, one day I've had a bit of a skinful, see. There wasn't nothing on at the pictures. The central heating's broken down again in the public library. Racing's abandoned at Plumpton owing to frost. So I thinks to myself, I knows what I'll do. I'll go and see old Hubert, see how he's getting on and have a bit of a laugh at the loonies at the same time. So I goes up to the loony bin, doesn't I? Well, they doesn't want to let me in. 'I'm a relation of his,' I says. 'Well, more like his uncle if the truth

176

be known.' They didn't believe me—suspicious bastards. So I goes round the back and tells this here janitor I've just come down from Harley Street to do a bit of the old brain surgery. Well, he wasn't for believing me—suspicious bastard. So I goes round the corner and nips in through the coke hole when no one's looking. Right?

"Cor blimey Charlie, I never seen nothing like it. Old Hubert? Lying on his back, he was. No bed clothes. No pyjamas. Black eye. Bruises all over his schonk. Legs covered in sores and you could see all his ribs sticking out. He looked more like a bleeding xylophone than a nut case. 'How are you, Hubert?' I says. 'Treating you all right, are they?' I says. Well, he takes one look at me and he starts to scream. I never heard screaming like it, and I seen the All Blacks play on the Arms Park often enough, I tell you. Raised the roof, he did. Well, I has to scapa quick, doesn't I? Course I does. Hears these footsteps, so nips into this here cupboard. Two nurses there was. Big bastards. One of them was the spitting image of Luis Firpa, the Wild Bull of the Pampas. Might have been him for all I know. So they comes into the ward, see. Grabs hold of old Hubert by the shoulders and starts to give him a working over. Icky Evans? Wasn't in it compared with them, man. They bangs his head on the floor, puts the boot in, bends his arms behind his back and takes him into the bathroom. I hears the water running in the bath, see, and old Hubert starts screaming again. Next thing I hears a splash and old Hubert's gurgling away like a drowning rat.

"Three days later old Hubert's dead. Snuffed it. Deceased more like. They has an inquest, of course. Double pneumonia they said it was. Natural causes. A week later Hubert's mam's walking round in a fur coat, and her fancy man's got a new fountain pen. They'd copped it on the insurance, see."

He drank his whisky, stood up and smiled broadly at Tom Manners.

"Smashing places, loony bins. I'm sure old Oliver would be very happy in one. Do him the world of good. Right? Like?" he said, and then just before he turned to go, he said: "I'll keep your proposition in mind, old flower. A couple of weeks or so and I'll give you my answer. Right?"

It was half past nine, when he called in at the Whippet. Ambrose was standing at the bar of the snug, talking to Mr Brandon. He excused himself when he saw Mog and went into

177

the saloon, where Mog told him everything that had been said that evening.

"What are you going to do then?" said Ambrose.

"I doesn't know yet," said Mog. "It's a tricky situation. I've got to make sure, ensure like, that I plays my cards right, hasn't I?"

"You'd never let them stick Oliver into a loony bin, would you?"

"Course not. What do you take me for? The bloody Gestapo, is it?" said Mog. "Besides you can't trust that bloody family not to welsh on you."

"How do you mean?"

"Well, I comes to an arrangement, a deal like, with old Philip Manners to cure Oliver and then collect my loot, and then, bugger me, the daft old bastard goes and dies on me."

"It wasn't his fault. He didn't do it on purpose."

"Don't you be so sure, my old short bread. There's people worked craftier flankers on old Mog than that, don't you kid yourself. Same thing would happen if I come to a deal with Tom Manners, wouldn't it? Course it bloody would."

Ambrose shook his head slowly and ordered two more pints of black and tan.

"He'd go and die on me sure as eggs are eggs if I come to an arrangement with him," said Mog. "Well, there's been some nasty fatalities in the House of Commons, hasn't there? Old Guy Fawkes nearly done for the lot of them, and there's a lot worse than him at the universities in Wales, I tell you."

"So you're going to try and cure Oliver, are you?"

"Try? What are you talking about? I could cure him tomorrow, if I wanted to. Course I bloody could," said Mog, nodding to Uncle Mort, who had just come in with Teddy Ward.

"Why don't you then?"

"I got my business commitments to consider, hasn't I?"

"You don't call making hares for greyhound tracks a business, do you? Bloody hell, you've only to cure Oliver, and he'd most likely let you run the whole of his business for him."

"True, true," said Mog. "But that's not what I calls a business. All they does is buy and sell property. Well, cor blimey Charlie, I'm doing a bloody essential service for humanity, aren't I? If it wasn't for me, they'd have to use live

178

hares at the greyhound tracks, wouldn't they? Well, that
wouldn't go down too well with the old hare community,
would it? They'd be up in arms about it. So would the bloody
flowers. It's because of me making artificial lily of the valley
that the real McCoy doesn't get picked and can live out their
lives in happiness and contentment surrounded by bloody big
dollops of horse shit. Right?"

"I sometimes think you're going off your bloody head,"
said Ambrose, and he nodded at Teddy Ward, who had just
returned from fulfilling an umpiring engagement.

Mog smiled at him and tapped the side of his head.

"The old noddle. The old napper. That's what I'm using, my
old son," he said. "I builds up my business, see. I becomes my
own boss, see. Gets Oliver so interested in it that when I cures
him, he sinks all his own capital in it. Right?"

"Mad. Bloody mad," said Ambrose.

"That's what they said about Galileo and look what
happened to him," said Mog. "I'm playing things my own way.
There's no hurry to cure Oliver, my old son. When I thinks the
time is right, that's when I'll bring the old trick cyclist caper
into action. Right?"

"It'll be too late by then," said Ambrose.

"That's just where you're wrong, smarty pants," said Mog.
"I'm going to see Mrs Mortensen tomorrow to make further
arrangements, aren't I? Course I bloody am."

13

Next morning Mog took the bus to Mannersville.

He walked slowly down the long driveway and rested for a
moment on the timber bridge, mopping his brow on his
handkerchief and watching the fish nuzzling the bank in a
deep, cool, stone-lined pool.

The cattle were lying in the shade under the trees. Bees were
buzzing above the tansy, the yellow pea and the spear thistle
in the grass verges. The sun beat down.

He went into the office and said to Nurse Mooseman, who was paring his fingernails with a paper knife:

"Is the gaffer in?"

"Bloody hell, look what the wind's blown in—Land of My Fathers and the horn of plenty himself," said Nurse Mooseman.

"You're just racially prejudiced," said Mog.

"Not me, sweetheart," said Nurse Mooseman. "I love it any shape or colour."

"Don't come that with me, you little puff," said Mog. "I knows all about your lot. I been in the Merchant Navy. Right? Drop your wallet in Cardiff, and you has to kick it all the way to Swansea before you dares pick it up. Right?"

"Now look what's talking about racial prejudice," said Nurse Mooseman, and he went into the surgery.

A few minutes later Mog was summoned into Mrs Mortensen's presence. She wore a navy blue shirt and white canvas slacks.

"What can I do for you, Mr Williams?" she said.

"It's what I can do for you what's the point at issue, Mrs Mortensen," said Mog, and he helped himself to one of her cigarettes.

"Tell me then," said Mrs Mortensen, easing the strap of her brassiere.

"Gets a bit sticky in the hot weather, the old danglers, don't they?" said Mog. "Right then, it's about these lunatics what are staying with my sister. Well, it's more like about the startling transformation what has transformed their general well-being since they moved from this place."

"They certainly have improved a lot, Mr Williams," said Mrs Mortensen. "Tell me more."

"Don't you bother yourself, my lovely, I will," said Mog. "Now the expert examining them, giving them a thorough shufti like, would say to his fellow head shrinkers: 'Smashing. Corking. They're coming along like a house on fire. Why not let them stay at Mr Williams's sister's place full time. Why not let the other loonies join them.' Right, Mrs Mortensen? Has I hit the nail on the head like?"

Mrs Mortensen nodded slowly and said:

"Continue."

"Right. Now I'm prepared to make a great sacrifice on their behalf, see. I'm prepared out of the goodness of my heart, no

180

thinking of Number One like, to allow them to stay on at my sister's permanent with no coming to Mannersville during the week and with the other two loonies joining them. Right? Like? I doesn't want them personal like. If it was left to me, I'd say: 'Goodness gracious, crikey bobs, what a silly idea.' But I'm thinking of them, Mrs Mortensen, my old flower. It's their interests what are paramount in influencing my mode of thinking at this very moment in time. It's not in my interests to have them round the house, is it? I got my tubes to consider. I got to do right by my bronchials. Right? I can't be running up and down stairs all day giving them breakfast in bed and cutting their toenails for them. I doesn't want to be waiting all day to use the lavatory, the toilet like, and having the smell of octopus through the house from that Chinky bastard, docs I? Course I doesn't. But what I'm doing, see, is thinking of them. If they comes and stops with me permanent, you won't see their backsides for dust when it comes to the question of getting better. Right? Like? So how about it, Mrs Mortensen. You scratch my back, I scratches yours. Well, metaphorically speaking like."

Mrs Mortensen stared at him silently for a while, and then she said:

"My first reaction, Mr Williams, is to say no."

"Well, if that's your attitude I'm off," said Mog, rising to his feet.

"Sit down," said Mrs Mortensen sharply, and Mog sat down. "However, under the circumstances I am inclined to say yes."

"There we are, my old lovely, I knew you'd see reason. I says to Megan this morning I says: 'She might be a sexy tart that Mrs Mortensen but she's not behind the door when it comes to using the old napper,' I says. Right?"

"I have certain plans of my own, you see, which would fit in very nicely with your plans for my patients," she said.

Then she stood up and extended her hand.

"It's a deal," she said. "I shall send Mr Lancaster and Mr Henderson to you later in the week."

Mog shook her hand warmly and left, singing happily to himself as he strode down the driveway.

He called in at the Rocket before he caught the bus to the city and had two pints of beer and a bottle of Jubilee stout.

In the city centre he stopped off at the Griffon for two pints of black and tan and, after taking another bus, had a bottle of lager at the Whippet. It was in there that he met Uncle Mort.

"Don't you do any work then?" said Uncle Mort.

"What's it got to do with you, hairy nose?" said Mog.

"Don't fly off the handle, mate. I were only asking a civil question," said Uncle Mort. "Do you fancy another bottle of that there jungle juice then?"

Mog smiled and nodded.

"Righto," he said. "Shall we be mates then?"

"Aye, we might as well," said Uncle Mort. "Beggars can't be bloody choosers."

They talked for a while about lobsters, zeppelins, cream crackers and communism, and then Mog told Uncle Mort about his home industry enterprises.

"You want to be careful," said Uncle Mort. "If the council finds out you're carrying on a business in your own home, they'll slap your rates up for you."

"But it isn't my own home, see. It's my brother-in-law's, see. That's the whole beauty of it. That's where the old grey matter's come in so useful. Right? Like? Have another pint, my old son, and if you wants to try your hand at sticking on stalks, just give us a shout."

On the way home Uncle Mort said:

"Are they really lunatics them blokes what are staying with you?"

"Lunatics? Maniacs? Nut cases? Whatever gave you that incredible idea?"

"That little Chinese git. He told me he was as mad as a hatter the other night. He says he was completely off his bean pole, but not to mither as he wasn't one of your pervert brigade."

"Don't mind him, boy, he's just a congenital pud-puller. Well, more like he spends all day on the old onanism caper. He'd win the Nobel Prize for it, if they had one, I tell you."

"Bloody hell," said Uncle Mort. "And he's not even in the army neither."

"I keeps telling him he wants to write a book about it. He'd make a fortune out of it. 'Write a book about your complaint, you Oriental twerp,' I says to him. Well, they'd read anything these days. Right?"

"So he's not a loony?"

"Course he isn't. There's none of them loonies. Them's
182

three genuine lodgers. Well, more like bona fide residents if the truth be known."

"Well, so long as they're bona fide, we can rest safe in our beds," said Uncle Mort.

That evening Mog gathered the lunatics in the front parlour and told them what had happened at Mannersville.

"Ripping," shouted Horace A'Fong. "Can I be hares monitor?"

"Don't it get you down sometimes making them all hares?" said Megan to Horace A'Fong after the meeting had broken up.

"Oh no, I think it's absolutely topping, and it's frightfully good for my complexes shoving horse hair stuffing up their little arseholes," said Horace A'Fong.

"And what does he pay you for all this work?" said Ambrose.

"Oh oodles, old bean. Simply oodles. Last week I earned two and six pence. Spent it all on tuck, too. Bought eight tins of Zubes with it. Absolutely scrumptious. Yum hairymacyum yum."

"But why don't you want to be cured, Oliver?" said Miss Miranda, her green eyes flashing.

"Because I'm very happy as I am," said Oliver. "If I was cured now, I'd have to start taking an interest in the business, wouldn't I?"

"Of course you wouldn't, you daft old bath bun," said Miss Miranda. "You could sell it, and then we'd have lots and lots of money and we could go on this tremendous cruise that Elaine Robertson's parents made last year in the South Seas and we could buy a simply enormous house and we wouldn't invite Oonagh Liddell to stay with us, and we'd have this simply enormous Newfoundland dog as a pet. You do like Newfoundlands, don't you, Oliver?"

"I think so," said Oliver.

They had been sitting in a public house in the Dales. It was the same one they had visited during the rain storm earlier in the year.

"Anyway, I think you're cured right now," said Miss Miranda. "I think you've been cured for ages and ages and so does Megan."

"I'm not, I'm afraid," said Oliver.

"Cor blimey Charlie, course you are, you bloody pudding head," said Miss Miranda. "You're as sane as anybody in this room. And, anyway, what makes you think you're not cured?"

"Your mother showed me this book."

"Which book? Was it a sexy book? Was it all about women wearing black lace panties and nothing else and men talking out of the side of their mouths and shooting each other with Micky Flynns?"

"It was a notebook written by my father," said Oliver quietly. "He'd written down what happened on the night my mother died."

"And she showed you it all?"

"Yes."

"And you didn't remember anything that happened?"

"As a matter of fact, I did."

"Oh, Christ," said Miss Miranda.

"It was rather peculiar really. My father had written down in the book how he'd found me standing on the bridge with my mother lying drowned in the stream below. He wrote down how I said I'd pushed her in and then held her head down when she struggled to get out."

"So that's what happened? How super!" said Miss Miranda, and then she added hurriedly: "I mean, how awful."

"But that's not what happened," said Oliver. "As soon as I read the notebook I remembered what really happened."

"What?" said Miss Miranda, and her eyes opened wide and she clutched hold of Oliver's arm tightly.

"We were having an argument about Tom, and my mother slipped and fell in, and I raced down the bank and tried to pull her out and I felt all faint and then I blacked out and then when I came to, I was standing on the bridge and my father was pummelling me on the chest."

"Did you tell the old bitch all this?"

"No."

"But why not? Cor blimey Charlie, why not? Once she knows you've remembered it all, you'll be cured," she shouted. "Oh, Oliver, you're cured, you're cured."

The landlord looked at them and then nodded to the man in leather waistcoat and gaiters, who was standing at the bar.

"At one time it was only sailors what got it," he said. "Now it's the turn of the bloody gentry, you mark my words."

Oliver put his finger to Miss Miranda's lips and whispered.

"I'm not cured, Miranda."

"Why?"

"Because I don't want to be."

Miss Miranda began to punch him on the arm.

"You do, you do," she said. "And if you don't, then I'll tell the old bitch all you said, and she'll jolly well make you be cured."

Oliver caught hold of her wrist and held it tightly.

"If you do, Miranda," he said. "I shan't marry you."

Miss Miranda was still sobbing when she arrived back at the Tierneys' with Oliver.

"Whatever is the matter, love you?" said Megan. "You've not run over a cat on your scooter, has you?"

Miss Miranda shook her head violently.

"I want to see Mog," she said.

"Well, he's out at the pub with Ambrose, my lovely," said Megan, patting her on the shoulder. "Won't I do instead as a substitute like?"

"No," said Miss Miranda, and then she burst into tears and flung herself into Megan's arms.

"There there, my lovely," said Megan. "You tell Megan all about your troubles, and she'll cheer you up, don't you worry your pretty head about that, my darling."

Miss Miranda sniffled and snuffled and buried her face deeper into Megan's bosom.

"I'll tell you a story if you like," said Megan. "Would you like Megan to tell you a story, my lovely?"

Miss Miranda sniffled again and nodded her head.

"Well, once upon a time in days gone by there was a beautiful princess, see. And she had long golden hair and green eyes, and her name was Miranda. Oh, dearie me, I've just remembered—it's the same name as what yours is. Isn't that a coincidence?"

Miss Miranda nodded again, and wiped her nose on the sleeve of Megan's blouse.

"Well, her father, the king, was a terrible old tyrant. He used to go out boozing every night and keeping bad company, and his wife, the queen, says to him she says: 'You wants to think of your resistance, my lovely, your majesty,' she says. 'It won't do your resistance no good at all going boozing in the

rain and sitting in a wet crown all night,' she says. But the
king, he looks at her, and he says: 'Off with her head,' he says
and the public executioner comes up and he chops off her
head with his hatchet, he does. Are you enjoying the story,
Miss Miranda?''

"Yes, thank you," said Miss Miranda softly.

"Well, the princess Miranda was very fond of her mammy,
see. So when she seen what her daddy done to her mammy,
she runs away from the palace into the forests where nothing
stirs but wolves and creepie crawlies. 'Oh dearie, dearie me,'
she says. 'I'm very frightened, she says."

"I'm not surprised," said Miss Miranda, wiping her nose on
Megan's sleeve. "Stick me down in a forest with a load of
wolves, and I'd be shit-scared, I tell you."

"Then you'll not need me to tell you how delighted she
was, happy like, when this handsome young man comes into
the glade and says: 'Hello, all right, is it?' he says. 'Don't you
talk to me like that,' says the princess. 'I'm a princess and
you're only a common old woodcutter,' she says. And do you
know what the woodcutter done then, Miss Miranda?''

"Yes," said Miss Miranda. "He got out his chopper."

"How did you know that?" said Megan.

"Oh, they're always writing about things like that in the
News of the World," said Miss Miranda.

"Oh, I didn't know that. I always thought it was a naughty
paper," said Megan. "Well, anyway this woodcutter takes out
his chopper, and it was the biggest chopper the princess had
ever seen in her life. It was so big he had to hold it in both
hands." "Gosh," said Miss Miranda.

"And then he lifted up and he twirled it round and round
and round above his head. And then do you know what
happened?''

"He probably bloody near strangled himself, did he?" said
Miss Miranda.

"No, nothing like that," said Megan. "He tossed his chopper
over his shoulder, he walked to the edge of the glade and he
lifted his chopper at arms length, and then he began to hack a
way through the trees with it."

"Oh, it was that sort of chopper, was it?" said Miss Miranda,
and at that moment the front door banged and she heard the
voices of Mog and Ambrose in the hall.

She kissed Megan on the cheek.

"Thank you for a super story, Megan," she said. "It has cheered me up. Really. Honestly."

And then she went into the hall and led Mog into the front parlour where she told him everything that Oliver had said to her that evening.

"No problems there, my old sweetheart," said Mog.

"Course there are, you silly bastard," said Miss Miranda.

"Don't you use language like that to me, sweetheart," said Mog. "I might have a rough tongue myself, but I've never been one to allow my parentage to be called into question. Right?"

Miss Miranda stuck out her tongue at him and threw herself onto the fireside rug.

"Oh, it's a sod, isn't it, Mog?" she said.

"Not at all, not at all," said Mog. "I got contingency plans for just such a contingency as this, hasn't I? Course I has."

"What?" said Miss Miranda.

"Simple. Simplicity itself, my old kipper fillet," said Mog. "What we does, see, is to pretend to Oliver that we agrees with him. Right? But all the time we're really curing him. Right? What we're doing is, in other words, we're practising a bit of the old subterfuge on him. One day he'll wake up all bright and cheery like and I'll say to him: 'Olly, my old sponge cake, I'm pleased to announce that you're cured. You're as sane as what me and Miss Miranda is.' And if he doesn't want to be, if he insists on remaining a lunatic, I'll give him such a clout round the ear hole he won't know what bloody hit him. Right? Tact, my lovely. That's our modus vivendi, the way we works. Right?"

"But what about the notebook?" said Miss Miranda.

"Leave that to me," said Mog. "I got contingency plans for that, too, hasn't I? Course I bloody has."

Miss Miranda threw her arms round his neck and kissed him on the ear.

"Honestly, you are super, Mog," she said. "If I didn't love Oliver so much, I'd marry you tomorrow, and we'd be happy ever after, wouldn't we?"

"Not with the state of my tubes, my lovely," said Mog.

When he went up to bed, he paused outside Oliver's bedroom. Then he opened the door quietly and looked inside.

Oliver was lying on his back in bed. He was breathing steadily and quietly, and on his face was a wide and gentle smile.

187

"Good for you, Oliver, my beauty," said Mog softly. "You and me's on the same wavelength for the first time, isn't we?"

And then chuckling to himself he went up to his bedroom and slept soundly.

When Wyndham Lancaster and F.K. Henderson arrived at the Tierneys' to take up residence, they were greeted with great affection by Megan.

"Come in, come in," she said. "I am glad to see you both. Got any more saner, has you, since I been away?"

"I didn't want to come, you know," said F.K. Henderson. "F.K. Henderson wanted to stay in the dormitory at Mannersville. He considered it to be extremely restful since the departure of Horace A'Fong and his ceaseless chatter."

"Beast," said Horace A'Fong.

"Don't you call F.K. Henderson a beast," said F.K. Henderson, and he raised his fists and advanced threateningly towards the minute Oriental onanist.

Unfortunately he caught his toe on his mandolin case, tripped over his bassoon, fell headlong and struck his head a violent blow on the corner of his timpani.

He was unconscious for two days, and when he came to, he said:

"I wonder if you'd be awfully decent and send for my wife. I believe she's living in Cheltenham at the moment."

"Cor blimey Charlie, he's cured now," said Mog. "I'm losing all my bloody labour force, and I got three dozen lily of the valley to complete before morning."

In the afternoon a chauffeur-driven Humber arrived at the Tierneys' and a small thin man in a pin stripe suit got out and said to F.K. Henderson:

"Good afternoon, Sir Kenneth. Lady Henderson is expecting you for dinner."

"Afternoon, Snickett," said F.K. Henderson, and he collected his bags, shook hands warmly with Horace a'Fong and was driven away to Cheltenham.

"There's only one consolation," said Mog. "Well, not exactly a consolation. More like a relief if the truth be known. Right? At least I didn't waste any time training him to lick bleeding envelopes."

"I don't like the way things are going, Tom," said Sir Peter.

"Neither do I," said Tom Manners.

They were sitting on the balcony of the cricket pavillion. There was an evening match, and the home side had scored 169 for 5 declared. The visitors were 27 for 4, and young Renshawe had taken three wickets.

"If this fellow Henderson can be cured so quickly, what is to stop Oliver being cured equally smartly?" said Sir Peter.

"Just so, just so," said Tom.

The thundery weather of the past few days had cleared, and the air was fresh. A flock of pigeons bobbed and cooed on the edge of the boundary. The groundsman's dog lay panting beneath the score box. There was a burst of applause as young Renshawe took another wicket.

"By gum, young Renshawe's on the quickish side tonight," said Alderman Samson Tufton, coming to join them on the balcony.

"Just so. Just so," said Tom.

"He's a real asset to the side is young Renshawe," said Alderman Samson Tufton.

"Aye, but will he go the same road as his brother?" said Hedley Nicholson.

Renshawe finished the match by taking seven wickets for 28 runs. The home side won handsomely, and in the bar afterwards there was much jubilation and hilarity.

Teddy Ward, who had been one of the umpires, came across to Sir Peter Wakefield and said:

"That young quick bowler of yours is well on the way to making the grade, Sir Peter."

"It certainly looks like it, Ward," said Sir Peter.

"Aye," said Teddy Ward. "Aye."

He stood there smiling at Sir Peter and Tom Manners.

"Aye," he said. "Aye."

Sir Peter turned to Tom to continue their conversation.

"Aye," said Teddy Ward. "He's not far short of making the grade."

Sir Peter dipped into his pocket and brought out two half crowns.

"Would you care for a drink, Ward?"

"Oh, oh, ta very much," said Teddy Ward. "I weren't expecting that."

He took the two coins and bolted back to the bar, where he

189

joined the crowd who were pouring pints of bitter down young Renshawe.

"I just don't know what that bloody woman is up to," said Tom.

"She's certainly got us in quite a spot with that blasted notebook of your father's," said Sir Peter, puffing hard at his cigar.

"I wish to hell I knew what she was up to," said Tom.

He did not have long to find out.

On the following afternoon he was in the study at Mannersville discussing the purchase of a plot of land next to the old Moffatt Street tram sheds with Sir Peter Wakefield, when Mrs Mortensen entered and said with a smile:

"I am going to get married."

The two men looked up startled, and Mrs Mortensen smiled again.

"May one ask who the fortunate man is to be?" said Sir Peter.

"I haven't decided yet," said Mrs Mortensen.

Tom coughed, tapped the bridge of his spectacles and said: "Perhaps you've got a short list, have you?"

Sir Peter chuckled.

"Very good, Tom," he said. "Is it a secret, or may we know who is on this short list, Mrs Mortensen?"

"Certainly," she said. "The short list consists of two. One is you, Sir Peter, and the other is you, Tom."

14

Next morning Mog assembled his working force in the front parlour.

"All present and correct, Herr Kommandant," said Group Captain Greenaway, and then he said out of the corner of his mouth to Horace A'Fong: "Keep moving round when the Goons make the count. The longer we can delay them, the longer it will take them to discover Brickhill has made a break for it."

"What are you whispering about, pudding head?" said Mog.

"Some bounder called Brickhill, old bean," said Horace A'Fong.

"Traitor," said Group Captain Greenaway. "I'll have you blasted well cashiered at the end of hostilities."

"Listen to me, wobbly gut, if anyone's doing any cashiering round here it's me. Right?" said Mog. "I'm the one what controls the purse strings. Right? I'm the one what attends to the finances of the business. Right?"

"Never could rely on Johnny Ghurka when the chips were down," said Group Captain Greenaway, glaring sourly at Horace A'Fong.

"Now then, listen this way, you lot," said Mog. "The purpose of this little get together is to put you in the picture, inform you like, about how things stand now you're not going to Mannersville no more. Right? Now then, there's to be no more visits to the surgery, no more snoozing on the old couch while Mrs Mortensen dangles her dingle dangles provocatively in front of your beady little eyes. Right? All that caper's stopped, see. From now on, in future like, I'm the one what's going to be in charge of your mental health. Well, to put it another way, I'm the one what's going to see you don't get any more crackers than what you are already. Right?"

"Absolutely, old sport," said Horace A'Fong. "School, three cheers for Mr Mog Williams. Hip, hip, hip . . ."

"Shut up, you little Asiatic pillock, or there'll be a strange face in heaven by the time I've finished with you. Right?" shouted Mog.

"Beast," said Horace A'Fong.

"Now then," said Mog. "There's no time like the present, so I'm going to start the treatment here and now by giving you all a bash at the old group therapy. Now those of you what reads *The Lancet* and *Titbits* will know what this is all about. For those of you ignorant bastards what doesn't read those two eminent journals I'll explain. What we does, see, is we all sits around and we starts to tear strips off each other. Right? If old Chu Chin Chow there have got a gripe against one of you lot, he stands up and says so. For example, he might say: 'Group Captain Greenaway's a right dirty sod cos he won't wipe the bath down when he's finished using it.' "

"I most certainly do," said Group Captain Greenaway.

"I didn't say you didn't, did I, you balmy sponge head. What I was doing was giving an example of the sort of gripe what might be held against you. Hypothetical, that's what it was. Right? Like?"

"As a matter of fact, he doesn't wipe the bath down after him," said Wyndham Lancaster.

"Oh, I say, Lancaster, don't be such a stinker," said Horace A'Fong. "I can't stand a chap who blabs to the beaks."

"Whether he do, or whether he don't is beside the point," said Mog. "What I'm trying to get over is that you've all got to make complaints against each other. That's the whole point of group therapy, isn't it? Course it bloody is."

"Well, I'm making a complaint," said Wyndham Lancaster. "I'm complaining that Group Captain Greenaway doesn't wipe the bath down after using it."

"Hello, hello, hello, we've got a right clever dick by here, hasn't we? We've got a right barrack lawyer in our midst. Right?" said Mog. "Listen to me, Lord bloody Birkenhead, who's running this session, you or me?"

"You," said Wyndham Lancaster. "Sort of."

"So help me, I'll pull the hairs out of his nose with a bulldog clip, if he don't shut up," said Mog, and then he smiled and said: "Now come on, boys, let's be serious. Right? Let's get them gripes rolling, shall we?"

"Group Captain Greenaway doesn't wipe the bath down after using it," said Wyndham Lancaster.

"That's not a bleeding complaint," screamed Mog at the top of his voice. "That's a hypothetical complaint. You're going to cock the whole thing up, if you doesn't make genuine complaints."

"I've got a genuine complaint," said Oliver Manners quietly.

"Good for you, my old buttie. At least someone's paying attention," said Mog, wiping the perspiration off his brow. "What is it?"

"Group Captain Greenaway doesn't wipe the bath down after using it," said Oliver Manners.

Mog jumped up and down with rage. He beat his head with a rolled-up newspaper. His eyes began to pop out of his head, and the veins swelled on his neck. Horace A'Fong brought him a glass of water, which he drank in a gulp. Then after a few minutes his rage subsided and he said:

192

"What size boots does I take? Size nines. Right? Has I got reinforced toecaps on them? I has. Right? What does I want reinforced toecaps on my boots for? I'll tell you. To plant up the backside of the next bastard what mentions Group Captain Greenaway and his ablutions activities in the bath. Right? Like?"

He walked round and round the room sniffing hard, and then he sat down and said quietly:

"Right then, lads, let's have your complaints."

No one spoke. No one moved. The clock ticked.

"Come on, men. Let's have a spot of the old griping, eh?"

Still the clock ticked. Still no one moved. Still no one spoke.

"I mean, everyone's got gripes, hasn't they? You wouldn't be human if you didn't have the odd gripe tucked up your sleeve, would you?"

Oliver Manners slowly scratched his left ankle, and Horace A'Fong yawned.

"You take Fat Bas for example. Nice bloke. Good sort. Right? Never laid a finger on his old mam except in anger. Pays his maintenance regular. Right? But I got a gripe against him, hasn't I? Course I has. Sends me to Barnstaple to see this lorry driver. Right? Name of Hodgkinson the driver is called. I'm to meet him in a local hostelry. Got to collect a parcel off him, see. Fit into an attache case, it will, says Fat Bas. And what happens? The lorry driver comes in with a trunkful of tinned pineapples. So what does I do? I scapas quick. Gets back to Cardiff, goes to see Fat Bas, and what happens? Duffed up by Icky Evans. That's the substance of my gripe against Fat Bas—he's the biggest shithouse walking the face of this earth. Right?"

No one spoke. No one moved. The clock ticked.

Then Horace A'Fong coughed and said:

"Well, actually, old bean, I've got a hairymacgrouse."

"Good for you, my old Oriental beauty. What is it?" said Mog.

"I think you're an old meanie."

"What?"

"I think you should pay us more hairymacpocket money."

"So do I," said Wyndham Lancaster.

"What do you know about it? You only just got here," said Mog.

193

"We should share out the profits," said Wyndham Lancaster.

"And we should put in a strong complaint to the Kommandant about the standard of your language," said Group Captain Greenaway.

"My language? What's wrong with my language?"

"It's absolutely foul," said Group Captain Greenaway.

"And look at the way you dress," said Wyndham Lancaster.

"What's wrong with the way I dresses?" said Mog.

"Well, for a start it isn't done to wear a muffler in summer," said Wyndham Lancaster.

"Listen to me, clever dick. I has to wear that on medical grounds, doesn't I? Course I does. One of the most eminent specialists in the country gave me that tip."

"And you're a liar to boot," said Group Captain Greenaway.

"Me? A liar?" said Mog. "I'll have Icky Evans down here with the old dusters on you, if you doesn't shut up."

"And you're a rotten old bully, too," said Horace A'Fong.

"Me? A bully?" said Mog. "I'm as gentle as a lamb, I am. It's Icky Evans you wants to complain about, boy, not me."

"And you don't wipe the bath down after using it," said Oliver Manners.

"Here here," said Wyndham Lancaster.

"Exactly," said Group Captain Greenaway.

"Spot on," said Horace A'Fong.

"All right, all right, all right, I sees the score. I sees what you're getting at," said Mog. "You're just using this as an excuse to work off all your complexes against me. Right?"

"You said we could make any complaints we liked," said Wyndham Lancaster.

"Not against me, I didn't. Cor blimey Charlie, I never been spoken to like that since that ginger-haired screw at Durham caught me with a pair of cycle clips and a blancmange mould."

"We're not interested in that," said Wyndham Lancaster.

"Exactly," said Group Captain Greenaway.

"We think this therapy caper is all a beastly old swiz," said Horace A'Fong.

"And I thinks it's high time you was all getting back to work, you skiving gang of closets," said Mog. "Stone the crows, I wastes valuable man-hours trying to give you a helping

194

hand on the road to recovery, and what does you do? Turns round and bites the hand what feeds you. Makes up, concocts like, a fabrication of trumped-up charges against me what no court of law in the land would uphold in a hundred years. A thousand more like. Where's your evidence? Where's your witnesses? You can't conduct a case on hearsay. They'd laugh you out of court. Right? The old clerk would stand up and he'd say: 'Piss off, or I'll have you up for contempt.' Right? Course he would. I knows how to look after Number One, don't you worry. There's nothing you can tell me about jurisprudence. Right?"

"You should clean your teeth more often, too," said Wyndham Lancaster.

"Get out," screamed Mog. "Get out and start licking them envelopes."

In the evening Megan picked up the paper and began to run her finger slowly down the Births, Marriages and Deaths column.

Suddenly she let out a cry of surprise.

"What's up?" said Ambrose.

"Oh, dearie dearie me," she said. "Look what's wrote here in the engagements column."

Ambrose took the paper from her, read it and then clicked his tongue rapidly.

"What's all this about?" said Mog. "They hasn't voted to bring back the cat, has they?"

Ambrose pushed the paper across the table to him. He read it and then whistled long and loud through his teeth.

"I think it's an absolute howl," said Miss Miranda to Oliver later in the evening.

"I'm not sure what I think," said Oliver, putting the paper down on the table of the pub.

"I shall insist on being bridesmaid," said Miss Miranda. "And you'll simply have to be best man."

"I suppose so."

"I wonder who'll give her away? Mog! That's it. Mog can give her away."

"You can just imagine his speech, can't you?" said Oliver.

Miss Miranda roared with laughter and hugged Oliver delightedly.

"It's a funny situation, though, isn't it? My mother
195

marrying your brother—I wonder what relationship you and I will be then?"

"God knows," said Oliver.

"Can you imagine Tom on his honeymoon night with the old bitch?" said Miss Miranda.

"Frankly—no," said Oliver.

"We were always talking about what it would be like on your honeymoon night at school. Oonagh Liddell said it's far more exciting than getting your colours for hockey. She said her sister bought this transparent negligee from Harrod's and it was still in its original wrapper when she came back from her honeymoon. Of course, Antoinette Lilley had to go one better. She said that was nothing. She said when she goes on her honeymoon she's not even going to take pyjamas with her. Some hopes she's got of having a honeymoon anyway. Honestly, could you imagine marrying Antoinette Lilley, Oliver?"

"I don't even know her."

"Well, I'll invite her to our wedding, and we can all have a jolly good laugh at her. I bet you anything she'll become an old spinster like Miss Naughton-Bailey from the pony club, and, oh crikey, all this talk about honeymoons is making me feel fantastically randy. I wish you could have periods of truce when you make a vow of chastity."

Back at Mannersville Tom Manners paced up and down the drawing room.

"Why me? Why me?" he said.

Sir Peter Wakefield, sitting back in an armchair, chuckled.

"I'm sure it's a most suitable match, Tom," he said. "A mature and beautiful woman like Mrs Mortensen is the ideal consort for a young MP about to make his way in the world. Much more suitable than Estelle, you know."

"Estelle! Oh my God, what the hell will she say?" said Tom.

"Oh, there are plenty more fish in the sea for Estelle," said Sir Peter. "A good few sharks, too, if the truth be known."

"There's nothing for it," said Tom, gulping down his fifth whisky of the evening. "We'll just have to think of a way of getting rid of Mrs Mortensen."

"But why, Tom? She's turning into the most powerful ally we've got. Once we've locked her firmly into the bosom of the family, we're absolutely safe."

196

"It's not your bosom she's going to be locked into," said Tom.

Mrs Mortensen walked into the room and said to Tom:

"Darling, don't you think we should be giving some thought to the list of wedding guests?"

"I'm going out for a drink," said Tom. "A lot of drinks, I might add."

When he and Sir Peter Wakefield walked into the bar of the Constitutional Club, the conversation stopped immediately.

The people in the room glanced at them with hostility, and then turned to look at Hedley Nicholson, who was slowly walking across the room.

"You bastard," he said to Tom Manners. "You big, lousy bastard."

"Now now, Hedley," said Alderman Samson Tufton. "Calm yourself down, lad. Language like that won't get you nowhere. Do you follow my meaning?"

Hedley Nicholson pushed Alderman Samson Tufton to one side and took hold of Tom Manners by the lapels of his jacket.

"I'll have you for every penny you've got," he said.

"Please, Hedley, behave yourself," said Sir Peter.

"You keep out of this, you big lousy bastard," said Alderman Samson Tufton.

"Marrying your father's mistress? That'll look bloody marvellous when the constituency party gets hold of it, won't it?" said Hedley Nicholson, pushing Tom Manners backwards towards the bar.

"I'll ruin your career for you, you big bastard," he said. "Your name will be mud by the time I've finished with you, you big bastard."

"Now, now, Hedley, less of that language," said Alderman Samson Tufton.

"Exactly," said Sir Peter.

"Shut your hole, you big bastard," roared Alderman Samson Tufton.

"Breach of promise? I'll have you for every penny you've got," shouted Hedley Nicholson, and the crowd round the bar scattered as he jammed Tom Manners against it. "After what you've done to Estelle, I'll have you drummed out of Westminster, drummed out of this club, drummed out of business, drummed out of the bloody city."

"Oh, my God," said Tom Manners, and he collapsed in a dead faint.

Three days later Oliver Manners came down to breakfast, smiled at his fellow lodgers and said:

"Lovely day again, isn't it?"

Breakfast was eaten in silence, although from time to time Group Captain Greenaway glanced across at Wyndham Lancaster, and Horace A'Fong giggled nervously.

As soon as Ambrose had left for Mannersville and Megan had returned to the kitchen to do the washing up Wyndham Lancaster said to Mog:

"I think you had better listen carefully to what we have to say."

"Righto, my old bath bun," said Mog. "Pour us another cup of tea, will you?"

"We do not intend to work today," said Wyndham Lancaster.

"You what?"

"We do not intend to work again until our demands have been met in full," said Wyndham Lancaster.

"You what? You what?"

"You heard."

"You what? You what? You what?"

"It's a strike," said Wyndham Lancaster.

"You bleeding what?" said Mog, and Horace A'Fong giggled again.

"You are no doubt aware, Herr Hauptmann, that by forcing officers to engage themselves in manual labour, you are in direct contravention of the terms of the Geneva Convention," said Group Captain Greenaway.

"Officers? Convention? Will someone tell me what he's talking about?" said Mog.

"Shan't," said Horace A'Fong.

"And I would remind you, too, of certain other factors, which are highly pertinent to the issue under consideration," said Wyndham Lancaster.

"Here we go," said Mog. "I knew you'd have to stick your great hairy schonk in where it wasn't wanted."

"Our rates of pay are scandalously low, our rest periods are grossly inadequate, our working hours are disgracefully excessive and the machinery for full consultation between

198

management and labour is non-existent," said Wyndham Lancaster.

"In other words, we think you're an absolute stinker," said Horace A'Fong.

Mog went white in the face. Then he turned scarlet. His mouth opened, but no words came out. He shut it, and turned white once more. He stood up, and then he sat down. He stood up again and without speaking left the room and went into the kitchen, where Megan was scrubbing the table top.

"Whatever is wrong with you, Mog?" said Megan. "You're not sickening for nothing, are you, boy? Does you want a laxative, cos if you does, we're right out at the moment."

Mog raised his hand weakly and shook his head.

"You're not crying, are you, Mog?" said Megan, wiping her hands on her pinnie. "You're not upset about nothing, are you, kid? Has you suffered a bereavement? You has. I can see it in your eyes. Someone near and dear to you have passed on recent, hasn't they? Does you want to send an in memoriam or suitable verse tribute to the paper? I got a lovely selection in my album, if you does. Shall I go and fetch it, and we can look through it together and pick out something real suitable for the occasion?"

Mog shook his head. Then suddenly he burst into tears and buried his head in Megan's bosom.

"Shall I tell you a story?" said Megan. "Would you like Megan to tell you a nice story about Prince Mog and the way he killed the lion with his chopper?"

Mog nodded and wiped his nose on the sleeve of her jumper.

Half an hour later he strode into the vaults bar of the Whippet and shouted across to Uncle Mort:

"Hello, boyo, smashing day, isn't it? Have a pint on me, my old fruit cake."

"What are you looking so cheerful about?" said Uncle Mort.

"Cheerful? Me?" said Mog. "I'm bloody distraught if the truth be known. Well, more like brassed off. Chokker. Right? Like?"

"Well, give us me pint before you start diluting it with your bloody tears," said Uncle Mort.

Mog bought two pints, and they leaned their elbows on the bar counter, staring silently at the blue bottle buzzing round the open top of the bottle of lime cordial.

"The trouble with me is I'm a tonic," said Mog.

"Oh aye?" said Uncle Mort.

"All my life it's been the same. Right? Someone's upset, down in the dumps like, and what does they do? Send for Mog. He'll crack a joke, he'll dispel the tears and the gloom with his own inimitable brand of high spirits. Right? Like? It was the same before El Alemain. Monty, Field Marshall Sir Bernard Montgomery like, comes round and you should have seen the kisser on him. Talk about gloomy. More like suicidal if the truth be known. So what does I do? Goes up to him and says: 'Hello, kid, been on the batter, has you? Got a hang-over, is it?' 'No,' he says. 'I'm a bit worried about the impending conflict of arms between us and Gerry,' he says. 'Don't you worry about Rommel, the Desert Fox like,' I says. 'Me and Icky Evans'll sort him out for you. We knows how to handle ourselves at stop tap,' I says. Well, he takes one look at me, and his eyes lit up. Like Blackpool Illuminations they was. 'Take the name of that man, Claude,' he says to Field Marshal Auchinleck, known affectionately to his butties as The Auk. 'What for, Monty?' says The Auk. 'Mind your own bleeding business, pudding head,' says Monty. 'That man's been a right tonic to me, he have,' he says. Right? See what I mean?"

"I've got a brother-in-law what's just like you," said Uncle Mort.

"Has you?" said Mog. "Is he a tonic, too?"

"No," said Uncle Mort. "He's a right bloody liar."

An hour later Mog was sitting on the banks of the canal. Opposite him was a timber wharf, where men were loading planks onto a narrow boat.

"There were no need to run off like that," said Uncle Mort, sitting on the tow path beside him. He was breathing heavily, and there were beads of perspiration on his forehead. "I bloody near ruptured meself trying to keep up with you. What's to do with you any road?"

Mog sighed deeply and threw a handful of gravel into the canal. It made oily ripples in the water.

"I don't wipe the bath down after using it," he said.

"Neither do I," said Uncle Mort. "There's nowt wrong with that. You never wash a frying pan after making an omelette, do you?"

"And I don't clean my teeth often enough."

"Have them all yanked out and get yourself a set of dentures," said Uncle Mort. "Teeth? They're more bloody trouble than they're worth."

"Then there's the question of the way I dresses. I doesn't dress proper, see. It isn't done to wear a muffler in the summer."

"You don't want to take no notice of these here fashion pundits," said Uncle Mort. "I bloody don't. That's why I never wore spats."

"But what about my language? You hasn't taken that into consideration, has you?"

"I shouldn't mither about that. I mean, every country's entitled to have it's own language, isn't it? The Froggies speak Froggie. The Wops speak Wop, and the Coons speak Coon. Well, it's got nowt to do with me if the Taffies want to yatter away in Taffy, is it?"

"I'm not talking about that, you daft pillock. I'm talking about my language. The way I'm always swearing. Right?"

"I've not noticed it," said Uncle Mort. "You don't swear no more than what I bloody do."

"I swear a bloody sight less than what you does," said Mog. "Cor blimey Charlie, you swears like a bloody trooper you does. It's bloody disgusting."

"I'll punch your bloody head in, if you talk to me like that," said Uncle Mort.

Mog smiled and patted him on the shoulder.

"Sorry," he said. "I swears just as much as what you does. Right?"

"Perhaps you can't express yourself proper."

"Me? Not express myself proper? Listen to me, boyo, I can express myself more proper than what you can any day of the week. I'd bloody lose you at expressing myself proper. Right? Nine out of ten—that's what I used to get for compositions at school. Right? 'My favourite Uncle,' 'What I wants to be when I grows up'. Right? Shit hot at it, I was. Don't you worry your head about that, my old son."

"All right, all right, keep your bloody wool on," said Uncle Mort.

Mog did not mention the strike over tea, and he completely ignored Group Captain Greenaway, when the ex-aviator told Megan that in many respects he was quite looking forward to a spell in the cooler.

"Have you decided anything?" said Wyndham Lancaster, when the tea things had been cleared from the table.

"What about?" said Mog, and he went out for a pint with Ambrose.

They walked side by side through the dusk. There was a crab apple tree laden with fruit at the corner of the street, and at the tram terminus there was the smell of stale electricity.

"I've a good mind to jack it all up and go back to Cardiff," said Mog, when he had bought the beer. "Well, my business interests there is bound to be suffering during my absence, while I'm away like. You got to be there yourself to see things is done proper. You put a manager in, and what happens? The bastard starts diddling you right left and centre. I worked behind a bar in Llandudno, kid. I knows what goes on. Right? What it is, see, is I knows for a fact Fas Bas have got something lined up in Usk. Well, he'll be crying out for my assistance, my help like, won't he? Look what happened with that load of South African prunes he nicked from Barry Dock. He tries to handle it on his own, and it's only through the grace of God that the flat-foot what nabs him is engaged to Nelly Barsotti's cousin. Lucky bastard he is. I've a good mind to get the train tomorrow and see he's not coming to no harm. I doesn't like to think of my butties getting into trouble. Right?"

"No one's stopping you," said Ambrose.

"I'm too bloody kind-hearted, that's my trouble. I wouldn't walk out now and leave my loonies in the lurch, if you was to pay me a couple of grand. Right?"

"It's you what's been left in the lurch now, mate," said Ambrose. "You're the one what's got to cope with the strike."

"Easy. Simple. A cake walk," said Mog.

"Oh aye?" said Ambrose. "Know how to end it, do you?"

"Course I does."

"How?"

"Pardon?"

Mog bought two more pints. He stared glumly at the calendar on the wall. It had a picture of a naked woman, grappling with a python.

"I knows what I'll do," said Mog, his face breaking into a smile. "I'll butter them up. Bribe them. Right?"

"How?" said Ambrose.

"I'll give them a treat, my old son," said Mog. "I'll take them on a day's outing. Right?"

202

15

At half past eleven in the morning a thirty two seat charabanc drew up outside the Tierneys' house. The driver said to Megan:

"Does Maurice Mansell Williams live here, me ducks?"

"You're not from HM prisons, are you?" said Megan.

"No, ducks," said the driver. "I've come to take him to the zoo."

At that moment Mog came bounding down the stairs, pushed Megan to one side and said to the driver:

"Won't keep you a minute, my old son. I'll just get my party together. Right?"

He went into the front room, where the four lunatics were reading the morning newspaper.

"Right," he said. "I got a treat for you. I'm taking you to the zoo. Right?"

"I say, how ripping," said Horace A'Fong.

Wyndham Lancaster looked up from his newspaper and said:

"I don't want to go."

"Neither do I," said Group Captain Greenaway.

"I do," said Oliver Manners. "I'd love to go to the zoo."

"Course you would, my old sport," said Mog. "It's smashing at the zoo. They got all these wild animals there. Well, not wild in the accepted meaning of the word. More like they're all behind bars so they won't bite you. Right?"

"Can we go and see Jumbo the elephant?" said Horace A'Fong.

"You can go and see Herbert the bloody hippopotamus for all I cares, my old son," said Mog.

"Oh, top hole," said Horace A'Fong.

"I don't want to go," said Wyndham Lancaster.

"Neither do I," said Group Captain Greenaway.

"Listen by here to me," said Mog, sitting on the sofa next to Wyndham Lancaster. "I knows you doesn't like me. Right. I knows you hates my guts. Right? All right then. Let's forget all about it for today. Let bygones be bygones. Right? I've worked you too hard. I've not given you enough pocket money. I admits it. Right? Well, out of the goodness of my heart and entirely at my own expense, out of my own pocket like, I'm taking you out on a day's treat. Right?"

"I think it's very generous of you," said Oliver Manners. "Don't be such an old misery guts, Lancaster."

"There must be an ulterior motive somewhere," said Wyndham Lancaster.

"Ulterior motive?" said Mog. "I never had a motive in my life never mind an ulterior one. Cor blimey Charlie, I doesn't know the meaning of the word ulterior."

Wyndham Lancaster and Group Captain Greenaway whispered to each other for a few moments, and then they stood up.

"All right, we'll go," said Wyndham Lancaster. "But I refuse to feed sausages to the llamas."

Just as the party was getting into the coach Miss Miranda drove up on her scooter.

"Does you want to go to the zoo with us?" said Mog.

"May I?" said Miss Miranda.

"If you wants to, course you can, my sweetheart," said Mog.

"Super," said Miss Miranda, and she climbed into the coach and sat next to Oliver.

The driver shut the door and started the engine. Before he had time to release the brake, however, Mog jumped and shouted through the open window at Uncle Mort, who was standing at the front gate:

"Do you want to go to the zoo, boy? We're going to the zoo, aren't we? Course we are. Hop in, my old son, and have a good day out all expenses paid at my expense. Right?"

"Hold on. I'll just fetch me cap," said Uncle Mort.

This he did, and when he had established himself in the coach, the driver released the handbrake, and they set off for the zoo.

After they had been travelling for an hour Mog made his way to the front of the coach and said:

"Is everybody happy?"

204

"Yes," shouted Miss Miranda.

"Rather," said Horace A'Fong.

"Smashing," said Mog. "And so you ought to be. I paid twenty quid for this coach not to mention the entrance fees when we gets to the zoo and provision of afternoon tea and a few bottles of ale on the way back. Right?"

"Oh, we're going to do some supping, are we?" said Uncle Mort.

"However," said Mog, ignoring the interruptions. "It's not all enjoyment. Right? There's a serious purpose to this trip which I shall now endeavour to explain by putting you in the picture, making you au fait like."

"Do you mind lowering your voice," said the driver. "I only had me ears syringed last Thursday."

Mog glared at him and continued:

"Now I am addressing my remarks to the lunatics amongst us. Them what is present and in their right state of mind has no need to take no notice of what I am about to say. Right?"

"That lets you out, Oliver," said Miss Miranda.

"No, it doesn't," said Oliver.

"Now I've been doing some detailed research into the subject of lunacy," said Mog. "I've been giving Pears Encyclopedia the once over, see, and I thinks I can say with all sincerity that I've got to the bottom of it. When you're a lunatic, see, you're not like the rest of us in the accepted sense of the word. Right?"

"Here here," said Horace A'Fong.

"To put it in medical terms, you're all bloody crackers. You've got everything arseways round, see. Now there's some people what would want to stick you behind bars, treat you like outcasts, not have nothing to do with you, wash their hands of you. Right?"

"That's what I'd do," said the driver. "Be rights I shouldn't be on the road with a party of lunatics, you know. This vehicle isn't insured for lunatics, you know."

"Shut your rattle," said Mog. "Listen to what I'm going to say, and you might learn something. Right?"

"Aye, give him a hearing," said Uncle Mort, and then he whispered to Oliver Manners. "He's a bloody sight worse than what you lot are. He's going right off his beanpole, I tell you."

"What I'm going to say is this," said Mog. "I believes

205

personal like, for myself in my own opinion, that you should all be treated as though you was as normal as what I am. Right? That's why I'm taking you to the zoo. That's why I doesn't biff you over the noddles, when you misbehaves yourselves. That's why I don't stick you in cold baths and put the boot in and generally behave like the bloody Gestapo like what they does in these here state asylums. I believes that you've just as much right to be a sex maniac as any normal person. Right?"

"Are they sex maniacs then?" said Uncle Mort.

"I should jolly well say we are, old bean," said Horace A'Fong. "And I'm top of the form."

"I'll kick your teeth in, if you doesn't shut up while I'm talking," said Mog, and then he smiled at the party and said: "So now you sees the reason why I'm taking you to the zoo, don't you?"

"So we can see the chimps tea party," said Horace A'Fong. "Hurrah."

"No, you balmy sponge head. I'm taking you to the zoo as part of your treatment. Right? Like?"

Blank faces greeted this statement. Mog smiled at them, shook his head and said:

"This is what happens, when you're faced with laymen, see. They doesn't cotton on as quick as what them in the trade would do. Now, you pay attention and listen to what I'm telling you. You're going to the zoo so's you can see the animals locked up behind bars. Right?"

"That's what old Hoo Flung Dung just said," said Uncle Mort, and then he whispered to Oliver Manners: "I should get his head looked at, when you get back, if I was you."

"The similarities between the animals and you lot doesn't need me to explain them, does they?" said Mog. "I'll explain what I means. Right? They're locked away because they're different from the rest of us. Right? They're not normal like what human beings is. 'Hello, hello,' says your average homo sapiens, 'there's a giraffe. He's not like what I am. I tell you what I'll do. I'll lock him behind bars.' See what I mean?"

"No," said Wyndham Lancaster.

"Let me put it this way," said Mog. "How many human beings does you know with long necks and covered all over in spots?"

"One," said Horace A'Fong. "F.K. Henderson."

206

"I might as well talk to a brick wall," said Mog. "I'll try another tack, a different way like. What is it that's got a great hairy swede, a tail with a tuft on the end and is known popularly as the King of Beasts?"

"The camel," said Horace A'Fong.

"That's got two bleeding humps on its back, you great Oriental pillock," screamed Mog.

"That's a dromedary," said Uncle Mort.

"I don't care if it's your Aunt Fanny," said Mog. "It's not a lion, is it?"

"I bagged a lion once," said Group Captain Greenaway. "A man-eater. Fearsome chappie. Been terrorising the bearers for weeks."

"I'll terrorise you with my boot end, if you doesn't shut up," said Mog, and then he said quietly and patiently: "All right, we've established that the subject about what I'm talking about is a lion. Right? Now where does you get lions? In zoos. Right? And why are they in zoos? Because they goes round biting human beings and generally making a nuisance of theirselves. But that's no reason to lock them behind bars, is it? Your average man in the street doesn't go round jumping through hoops at a circus and stalking wart hogs, I grant you. Course he don't. And that's all the more reason why he should be tolerant to them what does and not lock them behind bars and keep them away from their butties. Right?"

"I think I see what he's getting at," said Miss Miranda. "He's anti blood sports, the pig."

"Now that's what your average human being, Mr and Mrs Everyman like, wants to do to you lunatics," said Mog. "Because you're different from what he is, he wants to lock you behind bars. See what I mean?"

"Yes," said Oliver Manners.

"Right," said Mog. "So when we gets to the zoo, make sure you behaves yourselves or you'll get me locked up. Right?"

They reached the zoo at two o'clock.

"Hey up, they've got an extension," said Uncle Mort. "We can sup all day."

"I'm not wet behind the ears, boy, don't you worry," said Mog.

The coach party climbed down onto the pavement, stretched themselves and then went into the zoo.

Immediately inside the entrance was a lake in which

flamingoes paddled. There were black swans, too, and mandarin duck and red-breasted geese.

"All right," said Mog. "Have a shuffle round on your own, be back at the coach at six, and we'll compare notes on the way back. And if anyone gets mauled by a tiger, they won't get no sympathy from me, because tigers don't like having their tails pulled. Right?"

Then he and Uncle Mort repaired to the Audubon Bar and bought two pints of black and tan.

"I didn't know you was a medical man," said Uncle Mort.

"Served my time at it, didn't I?" said Mog.

"I thought you was taking the piss, when you told me first of all that your lodgers was lunatics."

"All part of the treatment, wasn't it, my old flower? Course it was."

"What I can't fathom out is why you don't cure them all like what you cured that bloke the other day."

"I could, I could," said Mog. "But what I'm taking into account is their own interests. I got to say to myself, would they be happier being normal like you and me, or would they be happier staying like what they are."

"I'd say they was better off as they are," said Uncle Mort.

"Precisely, my old herring bone," said Mog. "A very good diagnosis. Why doesn't you go in for this psychiatry lark yourself?"

"Ah, you'd have to go to night school, wouldn't you?" said Uncle Mort, ordering two more pints of black and tan.

"Not necessarily," said Mog. "I'll give you tuition. Six bob an hour reduced to half a dollar, if you doesn't pass your test first time."

They drank three more pints of black and tan, and then they went onto whisky. Behind the bar was a mural of a scene from the veldt. The ash trays were made from antlers, and the beermats were shaped like penguins' feet.

"It's more like being in a zoo than a bloody pub," said Uncle Mort.

They drank two more whiskies, and then they went onto bottled lager.

"I got my plans for them, see," said Mog. "I got it all lined up, hasn't I?"

"Course you have," said Uncle Mort. "You're no mug, are you?"

"Course I'm not. I uses the old noddle. That's what's got me where I am today in the position in which I finds myself in now. Right?"

"Right."

"Hobbies. That's what I got lined up for them. We, you and me like, has already diagnosed that it wouldn't be a kindness to them to cure them. Right? So what follows from that is that we might as well give them something to make them forget that they're loonies. Right?"

"What have you got in mind?"

"Boxing."

"Boxing?"

"The noble art of self defence, my old jam sandwich. Have another lager."

"Ta," said Uncle Mort, taking a gherkin from a bowl shaped like an elephant's head.

"I knows a thing or two about boxing, don't you worry," said Mog. "I fought them all, didn't I? Young Chocolate? Best lightweight ever to come out of Tonyrefail, he was. Stopped him in three rounds, didn't I? Course I did. Docker Swetman, Teddy Flood, Nat Wilkes, Kid Slingsby, the bruiser from Bala? Licked the lot of them I did. It's true. It's true. Look it up in the record books. Late nineteen thirties. Right? I was in contention then, don't you kid yourself. If I hadn't been a martyr to hay fever, I'd have had so many Lonsdale Belts I wouldn't have needed to buy a pair of braces for the rest of my natural. Right?"

Uncle Mort snorted into his lager and took another gherkin.

"Marquetry, ju-jitsu and raffia work—I got that lined up for them as well," said Mog.

"Do you fancy a trip to the parrot house?" said Uncle Mort.

It was cold outside. The wind was ruffling the feathers of the flamingoes. A heap of rubble was smouldering near the compound where the wolves prowled up and down. An emu prodded at a piece of silver cigarette paper with its bill, and there were long strings of saliva hanging from the mouths of the camels.

They put their heads round the door of the parrot house, and Uncle Mort said:

"Noisy bloody things parrots, aren't they? I can't understand what people see in parrots, can you?"

"No," said Mog. "They gives you myxamatosis, if you're not careful."

"Dirty pigs," said Uncle Mort. "Do you fancy another jar then?"

They went into the Linnaeus Tavern, where they ordered two pints of black and tan.

"The room always starts to go round and round on me, when I come out of the parrot house," said Uncle Mort.

"It's all that screeching effects your ear drums," said Mog. "It's not generally known, but that's where your sense of balance is—in your bloody lugholes."

"Bloody parrots," said Uncle Mort. "Do you fancy a gander at the reptile house?"

"Might as well," said Mog. "I got nothing against boa constrictors, has I?"

The visit to the reptile house was followed by a visit to the Peter Scott cafeteria, where they had sausage and chips washed down by three bottles of Guinness.

They returned to the coach at half past five, and when the rest of the party arrived, they were curled up on the back seat, snoring loudly.

"Ah, well, home James and don't spare the horses," said Group Captain Greenaway, and the driver started the engine, and they began the journey home.

"Gosh, I'm so sleepy," said Miss Miranda, leaning against Oliver Manners' shoulder.

He took hold of a strand of her hair in his teeth and tugged.

"Ouch," she said and smiled. "What did you like best of all the animals, Oliver?"

"The European bison," said Oliver.

"I liked the gibbons best of all," said Miss Miranda. "Did you see the mother gibbon swinging round like billyo with the baby gibbons clutched in one arm? I'll do that when we have our babies, Oliver. I'll go swinging all over the house from light shade to light shade with our children tucked under my arm, and Miss Naughton-Bailey will come for tea, and she'll think I've gone completely loopy and I'll say: 'You're only jealous, because you're an old spinster and no man would dream of marrying you and giving you babies.'"

"Poor old Miss Naughton-Bailey," said Oliver.

"And what will you do with your smelly old European bison?"

"Train it to carry the evening paper in its mouth."

"Super," said Miss Miranda. "And it can bring you your carpet slippers when you come home from work."

"And beg for bones."

"And chase sticks."

"And bark like mad when anyone comes to the door."

"Moo," said Miss Miranda. "It would have to moo because it's a cow."

"Of course. It would moo its head off, wouldn't it?"

"Silly old Oliver," said Miss Miranda, cuddling into his chest. "And I love you much more than the mother gibbon loves the daddy gibbon, and why won't you go and get cured?"

"Ssh," said Oliver.

Horace A'Fong giggled to himself.

"I bought him a bag of buns, a bag of peanuts and a wacking great ripe red apple, and he wouldn't eat a blinking thing," he said.

"Jumbo the elephant?" said Wyndham Lancaster.

"No, silly. Group Captain Greenaway," said Horace A'Fong.

"Oh, him," said Wyndham Lancaster. "I was much too concerned with the printing machines to bother about him."

"Printing machines? What are they, old horse?"

"They're machines that print your name," said Wyndham Lancaster. "You turn a lever to the letter you want, press a handle and so on and so forth until you've spelled out your name. Then you press a button and out comes a strip with your name printed on it."

"What a topping wheeze."

"They'd the best collection of printing machines I've ever seen in any zoo anywhere in the world," said Wyndham Lancaster. "I printed my own name thirty six times and another name twice."

"What was the other name?"

"Reginald Ostrich," said Wyndham Lancaster.

Group Captain Greenaway had not spoken since the coach left the zoo. He had been sitting on his own deep in thought. Suddenly he stood up and said:

"Well, the men were certainly bearing up well in captivity. Dashed well. A fine show. A great credit to the service. Just shows what can be done, when morale is high and discipline is strict."

211

"Absolutely, old horse," said Horace A'Fong.

"The CO's inspection went off awfully well. Awfully well. The billets were absolutely first class, all the bed boards were in order, and the chaps were in prime condition. 'Don't let the Goons get you down,' I said. 'Dumb insolence—that's the way to treat Gerry.' One chap there, though. Didn't like the look of him. Damned strange habits he'd got. Obviously hadn't shaved for five or six days and seemed to be having trouble with his arm pits. Sat there in a rubber tyre, scratching himself all the time. 'Keep your pecker up, old chap,' I said. Then, dash me, the blighter did something absolutely beastly and threw a grape at me. Poor show. Poor show."

The coach arrived outside the house at eleven o'clock. It took them five minutes to rouse Uncle Mort and Mog.

They stood in a group on the pavement, and Uncle Mort said:

"Well, it weren't a bad day out, even though he is the biggest bloody liar this side of Ashton-in-Makerfield."

"Who's a liar?" said Mog.

"You're a liar," said Uncle Mort.

"Me?"

"You."

"Who? Me?"

"Yes. You."

They advanced towards each other, fists drawn, heads hunched into shoulders.

"Say that again," said Mog.

"You're a bloody liar," said Uncle Mort.

"Me?" said Mog. "You sure you got the right person? You sure you doesn't mean someone else?"

"Young Chocolate! In contention! I don't need to look up no record books, mate,"

"Put your fists up."

"I've got them up."

"Oh, sorry. I couldn't see in the dark like. Right?"

"Do you give in?"

"Who? Me? Give in?"

"Come on, Mog, don't get involved in any fighting," said Oliver Manners.

"I'll bloody well murder him," said Mog. "I'll knock the living daylights out of him."

He pushed Oliver to one side.

"Ooops," cried Oliver, and he staggered backwards into Horace A'Fong. The minute Oriental was propelled backwards by the blow. He hit the back of his head on the side of the coach and collapsed in a heap on the pavement.

At that very moment Wyndham Lancaster ducked to avoid Uncle Mort's swinging fist and tripped headlong over the prostrate body of Horace A'Fong. He hit his head on the garden wall and blood began to pour from his nose.

"My God—blood," said Group Captain Greenaway, and he fell into a deep swoon.

16

"You've got to go," said Megan to Mog.

"Why?" said Mog.

"Fighting in the streets like that. I never seen nothing like it since the day dad give a pasting to Billy Montgomery, God rest his soul, for giving aniseed balls to his ferrets. 'Mind his dentures, Billy,' mam kept shouting. I never seen blood like it."

"Well, why get onto me about fighting then?" said Mog. "It's the old laws of inheritance you wants to take to task, not me. I comes from a violent family, doesn't I? Course I does."

"You've got to go," said Megan firmly.

Mog stood up and went to the window. They were in the kitchen, and it was two days since the outing.

In the next door garden Mr Brandon was planting his anemone bulbs. Megan had left the washing out on the line overnight, and the first frost of the autumn had pinched the sheets and chilled the pyjama cords.

Now the morning sun was warming up the lawn, and a few late butterflies that had crept out of the cracks in the dry stone walls were fluttering weakly above the tall clumps of Michaelmas daisies.

"There's nice. There's lovely," said Mog. "I was only having a fight as part of my treatment for the loonies. Right? I knowed that if we had a free for all, a bout of fisticuffs like, they'd be bound to get a few cracks on their noddles, and then they'd be cured. Right?"

"But none of them was cured, Mog," said Megan. "You fell down there, didn't you, my lovely?"

Mog poured himself a cup of tea and slumped down in the hard-backed chair by the fireplace.

"Ambrose and me have talked it over, and we've decided we're going to get rid of the poor gentleman lunatics," said Megan. "We're going to see Mrs Mortensen and tell her that we don't want no more to do with it and we wants to go back and live in our old cottage."

"Typical, typical," said Mog. "That's the whole trouble with the world these days. No one cares about no one else. No man is an island. Don't you forget that, my lovely, when you're kicking everyone out of house and home."

"I'm sorry, Mog, but you'll have to go," said Megan.

"What about my equipment? I can't go without that, Meg, can I? Fair play, my lovely, you can't expect me to leave my artificial hares behind, can you?"

"We'll send them on to you."

Mog stood up and went to the window once more. He rubbed the moisture off the glass with the sleeve of his jacket and sighed deeply.

"Before you and Ambrose come to Cardiff on holidays I was a happy man," he said. "What had I got? Sweet how's your father, that's what I'd got. Where was I sleeping, residing like? Under a tree in Sophia Gardens. What was my state of health? Decidedly dicky. But was I happy? The answer to that is in the affirmative. In other words—course I bloody was."

"Oh, Mog, my sweetheart. I'm sorry, my love. I didn't mean you no harm," said Megan.

"But what was my prospects, Meg? That's what you got to ask yourself," he said. "My prospects was unbounded. Well, there was no limit to them, was there? Course there wasn't. You think of all them tankers plying the oceans of the world. Well, sooner or later one of them's bound to break down, have a collision like. And that's where I comes in. Out I goes in my ocean-going tug, throws out a rope, pulls them back to port and claims a fortune in salvage. Simplicity itself."

214

"You never told me you had an ocean-going tug, Mog," said Megan.

"I hasn't. I hasn't, Meg. That's the whole point. That's one of the many possibilities what was open to me, wasn't it? I'm surprised at you, Meg. Since you been living up here you got the real genuine inlander's mentality. No romance. No adventure. No vision. That's what you hasn't got. I was born in Cardiff. Right? A seaport. Right? Well, I stands there on the head at Penarth, and I watches the ships. I knows them all. Right? I knows all the companies. Lamport and Holt, Houlder Brothers, Blue Star, Thos and Jas Harrison what gives their ships the names of trades and professions. Right? And I sees them setting out into the Channel with the sun glinting on the waves like, and the seagulls flying in their wake like, and I starts imagining to myself where they're bound for."

He moved from the window and stared into the empty fireplace. A dog barked, and a few specks of soot fell into the grate.

"I been down to the Ship in George Street, and heard the seafarers talking. Well, I'm a regular patron, aren't I?" he said. "I stands there in the corner, and I listens to them talking about their experiences at sea and in distant lands in romantic foreign climes. Right? And all the time I'm picturing it in my mind's eye. I got a clear mental picture like of the exotic places what they're talking about. There's Corky Maloney in the corner there. Right? What old salt's yarns is he spinning? What magic is he conjuring up? He's talking about this bit of tail he had in Durban for three weeks. Well, you can imagine what she'd be like, can't you? About five foot three, an arse like a battleship and athlete's foot. Right? Well, the way he's talking about it, you'd think it was more like Jayne Mansfield. 'Like ten bobsworth of rip raps it was in bed,' he says. Bloody liar. I knows for a fact he's lying. Well, I seen his wife, hasn't I? Big Jean, they calls her. Well, she've had so many bambinos from one source or another, they got a special bed for her at St David's maternity. It's true. It's true. Billy Mathias told me that. He seen it with his own two eyes, when he's in there to get his impetigo done.

"And there's another bloody liar for you—Billy Mathias. He's on this ship, see, running spuds from Marseilles to Cadiz. Right? Spanish Civil War. Right? Well, according to his story, they're two days out from Gib, when these here Gerry

215

bombers comes over and starts bombing them. So Billy runs up to the bridge, breaks down the door of the Old Man's cabin, takes out his Very pistol, dashes out on deck and shoots down three bloody Heinkels. Well, I knows for a fact he couldn't have done that. You seen how his hand shakes. Right? You orders him a pint of Brains' dark, and he's not got it up to his bleeding chest before half of it's spilled down his trousers."

"There's a train at half past six," said Megan. "Ambrose will drive you down, and we'll come and see you off."

"I'm looking at the situation from an outsider's point of view, Meg. The outsider, the impartial observer like, a bloke with no axes to grind like, would have took one look at me in Cardiff and he'd have said to hisself: there's a man with prospects, there's a man with the whole world at his webs. Right? Course he would. If I'd gone up to him for advice, asked him whether or not I should do you a favour and come up here and help you out, he'd have turned hisself inside out with laughing. 'Don't be such a foolish fellow,' he'd have said. 'You take my advice, old chap, and stay where you are. Look after Number One and start building up the old liquidity. Right?'

"But what did I do? I didn't take his advice, did I? Course I didn't. I laughed in his face, didn't I? Well, he was upset by that, see. I mean, you can see his point. I asks for advice, and when I gets it, I laughs in his face. You could see he was mad. One false move from me, and he'd have given me a dig in the chops, no messing. See what I mean, Meg? Them's the sort of risks I took for you. If Megan and Ambrose wants a helping hand, I says to myself, they has to look no further than yours truly. Right? Like? And so I comes. And so I stays. And so I'm booted out without so much as a word of thanks."

"Oh, don't say that, Mog. Don't say that, my lovely," said Megan. "We are grateful to you. We're very grateful for all you've done, and when you gets on the train, remember you got to change at Birmingham."

Mog went to the door of the kitchen. He stood there for a few seconds and then he turned and said to Megan:

"I shall leave with dignity. I shan't appeal to your sense of fair play. I shan't endeavour, try like, to make you see the injustice of your actions. No pleading. No begging. I'll go quietly, don't you bother yourself."

216

When Ambrose came home for lunch, Mog grasped him by the sleeve and said:

"Don't throw me out, boy. Don't send me packing. I got nowhere to go. You can't have me sleeping rough with a chest like mine. Don't throw me out. Please, please, please."

"It's got nowt to do with me," said Ambrose. "It's Megan what made the decision."

"What about Oliver? What will he do without me? You're not thinking of him, are you? Self, self, self, that's what you're thinking about, and all the time there's that poor misfortunate having the one consolation in his life ripped away from him and sent packing to Cardiff. You wants locking up, you does."

"Did Megan tell you you've got to change at Birmingham?" said Ambrose, and then he went into the kitchen and had spare ribs, cabbage and jacket potatoes for his lunch.

Later in the afternoon Miss Miranda came to the house on her scooter.

"Where's Meg?" she said.

"Out shopping," said Mog.

"Oh, what a pity," said Miss Miranda. "I was going to take her out to see the house Oliver and I are going to buy, when we get married. It's super, Mog. It's gorgeous, and Oliver's out there now visualising it all."

"Visualising it?"

"Visualising how it will be when we're living there with the children and having people round to dinner and being famous painters and potters and giggling over Antoinette Lilley because she still hasn't got married yet."

"You wants your bloody heads testing," said Mog.

"I tell you what. Why don't you come out and see it?"

"Me? On the back of that scooter? I had my bellyful of that last time, I tell you."

"Please yourself. I don't care, do I? Course I bloody don't."

"Go on then, being as how it's you, I'll do you a favour and come and give it the once over."

He grasped Miss Miranda tightly round the waist as she drove out of the city and headed for the village, where the house was situated.

They drove down country lanes heavy with the smoky scents of autumn. The wheels of the scooter mashed the dead leaves. A weasel ran across the road in front of them, and a flock of greenfinches flew up from the hedgerow. To their

217

right the river was outlined by double banks of beeches, which glowed golden in the sunlight.

They went through the village slowly. It had a main square with stocks in the centre, and a red and white bus was waiting outside the post office. There were five pubs.

The house lay half a mile outside the village. It was in the grounds of a crumbling Cistercian abbey. It had small mullioned windows, a studded oak door, a courtyard paved with flagstones, a rusting water pump, a small herb garden, and the lawns at the back rolled down to the river.

"Isn't it super, Mog? Isn't it just too gorgeous?" said Miss Miranda.

"I'll bet you half a bar it's riddled with dry rot," said Mog. "We had a house in Splott once, and the first day we're in my old dad goes out to the lavvy, the toilet like, pulls the chain when he's done, and half the bleeding back wall caves in. I knows all about property, don't you kid yourself."

"They say it's got a ghost," said Miss Miranda.

"It's supposed to be this old abbot, who was murdered by Cromwell's soldiers," said Oliver Manners, who had come up to join them.

"More like a family of rats living behind your skirting boards," said Mog.

The two young people showed Mog round the outside of the house. They were full of enthusiasm and excitement, and when they had finished, they went into the village and entered one of the pubs.

Oliver bought pints of beer for Mog and himself and a bottle of Coca Cola for Miss Miranda.

"Well?" said Miss Miranda to Mog. "What do you think about the house? Isn't it super? Isn't it gorgeous?"

"You could make a fortune doing bed and breakfast," said Mog.

"But we don't want to," said Miss Miranda. "We want it all for ourselves."

"You see, that's the whole trouble with the younger generation. No sense of vision. No sense of enterprise. Right?"

"Oliver's going to be a famous painter, and I'm going to be a famous potter, and he'll have his paintings shown all over the world, and my pottery will become an absolute must for people who want to be in fashion," said Miss Miranda.

"That proves my point," said Mog. "You've no imagination.

Thirty bob a night B and B, and you'd have liquidity to burn."

They sat on their benches outside the public house. There was a tangled orchard to their right, and they watched a spotted flycatcher hunting from the stump of an old apple tree. Shortly it would leave for its winter quarters.

Mog yawned and said:

"Does you ever wonder about growing old and dying?"

"What a horrible thought," said Miss Miranda.

"Well, I does. Sometimes I wonders about it a lot. I walks round the docks in the evening, and I sees the seagulls coming home to roost, to have a bit of the old shut eye like, and I sees the bobbies slapping their arms to keep warm, and I hears the tugs hooting and the trolleys swishing on the overhead wires. And sometimes I goes up the valleys. Well, I got a buttie at Treherbert, hasn't I? Course I has. And we goes up on the tops, see, and we looks out and we sees the sheep grazing and hears them bleating in the distance, and we sees the big black mountains and the slag heaps and the pit heads. And I thinks to myself, when I'm gone, snuffed it like, kicked the old bucket, it'll all be the same. Well, not exactly the same, cos I knows for a fact they'll get rid of the trolley buses in Cardiff sooner or later. But nothing stops, see, when your time comes. You snuffs it, and it makes no more impression than a moth farting. Yet at the same time I thinks to myself that when I was born, for a moment in time, a tiny fraction like, I was the youngest man in the world. I finds that very comforting, doesn't you? Well, I always was a bit of a philosopher, wasn't I? Course I bloody was."

"Gosh, you are being gloomy today," said Miss Miranda. "Is anything the matter?"

Mog took a long gulp from his beer, wiped his mouth on the sleeve of his jacket and in a single breath told them what Megan and Ambrose had said to him earlier in the day.

"The lousy bastards," said Miss Miranda.

"I knows," said Mog gloomily.

"You must come and live with us, when we get married," said Miss Miranda.

"Pardon?" said Oliver.

"You can be our butler," said Miss Miranda. "You can buttle away like stink while we're doing our painting and potting, and in the evening you can go down to the pubs in the village, and you'll meet this widow, whose husband has just

219

died under tragic circumstances, and she'll have a big black Labrador and she'll make a home for you and you'll be able to comfort each other in the twilight of your lives."

"Twilight of our lives? I'm not in the bleeding twilight of my life," said Mog. "And in any case I can't stand dogs. Their hairs gets up your nose and they're always rolling in horse shit."

"It was only a suggestion," said Miss Miranda.

"I knows it was, my lovely, and I'm very grateful. I'm very touched. The old ticker's really been moved by what you just said to me."

Miss Miranda looked thoughtful for a moment, and then she gritted her teeth and said:

"There's only one thing for it, Oliver. You'll have to be cured."

"What?" said Oliver.

"You'll be cured, we'll get married, you'll take over the business, and Mog will stay here and run it for you."

"But I don't want to be cured," said Oliver. "I'm happy as I am living with you and Megan and Ambrose and making artificial hares."

"You balmy sponge head, all that's over now, isn't it?" said Mog. "There won't be no more licking envelopes and sticking on stamens, when I'm gone, will there? They'll send you back to Mannersville, and you'll be locked away in that dormitory with that little ponce, Nurse Mooseman, trying to touch you up all the time. Right?"

"Right," said Miss Miranda.

"Oh, hell," said Oliver. "I hadn't thought of that."

"So you've just got to be cured," said Miss Miranda fiercely.

"I suppose I have," said Oliver glumly.

Then Miss Miranda smiled at him and led Mog away round the corner of the pub.

"How are we going to do it?" she said.

"Simple. Simplicity itself, my old cream cake," said Mog. "Just you pin back your lug holes and listen to what I'm going to tell you."

He spoke softly and rapidly for five minutes. As he spoke Miss Miranda's eyes opened wide and she said:

"Gosh. Super. Gosh. How absolutely super."

"All right then? You knows what you got to do?" said Mog.

220

"Course I bloody does," said Miss Miranda. "How absolutely super."

She raced back to Oliver, snatched the drink from his hands and downed it in one cascading gulp. Then she pulled Oliver by the hand to her motor scooter and roared off out of the village in a cloud of blue smoke.

Mog smiled to himself, and then he began to rub his hands nervously together.

He went inside the pub and bought himself a large whisky.

He had two more whiskies, and then he caught the bus back to the city. He called in at the Griffon, where he ordered a pint of black and tan and a whisky chaser.

When the hands of the clock showed it was eight o'clock, he rubbed his hands nervously together again and said to himself:

"Well, this is it, my old son. Good luck to you, Miss Miranda, my old beauty."

Over in Megan's cottage in the grounds of Mannersville Oliver Manners sat in the kitchen, smoking a cigarette. Miss Miranda was in the bedroom.

Outside it was growing dusk. A light burned in Mrs Mortensen's bedroom window. Tawny owls called to each other.

"You can come in now," shouted Miss Miranda.

When Oliver went into the bedroom, he found Miss Miranda lying naked on the bed rubbing herself with salad dressing.

"What on earth are you doing?" he said.

"Making myself desirable," she said. "You know India? Well, the concubines there rub their bodies with sweet-smelling oils to titillate the desires of their lovers."

"Salad dressing isn't a sweet-smelling oil," said Oliver.

"I know that, stupid. Megan hadn't got any bath oil or anything like that so I thought salad dressing would be the next best thing. I did put sugar in it."

Miss Miranda's body glistened with the oil, and Oliver began to shiver and tremble.

"The season of chastity is over," said Miss Miranda softly. "The season of mellow fruitfulness is about to begin."

Oliver stood there, and the tremblings became more violent.

"Oh, come on, Oliver, don't just stand there," said Miss Miranda. "Take your things off, and let's get seducing each other."

Oliver got undressed very slowly.

221

"Gosh, look at your Thing. It's enormous," said Miss Miranda. "You dirty old beast."

Oliver took off his wrist watch and flung himself on the bed beside her. He took her into his arms and began to kiss her nipples violently. She struggled free and slapped him on the chest.

"Don't be so rotten, Oliver," she said. "Just hold on for a minute, and let's do things properly. Oonagh Liddell lent me this book here, and it tells you all about it and what to do."

She began to read from the book, which was covered in brown paper, on which was printed in ball point pen: 'Oonagh Liddell, Form Five A, Scripture,'

"There's a lot of boring old stuff in the first chapters about respecting each other and how to get a mortgage," she said, flicking through the pages. "Ah, here's where it starts. Page 37, where all the thumb marks are."

Another owl hooted. A daddy longlegs crawled up the wall, and a moth beat at the window pane.

"Ah, I see. Well, I'd better read it to you," said Miss Miranda. " 'Before commencing the act of intercourse it is essential if full and deep satisfaction is to be derived therefrom by both partners that the male stimulate his partner by those various activities known collectively as love play.' Well, go on, Oliver, stimulate me."

"I don't know what stimulate means in that context," said Oliver.

"Well, I'd better look it up in the index then," said Miss Miranda.

She turned to the back of the book and ran her finger down the index.

"Shit. It's not in," she said.

"Try 'love play'," said Oliver.

"Good idea," said Miss Miranda, and she ran her finger down the index once more. "Ah, here it is. After 'loofah'."

She opened the book at the relevant page and began to read.

"Gosh. Crikey. Gosh," she said. "Gosh, it's no wonder Antoinette Lilley had an attack of the vapours after reading this. Okay, Oliver, move over to me and we'll do it together while I read the instructions. Now you do this, and I do that. Right? Good. Then you do this. And this. And this. Oh, Oliver, how super. Oliver, Oliver, Oliver, Oliver. Then I do this. And this. And . . . stop wriggling, Oliver. Then you do this.

Then I . . . blast, I've turned over two pages. Gosh. Crikey. Super. Fabulous. Yes, we can skip these two pages and carry on from here. And you do this. And this. And . . ."

And so tentatively and clumsily, painfully and tenderly, fearfully and excitedly they made love.

When they had finished, Miss Miranda said:

"I love you, Oliver."

And Oliver said:

"And I love you, Miranda."

17

"I'm cured, I'm cured. Whoopee," shouted Oliver, rushing into the Tierneys' front parlour later in the evening.

"And I've had my oats, and it was super. Whoopee," shouted Miss Miranda dashing in behind him.

"I say, old beans, hearty congratters," said Horace A'Fong.

"I'm cured, I'm cured," shouted Oliver, and he took Megan in his arms, lifted her up and twirled her round and round.

"And we're going to get married, and Oliver's going to take over the business and Mog's going to run it for him, and where is Mog by the way?" said Miss Miranda.

"Search me. He hasn't been back since the afternoon and we've got all his things packed for him," said Ambrose.

"Well, you'll just have to unpack them, won't you?" said Miss Miranda. "Course you bloody will."

"I'm cured, I'm cured," shouted Oliver, and he pranced round and round the room with Megan in his arms.

"Oh, I am happy, Oliver," she said. "Oh, I'm so happy for you, my lovely. This is the happiest day in my life. It is. It is."

She collapsed on the sofa, put her hand to her bosom and sobbed unrestrainedly.

Oliver sat down beside her, and his eyes were full of tears, too.

"This calls for a celebration," said Horace A'Fong. "How about cracking a bottle of Tizer?"

"I'll crack a bottle over your Oriental noddle, if you doesn't shut up," said Mog.

They turned to the door, where Mog was standing, shirt undone to the waist, trousers ripped and with an enormous grin on his face.

Miss Miranda dashed across to him and kissed him passionately on the chin.

"It worked," she said. "It really worked."

"Course it did," said Mog. "You leave it to old Mog, he knows a thing or two about what's what, don't he?"

"Course he bloody do," said Miss Miranda, and everyone laughed.

"Just look at the state of your clothes, Mog," said Megan. "Wherever have you been?"

"I had a bit of an altercation with a lamp post, didn't I?" said Mog.

They all laughed again, and Ambrose went out to the local pub to buy beer and pop for the celebration.

Megan looked at Miss Miranda gravely and then said:

"You been a very naughty girl, hasn't you, Miss Miranda?"

"Why?" said Miss Miranda.

"Well, you been and gone and done what you didn't ought to do until after you got married, didn't you?"

"Yes," said Miss Miranda. "And it was absolutely super. Antoinette Lilley will go green with envy when she finds out. I'll write to her tomorrow and tell her it's streets and streets better than mucking out Miss Naughton-Bailey's smelly old ponies."

"I don't know what the world's coming to," said Megan. "All you young people seem to think about these days is sex. We never had things like that when I was a little girl. I never knew what sex was until I had to fill in this form to join the Land Army."

"The whole world's bothered about sex if the truth be known," said Mog. "That's all people thinks about these days. Bloody fools. If you wants my opinion, I thinks it's all a bloody good laugh. That's the way to treat it. Have a bloody good laugh about it. Well, that's all its worth, isn't it?"

They all followed Mog's advice and had a very long and very loud laugh. Then they applied themselves to the festivities.

Horace A'Fong drank fourteen bottles of cream soda and ate seven tubes of Smarties. Group Captain Greenaway gave an

224

impersonation of Gracie Fields and Wyndham Lancaster gave a selection of readings from the British Railways (Midland Region) timetable. Mog drank three quarters of a crate of Guinness and, chased by Oliver and Miss Miranda, ran round the garden with a half-completed hare tied to his braces. Megan sat on the sofa and smiled.

"Tomorrow it'll be all over, Oliver," said Miss Miranda.

"Yes," said Oliver.

"You'll go to Mannersville, and the old bitch will pronounce you officially cured."

"You know, I'm rather looking forward to it," said Oliver. "It'll be quite nice to be sane again."

"Super," said Miss Miranda, and she bit him on the neck.

"I see young Renshawe's brother's in trouble again," said Sir Peter Wakefield, pointing to a report in the local morning newspaper. "He was had up in court yesterday for receiving half a hundredweight of copper piping. Tragic. Absolutely tragic."

"Tragic? What about me?" said Tom Manners. "You don't need to look outside this room to see a prime example of tragedy."

"Calm down, Tom," said Sir Peter. "Please will you calm down."

They were sitting in the drawing room at Mannersville. In another part of the house Mrs Mortensen was examining Oliver to discover whether he had, in fact, been restored to sanity.

"I don't trust that woman one little inch," said Tom. "When women start to meddle in politics, you can bet your life that trouble is certain to ensue."

"Politics?"

"The politics of ruining this family and, more specifically, of ruining my career as a businessman and a politician."

Sir Peter folded up the newspaper and smiled at Tom.

"There's not the slightest reason for you to worry, Tom," he said. "It just wouldn't be in her interests to pronounce that Oliver is completely cured."

"Why not?"

Sir Peter sighed, stood up and poured himself a large gin and bitter lemon.

"Because, my dear Tom, if Oliver is cured, the business goes to him, and, I do assure you, Mrs Mortensen is not the sort of woman who would countenance marriage to a penniless ex-businessman and a discredited ex-politician," he said.

"I wish you wouldn't say things like that," said Tom. "The merest suggestion of penury or discredit is enough to bring me out in a cold sweat these days."

"There is, of course, another solution," said Sir Peter, tugging the lobe of his left ear.

"What's that?"

"She might decide to marry Oliver instead."

"Oh, my God," said Tom, and he reeled backwards into the sofa and sank down, tugging at the knot in his tie.

"Oliver's been a frightfully long time in there with her, hasn't he?" said Miss Miranda.

"Well, she's got to give him a thorough overhaul, haven't she?" said Mog. "It's the same as putting a car what's had an accident on the road again, isn't it? Course it is. We don't want old Oliver to come out with a wonky gear stick, do we?"

They began to walk down the driveway towards the lake. They passed by a mound of earth. It was the newly-dug final resting place of the old English sheepdog, Quimby.

"Poor old Quimby," said Miss Miranda, pausing to look at the grave. "I wonder if dogs go to heaven, Mog."

"If they've behaved theirselves, I suppose they does," said Mog.

"Why? Do you think they have to stand at the judgement seat?"

"Course they bloody does. They has to account for theirselves same as you and me. Right?" said Mog. "I mean, if they've been naughty and spent all their lives rolling in horse shit and sticking their hairs up people's noses, they don't stand a dog's chance of getting in, does they?"

"I bet Quimby got in," said Miss Miranda. "He never did anything like that."

"Don't you be so sure," said Mog. "You never knows what dogs gets up to, when you're not with them. You take that corgi what Fat Bas owns. Cor blimey Charlie, you never seen such a vicious little bastard in the whole of your natural. Take the arse out of your trousers he would as soon as look at you. Well, that's what comes through sleeping with Fat Bas. Uses him as a hot water bottle, see. Dirty pig. I kept telling him it was unhygienic. I kept telling him that was the reason why he

226

was always scratching hisself. And what happens? Duffed up by Icky Evans, and the bloody corgi uses my hands as an ham sandwich next time it sees me."

"Well, he'll go to hell for sure, won't he?"

"Yes. And he better not bite me there, or I'll throw him in the bleeding furnace, won't I? Course I will."

They came to the summer pavilion. The chestnuts fringing the opposite bank of the lake were turning golden, but the colony of sand martins was still active, quartering the surface of the water, which lay still and steely grey.

A rowing boat was moored to the jetty. There were dead leaves on the seats and bird droppings on the oars.

"Shall we go for a row?" said Miss Miranda.

"Not with my tubes in their present state, my lovely," said Mog. "Well, it wouldn't be playing fair with them, would it?"

Miss Miranda sighed deeply.

"Gosh, she is keeping him a long time with her," she said.

"Probably having a bit of trouble with his brake linings," said Mog.

They sat down on the steps of the summer pavilion.

"Won't it be super when we take control of the business, Mog?" said Miss Miranda. "Can I be your private secretary, when you become the boss?"

"If you wants to," said Mog.

"Super," said Miss Miranda. "But you've got to promise not to try to get your end away with me, because I shall be married by then and even though I shall be wearing these sexy skirts which show half a yard of thigh, it won't be for your benefit, it'll be for Oliver and to impress all the important clients who come to see you."

"It won't bother me, my lovely," said Mog. "I'll be too busy sorting out the old liquidity, won't I?"

"Well, you could show a bit of interest," said Miss Miranda sulkily.

"I am showing interest," said Mog. "You wear one of them plunging necklines, right, and I'll have a bit of a dekko down the front from time to time, if you wants."

"Super," said Miss Miranda. "And Sister Concepta can be head of the typing pool, because she must have had her baby by now, and she'll be bound to be looking for a job."

"Not on your bloody life," said Mog. "Never have nuns in your typing pool, that's my motto. Well, they gets their

227

rosaries stuck in the typewriter keys all the time, don't they?"

Miss Miranda giggled. And then she hugged herself and said:

"Have you got all sorts of super plans for the business, Mog? I bet you have."

"Plans? I got hundreds of them. Well more like thousands if the truth be known. Right?" said Mog. "I'll buy myself a new bloody wrist watch for a kick off and then I'll consider the purchase of a fleet of ocean going ore carriers."

"Gosh," said Miss Miranda. "What do ore carriers carry?"

"Ore, you daft pudding head," said Mog.

"What's ore?"

"Cor blimey Charlie, didn't they teach you nothing at school?" said Mog. "For your information, just so's you know like, ore is what . . . well, ore is the same thing as what . . . and then I'll buy out Tommy Ishmael's cafe and buy a new bloody tea urn for it. Well, you got to think big when you're in business, hasn't you?"

"Could we buy out my old school?"

"Why?"

"Well, I've got this super idea. You know Paris and all the houses of ill repute they have there? Well, we could easily turn the school into a high class house of ill repute and we'd make a fortune out of it. I mean, all the girls from form three upper and above are just gasping for it, and Oonagh Liddell says that in the Middle East you get concubines who aren't even old enough to be in form two beta, so if the business went really well and all the girls got fantastically knackered, we could always ask for volunteers from Sister Clemency's form, couldn't we?"

"What about Antoinette Lilley? You hasn't thought about, considered like, what she'd have to say, has you?"

"Oh, fiddle dee dee and bollocks to Antoinette Lilley," said Miss Miranda. "Anyway, I know for a fact she'd make excuses so she wouldn't have to take her turn. It'd be just the same as when we have hockey. When it was her turn to be stuffed, she'd get her father to send a note to say she'd got to be excused because she'd got a cold."

"Typical. Typical," said Mog.

Miss Miranda looked at her watch again.

"What can she be doing to Oliver all this time?" she said.

Oliver was lying on the couch in Mrs Mortensen's office.

228

She was sitting by his head. She was wearing a green silk blouse with wide sleeves and maroon velvet trousers.

"Go on, Oliver," she said. "Tell me more."

"Well, Lieutenant Quimby came into the mess one evening, and asked me if I'd like to go rowing on the lake with her the next day."

"Why did she do that?"

"I rather think she liked me."

"Did you like her?"

"No."

"Then why did you say you'd go with her?"

"Her sister knew a friend of mine, who lived in Wakefield."

"I see," said Mrs Mortensen. "Well, continue, Oliver."

"We drove out to the lake in Bunty Costello's Volkswagen. My old crate had broken down, you see, and in any case you couldn't get the hood up, if it rained."

"What a nuisance."

"Well, she'd turned up in uniform, which I thought was bloody silly. I told her I thought it was bloody silly to turn up in uniform to go rowing on a lake, and she started to cry and said I'd only said that because she didn't look nice in uniform."

"Did she?"

"She didn't look nice in anything. Her fingers were covered in nicotine stains for a start, and she was always eating bars of chocolate."

"What happened next? "

"We hired a rowing boat and went out on the lake."

"And that's all you can remember, is it?" said Mrs Mortensen. "Your mind is still a blank about what happened, is it?"

"No, of course it isn't," said Oliver, sitting up. "That's why I've come here to see you, isn't it? Course it bloody is. Right? "

"Tell me then," said Mrs Mortensen quietly.

"Well, there were lots of little islands on this lake, you see, and she suggested that we tie the boat to a tree and have a smoke. I didn't want to really, because it was bloody cold for the time of the year, and I thought I'd catch my death of cold if I stopped rowing."

"But she insisted?"

"No. But she looked as though she was going to start crying

again, and I can't stand women crying, so I rowed the boat to this little island and tied up to this tree."

"And then?" said Mrs Mortensen, lighting a small cigar.

"Well, we lit up cigarettes and started talking."

"What about?"

"And then suddenly she stood up and said she wanted me to make love to her. Christ, it was awful. I didn't know what to do. Could you imagine making love to somebody wearing the uniform of . . . God, it was dreadful. I just didn't know what to do."

"And what did you do?"

"I picked up the oars, and I gave a tremendous heave on them. Well, she fell back in the boat with the most tremendous clump, and I just couldn't rouse her. It was horrible. She was lying there all white in the face and her neck was at this funny angle. I rowed and rowed like hell back to the hut, and they called an ambulance. And all the time this German who ran the place kept looking at the front of her tunic and then at me. She'd ripped open the front of her tunic, you see, when she'd tried to get me to . . . and I went back in the ambulance with her, and I was certain she was going to die. But she didn't die. She came to after about three hours and she told them . . . well, she told them that I'd tried to assault her and when she wouldn't give in, I'd hit her on the head with an oar and they court martialled me, and when I got up in front of them, I couldn't remember a single thing that happened. I just stood there and listened to her evidence, and I didn't know whether it was true or not. It was awful. It was bloody terrible."

He slumped back onto the couch. Mrs Mortensen tapped Philip Manners' notebook on her knee.

"Is this true, Oliver?" she said quietly.

"Yes."

She looked down on him, ran her hand lightly across his brow and held up the notebook in front of his eyes.

"And what your father wrote in this about your mother's death is untrue, is it?" she said.

"Yes," said Oliver. "I told you what really happened."

Mrs Mortensen ran her tongue round the edges of the notebook. She stood up and sat down on the corner of her desk. She smiled at Oliver.

"Then, Oliver, I am sorry to say, but you are not yet cured," she said.

230

18

The whole of the Tierney household was stunned by the news.

Mog and Miss Miranda wept openly, and Miss Miranda said: "That's me finished with the old bitch and Mannersville for ever and ever. Can I stay on here and live with you, Megan?"

"Course you can, God love you and keep you," said Megan.

When Wyndham Lancaster heard the news he came out in a rash on the back of his neck, and Horace A'Fong said he would lend Oliver Manners his collection of 'Rupert' annuals by way of consolation. Group Captain Greenaway sat down and began to write a strong letter of protest to the International Red Cross. Halfway through he ran out of ink, so he screwed up the letter and ate it, saying:

"It's the only way, men. We'd all be slapped in the cooler, if the Goons set eyes on it."

It was Megan, however, whose feelings on the subject were most violent. What incensed her more than anything was Mrs Mortensen's insistence that Oliver and his fellow lunatics should return to Mannersville immediately.

"They're not going," she said. "I'm not going to allow them to return, go back like, now they've got used to the way I cook my vegetables, and I knows for a fact no one would think of rubbing Group Captain Greenaway's chest with Vick before he goes to bed at night."

"Good for you, old horse," said Horace A'Fong. "School, three cheers for matron. Hip, hip, hip . . ."

"Oh, go and get stuffed, you great Oriental pillock," shouted Miss Miranda.

In the afternoon they were visited by Estelle Nicholson. She took one look at Oliver and burst into tears.

"Bloody hell," said Ambrose. "It's like the Wailing Wall of Jerusalem in this house."

231

And then he went out for a pint with Mr Brandon from next door.

"Now then, Miss Nicholson, don't upset yourself, my lovely," said Megan handing her a cup of tea. "You wants to think yourself lucky you're out of Mr Tom Manners' clutches in time. He'd have slapped you in the loony bin as fast as look at you, sure as eggs are eggs."

"The big fat bastard," said Estelle, and then she blushed and started to cry again.

Mog looked at her, and his lower lip quivered, and he started to sob once more.

"What about my ore carriers?" he said. "There's none of you thinking about them, is there?"

Miss Miranda took Estelle up to the bathroom, and when they returned, Estelle said:

"The reason why I came was to tell you that daddy says that if there's anything he can do to help, you mustn't hesitate to ask him."

"He couldn't chip in for a bit of an ore carrier, could he?" said Mog. "Well, a new tea urn for Tommy Ishmael's cafe would be better than nothing, I suppose."

"That's very nice of your father," said Oliver. "Thank your father very much, will you?"

"Oh, Oliver, you poor boy," said Estelle, and she kissed him on the cheek before getting into her car and driving away.

"Well, it's up to you now, Mog," said Miss Miranda.

"What do you mean, it's up to me?" said Mog.

"You're the one that's full of ideas. It's up to you to think of something."

Mog blew his nose and wiped his eyes. And then he sighed deeply.

"I can't think of nothing," he said. "All the stuffing's been knocked out of me."

The respective stuffings of Sir Peter Wakefield and Tom Manners, however, had not been knocked out.

Sir Peter was jubilant.

"Marvellous, Tom," he said. "What did I tell you? I knew she'd be on our side."

His mood was so buoyant that he invited Tom and Mrs Mortensen out to dinner that evening. He took them to the Cafe Royal.

"To you, Mrs Mortensen," he said, raising his glass of sherry as they sat in the bar.

Mrs Mortensen nodded and accepted his toast with a smile.

The head waiter came to their table with three menus and handed them round. Tom began to lick his lips. He sat back in his chair and held the menu in front of him, smiling contentedly.

Mrs Mortensen, however, leaned and snatched it out of his hands.

"No more of that stuff for you, my darling," she said. "Your father never touched meat from the day he met me, and look how well he thrived on it."

Tom Manners groaned, and Sir Peter chuckled to himself.

Back at the Tierneys' the household sat silently in the front parlour. Horace A'Fong was sucking a stick of liquorice root, and Group Captain Greenaway was making out a forged travel document enabling an Estonian chemical worker to travel from Danzig to Calais.

Suddenly Mog jumped out of his chair and said:

"We'll organise a petition."

"What for?" said Miss Miranda.

"For Oliver, you great steaming nit," said Mog. "We'll go round all the houses in the street and we'll get them to write their names, append them like, on a document saying they thinks Oliver isn't a loony no more. Right? Like?"

"They'd think it was you what was the loony going round with a document like that," said Ambrose.

"And in any case they don't even know Oliver," said Miss Miranda.

"Typical. Typical. That's what I've been faced with all my life—lack of foresight, enterprise and vision on the part of my butties," said Mog. "You take Cuthbert Loosemore. No bloody vision. Well, I knows he had to wear bi-focals, but I'm not talking about vision in the literal sense. I'm talking about it in the metaphorical sense, aren't I? Course I am."

"And I'll tell you why Cuthbert Loosemore had to wear bi-focals," said Megan. "It was because his mam, God rest her soul, didn't keep him in a dark light when he'd got the measles that time just after the Corpus Christi procession."

"I don't care if she kept him in a vat of bloody blanc mange," said Mog. "What I'm saying is that he had no vision in the metaphorical sense of the word. I knowed for a fact Nickel

233

Coin would win the Grand National in '51. Forty to bloody one he come in at. Cor blimey Charlie, we'd have been laughing. But no, Cuthbert wouldn't have it. A friend of the postman had told him Arctic Gold would skate in. He bloody did, too—flat on his nose at the Canal Turn, the bastard. Two five pound notes down the drain there. I'd have had Silver Fame in the Cheltenham Gold Cup that year, too, if I hadn't been inside for nicking tangerines at Pontypridd market. Right?"

"I'm fed up with your stories," said Miss Miranda. "You're all wind and no action."

"No action, is it?" said Mog. "Right, my old lovely, we'll soon see about that."

And he went outside into the back garden and called over to Uncle Mort, who was sitting in the wheelbarrow, smoking a cigarette and reading the evening paper.

"Hey, hairy nose," he shouted.

"I'll punch your teeth in, if you talk to me like that," said Uncle Mort.

"Cor blimey Charlie, you're worse than Rocky bloody Marciano," said Mog. "You've only got to look at you crooked, and you got the old maulers up thirsting for a punch up."

"What do you want?" said Uncle Mort.

"Come in by here for a minute. I got a favour I wants you to do for me."

Uncle Mort folded up his evening paper, pushed his way through the gap in the privet hedge and was led into the front parlour by Mog.

"Now then," said Mog pointing to Oliver Manners. "What's the first thing that strikes you about him?"

Uncle Mort looked Oliver up and down for a few moments, and then he said:

"He needs a bloody hair cut."

"I'm not talking about his physical appearance, prune head," said Mog. "I'm talking about his bloody mental appearance. I'm talking about his grey matter, the state of his noddle and what goes on inside it. I'm asking you, inquiring like, whether or not you think he's off his bloody chump."

"If you ask me, it's you what's going off your bloody chump," said Uncle Mort.

"Here here," said Ambrose.

234

"Bloody laymen," said Mog with a sigh. "I've been surrounded by them all my life. Well, look what happened when me and Icky Evans took Cuthbert Loosemore with us to do that job in Lyme Regis. We'd only been gone . . ."

"Oh, shut up," said Miss Miranda, and Mog looked at her and his lower lip began to quiver.

"What's all this in aid of any road?" said Uncle Mort.

"I thinks my brother wants you to say whether or not you thinks poor Mr Manners is lunatical or not," said Megan.

"Course he isn't," said Uncle Mort.

"There you are. See what I mean?" said Mog. "So now you can be the first one to stick your name to the petition. Right?"

"What petition?" said Uncle Mort.

"Tell him, Meg. Tell him," said Mog.

Megan told Uncle Mort about the petition. She also told him about the actions of Mrs Mortensen and Tom Manners.

"Bloody Tory dog. It doesn't surprise me in the least," said Uncle Mort. "Look what Lord Woolton did inventing British Restaurants. I went to this one in Stretford and I had fried snoek and chips. Bloody hell, I were off work with the screaming yim yams for three week after that lot."

"Bloody Tory bastards," said Mog.

"I bet Anthony Eden never had to have fried whale meat for his dinner," said Uncle Mort.

"Course he didn't," said Mog. "And where did he get all the coupons from to buy all them bloody hats of his?"

"True. True," said Uncle Mort.

"You lot make me sick," said Miss Miranda.

Startled, they turned to look at her. Her eyes were flashing and her cheeks had turned scarlet.

"Why don't you get up and do something instead of spouting off about Anthony Woolton and having the screaming yim yams and inventing British Restaurants and eating whale meat?"

"Standing up and doing something? That's precisely what I am doing," shouted Mog. "What about my bloody petition?"

"You can stuff that up your arse," shouted Miss Miranda.

"Oh, dearie dearie me, Miss Miranda," said Megan, putting her hands to her eyes. "Bottie—that's the word you should use if you wants to be suitable."

235

"Suitable? She doesn't know the meaning of the word," screamed Mog.

"It's like being in a bloody nut house," said Uncle Mort, and he turned to Ambrose and said: "Do you fancy a pint?"

"Not half," said Ambrose, and he stood up and left the room with Uncle Mort.

Mog glowered at Miss Miranda and said:

"You're a right clever dick you, aren't you? I hasn't noticed you bursting your boilers coming forward with suggestions, has I? Course I bloody basn't."

"Well, I have got a suggestion, if you must know," said Miss Miranda.

"That's a clever girl," said Megan. "I knew you'd have a suggestion sooner or later if you tried hard enough."

"A suggestion!" said Mog scornfully. "I'll give you a suggestion. Why don't you go and take a running jump at yourself?"

"Sticks and stones may break my bones, but words can never hurt me," said Miss Miranda, and she stuck out her tongue at Mog.

"What is your suggestion, Miranda?" said Oliver.

"I've a good mind not to tell you now," she said.

"Oh, go on," said Oliver. "Please."

"Well," said Miss Miranda. "I think we should steal your father's notebook from my mother, and then we'd have all the evidence we need to prove that you're sane."

"But how?" said Oliver.

"We'll take it to an independent pys . . . pysch . . . pys . . . oh, shit, what's the word?"

"Head shrinker," said Mog.

"We'll take it to an independent head shrinker, he'll examine you, and he's certain to say that you're back to normal again," said Miss Miranda breathlessly. "And in addition we'll have a terrific hold over Tom and fat old Sir Peter Wakefield because they'll know we know what's in the book and it isn't at all certain that they know what's in the book, is it?"

"Oh, I don't know, Miss Miranda, love you, you got me beat," said Megan. "Can you make head nor tail of it, Mog?"

Mog nodded slowly and said:

"It's not a bad idea."

Then he jumped up in the air, raced across the room to Miss Miranda and hugged her.

"It's a bloody bramah of an idea," he said. "Fat Bas couldn't have thought of a better one, I tell you. It's true. It's true."

"How are we going to steal it?" said Oliver.

"Simple. Simplicity itself, my old fruit cake," said Miss Miranda. "Mog will steal it."

"Me?" said Mog. "Why me? What's so special about my knowledge of the subject of larceny that you wants me to do a nicking job for you?"

"Well, you're always telling us how terrific you are at it, aren't you?" said Miss Miranda. "Now's your chance to prove it."

"Cor blimey Charlie, give a dog a bad name," said Mog.

"Well?" said Miss Miranda challengingly.

Mog looked from her to Megan. And then he looked from Megan to Oliver. And then he looked from Oliver back to Miss Miranda.

They were all staring at him with their eyes glinting.

"All right," he said. "Being as how it's family."

Two hours later Mog's spirits had risen considerably. Three pints of bitter beer and two glasses of rum and peppermint in the local public house had worked wonders on him, and he was full of enthusiasm by the time he returned to the Tierneys'.

"Right," he said. "I shall need an assistant."

"Bags me," said Miss Miranda. "You'll want me to drive the getaway car, won't you? Well, more like the getaway scooter if the truth be known. Right?"

"Right," said Mog.

"Oh dear, Miss Miranda, I don't think its right and proper for a girl of your age to be getting involved in nefarious activities at your age, my lovely," said Megan.

"She'll be all right with me, don't you worry," said Mog. "I'll see she don't wear squeaky shoes. Right?"

An hour later Mog and Miss Miranda were creeping through the grounds of Mannersville.

It was pitch black, and, as they crossed the timber bridge, Mog put his foot right in the middle of a large pancake of cow dung.

237

"Bloody cows," he said. "Why can't they get them house-trained?"

"Ssh," said Miss Miranda.

There was only one light on in the house. It came from Nurse Mooseman's bedroom. They crept round the front of the house and tip-toed along the terrace which ran the whole length of the back.

Miss Miranda pointed up at a window on the second floor.

"That's where the old bitch sleeps," she whispered. "The notebook will be locked away in her dressing table."

"Okay, up you go then," said Mog, pointing to the drain pipe.

"I'm not climbing up that," said Miss Miranda. "You're supposed to be the cat burglar round here."

"Me?" said Mog. "Whatever gave you that incredible idea? I got no head for heights, see. Cor blimey Charlie, I gets vertigo just through tying my shoe laces, doesn't I?"

"Ssh," said Miss Miranda.

"Who are you bloody shushing?" said Mog. "Listen to me, you're in the presence of an expert now so don't you go throwing your weight around trying to pretend you knows more than what I does. Right? Like?"

"Ssh," said Miss Miranda, and at that moment a light went on in Tom Manners' bedroom.

They flattened themselves in the shadows against the wall. Their hearts began to pump rapidly.

The window opened and Mrs Mortensen looked out.

"It's all right, Tom," she said. "There's no one there. It must be the foxes again."

The window closed, and Miss Miranda said:

"The randy old faggot. She's having it away with him now."

She had hardly finished speaking, when Mog let out a loud volley of hiccups.

"Ssh. Ssh," went Miss Miranda.

"Don't you bloody hic-hic-hic shush hic-hic-hic me," said Mog.

Miss Miranda began to slap him violently on the back.

"Mind my hic-hic-hic-bloody hic-hic-hic-tubes," said Mog.

He staggered away bent double and crouched in a corner of the verandah.

"Hic-hic-hic-hic-hic," he went.

"Hold your bloody breath," hissed Miss Miranda.

238

"That's just what I am hic-hic-hic-d-hic-hic-hic-ing," hissed Mog back at her.

She stood there, screwing and unscrewing her fists into tight little balls.

Presently Mog stood up and whispered:

"I must have eaten something what disagreed with me."

Miss Miranda looked him up and down scornfully. His hair was awry, and his face was purple through having held his breath so long.

"Useless. Bloody useless," she said. "Well, I suppose I'll have to go up the drain pipe myself now. At least, the old bitch isn't in her bedroom."

"That's right, you're in clover there, my old sweetheart," said Mog. "I'll act as look out, don't you worry. You're in the presence of an expert look-out here. Right? It's true. It's true."

She tucked her skirt into her knickers, spat on the palms of her hands and then began to climb up the drain pipe. At first her movements were tentative and nervous, but as she gained confidence they became more fluent and supple, and within a few minutes she had opened the window and slipped inside.

Five minutes passed. There was complete silence. Mog nodded to himself and pulled his coat collar round his neck.

An owl hooted, and he started and hunched his head further into his coat collar. Then he heard a snuffling sound. It grew louder, and there was a scratching noise too.

His whole body froze. There was a soft, low growl. Slowly he turned his head, and there staring at him out of the darkness was a pair of eyes, glowing greeny-red.

"Cor blimey Charlie, a bleeding fox," he shrieked.

And with a single bound he hurled himself over the verandah and landed with a crash of shattered urns and plant pots into the flower beds below.

The light in Tom Manners' bedroom flashed on again. The window opened, and Mog was pinned against the earth in the beam of a flashlight.

"Williams! What the bloody hell are you doing here?" shouted Tom Manners.

Mog scrambled painfully to his feet, shielded his eyes from the beam and said:

"I seem to have lost the top of my fountain pen."

"What?" bellowed Tom Manners.

239

"Well, it could happen to anyone, couldn't it? I must have dropped it by here some time last week. Right? Well, I'm in the middle of writing a letter to my old grannie what's been run over by a trolley bus at a point to point meeting and . . . hic-hic-hic-hic."

"Put that gun away, Tom, for God's sake," shouted Mrs Mortensen.

"Gun?" screamed Mog. "Don't be such a bloody maniac, man. I'll come quietly. Hic-hic-hic-hic-hic. Hold on while I gets my white hankie out. Right?"

"I'll give you just two minutes to get out of here, Williams," shouted Tom Manners. "If you're not out of here by then, I'll pepper your backside with shot and ring for the police. Do you understand?"

Out of the corner of his eye Mog caught sight of Miss Miranda's startled face peering out of her mother's bedroom window.

"Right. Leave it to me. Right," he said, and then he began to limp away.

The beam of the flashlight followed him as he picked his way across the lawns. He paused, turned and shouted:

"If you finds the top of my fountain pen, pop it into the post for me, will you? Hic-hic-hic-hic."

"Get out," bellowed Tom Manners.

Half an hour later Miss Miranda found Mog huddled up in the grass by the side of her motor scooter. He was snoring.

She prodded him with her foot, and he sprang to his feet, shouting:

"Grannie, grannie! Watch out for the fox."

She thrust the notebook into his hand.

"There. Keep a tight hold on that, if you're capable," she said. "You bloody messer you."

19

"It was easy. Simplicity itself. Well, more like a piece of cake," said Mog, strutting into the kitchen, where Megan was washing the breakfast things.

"I heard all about it from Miss Miranda," said Megan.

"Lying dog, she is," said Mog. "That's tantamount to perjury what she told you. What did she tell you then?"

Megan pushed him to one side and went into the back parlour to collect more dirty ware.

There was a knock at the front door. Megan answered it. Then she returned to the back parlour, shut the door behind her and said:

"It's Mrs Mortensen. She's come to see Miss Miranda and Oliver."

Mog puffed rapidly at his cigarette and walked up and down the room.

"Don't panic. Don't panic," he said, and then sat down, stood up, sat down again, stood up and resumed his rapid pacing of the room.

"She'll be wanting to take them back, and they're upstairs now with that notebook," said Megan. "She mustn't know they're here."

"Cor blimey Charlie, don't panic, woman," said Mog, and he sucked so hard at his cigarette that he burned his fingers and cried out in pain.

Megan looked at him scornfully.

"Well, you'll have to think of something," he said.

"I has," said Mog. "I got the answer to it. I'm suffering from one day flu. Right? I'm riddled with germs and I can't stop sneezing and being sick. Well, it wouldn't be fair to see her in my condition, would it? Course it wouldn't. She'd take all my germs back to Mannersville, give them to Tom Manners and before you knew where you was, see, he'd have snuffed it and they'd have to hold a by-election. Well, I doesn't want to

241

embarrass the government, does I? I'm not thinking of Number One here. I'm thinking of the whole fate of parliamentary democracy. Right? You'll have to see her."

Megan moved across to him, her mouth tightening, and her eyes flashing.

"Are you going in to see her on your own accord, or does I have to drive you into the front parlour with the coal shovel?" she said.

"All right, all right, I'll go," said Mog, and then he paused by the door. "Panic? I never seen so much of it in all my life. Don't blame me if the whole of the city's wiped out, exterminated like, by one day flu. Right?"

Mrs Mortensen was sitting on the sofa in the front parlour. She was wearing a navy blue linen suit, and she had a pink chiffon scarf round her hair.

"Atishoo, atishoo, atishooooooooooooooooooooo," went Mog. "Don't blame me, if we has to have a by election, my old beauty. Atishoooo."

Mrs Mortensen stared at him coldly and said:

"I should like to see my daughter, please."

"She's out."

"Her scooter's outside in the drive."

"Pardon?"

"I said her scooter's out in the drive."

"That's because she's gone out with Ambrose to collect some spares for it owing to the simple fact that it's broken down and won't go without the spares what she's gone to pick up with Ambrose. Right?"

Mrs Mortensen's lips curled into a slight sneer. She lit a small cigar and said:

"Then I should like to see Oliver, please."

"Who?"

"Oliver."

"Oliver Manners, is it?"

"That's right."

"Oh, Oliver Manners, I see, my old lovely. Well, why didn't you say so in the first place? You had me labouring under a misapprehension there. Well, more like I hadn't a bloody clue what you was talking about. Right?"

"May I see him then?"

"No."

"Why not?"

242

"He's out."

"Where?"

"Pardon?"

"If he is out, as you say, where is he?"

"Pardon?"

Mrs Mortensen stood up and began to walk towards the door. Mog, however, limped across the room and barred her way.

"I'm a liar," he said. "He's in."

"I knew he was," said Mrs Mortensen. "Will you call him for me, please?"

"I can't," said Mog.

"Why not?"

"Don't panic, don't panic," said Mog. "Be calm like what I am, will you?"

"Why are you unable to call him?" said Mrs Mortensen slowly.

"He's got his girl friend up in the bedroom with him, hasn't he? Course he have."

"Pardon?"

"Been there for the past two hours, hasn't they? Well, you're a man of the world, aren't you? You knocked about a bit on the sly, eh? You knows your onions, if anyone do. Right? Well, between you, me and the gatepost, see, he wouldn't bless you if you was to disturb him now. A man gets violent on occasions like that. You take Hubert Morgan. On the job with this little Polak bint he was, and in walks Fat Bas and shakes his umbrella all over them. Well, I never seen such a set to. Fat Bas couldn't collect his dole for three weeks. I has to do it for him, on his behalf like. Then the bastard turns round and says I'm diddling him out of seven and nine. What he didn't take into account, see, was bus fares. Right? Like? Cost me all of seven and nine on the bus not taking into account the wear and tear on my boot leather, when I didn't catch it. Right?"

Mrs Mortensen sat down and smiled thoughtfully.

"So Oliver has got a girl friend, has he?" she said. "Does my daughter know?"

"Cor blimey Charlie, no she don't," said Mog. "It'd be more than my life's worth to tell her. Course I doesn't like to see such deceptions going on, but old Olly's the gaffer now, and I just has to do as I'm told. Right?"

243

"Who is she?"

"Who?"

"Oliver's girl friend."

"Pardon?"

"What is her name?"

"Jean Moloney. That's right. Jean Moloney's her name, isn't it? Course it is. A beautiful girl. Talk about chaste. You never seen no one more chaste than what she is. Brought up in a convent she was, see. Lovely way with her she have. Artistic, see. Clever with her maulers. Right? Does this here pottery and a bit of the old painting as a side line. Her painting's known all over the world, isn't it? And her pottery? Well, it's a must for anyone what wants to be in the fashion. Right? Play your cards right, and I'll get her to make you an egg cup at cost."

"Where did Oliver meet this Jean Moloney?"

"At the Merchant Navy Hostel."

"Where?"

"Well, not exactly the Merchant Navy Hostel. More like next door. That's right, isn't it? He met her next door. She's a friend of this feller, Mort. He's a bit handy with the maulers, too, on the quiet. Statues—that's what he does. With their clothes on, see. None of this down to the canvas malarkey. Well, knowing that Oliver's out of the top drawer, from a good family and well-educated like, he asks him in to see this here Jean Moloney. Love at first sight it was. Talk about romantic. Talk about the first flowering of young love. Talk about delicacy of feeling. Cor blimey Charlie, I almost had to drag him off her. Like a wild bull he was. I been in the Andrew twenty years, and I never seen nothing like it. Right?"

Mrs Mortensen nodded slowly.

"Good," she said. "Whoever she is, I am glad he is taking such an interest in the opposite sex."

"Oh, she's the opposite sex all right, don't you worry your head about that," said Mog.

She stood up and walked quickly to the front door. She paused there and said:

"I don't believe a word of what you've said, Mr Williams."

"Pardon? Are you accusing me of being a liar, telling untruths like?"

"I am."

"Ta. I just wanted to get it clear in my own mind. Right?"

"You'll be having another visitor very shortly, and I assure

244

you he won't be as gentle with you as I was," she said. "I should hand him the notebook, too, when he asks for it. Good bye."

"What did the old bitch want?" shouted Miss Miranda from upstairs, when the front door had been closed.

Mog told her.

"Well, who the hell is the visitor going to be?" said Oliver Manners.

He did not have long to find out, for within half an hour Tom Manners had knocked at the front door and been shown into the front parlour.

When Mog entered the room, he said:

"Ah, Williams, will you send my brother down."

"Don't you 'Williams' me, you Tory vermin," said Mog. "Who's never had it so good? I bloody well hasn't, I tell you."

"I'm not here to bandy words with you, Williams. I'm here to see my brother. Now kindly bring him to me this minute."

"Now we sees it all, don't we? Now we really sees you in your true colours. Listen to me, flabby chops, the days when the likes of you could boss round the likes of me is long since past. Right? Nye Bevan? Clem Attlee? They sorted your hash out for you, don't you kid yourself. I didn't go on the Jarrow hunger march for nothing. I'd have chained myself to the railings at Downing Street, if I'd been old enough to be a suffragette, wouldn't I? Course I bloody would."

"Where is my brother?"

"Out."

"Where?"

"Upstairs in his bedroom."

"How can he be out and upstairs in his bedroom at the same time?"

"There you are. You talks just like a politician, doesn't you? Argumentative. Always wanting an argument, isn't you?"

"Send him down at once."

"I can't."

"Why not?"

"He's with his girl friend, isn't he?"

"Well, send Miss Miranda down, too."

"It's not Miss Miranda."

"What?" said Tom Manners. "Well, who is it then?"

"Pardon?"

"What is the name of the woman who is upstairs with my brother?"

"Mrs Mortensen."

"Good God," said Tom, sinking back into his chair. "Sir Peter was right after all."

"Comes round every Tuesday, she do. Regular as clockwork, she is. Knock, knock, knock on the front door. Tip toe tip toe tip toe up the stairs. Two hours in the bedroom. Tip toe tip toe tip toe down the stairs. Smile smile smile at the front door. Out she goes, and Bob's your Uncle, Fanny's your Aunt."

"Good God," said Tom.

"Well, I don't think there's much to it, see. She calls it therapy. You and me knows it under another name, doesn't we? Course we does. But it's all harmless. Relatively. And I never seen him looking so well. It's got rid of his shaving rash, I tell you, boy."

"Mrs Mortensen!" said Tom. "Good god."

"Better than the other one what he had, my old son. What? I should say so. Jean Moloney. Big Jean, they called her. Where he picked her up from I'll never know. Let's be honest, fair play's, old Corky wasn't particular when it come to the old crumpet, but even he wouldn't touch it with a barge pole. It wouldn't be so bad, mind, if he'd taken a fancy to her sister-in-law. Smashing little bit of stuffing, she is. Half Indian. Black eyes. Hairy legs. She'd eat you up for breakfast and still have room for bacon, eggs and curry. Right?"

"You're a liar," shouted Tom Manners.

"Who? Me? A liar?" said Mog, backing away from Tom, who was advancing towards him.

"Yes, you," shouted Tom, and he grasped Mog by the scruff of the neck.

"Don't hit me, don't hit me. Mind my dentures," shouted Mog.

"It's all lies about Mrs Mortensen, isn't it?" shouted Tom.

"Yes," said Mog, and Tom dropped him to the ground.

"What a pity," he said softly, and then he strode out of the room to the foot of the stairs and shouted:

"Oliver. Come down immediately. I'm here to take you back to Mannersville."

"He's not coming," shouted Miss Miranda. "Piss off."

246

"I'm not coming," shouted Oliver.

"If you asks me, I'd say he didn't want to come," said Mog.

Tom took hold of him by the shoulders and said:

"I have a court order demanding that Oliver be returned immediately to Mannersville. If he is not back there by six in the evening, I shall see that it is executed at once. Do you understand?"

"You bastard," said Mog, and Tom smiled at him and marched out of the house.

"I'm not letting them take you away, Mr Manners, sir," said Megan, when she heard what Tom had said.

"Neither am I," said Miss Miranda.

"But what can we do about it?" said Ambrose, who had just returned for his lunch. "Talk sense, woman. Talk sense."

"We'll organise a siege," said Miss Miranda.

"What are you talking about?" said Ambrose.

"We'll barricade the house, and we'll defend it to the last man against them," said Miss Miranda. "We'll make them besiege us, and they'll never get Oliver out."

"Great idea," said Mog. "Now you leave it all to me. I knows a thing or two about sieges, doesn't I? Course I does. Well, I wasn't in the marine commandos for nothing, was I?"

"You won't have nothing to do with it, Mog Williams," said Megan.

"Not after the balls-up you made of the Mannersville job. Right?" said Miss Miranda.

"We'll take charge of everything, don't you worry," said Megan.

"You can help lug the furniture round, if you want to make yourself useful," said Miss Miranda.

"Charming. Marvellous. Corking. There's gratitude for you," said Mog. "Talk about looking a gift horse in the mouth. Ingratitude isn't in it. More like a kick in the bleeding teeth. Well, you sort yourselves out. I'm having nothing to do with it. Right?"

"And neither am I," said Ambrose. "You must be bloody mad."

All afternoon Miss Miranda and Megan directed the siege operations.

Oliver Manners and Wyndham Lancaster barricaded the front door with two wardrobes and a Welsh dresser. Group Captain Greenaway and Horace A'Fong dragged the kitchen

247

table, the front parlour sofa and the back parlour sideboard into the kitchen to make a barricade for the back door.

"What about your bloody windows?" said Mog. "You hasn't thought of them, has you?"

"I'll have you damn well cashiered, if you talk to the CO like that," said Group Captain Greenaway. "Now stir yourself, man. Stir yourself. Show a bit of spunk."

After they had finished the barricading operations Miss Miranda issued each of them with a weapon to repel boarders. She also supervised the manufacture of water bombs, flour bombs and stink bombs.

Megan went out to the shops and returned with four cardboard boxes packed with food.

"That's right," said Mog. "Don't forget the old victuals. Can I have one of them digestive biscuits?"

Megan slapped him on the wrist, as he tried to rifle one of the cartons.

"You keep your hands out," she said. "An army marches on its stomach. Right? I doesn't want you tampering with my logistics. Right?"

"Logistics? What are you talking about, woman?" said Mog. Megan giggled.

"I doesn't know, my lovely. That's what Group Captain Greenaway calls them. That's all I knows about the subject, isn't it?"

Mog stuck his hands in his trousers pockets and shuffled out of the kitchen and into the hall.

"Get out of here," shouted Miss Miranda. "I don't want you fouling up my lines of supply."

"Lines of supply? What are you talking about?"

Miss Miranda giggled.

"I don't know. That's what Group Captain Greenaway calls them. Isn't it super?"

Mog shook his head and shuffled into the front parlour.

"Grab that man," shouted Group Captain Greenaway, and Horace A'Fong and Wyndham Lancaster leapt on Mog's back and pinned him to the floor.

"Mind my bloody tubes," shouted Mog. "What are you on about, you bloody madmen?"

"Caught you at last," said Group Captain Greenaway looking down on him.

"We've been waiting for this moment for months," hissed

Wyndham Lancaster and he twisted Mog's arm behind his back.

"What are you playing at, you silly buggers?" said Mog, struggling to free himself.

"We've known for some time that the Goons had got wind of our plans," said Group Captain Greenaway. "Now we know who the traitor is."

"Traitor? I'm no bloody traitor," said Mog. "I'm on your side, my old wingsy bash. Let go of me, and I'll give you a hand with the old stink bombs, won't I? Course I will."

Wyndham Lancaster increased his pressure on his arm, and he cried out in pain.

"When a man betrays his fellow officers, Williams, there is only one thing to be done with him," said Group Captain Greenaway.

"Summary execution," said Wyndham Lancaster.

"Now then, now then, lads," said Mog. "You've had your little joke. Now let me get up, and we'll forget all about it, eh?"

Horace A'Fong took out a curved knife from the inside pocket of his jacket and held it at Mog's throat.

"Tippet betrayed us over Ethel, and you know what happened to him," said Group Captain Greenaway.

"Ethel?" said Mog, and he began to tremble.

"The tunnel from the latrines," said Wyndham Lancaster.

"There was only one thing to do with him," said Group Captain Greenaway.

Wyndham Lancaster ran his finger across his throat and cackled.

"Brother Herbert betrayed us over Mable. F.K. Henderson betrayed us over Violet," said Group Captain Greenaway. "And what happened to them?"

Horace A'Fong pressed the point of his knife lightly against Mog's Adam's apple.

"Now, listen to me, lads, you got hold of the wrong end of the stick, hasn't you?" said Mog. "I mean, it wasn't me what split on you to the Goons, was it? Course it wasn't. The bloke you should be looking for is Oliver Manners, isn't it? Course it is. He's the bloke what done the old dirty on you. I seen him only yesterday whispering in the corner with the old Kommandant. Right? Cor blimey Charlie, you could see he was up to no good. It was as plain as a pikestaff, wasn't it?

Course it was. The reason I didn't tell no one was I was going to deal with it myself, see. Tell you what I'll do. You let me up, I'll go and deal with that traitorous bastard, Manners, and I'll do you a favour and forget all about what's gone on by here. Right?"

"Is there anything you wish to say before the execution is carried out?" said Group Captain Greenaway.

"Execution?" said Mog, and then he screamed at the top of his voice: "Help! Help! Help! Help!"

Footsteps sounded on the stairs. Wyndham Lancaster and Horace A'Fong jumped up, and the minute Oriental hastily slipped the knife into his pocket as Miss Miranda came rushing into the room.

"What's going on?" she said. "Have they started the siege?"

"Siege?" said Mog. "What are you talking about? More like a bloody execution. These bastards here were just about to slit my bloody throat for me."

"I think he's a bit over-excited," said Wyndham Lancaster. "All these preparations for the siege seem to be too much for him."

"Listen to me, pudding head," said Mog. "I knows for a fact Tippet didn't split on Mabel."

"Mabel?" said Miss Miranda.

"The tunnel from the bloody latrines. Well, more like the bogs if you wants the proper word. Right?" said Mog.

"What on earth is he talking about?" said Miss Miranda.

"I really don't know," said Group Captain Greenaway.

"Oh yes, you does, colonel," said Mog. "You're the one what started all these filthy rumours about me blabbing to the Goons."

"The Goons?" said Miss Miranda. "Will someone please tell me what he's talking about?"

"Tell her," said Mog, pointing to Horace A'Fong. "Tell her what you lot just told me."

"Don't know what you're talking about, old bean," said Horace A'Fong, smiling at him.

"Right," snapped Miss Miranda. "Grab him."

Wyndham Lancaster and Horace A'Fong sprange forward and grabbed hold of Mog.

"Don't knife me, don't knife me," cried Mog. "I done nothing. It wasn't me what done the dirty on Violet."

"Now get him out of here," said Miss Miranda.

They hustled Mog out of the front parlour and took him to the front door, where Oliver Manners and Group Captain Greenaway struggled to remove the barricades. When they had finished, Miss Miranda said to Mog:

"Useless. Bloody useless. Right?"

And then they threw Mog out into the front path and slammed the door in his face.

As he struggled to his feet, he heard them dragging the furniture back into place in front of the door.

He dusted himself down and began to walk slowly away down the street. He had not gone far, when he bumped into Ambrose.

When Ambrose heard what had happened in the house, he took hold of Mog by the arm and said:

"Well, we might as well have a few jars, mightn't we? There's no point stopping in tonight. We'd not be able to watch the telly, would we?"

They went into the Whippet and bought two pints of beer.

"Bloody women," said Ambrose.

"Cor blimey Charlie, they're more bloody trouble than they're worth," said Mog.

"I never thought I'd live to see the day when Megan would be besieged in her own home," said Ambrose.

"Anything's possible with women," said Mog.

"True," said Ambrose.

At half past seven Uncle Mort walked into the bar and said:

"What's going on at your house?"

"You tell me," said Ambrose.

"Well, there's a couple of bobbies and a bloody tipstaff been hammering on the door for the past half hour. They won't let them in," said Uncle Mort.

Ambrose explained the situation, and Uncle Mort said:

"That's bloody women all over, isn't it?"

They drank steadily until a quarter past nine, when Mr Brandon came in with his son, Carter.

"What's going on at your house?" he said to Ambrose.

"You tell me, boy," said Mog.

"Well, there's a couple of police cars and a black maria outside, and your sister's throwing water all over the bobbies."

Ambrose explained the situation to him, and he said:

"That's just the sort of behaviour you expect from women."

"Mm," said Carter Brandon.

Uncle Mort bought the next round, and they were halfway through it, when Teddy Ward arrived and said to Ambrose:

"There's a bloody fire engine outside your house, mate."

"That don't surprise me," said Mog. "What do you want to drink then?"

"Give us a half of bitter, will you?" said Teddy Ward. "This new suit I'm wearing's really taken the edge off me drinking. Funny, in't it?"

"That's new suits all over," said Uncle Mort.

A quarter of an hour later Derrick Warrender came into the pub and said to Ambrose:

"Hey up, there's a rare old battle going on outside your house. They've got the bloody television cameras there."

"They better not tread on my anemones or I'll bloody sue them," said Mr Brandon.

Ten minutes later Sid Skelhorn came in and said:

"How do, Carter? How's the world treating you?"

"Not bad," said Carter Brandon.

Sid Skelhorn bought himself a pint and then said to Mr Brandon:

"There's a right old shemozzle going on next door to you. There's two fire engines, half a dozen police cars and a tender from the Civil Defence outside. The people inside are throwing flour and bloody stink bombs. There's a woman inside yelling her bloody head off at the bobbies."

"That'll be my wife," said Ambrose.

"Typical, typical," said Sid Skelhorn. "Mine's just the bloody same."

They heard sirens wailing in the distance, and an ambulance flashed past the pub, its bell jangling stridently.

"Do you think we'd better see what's happening there?" said Ambrose.

"Aye," said Uncle Mort. "Shall we have one for the road?"

"Go on then," said Mr Brandon.

Mog excused himself and went out into the corridor. He stood there for a moment, looking at the telephone. He made a step forwards to it, and then he stopped and stepped back.

"Go on, Mog, my old son, you might as well," he said to himself, and he went to the phone, thumbed rapidly through the telephone book, made a call and returned to the bar just in time to accept a newly-drawn pint of best bitter beer.

The men ambled slowly homewards. They turned the corner of the street where the Brandons and the Tierneys lived and saw a great crowd of people milling around in the road.

There were fire engines, ambulances, police cars and a Civil Defence van. The lights for the television cameras lit up the whole front of the Tierneys' house.

In their light could be seen Tom Manners climbing up a ladder to the front bedroom window.

"He's going up there to try and persuade his brother to give himself up," said Mrs Warrender, the neighbour from Number 36. "In't he brave?"

Tom was just about to knock on the window pane, when three police cars, lights flashing and bells ringing, screeched up in front of the house.

Out of the leading car stepped the chief constable and Hedley Nicholson.

The chief constable looked up at Tom, and then shouted to the policeman standing at the foot of the ladder:

"Arrest that man."

Tom turned suddenly. The lights blinded him. He struggled wildly to keep his balance. For a moment the ladder seemed to be suspended in space and then slowly it began to topple backwards.

With a howl of terror Tom tumbled earthwards and landed on the back of his head in the Tierneys' front garden.

"Right on my bloody fuschia bush," said Ambrose.

Hedley Nicholson turned to Mog and said:

"You did right to call me, Mr Williams. You did right."

20

Three eminent specialists pronounced that Oliver Manners was perfectly sane.

The same three specialists pronounced that, owing to the severe blow he had taken on the back of his head, Tom Manners was insane.

An eminent judge sentenced Sir Peter Wakefield to three years imprisonment for embezzlement of funds belonging to the Manners Property and Development Company.

The same eminent judge sentenced Mrs Mortensen to one year's imprisonment for conspiring to pervert the course of justice.

By a strange coincidence the eminent cleric who married Oliver Manners and Miranda Mortensen in the cathedral was the younger brother of the eminent jurist who had passed sentence on the bride's mother.

"Well, these eminent people all gang up together, don't they?" said Mog. "That's the whole bloody trouble with the world today—it's run by bloody eminent people."

At the first meeting he chaired of the Manners Property and Development Company Oliver Manners introduced the new managing director.

"Ta very much, Olly," said Mog Williams. "Now then, listen this way. As managing director I have news of a very important transaction what is just about to be transacted."

"Hurrah," shouted the company secretary. "School, three cheers for Mr Mog Williams, Hip, hip, hip . . ."

"Shut your rattle, you great Oriental twerp," said Mog.

"Here here," said Wyndham Lancaster.

"Now then, this transaction what I'm talking about involves the purchase of one of the most famous catering establishments in the whole of South Wales. Well, more like the whole of the bloody country if the truth be known. And you doesn't need me to tell you that the name of the said establishment is none other than Tommy Ishmael's cafe."

There was a burst of applause from the board of directors, which was led by the company vice chairman, Mr Basil Yorath. The corgi lying at his feet snarled.

The applause was interrupted, however, when the doors of the board room were flung open by a uniformed inspector of police and two sergeants.

The inspector pointed his finger at Mog and said:

"F.S. Seymour?"

"Cor blimey Charlie, it always happens," said Mog. "Just when I gets my hands on a bit of the old liquidity, my bloody luck runs out."

He was escorted out of the building and placed into the back seat of a black Wolseley police car.

One of the sergeants handcuffed him to a broad-shouldered, fair-haired young man, who was already sitting in the car.

"What have they nabbed you for then?" said the young man.

"Impersonating a bloody clergyman in Builth Wells," said Mog.

"Hard luck," said the young man.

The car drew up outside the central police station. The sergeant opened the door and Mog and the young man climbed out.

As they crossed the pavement and walked up the steps of the police station a passer by pointed at the broad-shouldered young man and said to his neighbour:

"I see young Renshawe's gone the same way as his brother then."

Peter Tinniswood's first novel is
A Touch of Daniel.
If you haven't read it yet see what you've missed.

"A humorous gem from a novelist of rare talent"
Sunday Express

"Mr. Tinniswood has done a rare thing –
created a new, big comic world"
Financial Times

"A brilliantly inventive writer, a master of
situation and character, he has delivered a
book which is both awfully funny and funnily
awful"
Illustrated London News

Hunter Davies' choice as book of the year in
The Sunday Times

"Very funny indeed . . . he juxtaposes the banal
and the bizarre with extraordinary delicacy
and precision"
Sheffield Morning Telegraph

"Gorgeous barrage of humorous improbabilities"
Evening News, London